SHADES OF
BETRAYAL

U. W. BAKER

 FriesenPress

One Printers Way
Altona, MB, R0B 0B0
Canada

www.friesenpress.com

Copyright © 2022 by U. W. Baker
First Edition — 2022

All rights reserved.

ISBN
978-1-03-911429-6 (Hardcover)
978-1-03-911428-9 (Paperback)
978-1-03-911430-2 (eBook)

1. FICTION

Distributed to the trade by The Ingram Book Company

To the memory of my parents.

Born deeply rooted, soaked in the memory of generations
Walked the streets painted with the patina of centuries
Touched the imperishable walls of old buildings
Dreamed in gardens under the majestic trees
Rested in the grass smelling of heroes' blood
Walked cemeteries with forefathers' souls in the tombs
Listened to whispers of strength, love, and death

Part One

— NEW BEGINNINGS —

August 1927.

Monday, August 15, 1927, was the Assumption of Mary holiday in Poland, popularly known as the Feast of Our Lady of Herbs. The holiday celebrations that started on Sunday, continued through Monday, reaching the culmination point during the noon Mass in all churches across the country.

Teddy Novak, together with his parents and two-year-old sister Ania, took part in the festivities in the town square, but nothing could make him happy on that day, not even the cotton candy his father bought for him and Ania. He loved this treat, but the taste of it was bitter mixed with the tears that he tried to conceal from his father.

It was his sixth birthday and he'd anticipated it to be an affirmation of his maturity and moving from his child years into becoming a pupil at a local primary school. Instead, his father was leaving him and the family to go to France. Teddy decided that he would never celebrate the Day of Assumption again; it would always be a reminder of the saddest day for him.

Together with many people in Brusk, a small town south of Warsaw, Teddy and his family participated in an old tradition of carrying bouquets of herbs to church and walking in a procession across the town. The bouquets were blessed during the Mass and kept at home, signifying a good harvest for the farmers and the prosperity of all the people.

After the official church celebrations, the revelries moved to the main square in town, where stalls with trinkets, sweets, toys, and fresh pickles had been erected. The holiday was an occasion for friends and family to get together and take part in the local festivities and tastings of the freshly made pickles, which was a tradition in this part of Poland.

At the end of the day, the family sat at the table to share supper together. With a fork, Teddy pushed his food on the plate, unable to eat, his headache growing with every word spoken by his father.

He looked at his mother pleadingly, desperately avoiding his father's eyes. "Can I go to bed?"

"Ania, it is time for you to go to bed too." Mother hugged Ania and Teddy disappeared behind a curtain separating the kitchen from the kids' bedroom.

He could not sleep and the quiet conversation between his parents was like a heavy weight pressing on his head. All he could think about was life after his father was gone. His thoughts were dark and the anger at his father was growing in his heart.

"Why can't he work in Poland? What will happen to us?" Teddy whispered, but then he stopped before anyone could take notice.

The beautiful August holiday had been a good opportunity for Joseph Novak to say goodbye to family and friends; the mood was happy and hopes were high for a good harvest. The next day he was leaving his home and family to work in a foundry in the town of Thionville in the northern region of Lorraine.

Joseph was a blacksmith but there was not enough work in Poland to provide for his family and to finish building their house. He was very skilled at his profession and occasionally earned extra money by making iron gates, window shutters, or even small items like doorknobs and other ornaments, but it was still not enough.

Earlier that year, Joseph had read an article in a national newspaper about France rebuilding its industry after the Great War and looking for foreign workers to work in smelters, mines, and factories in the Alsace-Lorraine region. With a heavy heart, Joseph applied for a job and received a work permit from the Rhine Foundry in Thionville.

The last few days before travelling to France were very emotional and tough for him and the family. He loved his wife Maria, son Edward, who was affectionately called Teddy, and daughter Ania. Leaving them was very difficult and they all worried about the future, though he promised to send money and visit them as soon as possible.

After supper, when both children were in bed, Joseph and Maria sat at the table looking at each other.

"Maria, I'll send money as soon as I'm paid by the foundry."

Maria held Joseph's hands. "My love, I hope that we're making the right decision and won't regret the choice of leaving Poland."

Suspecting that their families would strongly object to the idea, Joseph and Maria kept their plan to move the family to France secret.

"Once I work there, I'll decide if bringing you and the children to France is a good decision. In the meantime, use the money to support the family and save some for the future either here or in France."

Both had tears in their eyes when Joseph took his wife's hand and led her to their bedroom. They had been very much in love since the first day they met. Joseph was always gentle, almost shy, while making love to Maria. She, on the other hand, was the passionate one, pushing for more, enjoying the pleasure of love and physical contact.

On that last night before his departure, the passion, tenderness, tears, and kisses didn't stop until the first rays of sun put a dancing shadow on the wall of their bedroom.

"The sun is looking at us through the window," Joseph said as he kissed Maria. "It's a good sign of a better life ahead."

Maria made a sign of the cross and rose from the bed. "I hope you're right. I'll keep this sunny image in my heart."

The breakfast of eggs, bread, and coffee was more cheerful than the supper; only Teddy sat at the table stone-faced, trying to hide his emotions.

Joseph hugged his wife and daughter but his most meaningful words this morning were for his son. "Teddy, you're the head of the family until I come back. Take care of your mother and sister." He put his arm around Teddy's shoulders.

"I'm not Teddy anymore. I'm Ted," the boy said defiantly with his eyes fixed on the ground.

Although he was only a six-year-old, Ted remembered a lot from his early childhood. He remembered moving to this new house when he was four years old. It was such a happy time for the family and soon after, Ania was born, capturing Ted's heart from the moment he saw her tiny face and the small hand that grabbed his finger and didn't want to let it go.

The house had two finished rooms on one side of the hallway that ran from the front door to the back door, separating the house into two parts. One room was a kitchen with two bunk beds, where the kids slept, and an alcove with a good-sized basin for personal care. The toilet was in an outhouse next to the storage shed.

The second room was his parents' bedroom.

Ted often babysat his little sister, especially in the evenings and on Saturdays while his parents worked on finishing the part of the house that they already lived in. He liked the smell of fresh paint, new floors, and the stove in the kitchen. Mother always found a little sugar and flour to bake cookies for him.

Whenever Ted had free time, he loved to play on the other side of the house. It was a big empty room with a roof over it, boarded windows, and unfinished walls and floors. Ted didn't have many toys, but his imagination was enough to have fun and to make-believe. Like other boys, he liked to play war.

Occasionally, his father took him for walks outside the town, telling him Poland's history. "Our country suffered a lot at the hands of its neighbours."

Ted looked at his father with anticipation. "Because the Russians occupied Poland?"

"Not only the Russians but also the Germans and Austrians. For over a hundred years, Poland was divided between the three countries," Joseph would say, as much for himself as for Ted. "In 1914, the Great War started. Our town, located between the hills on the east and the river on the south-west, was vulnerable to attacks from all enemies ..."

Although Ted had heard this story many times, he still asked, "Why was the town's location so bad?"

Joseph always looked beyond the river, searching the horizon of the western sky. "The Russians built their trenches in the hills on the east side and the Germans and Austrians behind the river on the south-west."

Sometimes father and son would continue to walk in silence as Ted thought about the stories of the Great War, which had ended with Poland taking back its independence. His parents' generation remembered the devastation, hunger, and bullets flying over their heads. Most of their houses had been burned and food was scarce.

All those war stories fuelled Ted's imagination and the wooden planks in the unfinished part of the house were his make-believe armies, trenches, and fortifications. Ted was always the general directing his armies into battles and always winning.

As he was alone in the unfinished room on the morning his father was to leave, memories flooded Ted's mind, and he felt hopeless and afraid. He knew he had to be strong and not cry. His father expected him to be responsible for the family while he was working in France. Ted was mature for his age, but now he had to become a grown-up man while his father was away. "What should I do to take care of my family?" he screamed, and he kicked at the planks that were his make-belief fortifications. "I'll never play here again."

He left the room without looking back.

On Tuesday, August 16, 1927, when Joseph left his house to take the train, he didn't know that his life would change forever. He and another man, Jan Lech, who'd been hired by the same foundry, travelled together to France. The fifty-kilometre journey to Warsaw by train took them two hours and they arrived at the main station in the early afternoon.

"I'll miss coming to Warsaw every week, meeting people at the market, doing business with them, and buying little gifts for my children," Joseph said to Jan.

They purchased train tickets to Poznań and from there they would take the trains as far as Luxemburg. The train to Poznań left at ten at night. It was very crowded, but they were able to get one seat and one standing spot by the window.

At four a.m., it was Joseph's turn to stand by the window while Jan rested in the seat. It was a beautiful morning and they were already quite far from Warsaw. He noticed that the farther west they travelled, the bigger the farms got and the more solidly built the houses were. Even the barns looked better than many houses in his part of Poland.

A hundred years of occupation by Germany, Austria, and Russia had influenced the way each part of Poland developed. The Russian-occupied parts were poor, with small farms divided into strips of land growing potatoes, cabbage, rye, and beets. Each farmer produced a little of everything, just enough for their family and to sell in the nearby towns. Many folks were poor and winters were the most trying times to feed families.

Leaving the eastern part of Poland behind, Joseph liked what he saw: the farms with people harvesting the fall crops, houses with nice front yards full of flowers, and towns with red-brick houses.

In Poznań, they switched trains and headed to Hamburg, where they would change trains again to take them to Luxemburg. The train to Hamburg was not crowded and both men had comfortable seats by the window. As they travelled farther into Germany, their spirits rose high at the sight of more prosperous country.

"I read about high unemployment in Germany after the Great War and the German people's feeling of injustice resulting from the Treaty of Versailles in 1919," said Joseph.

"Seeing the prosperous farms and beautiful cities, you could wonder if Germany was as poor as the newspapers say," replied Jan.

"Maybe there are different levels of poor and ours is much greater. Let's hope it will all improve with time."

On the fourth day, they arrived in Hamburg.

Every summer, Erik spent one month with his paternal German grandparents and one with his maternal Polish grandparents.

He rotated the months every year, allowing both grandparents to celebrate his birthday on August 15th.

Erik and his parents lived in the free city of Gdańsk, where Polish and German citizens lived in harmony, although often in separate neighbourhoods. The city was one of the oldest in Poland, founded in the tenth century. At the beginning of the fourteenth century it fell under the rule of the German Teutonic Knights for 150 years. Taken back by Poland it became a vital port and it attracted people from all over Europe. As the city switched hands several times through the centuries, its citizens wanted more autonomy and after WWI the Free City of Gdańsk known as Danzig to the German citizens was created under the administration of the League of Nations.

Otto and Rita Hermann's apartment was in the German part of the city where Erik's father had a good job as an accountant at City Hall. It was close to the Polish neighbourhood and both Polish and German friends frequently came to parties or just for a coffee and small talk. Erik's mother, Rita, loved to entertain, always baking to make sure that when friends dropped by unexpectedly, there was a cake and coffee on the table.

In the summer of 1927, Erik was spending his August vacation with his Polish family. His birthday was always a special time for him, but on his eighth birthday, he was allowed to invite many of his friends from town and Grandfather planned special games for them.

Erik spoke both German and Polish fluently, and his conversations at home were often spoken using both languages intermittently.

"Erik, remember that you have to speak Polish only when you're with your grandparents," said his mother when they'd settled into their seats on the train from Gdańsk to Gniezno,

"Yes, Mom, I know that. Father always tells me to speak only German when he takes me to my German grandparents."

"How was your summer vacation on the farm with Oma and Opa?"

"It was good. Opa insisted that I exercise every morning," Erik replied.

"I'm glad you exercised and hope you were helping with the work there. The farm is doing well and they had to hire more seasonal workers this year."

"Yes, I helped a lot. Opa always said that it was good to be disciplined, organised, and hard-working," Erik said, beaming with pride. "He was serious during the day but always hugged and kissed me goodnight."

Mother smiled, looking at Erik with love in her eyes. "They'll visit us in September. Father got a promotion at work and he wants to celebrate with family and friends."

In less than three hours, they arrived in Gniezno. Erik's grandparents, Zofia and Fred Pasiak, waited at the train station like they did every year.

Erik ran into his grandfather's arms, and in his best Polish, he shouted, "I'm here. When are we going fishing?"

Fred Pasiak was a schoolteacher and the family lived modestly on his small salary on a quiet street not far from the school. Fred was a scout and organised many hiking and fishing trips with Erik and other boys. In their free time, the boys played football in the field behind the school.

On many evenings, neighbours would gather on their veranda and talk, mostly about politics. "Fred, perhaps you could ask your daughter about her husband's opinion of the current political situation in Europe."

Fred's answer was rather terse. "We don't discuss politics with her and Otto."

A younger neighbour voiced his concern. "We should keep an eye on the Germans living in our area. Many times, they are not friendly towards us."

Often the conversation would steer towards stories about life during the Great War. Erik liked listening to those stories while sitting on the steps of the veranda.

In the middle of August, the family was getting ready to celebrate the Assumption of Mary holiday and enjoy the festivities with friends.

Erik's mother always visited her parents on that holiday and this year Erik's father was coming as well, to join in celebration of Erik's eighth birthday.

The morning of August 15th, Mr. Pasiak left early to work on construction of the stage for the day's festivities. For Erik, the day started as always with a breakfast of hot oatmeal sweetened with honey and a cup of tea. After breakfast, Grandma and Mother started baking Erik's birthday cake. They talked about the festival they were all going to enjoy.

Erik was cleaning the kitchen table when somebody knocked loudly at the door.

It was their neighbour, panting and gasping for air. His face was twisted in pain, eyes cast down hiding some dark news. "Mrs. Pasiak, there was an accident and your husband was hurt."

Erik heard Grandmother's alerted voice. "What happened? How badly is he hurt?"

"Mrs. Pasiak, please come with me to the hospital," he answered, still unable to look into her eyes.

The hospital was two kilometres from the house. They walked briskly and when they arrived, Erik waited in the hallway while his grandmother and mother went to talk to the doctor. In the next few minutes, he heard a cry. Then his mother came and hugged him for a long time.

"What is it, Mom?"

"Your grandfather is dead—killed by a beam that fell from the stage he was helping to build." She wiped the tears from her eyes while hugging Erik with one limp arm.

Erik could not believe what he'd heard. It was unimaginable that his grandfather was dead. He began to cry uncontrollably. "Can I see him?"

"Not now. Grandma is with him, and she needs some time to say her prayers."

They sat on the hospital bench and cried, both lost in their grief.

Erik's life changed forever after the accident. His summer vacations with his Polish grandmother were cut to one week, as she had to sell her house and move in with her son. Most of the other summer vacations Erik spent with his German grandparents, listening to German radio with his grandfather, playing with German boys, and being slowly influenced by the growing nationalism in Germany.

The French customs officer was suspicious of two Polish men crossing the border from Luxemburg to France. "What is your business here?" he said, looking sternly into Joseph's eyes.

"Work in foundry," Joseph answered with the few French words he knew.

"Follow me." The officer gestured with his arm and took them to a small waiting room.

After over an hour of waiting, the officer came back. He was polite but unapologetic. "Your papers are in order and we confirmed with the Rhine Foundry that you're employed by them. Often we get people crossing the border with illegal documents and we need to check everybody carefully."

Joseph smiled with relief. "Thank you."

After arriving in Thionville, Joseph and Jan cleaned up in a public washroom at the train station and got ready to report to the offices of the company that was to employ them. Joseph changed into a brown suit. It was the latest fashion in Poland but he was somewhat apprehensive about his look, not knowing if it would be considered old fashioned here. Joseph and Jan, who dressed in a grey suit and was not nearly as concerned about how he looked, asked for directions to the foundry and walked for half an hour, carrying their small suitcases with their belongings. They were looking forward to starting their new jobs.

When they arrived at the offices of the Rhine Foundry they presented their passports and work-offer letters to the male assistant sitting behind a big wooden desk. There were other people in the large room, either sitting in chairs along the wall or standing with their belongings by their sides.

Jan shuffled his legs restlessly. "Look how many people are looking for a job here. I'm getting nervous they may not have enough work for everybody."

Despite being anxious, Joseph sounded confident. "We have the employment letters from the company. We shouldn't have any problems." He surveyed the room carefully while the clerk was inspecting their papers.

Joseph was pleased with his appearance and more confidence was building inside him. "I'm glad we changed into our best suits. Look around. We look better than the others."

The other men in the room lacked confidence. He could see it in their eyes and the way they carried themselves.

The clerk inspected Joseph and Jan's documents and with a gesture of his hand, ushered them through a door on their left. Soon, a Polish man, who appeared to have some rank in the company, greeted them and the other few men in the room, all of them Polish. Joseph relaxed, happy to meet more of his countrymen.

"Good afternoon," said the man, introducing himself as Kazimir. "I'm responsible for making all the arrangements for accommodations and introductions to your workplace. I'll also arrange French lessons for you."

The men followed Kazimir to their housing compound, not far from the foundry. After touring the common areas of living room, kitchen, and bathrooms, Joseph was given a key to his private room.

He stood in the middle of his room, assessing it. It was furnished with a single bed, a dresser, and a table that he could use for eating, writing, and reading newspapers.

He opened his suitcase and looked at his belongings with feelings of sadness and love. On top of his best shirt was a dried flower from the garden his wife Maria cultivated at the back of the house.

Longingly, he thought about his marriage and the time they'd bought the little parcel of land across from the church and built their house. He vividly remembered the small garden where Maria had planted vegetables and her beautiful flowers and he thought sadly that he might never see his house again.

"I have to succeed here," he said out loud, looking at the picture of Maria and his children. He gently placed it on the table and said, "Maria, one day when you're here, I'll tell you about my past, hoping that you can understand and forgive me for the sins of my youth." He kissed the picture. "I love you very much."

An hour later, he'd finished unpacking and went to the living room. It was a big room shared by all the men in the compound. It served as a meeting place where everybody relaxed, played games, and talked about their lives. Joseph was happy that some French men shared the same accommodation. It was an opportunity to learn and practice the language of his new country.

A few men were already sitting comfortably and drinking tea. It was early afternoon and nothing was expected of them until the next day. The evening was very enjoyable, with wine, cheese, and fresh bread provided by the company.

As the evening wore on, four men sat at the table in the centre. The wine bottle was empty. Two other bottles: a vodka with Russian letters and one with Polish letters on the label, were half empty. The men were not drunk, but the alcohol made their conversation very lively. Joseph observed them with amusement. He could hear the different languages spoken at the table, but he noticed that the hand gestures were like another living language that could describe the meaning of every spoken word, especially after a few drinks.

A middle-aged man sat at Joseph's table. He was sober and spoke in accented French. "Hi, my name is Kenneth Long."

"I'm Joseph Novak," Joseph replied. His voice was shaking, a little afraid that he might disappoint the stranger with the few words he could say in French. Fortunately, the man was skilled in talking to foreigners who knew very little French; he even used some Polish and Russian to make it easier for Joseph to understand the conversation. Kenneth was an Englishman and had lived in France since the Great War. He'd arrived in Thionville from Normandy and worked in the foundry for the last two months.

Kenneth hadn't had anything to drink all evening, and after he left Joseph's table, he kept to himself, observing everybody with his penetrating eyes. Joseph became uncomfortable, thinking that maybe Kenneth was being used by the company to assess the newcomers in their private hours. He decided to be on guard not only at work but also during his social hours.

The second half of the summer of 1927 was very hot in most parts of England, particularly in London. William was ten years old when he and his parents went to the seashore on a short, one-week vacation. It had been a last-minute decision when an invitation from a distant aunt had arrived in the mail. Although the relationship with Aunt Maggie was largely estranged, accepting this invitation and going to the sea for a week was a great opportunity to take a break from the London heat and allow the kids to enjoy the end of summer.

William had two younger sisters. Sadly, one of them was disabled as a result of polio, which had struck her at the age of two.

The trip by train was long and everybody was tired, except for William, who was very excited, thinking about the sea and swimming in the salty water. He and his sisters had never been on a vacation by the sea and this was a big adventure for them.

Aunt Maggie received them warmly and after polite greetings, she turned her attention to William. "Hello, William, you may not remember me. The last time we met, you were just four years old and your sister was sick."

William, called Billy by family and friends, was a tall, slender boy, who looked people straight in the eyes when talking to them. He looked at his aunt and smiled with confidence. "I do remember you a little. You always wore beautiful hats."

"What a great memory."

His sisters looked up to him with admiration and unconditional love; they would do anything for Billy. This exchange with Aunt Maggie reaffirmed their conviction that Billy was the smartest boy in the world.

Aunt Maggie showed them their two rooms, one for his parents and one for the three kids. The rooms were small but Billy and his family were used to living in an apartment and this house by the sea was like a palace to him.

The butler announced that lunch was ready and all went to the dining room. The meal was simple but delicious, little sandwiches, fruit, and lemonade.

When lunch was finished Aunt Maggie stood up and walked towards the back door, which led to a big veranda. "I'll show you the way to the beach."

After a short walk on a wooden boardwalk, they stepped onto the warm sand of the beach. It was like a paradise to Billy and his sisters. He helped his younger sister to get around on her crutches as they played in the water, built a sandcastle, and covered themselves with the sand.

In the late afternoon, the family went back to the house, and after a short rest Aunt Maggie took them to a big barn near the house. Billy could not believe his eyes—covered with a khaki canvas, an old airplane was resting like a strange being frozen in time.

"It's a seaplane. Beardmore W.B. III, nicknamed the 'Folding Pup,'" said Aunt Maggie.

The seaplane was built for use on aircraft carriers as a naval scout. It was small with redesigned wings that allowed folding for storage.

Billy had heard stories about the war and his uncle and grandfather fighting the Germans. "Is it the plane that Uncle Winthrop flew during the war?" he asked eagerly.

Aunt Maggy looked at it with teary eyes. "Yes, it is."

The plane was magical and beautiful, despite the rust showing on the wings. "Aunt Maggie, could I go inside the plane?" he asked politely.

"Billy, let's agree that during your stay here, the plane is yours to play in as much as you would like." She put her arm around his shoulder and said, "Perhaps you could be a pilot one day."

Billy spent long hours in the plane, smelling the damp, musty air of the cabin and imagining flying it high in the sky. He could almost hear the propeller rotating in the air and see the land below, full of summer colours.

It was the week of discovery. He had found his calling. He decided to do everything he could to become a pilot.

His sisters were not happy that he spent most of his time daydreaming. He tried to be with them on the beach, but instead of castles, they built planes and fortifications and fought imaginary battles.

"Aunt Maggie, could you please tell us some stories about Uncle Winthrop flying this airplane?" asked Billy on the last day of their vacation.

There was a silence at the table and his aunt and parents became very serious.

"Another time Billy. It is our last evening here. Let's enjoy our supper and play some games."

He thought for a moment that there was a sadness in her eyes.

Joseph's first day at work was spent on general orientation, visiting all departments of the foundry and assigning people to different work areas. He was allocated to the smelting department and introduced to the worker responsible for his training.

Jean Navarre was the senior employee in the foundry who was often given the responsibility of teaching newly hired Polish workers. He spoke good rudimentary Polish. His regular job was in the warehouse where he operated a crane moving heavy loads of the raw materials used in the smelters. "Hello, Joseph. Can I call you Joe?" he asked.

"Yes," answered Joseph. He added nervously, "I hope I can learn my new responsibilities quickly."

"It is up to you Joe to observe and learn." Jean's Polish was endearing to

Joseph and he instantly liked him.

After an explanation of the basic principles of smelting, they stopped by the furnace where Jean explained, "We use a metal extraction process in which crushed and refined iron ore called concentrate is mixed with coke and limestone, and then heated to high temperatures in an enclosed furnace called a smelter."

"I see four smelters here," Joe said as he pointed out the big furnaces in the hall.

"This foundry is one of the biggest in the area and produces a high amount of steel, mostly for the military and the newly growing automobile industry."

After the training, Jean invited Joe for a glass of wine at the local bar. It wasn't long before this became routine and they grew to be friends. They both were passionate about politics and their discussions were often about the situation in Europe after the Treaty of Versailles.

"Joe, what do you think about Europe's stability?" Jean asked, sipping the wine from his glass.

"The political landscape is very unstable, and although governments paint a positive picture of a peaceful Europe, I think that the peace won't last."

"How so?"

"In Poland, we don't trust our neighbours, Germany and Russia. We believe that it is important to be always on guard."

The French language classes were conducted every day at a local school in town. Joe was very good at grasping the language and dedicated most of his free time to learning. His growing friendship with Jean and their frequent conversations allowed him to practice French and progress at a fast pace.

"Jean, I have to move out of the compound by the end of the year. Do you know of any rooms for rent at an affordable price?"

Jean's face broke into a big smile. "I have one room for rent in my house. I would be happy if you rented it from me."

In the middle of December, Joe moved into Jean's small house on the outskirts of Thionville. They celebrated Christmas together with two other workers who were not able to visit their families. After a few glasses of wine, nostalgia overtook Joe and with teary eyes, he talked about his wife and children in Poland. The other two men shared their stories of leaving families behind in search of a better life.

Joe looked towards his friend. "Jean, what about your family?"

"It's a sad story. Now isn't the time to talk about it." Jean stood up, went to the kitchen, and brought another bottle of wine to the table.

When the evening was over and the two invited men stood up to leave, one of them looked closely at Jean and Joe with a slight surprise on his face. "You two look like brothers."

Jean laughed while Joe answered with embarrassment. "Perhaps I try too much to become a Frenchman."

Christmas 1927 was a blend of many emotions for Maria. It was the first time since her marriage that she'd celebrated without her husband, Joseph. In December, she received a parcel from him with warm clothes, chocolates, and money stuffed into the pocket of a new sweater for her.

Maria stroked her son's head. "Ted, we're going to celebrate Christmas Eve with your grandparents and your uncle and his family."

Since August, Ted had been very serious, often making Maria sad for him and his abruptly ended childhood. She hoped that a family dinner would cheer him up.

Ted's face brightened with a big grin. "Are they coming here?"

Maria looked at her son lovingly. "Yes, they are. I'll need your help to clean the house and look after Ania."

She worked all week preparing the traditional supper consisting of thirteen dishes. It would be the most lavish Christmas Eve supper they'd ever had, in some ways a compensation for her husband not being with them and sitting at the head of the table. Everybody arrived early, bringing chairs, dishes, and cutlery to accommodate them all for the supper. The children's beds were removed from the kitchen to Maria's bedroom, making room for the dining table. The small dining table was extended by placing long wood planks on top and covering them with a white linen cloth.

"Children, we need to finish decorating the Christmas tree," said Ted with authority.

Ted's cousin looked at the confident Ted. "Can we sing carols?"

"Let's sing and keep an eye on the sky for the first star. We must follow the tradition of starting the supper after the first star brightens the sky."

Ted had a beautiful voice and singing was his passion. Soon, the whole family joined in the singing while setting the table.

The women placed twelve plates around the table, and Ted noticed that his mother kept one plate close to her heart before placing it at the head of the table. There were only eleven of them but traditionally one empty plate was placed on the table for a stranger who might knock at the door on Christmas Eve. Nobody said it, but all knew the plate was for Joseph and they left the chair at the head of the table empty.

"I see a star," Ted's cousin shouted excitedly.

"It is time to sit at the table," Maria said in a sad voice.

Once they all were comfortably seated, Maria asked Joseph's father to say a prayer.

Sharing a traditional thin wafer blessed in church, he wished everybody health, love, and prosperity. Addressing his last words to the empty chair, he said, "Dear Joseph, Maria and the whole family are thinking of you on this Christmas Eve Day. We hope you're in good health and will be back soon."

"Amen," all answered and the supper started.

The first dish was a delicious soup made from dried wild mushrooms with square noodles. It was a traditional soup Maria remembered from her childhood. The pierogis with cabbage and wild mushrooms were equally delicious. After all the other courses, when poppy seed cake and a fruit compote were placed on the table, Maria left the room for a few seconds.

When she came back, she said, "Kids, I have something special for you." She opened a box full of chocolates.

"Are they from Dad?" Ted exclaimed.

"Yes."

The kids could not believe their eyes; even Ted and Ania had not known about the chocolates. It was a treat almost unknown to them. Everybody enjoyed the evening, often talking about Joseph and wishing he were at the table.

At 11:30 p.m. they all dressed warmly, Maria and the kids in their new scarves, hats, and mitts, and went to Midnight Mass.

After the celebration of Mass, the relatives left and the kids went to bed while Maria sat at the table for a little while. She was not ready yet to go to her empty bed. She missed Joseph very much, not only the conversations with him but the physical presence and the closeness in bed. She closed her eyes and imagined him taking her by the hand and closing the door of the bedroom behind them.

She missed his gentle kisses and his shy approach to making love to her. She put her head on the table and gently wept.

Joe liked living in Jean's house. Most of the time they were able to arrange to work the same shifts and either walked or biked together to the foundry.

They were known as J&J by the other workers, and sometimes Joe was called Jean, which pleased him.

"I'm becoming a Frenchman. It will be easier for Maria to assimilate when she arrives." Joe was satisfied with his own assimilation into French society.

He didn't trouble himself with developing any strong friendships with other workers in the foundry. Many of them came to Thionville for a year or two and went back home with their savings. Even Jan had left after just a year. Jean's company, working many hours, and improving his language were enough for Joseph.

"Joe, let me show you the various buildings and statues that are a testimony to the hundreds of years of French and German influence on this region," Jean said on the first Sunday of spring 1928.

"That would be great. The weather is beautiful, perfect for exploring."

As they rode their bikes through Thionville, Jean pointed to the smaller buildings with porches that were characteristic of the French influence and the neo-Romanesque architecture typical of the German Empire.

"After the Franco-Prussian War of 1870, the area of Alsace-Lorraine was annexed to the newly created German Empire by the Treaty of Frankfurt and became a Reichsland. Thionville was renamed Diedenhofen and became a prosperous German city."

"The German buildings are larger than the French," observed Joe. "They always liked everything big and powerful."

After looking at the town's buildings, they biked to one of the three forts built by the Germans in the nineteenth century.

Jean's hand swept along the line of the fortifications. "The German Army decided to build a fortress line from Mulhouse to Luxembourg to protect the new Reichsland."

Joe's knowledge of history was quite extensive, reaching beyond the borders of Poland. "Is this the Fort de Guentrange?"

"Yes, it is. Another time we'll visit the other two forts and look at fortifications built around Thionville."

Joe was fascinated by the fortifications and the size of the fort.

"Magnificent defence system."

Jean looked at the distant horizon beyond the fortifications. "I don't like the ramparts, such a reminder of the constant wars. I was very happy after the armistice with Germany ending the Great War. As you probably know, the French Army entered Thionville in November 1918, and the city was returned to France by the Treaty of Versailles in 1919."

Through many expeditions with Jean, Joe became familiar not only with the town of Thionville but the large area of northern Lorraine and Alsace with its beautiful wineries, farms famous for their cheeses, and bakeries that were the landmark of every little town.

In November 1929, he decided to visit his family in Poland during the upcoming Christmas holidays. In addition to seeing Maria and the kids, he wanted to discuss their final plan of emigrating to France. He sent a letter to his wife with the latest picture of him, which had been taken by a professional photographer, with the inscription, "To my wife, Maria." At the bottom of the picture, he'd added, "From a place of our future."

Every day since his arrival in France two years ago, Joe had missed his wife and children and time didn't diminish his love for them.

The afternoon of November 15th, Joe and Jean left the house for their afternoon shift at work. The weather was still very nice and they rode their bicycles to the foundry.

"Joe, I asked the superintendent, Marc Kurtz, about your chances of getting a month off to see your family. He was very optimistic," Jean said as he parked his bicycle.

"Thank you. I hope to repay you for your kindness one day."

Marc Kurtz was in the locker room when Joe entered it. "Hi, Joe, I need to talk to you."

"Do you want me to work a double shift today?" asked Joe, as it was a frequent request here at the smelter. Joe didn't mind the double shifts; he was able to save more. He was frugal with the money he earned, and after sending part of it to his wife and spending very little on himself, he had a good amount put aside for a possible future in France and building a house here.

"No, it isn't about work," said Marc. "The company agreed to give you one month off to go to Poland, and they'll buy a train ticket for you in appreciation of your good work in the last two years." Marc was very pleased delivering the message.

"Thank you. I'm so grateful. I almost can't believe it is happening." He extended his hand to Marc.

Joe was a little late when he entered the smelter hall. The other men were already busy moving the raw materials, stacking them close to the furnaces.

The air that emitted from the smelters was very foul but Joe didn't notice it today. Happiness filled his heart and his thoughts were with Maria and his children.

He and four men operated the smelters in this hall. Each one of them took a break every hour to rest from the heat and hard labour. During his break, Joe went to see Jean in the warehouse.

He entered through a big gate as Jean was moving a load of lime with the crane. "Hi, Jean. I have great news."

"Wait a moment, Joe. I'll be there in a moment." He stopped the crane with the load up in the air and went to see Joe.

"Great news, I can go to Poland. The company will also pay for my train ticket."

"I'm happy for you."

"I can't wait to tell my family about you, our friendship, about my life here. I could not have achieved what I have without you."

"I didn't do much; it was your hard work and smarts that made you who you're today."

"Maybe it was fate that we met here and became friends. My wife Maria would like to meet you. She may even emigrate to France when I save enough money."

"I envy you. You have a clear mission ahead of you. I'm still a free spirit but hope to meet the right woman one day and settle down."

"My life wasn't so clear a few years ago. I made mistakes. I hurt people. I'll tell you more about my life one day, over a bottle of wine."

"Look at you, becoming such a Frenchman, loving wine and cheese. We like women as well; this is why I'm not settled down yet."

"Wait until you meet the right one; everything changes for the better."

They embraced, looked at each other, and started to laugh. They were not comfortable openly showing their emotions and the laughter curtailed their embarrassment.

They didn't hear the squeaking noise above them until alerted by a loud snap of the wires. They looked up for a terrifying split second that seemed to last for a long time as Joe watched the load of lime coming down on them. He moved one step and lost consciousness.

When he opened his eyes, they were burning and the pain of it was excruciating. He willed himself to keep one eye open and looked slowly around. He was partially covered by the broken bags of lime and the splinters of the wooden pallet. Gathering all his strength and despite the unbearable pain, he wriggled out from under the debris. His left leg was badly broken but it didn't stop him from moving a little away from the crash scene. He looked back and saw Jean's leg sticking out from underneath the broken pallet.

The terrifying scene gave him supernatural strength and he crawled to the cabin of the crane in hope of moving it. He lifted himself on his elbows, trying to reach the door of the cabin. The pain that gripped his body was paralysing … and then his vision blurred and he fainted.

The collapse of the crane had been heard in other departments in the company and some of the guards and superintendents rushed to the warehouse. The scene in front of them was terrifying. The crane cable was broken and the heavy load of lime was on the ground. A man's body was partially visible under the load.

"Raise the alarm," ordered the chief guard.

Soon they discovered another man near the crane cabin with a badly broken leg and a face covered with blood. He was unconscious but alive. The other man under the load of lime was beyond recognition. He was already dead.

The warehouse superintendent knew that Jean Navarre was the operator of the crane on that day but he didn't know who the other man was. After the count of all the men in the foundry, it was discovered that Joe Novak from the smelting department was missing.

Marc arrived at the accident scene with the director of the company. "The dead man could be Joe Novak." His voice was very distressed.

"Why do you think it's him?"

"He was close friends with Jean Navarre, the crane operator. Most likely Joe came to talk to him. Judging by the positions of the two men, I would say that the one near the crane must be Jean."

They stood silently for a while. Marc could not believe his eyes. Only two hours ago he had spoken with Joe about his visit to Poland.

"How long had he been working in the company?" asked the director.

"He started over two years ago. He was a hard-working man saving money, hoping to bring his family to France."

The director nodded to Marc to continue.

"He was one of the smartest foreign workers in the foundry. He learned our language and immersed himself in our culture. I was planning to promote him after his return from Poland. Few of the foreign workers stay longer than one year and we always have to train new ones. It will be a great loss to us."

The director turned to Marc. "We need to inform his family in Poland. Please come to my office tomorrow, we need to write an appropriate letter to his wife."

"The company should consider sending some compensation to his family."

"We will discuss everything tomorrow."

The ambulance arrived at the door of the warehouse and the unconscious man was transported to the hospital.

It was a grey, cloudy day in November. Ted was outside raking leaves in the garden when he heard his mother wailing in the kitchen. He ran quickly into the house.

She was kneeling on the floor crying, her face buried in her hands.

"Mom, what happened?"

Ania was standing behind, trying to hug her mother, confusion painted on her face.

Ted noticed a letter stained with tears on the floor. He picked it up and read. Horror twisted his face.

Dear Mrs. Novak,

It is with a feeling of great sorrow that we inform you of the death of your husband, Joseph Novak. He was involved in a very unfortunate accident at the foundry. He was buried according to Catholic tradition in a local cemetery. Joseph's savings of 1200 Francs and his possessions will be sent to you shortly. We humbly ask that you accept compensation in the form of 1000 Francs and gifts for you and family to brighten your Christmas a little.

We're very sorry for your loss.
Rhine Foundry Company

Ted finished reading and fell into a state of shock, oblivious to his mother's cries and Ania's tugging on his sleeve. He could not cry; he just stood there motionless. All his dreams of seeing his father vanished. They would never again walk hand in hand the way they had, talking about history.

Ted's emotions turned into anger and resentment. "How could he leave us and then die?" he said out loud. He knelt beside his mother and put one arm around her and the other around his sister. In that moment, he realised that he was not a child anymore and the weight of becoming a grown-up scared him. He was now responsible for his mother and sister. "Mother, go to bed. I'll look after Ania."

There was no answer, only quiet sobs and words repeated over and over again. "Joseph, my love."

Later at night, Ted tried hard to envision the responsibilities of a male head of the family, but he knew that all his thoughts were just childish perceptions of an adult life. Feeling sorry for himself because of his stolen youth and the realisation that he didn't have a father to guide him through the years ahead, Ted could not fight the tears anymore. He cried for a long time, until his pillow was wet under his face. When the tears stopped flowing and his heart grew calm, he resolved never to cry again. His thoughts turned to Father Karol, the local priest who lived across from their house. He decided to talk to him about a sermon in his father's memory and to ask him for his counsel through his life.

Joe opened his right eye and was instantly blinded by the light that flooded the room through a small window.

He was lying on a bed, unable to move; his leg was elevated and the pain in his body was excruciating. A chill went through him and the brightness of the light was unbearable. He closed his eye and realised he could not remember anything. "Where am I? Who am I?"

He was panic-stricken, not remembering anything about who he was or where he lived. He looked around the room with his one eye, realising that the other one was covered with bandages.

I need to keep my eyes closed and soon all will come back to me, he thought before he lost consciousness again.

The next time he woke up, a serious-looking young woman was bending over him, changing the bandages around his ribs. The pain of any movement and the feeling of desolation were paralysing, both physically and mentally.

The women in a white apron and a nurse's hat smiled at him. "Good, you're awake."

He could not understand what she said and stared at her with his one eye open.

"Can you hear me?" she asked.

The words were faintly familiar but he could not make sense of them. Panic set in. He closed his eye and pretended to lose consciousness again. *What is happening to me? Who am I?*

In his mind, he repeated the same questions over and over again. Any effort to remember anything about his life failed.

He was in a hospital bed, unable to move most of his body parts other than his head and one arm. He examined his body, hoping that it would help him remember what had happened. A heavy cast immobilised his left leg, including the hip; his torso was bandaged; and the pain he felt in his rib cage indicated broken ribs. His head and most of his face were covered with bandages and he could not open his left eye under them. Checking his body, he realised that the words forming in his head sounded different from the ones the nurse had spoken to him. This compounded his confusion and he decided to just listen and try to figure out more about himself before he said anything. Other medical staff came to the room and spoke to him, but he just stared at them without responding.

Sedated by the drugs, he slept through the night, until the gentle touch woke him up. It was the nurse he remembered from the other day. *Good sign,* he thought, *at least I remember her.*

"Good morning. Are you feeling better today?"

He blinked, looking at her with his one eye.

"Do you remember anything about the accident?"

Although he could not fully grasp what she said, he understood most of her words.

"Is your name Jean Navarre?" the nurse asked.

The name sounded familiar and he smiled at her. She was a slender, plain-looking woman with a beautiful smile. He thought he would have to trust her; there was no other choice if he wanted to know his identity and to remember his past. For now, he was relieved that his name might be Jean Navarre.

His face scarred on one side; his broken jaw still swollen; his nose healed, but distorted; and his left eye droopy and half closed made him unrecognisable. He stayed in the hospital for three months, while his body recovered and his French partially returned, albeit unclear due to the broken jaw making him speak with a slur.

The nurse, whose name was Emilie Garnot, told him about the accident; about his Polish friend, Joe Novak's, death; and Joe's funeral in a Catholic church attended by the company representatives and some workers. She came every day to his room, taking care of him and telling him a little about his life. One day, she brought a small mirror, and he looked in disbelief at his disfigured face. *Nobody who knew me in the past would recognise me now,* he thought. Tears wet his cheeks and he looked away from the nurse.

Marc Kurtz visited him once in a while, bringing news about current events. The hospital room was small, smelled of disinfectant, and was devoid of any colour except for the bright light coming through the window on the opposite side of the door. Each time Marc came to visit, he wore the same scarf with a blue and white design of a starry night. One day, Jean, as he was now known, pointed at the scarf and said, "It is beautiful."

Marc was slightly nervous when he answered. "I wear it each time I visit you to make sure you recognise me. The doctors worry that you may relapse and lose even the little memory you have."

Jean moaned at the thought of such a possibility.

"The company is paying for your stay here, making sure that you have good care."

"Thank you." He was mostly silent, just listening to Marc talking.

"You and Joe were very good friends and I'm sad that he died in the accident. The representative of the company's management and I went to your house, collected most of Joe's belongings and sent them to his wife in Poland. Joe had planned to visit his family at Christmas and had already bought presents for his wife and two children. We sent them as well, but it was not the presents they expected for Christmas. Perhaps, one day you may want to write to them as a friend of their father."

Jean felt a connection to the family that Mark spoke of. It was a strange feeling and he hoped to understand more as he recovered.

After a long silence, Marc described the scene of the accident and assured Jean that it was not his fault.

"The crane was new and the investigation is still ongoing to determine the cause of its collapse. The company is very eager to get to the bottom of this disaster. I think they want to recover money from the crane supplier and maybe send more money to Joe's widow in Poland."

Jean didn't say anything; he just thought about the widow and her two children.

Marc looked intently at Jean, trying to evaluate his reaction to any news about the Polish family. The accident scene and the bodies' positions were strong proof that it was Joe Novak who had died, but Marc had a nagging feeling that the fast decision made at the scene could be wrong. He had known Jean Navarre longer than Joe, and looking at the partially uncovered face and particularly the eye, he didn't get any sense of the closeness he'd felt in the past when he was in Jean's company.

I may never know for sure who died, but everything I knew about the two men points to the death of Jean not Joe, Marc thought. Each visit brought him closer to his conviction that it was a case of mistaken identity, but it was too late to undo the course of the last two months. Being the one who had assumed that it was Joe who died, Marc could find himself in the middle of a possible new investigation into the accident, creating chaos and perhaps incriminating himself.

Jean brought him back from his thoughts. "Marc, what is it?"

"Nothing, just thinking about your life ahead." In that instant, Marc made a decision not to act on his suspicions about the injured man's identity and to let him live as Jean Navarre.

Three months later, Jean was able to walk and was released from the hospital. He could not remember his past and his strongest connection to the real world was the nurse, Emilie.

"I hope you'll help me with my recovery at home," Jean said to her on his last day at the hospital.

Emilie liked Jean. He was a kind and gentle man. The left side of his face was lacerated with scars and his eye was slightly closed, but he smiled often, trying to compensate for his limited ability to communicate. He was aware of his slurred speech and made an effort to be as clear as he could by speaking slowly, pronouncing every word separately to the point of making them sound non-natural. He preferred to listen to Emilie, avoiding talking unless it was necessary, giving him an aura of secrecy that she accepted as a natural result of the trauma of the accident and his loss of memory.

"The company agreed to pay for your care at home. I'll come to your house to help you with your recuperation."

The transportation from the hospital to Jean's house was arranged by Marc, who spent the first day and night at the house making sure that Jean had everything needed to live independently. The bed was moved closer to the door of the bedroom and clean towels were arranged in a small bathroom adjacent to the bedroom. The pantry in the kitchen was stocked with plenty of food, and fresh bread and cheese were set on the table. The house felt familiar to Jean and he was hopeful that his memory might come back to him with time.

Emilie visited Jean almost every day after work, helping him to recover his mobility and speech. She had the patience to work with him on his speech by asking him to repeat common phrases and read aloud small passages from the book collection in the house. By the spring of 1930, his speech had improved but the slight slur remained, making him sound peculiar as he enunciated every word.

With every day passing, their conversation was livelier and Jean felt at ease in Emilie's presence. They talked about the books Jean read recently and Emilie's job in the hospital and her love of flowers. She knew a lot about many of them and dreamed about having her own garden.

He found comfort in her company and the courage to ask questions about his past. "Emilie, do you know anything about my family?"

"As per the company records, you don't have any known family. Your parents and two sisters died during the Great War of malnutrition and influenza," Emily said with genuine sadness.

"Do they know where they lived?"

"They had lived on a farm in southern France. Perhaps one day you could go there and visit their graves. Maybe it could help with your memory."

Every day Jean looked forward to Emilie's visits.

"It's a beautiful day. Let's go for a longer walk today." Emilie extended her hand invitingly.

Jean stood up and took her hand. "Let's try. I think I can do it."

She didn't withdraw her hand but looked at him smiling and squeezed his hand gently. She looked radiant; her short hair bounced as she lifted her face towards his.

Jean felt happy for the first time since the accident.

Before the death of her husband, Maria had been a very industrious woman, supporting her family by buying eggs, milk, cheese, and cream from farmers outside the town and selling them at the local market. She had earned enough money for everyday life, allowing her to save the money that Joseph sent to her from France. After his death, her desire to live vanished and she stayed mostly inside the house, leaving only to attend daily evening Mass and Sunday morning Mass in the local church.

Life had become difficult for Ted since the accident. He didn't complain, but the responsibilities for his family were pressing down on him. Half a year had passed since the dreadful letter arrived from France.

Dressed in his Sunday clothes, Ted called impatiently to his sister struggling to put her dress on. "Ania, hurry up. We'll be late for Sunday Mass."

"I need some help. Is Mom already at the church?"

He turned with annoyance on his face. "Yes, she's already there. I'll help you."

He looked at his five-year-old sister and his anger disappeared. He loved her more than he wanted to admit. She was the only person that he truly cared for in his young life.

"Will Father Karol talk to us after Mass?" she asked, taking Ted's hand as they left in a hurry.

Ted and Ania liked the priest, who was like a father to them. He always had a little sweet treat for Ania and was very helpful guiding Ted in his young life.

"Perhaps I should talk to him about Mother. Maybe he could help her to recover from the tragedy and look after the family more. He needs to know that we're using the last savings from Father." Ted was talking more to himself than Ania, who was already distracted by the blooming trees on this beautiful June day.

After the Mass, when Maria and the kids met with the priest, Ted was surprised at the turn of the conversation. "Ted, soon you'll be ten years old, and your mother and I decided that you would take over her business." Father Karol looked at Ted while his mother stared absentmindedly into space. "Summer vacation is a good time for you to start to go to the farms. You're familiar with the route and know some of the farmers. Your mother still needs more time at home and cannot walk the route." Father Karol appeared uncomfortable.

"Will Mother sell the produce at the market?"

"With your help, she will try."

Ted was familiar with the farmers' route and with the market, not only in town, but also the big one in Warsaw. Before the death of his father, he'd often helped his mother carry the food from the farms and sell it at the markets. It was hard work. Three times a week, they walked up to thirty kilometres to various farms to buy products. They sold the milk and cream to the town's people and took the cheese and butter to Warsaw every Saturday. Now, he would have to do it on his own.

Soon he was able to recover some of the business lost after his mother had stopped buying from the farmers, but he resented the summer that dragged slowly by, one day at a time. He made money that the family needed for everyday expenses and when September came, he continued his rounds to the closest farms. Three times per week, he got up at 4 a.m. and came back just in time to go to school. He grew resilient to the hardship of his life, becoming strong-minded and able to carry on with the responsibilities that had been so unfairly presented to him by life.

On the anniversary of Joseph's death, Maria went to see the priest. "Father Karol, my savings are almost gone. I'm so sorry that I cannot recover faster from my grief. It's not fair to Ted."

"Maria, you're lucky to have such a responsible young son; he will always look after you."

"We cannot continue like this anymore. Maybe we should go to my mother's house to stay with them." Maria's voice was full of anxiety and Father Karol knew she didn't want to make such move.

"What about applying for a pension from the French Company?" suggested Father Karol.

He helped her with the application and even hired a lawyer to draft a letter. To their surprise, Maria started receiving the pension as of January 1931.

Life improved with the money from France. Ted continued buying from the farmers, but the pressure of providing for the family was gone and he started saving the money for himself. He was a leading voice in the school and church choirs and was learning to play the church organ every Sunday after Mass. He thought that he could be an organist at the church and maybe even a music teacher at a local school. Things were looking up for him. The dark clouds hanging above his head were slowly disappearing.

Every summer for the last three years, Billy and his family had gone to Aunt Maggie's for a week of vacation. The time they spent there was full of beach outings, lunches on the big veranda, and visiting the countryside. Billy reluctantly took part in the family activities, always looking for free time that he could spend in the barn where the plane was.

On the last day of his summer vacation in 1930, Billy was cleaning the airplane while everybody else was at the beach.

Quietly, Aunt Maggie came to the barn. "Billy, I would like to tell you the story of our family. You're thirteen years old now, and it is time for you to know the truth."

Billy nodded eagerly.

"Let's sit here near the airplane," she said as she opened an album full of pictures. "The seaplane that you love so much was one of four that were flown by my husband, Winthrop, and your grandfather, William."

Billy turned to his aunt, smiling with pride. "I was named after him."

Aunt Maggie sat silently and appeared lost in her own thoughts for a while. Billy looked at the album, but her hands were resting on the opened pages, covering most of the photos. He noticed a beautiful ring adorning a finger on her left hand. He stared at the ring, imagining her as a young and beautiful woman. He regretted not knowing her during those times and wondered what had kept the family separated for so many years.

His thoughts were interrupted by his aunt's voice, which continued in the same soft manner. "Your grandfather was a younger brother of my husband, who was the commanding officer on the aircraft carrier during the Great War. Your grandfather and many younger pilots served under his command. During one of the final sea battles of the war, your grandfather was killed in the battle. Death was a frequent occurrence during the war and many men died at sea."

Billy's voice was very quiet. "We learned a lot about the Great War at school."

"Your grandfather's death was difficult to accept for the family because my husband decided to send several of the scout planes to find the exact position of the German fleet, knowing that it was a very dangerous mission and the chances of dying were high."

Billy saw the emotions painting her face: grief, love, regret, and sadness.

"Two planes came back but two went down—one with your grandfather. He was forty-eight years old and you were just one year old. It was a devastating tragedy for your grandmother. She and her family could not forgive my husband for approving this dangerous mission."

"But it was war ..." Billy stopped in mid-sentence as he realised that his aunt didn't hear him.

"Your Uncle Winthrop died soon after the war of tuberculosis and also of a broken heart." Tears rolled down her face. "I lost direct contact with your family for many years. Fortunately, a mutual friend kept me informed about all of you. Three years ago, I got the courage and contacted your father. That was the first time we met here in this house." Aunt Maggie stopped talking and closed her eyes.

They sat in silence and when long minutes had passed, she removed a picture from the album and gave it to Billy. "Let's hope that the world will be at peace forever, and you never have to make a decision like your Uncle Winthrop."

She closed the album and put her arm around Billy.

The picture was of two brothers in military uniforms. Billy had no difficulties recognising his grandfather. He looked like him.

Emilie and Jean got married in June of 1930 in a small church in Thionville.

Before the wedding, his nervousness increased as he worried about exchanging their vows in front of family and friends.

"Jean, don't worry about your speech. It has improved significantly and the slur is gone."

"But I sound different from you or Marc."

"You sound fine and everybody understands you. You've learned to pronounce every word carefully, making your speech clipped. Sometimes, I can hear a Germanic accent when you speak."

"Germanic accent?" Jean was taken aback.

"Nothing wrong with it. Many people here have German roots and speak with different accents. You belong to this part of France."

Emilie's parents and two brothers came to the wedding from northern France. Marc was Jean's best man, which was not surprising to anyone, as they had grown close during Jean's recovery.

Jean was very nervous waiting for Emilie to enter the church, led by her parents. His memory, wiped out by the accident, made him unsure of himself and the decisions he was making. He was aware of this weakness and afraid that Emilie's father might not fully approve of him. It wasn't only the thought about approval. There was something else that lingered in the deepest parts of his mind, some glimpses of his previous life that seemed very different from the one he lived now. Vague fragments of memory, which he'd been afraid to explore in the past year, flooded his mind while he was waiting for Emilie. He closed his eyes, seeking refuge in the darkness and hoping for the end of his unwanted thoughts.

The sound of the church organ playing soft, beautiful music brought him back to reality. He opened his eyes and looked at Emilie approaching the altar. She looked radiant in a white gown with a lace veil swept to the back of her head. His uncertainty left him, and happiness filled his heart. At that moment he was sure that the wedding was the beginning of a good new life. Emilie's father smiled at Jean and shook his hand firmly, looking with warmth into his eyes. Jean had no doubts anymore about the approval of his future father-in-law. The wedding reception was held at the house with Emilie's family and a small group of their friends attending.

After the reception, they left the house and took the train to Strasburg. It was a modest honeymoon, but they enjoyed every moment of it. Emilie's favourite time was walking through the markets and looking at the multitudes of flowers displayed in various shops, some still in buckets of water and some already made into beautiful arrangements.

"Darling, I hope to be better soon and start working again at the foundry," Jean said. They were sitting in the small café on a main street of Strasbourg. "In the meantime, I can fix the fence and make some improvements on the house."

"My love, I know that you'll be well very soon. I would like to continue working in the hospital until you are fully employed." Emilie took his hand in hers and kissed him gently on the mouth. She was a modest person but after the wedding, she often showed her affection in public. At first, he was a little uncomfortable but soon liked her spontaneous kisses and hugs.

They quickly established their life together in Jean's house. Emilie continued to work in the hospital and Jean slowly worked on house improvements. In the evenings, they talked about their future modest but happy life, hoping that they would be blessed with children.

Jean had not recovered his memory and secretly didn't want to, as if afraid that something from the past might affect his state of happiness. The left side of his face was scarred, but he covered it with a well-trimmed beard that suited him well. His left leg, which had been damaged during the accident, had left him with a permanent limp and he often had to use a cane to move around.

During his recovery at home, Jean discovered that he was very skilled at metalwork and woodworking, and he applied his new skills to house improvements. It was a small, two-storey stucco house with an attic and was built on a corner lot at the end of the street. The size of the lot was bigger than the other lots, and the land on the east side was owned by the town. A football field and a park were the focal points of the public area and Sundays were popular days for the townspeople to gather there.

The main entrance to the house was located on its side, away from the street. Two windows on the main floor and two smaller ones on the second floor faced the street. Blue shutters affixed to the windows showed signs of chipping paint but looked solid and well attached to the walls. The front of the house facing the garden had two windows on each side of the door and three on the second level. Like the windows facing the street, they were adorned with blue shutters in a similar fashion to many other houses on the street. Three very small windows were located just under the roof, letting some light into the attic. The fence that ran along the street was made of wooden pickets attached to stone pillars. A keen-eyed passerby could notice that some pickets were rotting and few stones were crumbling. The other sides of the property were enclosed by a chain-link fence that was in good condition. The small wooden gate leading to the garden and the main entrance to the house was in good repair, but the latch was broken and rusted. Jean wondered why he had not taken more pride in his house and kept up with the repairs. Perhaps being a single man and renting rooms to seasonal workers was the reason behind the disrepair.

"Everything has changed now. I'm a happily married man and I want my wife to be proud of her house," he often whispered to himself as he worked on the improvements. With the help of Marc he purchased some old equipment from the Rhine Foundry and installed a small forge in the open air at the back of the property.

When the repairs were done, the fence was freshly painted, and the small gate replaced with an ornate one made of wrought iron, Jean and Emilie liked to sit at the outside table and talk about their future.

The new fence with a beautiful iron gate and the small shed in the back of the house were the best in the neighbourhood. Soon, many people asked Jean to improve their fences or build simple furniture, doors, and sheds. His skills of woodworking and wrought-iron ornaments became known in the area.

In May 1931, their son Jean-Marc was born. Emilie stopped working at the hospital as Jean's earnings, although modest, provided for a comfortable life.

Over a year later, on November 1, 1932, their daughter was born. She was named Marie-Ann. Jean chose the name for his daughter because the sound of it was familiar to him. Something from his past echoed in his mind and occasionally names came to him, which he couldn't explain.

With Emilie's help and care, he had recovered his health but his injured leg was shorter and the limp was a serious obstacle to going back to work in the foundry. Before his daughter was born, he had found steady employment as a cooper with a prominent winery, making barrels for their wines, shelves for the cellars, iron gates, wrought-iron rod ornaments, even furniture. As part of the settlement with the foundry, in addition to some money, Jean was given the opportunity to buy one of their used trucks, an older version of the Berliet. He was making a good living working for the winery and saved enough money to consider opening his own business. Emilie supported his idea and in 1933, Jean started his own cooperage business, making and supplying barrels to wineries in the Alsace-Lorraine region. The wines from this area were well known across France and other countries, and his product was in high demand.

"Emilie, I'm thinking about expanding our business." Jean was beaming with self-satisfaction.

She looked at him with anticipation, expecting further explanation.

"The vacant lot at the back of our house is for sale. We could buy it and have enough land to expand the cooperage business. Maybe you would like to expand your garden?"

They purchased the vacant lot, and Jean hired people to build a big shop and a warehouse. By the end of 1934, he was employing fifteen people and had plans to expand even further. The house they lived in was enlarged by adding an extension, creating an L-shaped building that obscured some view of their back property. Emilie created a beautiful garden, growing flowers and vegetables. Soon, she owned a stall at the market, selling her flowers and vegetables. Life was taking the right turns for Jean and his family. The accident and his recovery were a distant memory and he stopped dwelling on his forgotten past.

On an early afternoon in March 1934, Jean met with Marc in the local pub. Marc had continued to work at the foundry, earning his promotion to the position of operations director. He had married in 1931 and had one son, Pierre. Jean and Marc continued their friendship and met frequently.

Jean was happy to see his friend. "How are you, Marc? Let's get a glass of wine."

They sat at the corner table, away from other patrons. Marc looked a little hesitant but after a glass of wine, he relaxed and looked at Jean for a long while in silence.

"I'm concerned about Hitler coming to power in Germany. He is very nationalistic and may want to oppose the Treaty of Versailles," Jean said, breaking the silence and continuing to prophesise the possibility of dark times in Europe.

"Jean, you're still passionate about politics. You and Joe would spend hours talking about the affairs of the world; your lack of memory didn't erase your passion for politics." Marc raised his glass of wine, laughing. "*Salut.*"

Jean continued with a gloomy voice. "The rise of Hitler is a very serious matter, and I'm afraid for the future of the neighbouring countries, including France."

"I agree with you. It is a very serious situation. I was laughing because it was like hearing Joe instead of you. He always saw the negative and dark side of politics and you were always the optimistic one."

"Sometimes I feel guilty about his death and maybe I try to think like him," Jean responded quickly. "Is the company sending a pension to Joe's widow in Poland?" His heart pounded a bit more as he talked about the Polish family.

"Yes, they send a monthly pension and I make sure that they send small gifts every Christmas." Marc hesitated for a moment as if wanting to say something ominous, sending a shiver through Jean's spine.

"Is something wrong, Marc?"

"Everything is fine, Jean. Going back to politics, what do you think about the expansion of the fortifications on the German border? The Maginot Line."

"I think that defence fortifications are necessary as part of our military strategy. The newspapers write about the senior members in the French military believing that the German anger over Treaty of Versailles is a clear sign that Germany could seek revenge." Jean always prided himself as very current in world affairs, and he read at least a few newspapers every week.

"Rhine Foundry was contracted to do a lot of work for the government. Recently, I heard that they need a small company to produce hinges, locks, and other items for the concrete bunkers—perhaps you would be interested?"

"I'm busy, but expanding into ironworks for the military could be profitable." Jean was certain that he would accept the proposal but after a moment of silence, he added, "I need to discuss this with Emilie."

By July 1934, Jean had purchased more land and built a new shop specialising in small hardware for military application. He hired twenty people to work two shifts and a superintendent to assist him in managing his substantial enterprise. Business was really good.

Jean liked to personally deliver his hardware to the building site on the other side of Thionville along the Moselle River. He liked to look at the construction site and especially at the military fortifications. As a supplier, he was allowed to enter the building sites at various points of the defence construction area.

Unloading his truck with the help of two workers, he was approached by a tall man in military uniform. "Good morning," the man said. "My name is Michel Parrot. Can you please come with me to the office?"

"Is something wrong with my hardware?" Jean asked with concern in his voice.

They entered the barrack where the office was located and Michel closed the door behind them. "This is a very confidential conversation. Please don't repeat it to anyone, not even Emilie, your wife."

Jean was uneasy that this stranger knew his wife's name. He became a little apprehensive about this meeting.

"Your hardware is good but France needs your services beyond supplying your products for the fortifications. We know that you're from a southern part of the country and a loyal French citizen."

Jean looked at Michel with uncertainty. "I'm listening."

Michel talked looking through the window. "As you know, Alsace-Lorraine was always a disputed territory and for generations, many

Alsatians maintained that their traditional loyalty belongs to the region, rather than to French or German governments. We suspect that some people are spying for the Germans in hope that the region will gain an independent status in case the Germans invade France. Some families prospered under the German government and would prefer Alsace-Lorraine to be either independent or part of Germany again."

"Thank you for the history lesson, but what this has to do with me?"

Michel turned from the window to look straight at Jean. "I'll be very direct with you. Your friend Marc Kurtz is on our list of those we suspect of spying for the Germans. He works for the Rhine Foundry and often has meetings on their behalf with our officials. They supply many parts and the railway tracks for us."

Confusing thoughts raced through Jean's head. He was uncomfortable listening to the accusation; Marc was his close friend and the conversation was not heading in the right direction. If Marc was a spy helping the Germans, Jean's friendship with him could be questioned by authorities.

Michel saw the emotions on Jean's face. "You could help France by getting involved."

Jean was taken by surprise, not knowing what to say. He was hoping that Michel would continue.

"Please come with your next delivery in two days. A young man with dark hair and a thin moustache will meet you on the site and bring you to the office.

Two days later, Jean arrived at the barracks. When workers were busy unloading boxes of hardware from the truck, a young man fitting the description given by Michel approached him.

Michel didn't waste any time with pleasantries. "As a close friend of Marc's, you'll find out about his family background and his thoughts about France and Germany."

"That should not be difficult." Jean was relieved that the task was rather easy, but Michel continued.

"We need to know more about his organisation. You should suggest to Marc some improvements on his house to be there frequently and look around for some evidence of spying."

Jean looked at Michel, expecting more information.

"It would be good if Marc tried to recruit you to work with him as a spy. Most likely he won't reveal that he works for the Germans, but he may ask you to work with him for an independent Alsace. You have to agree to work with him."

Jean was horrified, but had no other choice but to agree to the plan. He wanted to be seen as a true Frenchman and patriot.

Thirteen-year-old Erik was in his room reading a book when his father, Otto Hermann, came home from work full of excitement, singing, "*Deutschland, Deutschland über alles.*" Erik put the book down and opened the door, but the scene in the living room stopped him from entering it. His mother Rita looked at her husband bewildered, her hands on her hips waiting for some explanation.

Erik heard their hushed conversation, then he heard his mother cry, and minutes later, the slam of the door behind his father as he left the house.

"Mom, what happened?"

"You're too young to understand."

"Mom, will something happen to us because you're Polish and the Germans don't like them?"

She put her arms around him, kissing his head gently. "Hitler has become the chancellor of Germany. Maybe he isn't as bad as some people say."

"Is that why Father was so happy?"

"Don't worry, your father is a good man and will make sure everything will be fine. Let's not talk about it now." She left the room, blowing her nose into a handkerchief.

Life changed in the Hermann family from that day. Father was always in meetings and Mother grew quieter over the months.

To escape the tension in the house, Erik often spent hours in his room, reading books. Jules Verne was his favourite author. He visualised the adventures of Captain Nemo and other heroes from the books. "I want to travel the world," he would often whisper as he looked at the pictures in the book.

He spoke German and Polish fluently and had friends from both backgrounds. He loved football and enjoyed playing with other boys in the neighbourhood. Erik could play on both sides. Whenever some of the boys on either the German or Polish team were not available, he stepped in.

Over the next few months, he started to notice changes; the German boys became more aggressive and called others disrespectful names and football matches often ended in fights.

At the end of summer, Erik's father shocked Erik and his mother while they were eating breakfast. "Erik, in September, you'll attend a boarding school with military training after classes. You will live with the other German boys."

Rita's eyes became glossy with tears. "He is too young to be away from home."

"The decision is made; I already enrolled him. He is spending too much time reading fantasy books." The conversation ended abruptly and Otto left the room.

The fact that Jean had lost his memory and had no recollection of the political struggles of Alsatians made it easier to convince Marc that he was sympathetic with his cause of an independent Alsace. From earlier conversations, Jean had gained a good knowledge of Marc's family and their past.

The Kurtz family history traced back to the ninth century when the Alsatian region had been part of Lothringia, and later of the duchy of Swabia. Their family name was Von Kurtz. They owned substantial lands and were part of the influential political group of the gentry in the region. The Von Kurtzes were Protestants and like many others, were subjected to persecution by Catholic France after the whole region became part of France at the end of the Thirty Years' War in 1791.

It was during those times that the family lost their titles and considerable landholdings. Some of the Von Kurtz family emigrated to Russia when Catherine the Great proposed a plan to settle the vast plains in the Black Sea region. Thousands of farmers from Alsace took the opportunity to resettle with the promise of free land, religious freedom, and exemption from military service. The Von Kurtz family prospered in Russia, but it all changed during the devastation of the Great War and later the Bolshevik Revolution. Many Alsatians were executed or sent to Siberia's mines, and Marc's family lost contact with the Von Kurtz clan in Russia.

Although the Von Kurtz roots were Germanic, in his childhood, Marc often heard his grandfather say, "The Von Kurtz are supporters of an independent Alsace."

After the Great War, when France took control of the region and started repression of Germanic culture, strong political movements resulted in the formation of parties seeking autonomy or even separation and self-rule. Through the late 1920s and early 1930s, these movements reached their height, and the Kurtz family were prominent players in seeking independence.

The next time Jean and Marc met, their conversation was light, mostly about work and summer plans.

Marc started to talk about his plans. "I would like to renovate our house this summer."

"Do you need my help?"

"Yes, my wife likes the window shutters in your house. She would like to replace our old ones with ones similar to yours."

"I can make them for her," Jean said. He was thinking about the access he could have to Marc's house.

"Jean, please stop by our house any time you need to take measurements or start the installation. Don't worry if we're not at home; here's a spare key."

"That would be convenient, thank you." Jean put the key in his pocket.

During one of his visits in July, when Marc was at work and his wife and their son were out at the market, Jean discovered a loose brick under the window in the main room. Hidden inside the wall was a canvas bag. He removed it carefully and placed it on the windowsill. Inside, he found maps and detailed plans of the fortifications built in Thionville. The information on the maps and plans were written in German. There were other documents in the bag, all in German. After a quick scan of the content, he put the canvas bag back inside the wall just as the front door opened and

Marc's wife entered the room.

Jean stood in front of the window with the measuring tape in his hand. "I finished measuring the windows and will start working on the shutters soon." He smiled and left the house, afraid that she might discover his snooping.

Three days later, he made a delivery to the construction site and met with Michel Parrot.

"Marc is into something. I found maps and detailed plans of the fortifications, all in German."

"Can you watch him for a while, see where he goes and who comes to his house?"

"I'm not a spy; how can I do it without being noticed?"

"Perhaps it is time for Marc to include you in his network. We need to discover the whole network of spies and Marc can lead you to them."

The next time Jean and Marc met at the pub, Jean had an idea. "The bloody French are behind with the payment for the hardware I delivered to the construction site," he complained bitterly.

"Are you fine financially?"

"Not really. Is it possible that I could get some iron from the foundry on credit? I have some orders to make for the winery but don't have the cash to buy the iron."

Marc put a piece of cheese in his mouth and took the time to swallow it. "Let's meet next week. Perhaps I may have an answer for you."

The week dragged on at a snail's pace, making Jean more uncertain about his mission with each passing day. The mid-July day was hot and humid, and Jean was sweaty under his shirt as he entered the corner pub. Marc was already waiting for him at the table with two other men. They were drinking a local beer and Jean ordered one for himself. The conversation was about work, France, Germany, and the fortifications on the Moselle River. At the end of the evening, Jean left with the promise of a supply of iron on credit and agreed to meet with Marc at his house the next day.

Emilie was sitting at the dining table when Jean came home late in the evening. She was annoyed. "Jean, where were you tonight?"

Jean looked sheepishly at her. "At the pub with Marc."

"Is everything alright? You're never home lately. I worry when I don't know what you're doing. The kids are always asking for you."

"The work on Marc's house will be done soon. I promise I'll be home every evening after that," Jean answered, feeling uncomfortable about lying to his wife.

When Jean arrived at Marc's the next day, Marc was sitting alone at the kitchen table reading a newspaper. "Please sit down before you start your work," he said.

"Is something troubling you?" Jean said, taking a seat at the table.

"I'm just thinking about my life and the land I love."

"Please tell me."

Marc talked about his family history, about their love for Alsace, about the influences of the Germans and the French. "I believe in an independent Alsace." Marc almost seemed to have forgotten that Jean was sitting next to him. "The French changed their approach to Alsatians and they are demanding that we assimilate. There are more and more people from other parts of France and Europe that are coming here for work. It is good for our economy but bad for the survival of our culture." He looked eager to talk more about family history when he realised that Jean was sitting at the table with an uncomfortable expression on his face. "Sorry, Jean, to drag you into this. After all, you and your wife are French and prosperous here. I didn't mean to go on this way, but I hope you understand my feelings."

Jean trod with caution. "I think I do understand."

"You're my friend; you could help me a little in the pursuit of my cause." Marc poured another glass of wine.

At the end of the evening and a few glasses of wine, Jean agreed to get some information about the French defence plans for Marc.

Late in the evening, when Emilie was in bed, he wondered why Marc asked for this, since he already had a lot of information about the fortifications. He suspected that it was a way to get him involved. He was torn between his friendship with Marc and his duty to France. He knew that eventually, he might have to betray Marc. He shivered thinking about it, but at the same time, he felt betrayed by Marc. He had no right to involve Jean in Alsatian conspiracies, to drag him into a world that Jean didn't belong to and didn't want to be part of. On the other hand, Jean had created the opportunity to be involved with premeditation and under pressure from Michel Parrot. He felt stuck between the two wrongs and was unable to make his own decision. He had a feeling that his whole life, he had been pushed into actions by others and extraneous situations that were to a great degree out of his control. He shrugged his shoulders and resigned himself to a life of doing what others considered important.

It was a warm, sunny day in May 1936. Ted was fixing a broken rake, sitting on the front porch of the house. He was fifteen years of age, and medium-built with dark, intense eyes. He hoped he might resemble his father. The picture Joseph had sent from France depicted him as a slender man, with dark hair and dreamy, dark eyes. Ted's eyes were always alert and penetrating when he talked to people. Ania called them scary eyes. Perhaps they were, he thought, but they never missed anything that was important.

He looked up from the rake, alerted by a stranger approaching their house. The man was middle-aged and well dressed. He wore a dark coat that looked new and a fedora hat, looking nothing like the people in Ted's neighbourhood. Ted felt uncomfortable, frightened that the man was going to bring trouble. He could not explain this strange feeling and decided to go inside the house. At that point, it was too late.

"Is your mother at home?" the man in the fedora hat asked, putting one foot on the steps of the porch.

Ted's voice betrayed his discomfort. "She's not at home. What would you like from her?"

"Is your father around?" He looked straight into Ted's eyes.

"My father is dead. Who are you?" Ted stepped forward with the rake in his hands like a weapon. "He died in France. Please leave."

"Are you sure your father is dead? I would like to speak to your mother," the stranger insisted.

"He died in France. Please leave." Unexpectedly, Ted pushed the man away from the porch and went into the house, slamming the door in anger.

Who was that man? Why did he question my father's death? Ted looked through the window as the man walked back the way he came.

After the man left, Ted took Ania and went to the church, knowing that his mother was there. "Look after Ania," he said to his mother. "It's time for you to act like a normal person again."

Ted left the church in a hurry, desperate to find the stranger. He needed to know why the man in the fedora hat had come to their house and inquired about Father. He decided to check the diner on the main street not far from the church. To his surprise, the man was sitting at a table by the window with another, much younger man.

Ted crouched under the open window to eavesdrop.

The two men ate in silence for a while and then the young one asked, "Father, what did you find out about Joseph Novak?"

"I talked to his son; he is convinced about his father's death."

"Maybe there are just rumours that he survived the accident and lives in France under an assumed name."

"But the two men in my shop talked about Joseph being alive."

"Father, the two transient workers in your shop most likely were liars looking for some information about his family. Maybe they want to take advantage of the widow?" The young man turned his attention to the plate of food in front of him.

Their conversation confused Ted. Why would anyone doubt that his father was dead? Looking at the two men at the table, he realised that he was longing for his father. He wanted to sit at the table with him, talk the way the young man talked with his father, with respect and love. He thought about the last day he'd seen his father, about his anger, almost hate. Ted wished he could change their last meeting and tell his father that he loved him. Joseph must have been sad to leave seeing his only son resenting him.

Ted looked at the two men at the table and his admiration for them changed into anger. Why were they so lucky to have each other while he was lonely and tired of looking after his family? He wanted to harm them, let them know that they were not welcome in his town—tell them to go away and never come back to Brusk.

He entered the diner and went to their table with his fists clenched. "I don't know who you are, but leave and never come back here again. I heard your conversation." He wanted to scream at them but was only able to say quietly, "Our lives changed forever when my father died in the accident. Don't talk senseless things about his death. That would destroy my mother. She has not recovered after losing her husband and any gossip about him may kill her."

The older man looked sadly at Ted. "We understand your situation and won't bother you and your mother again."

"I hope so. You're not from this area," said Ted. "I know many farmers and townspeople. I've never seen you here before."

"No, Edward, we're not from this area and will be leaving on the next train to Krakow."

The young man silently nodded at his father's words. He was around eighteen years old with light-brown hair and blue eyes, not like Ted's.

"Perhaps, you would like to visit us one day. I knew your father," said the older man. He gave Ted their address and they left the diner.

On August 2, 1936, Jean met with Michel Parrot in the office of the Maginot Line fortification. The last time they'd met was in May, and Jean wondered if something unexpected had happened to Michel or their mission. He was relieved when he was called to the meeting.

"Jean, you're doing great work. We have many names of the conspirators, but we still don't have enough information about their collaboration with the Germans."

Jean became slightly annoyed. "Marc does not include me in every meeting, nor does he disclose all their plans. What else can I do?"

At the end of the meeting, they agreed that Jean would invite Marc to the pub and Michel's men would instigate a brawl. Jean feared that some harm might happen to Marc but despite his reservations, agreed to the plan.

The meeting in the pub happened a week later. It took Jean a great deal of effort to stay calm; most of the time, he kept his head down, eating cheese and filling his and Marc's glasses with local wine.

Three men sitting at the next table started arguing and soon a brawl started among them. In the next few minutes, another two men sitting in the corner joined the scuffle. Jean and Marc quickly finished their meal, washed it down with the rest of the wine, and stood to leave the pub. They were still near the table when two of the fighting men attacked them from behind. Jean didn't like to fight and quickly covered his face with his hands to avoid any confrontation. Somebody kicked him in the legs and soon he was on the floor. He could see three men surrounding Marc and closed his eyes, anticipating what might happen next.

In the next few minutes, everything was over and there was no sign of the hooligans. Jean's head was hurting as he listened to Marc's moaning on the floor on the other side of the table. He lifted himself from the floor and crawled towards his friend. The owner of the pub was already helping Marc to lift his head. Marc was bleeding from the nose and could not move one leg. Jean felt terrible about the incident. He was glad that the hoodlums had attacked him as well. His leg was hurting but was not broken. It was a small punishment for his involvement. Jean assisted in transporting Marc to the hospital.

A few hours later, Jean was sitting on the side of a hospital bed, looking at Mark's leg in a cast. "How are you, Marc? We were badly beaten by those strangers."

"Jean, I'm glad that you're not seriously injured."

"I was luckier than you." Jean smiled meekly. "Your wife was informed about your injury and came back home from visiting her parents."

"She will be angry with me for foolishly getting involved in the fight."

"She is more concerned than angry at you. Emilie is helping her to prepare the house for you to be comfortable there. It may take several weeks before the cast is removed."

Jean left the hospital with a heavy heart. He didn't like deceiving Marc. The plan to be more involved in Marc's organisation could work, but he was uncomfortable with this turn of events.

"Is it wrong to want to be free and live in someone's own country?" On the way home, Jean was anguished by his thoughts. They seemed familiar to him, as deeply inside him, something steered his past. He could not explain this strange feeling.

A month later, Jean travelled to Germany to meet with Marc's contact there. The man was a middle-aged German of Alsatian background. He was dressed as a civilian but Jean sensed that he served in the army.

They talked about an independent Alsace and told stories about many families emigrating to Russia and South Africa.

By the time Marc recovered from his injury, Jean was acquainted with several people in Germany involved in the conspiracy. He worked as an agent and provided information about the French fortifications to the Germans. All information he passed on to the Germans was approved by Michel.

Father Karol invited Ted to his office in the parish house. "Edward, I have good news for you. Please, sit down." He always had a habit of calling him Edward, never Ted like most of the people in town.

Ted liked the name. It gave him the feeling of being respected by the priest and most of all, taken seriously.

The big and very ornate desk made of mahogany looked out of place in an office sparsely decorated with just a plain cross on the wall behind the desk and shelves with books, mostly devoted to the Catholic religion. Ted wondered about the origins of this desk; maybe one day he would ask about it. He often met with Father Karol but never in such a formal setting—he was anxious to hear the news, hoping it would be about his further education.

Ted's mother didn't have money to send him either to high school or trade school after he completed grammar school in June 1935. Ted was still dreaming about becoming a musician, when earlier in the year, Father Karol proposed he apply to a trade school and become a master tailor. Ted knew that his dream of music school was just that, a dream, and agreed to the priest's offer. He loved Father Karol like his own father and respected his advice. The priest paid frequent visits to Ted's family, providing emotional support and occasionally financial help.

"The school is run by the Salesians order in Warsaw. They accepted your application and you'll start in September," he said.

"What about money?" Ted asked uneasily.

"Don't worry about the money. The order pays for most of it and I'll pay for the rest. I know it's not exactly what you would love to study, but it's the only option."

"Thank you, I appreciate this." Ted's eyes glossed a little but he quickly fought the tears.

"It is a two-year programme and you'll stay in the dormitory in Warsaw during school. You can come home for the weekends and continue to play the church's organ. The school has a musical band and a choir—you can sign up for that."

Ted's face brightened. "Yes, I would love that."

On the first of September 1936, Ted packed his belongings in a suitcase, a gift from Father Karol and went to the train station with his mother.

"Ted, nine years ago, I said goodbye to your father."

"I said goodbye to him too," Ted responded defensively.

"Don't be angry. I just wanted to say that he would be very proud of you, Ted. You're a very good son. Be a good student too."

Ted arrived in Warsaw in the early afternoon. He went straight to the school and reported to the office. An older priest greeted him, checked his documents, including the letter of admission to the school, and directed him to the waiting room. Twelve boys were already sitting there in silence and a few more arrived in the next two hours.

They were taken to the dormitory and Ted was assigned to a room with three other boys. All boys on the second floor shared a kitchen and a bathroom with five shower stalls. Ted liked the arrangements.

The first week of school was difficult. Ted missed his family and friends. At first, he had trouble getting used to the preordained everyday life in the school, but soon he found peace in the strict schedule and embraced everything the school had to offer. Within a month, he had signed up for the orchestra and the choir and started learning the saxophone. With his ability to play the organ and having a beautiful voice, he became involved in the school choir as well.

"Ted, I saw you in the principal's office. Are you in trouble?" his friend Zenon, who he shared the room with, asked.

Ted looked uneasy. "No, to the contrary, he asked me to assume a leadership role among the boys in our class. What do you think about it?"

"You'll be a great class leader. Many of the students respect you."

The boys embraced and a smile crept across Ted's face. For a brief moment, he had forgotten about home, about his childhood. He felt like a grown-up man taking charge of his life.

Ted's home visits on weekends were the happiest days for Ania. He always brought something small for her, and she rewarded him with kisses and unconditional love. She adored her brother and his visits were the highlight of her life.

During one of the visits in the spring of 1937, he brought her a book about the history of Poland with many pictures in it. Ted knew that she shared the books with her best friend, Rose, and hoped that both girls would like it. Late in the evening, he was going through the book himself, and he spotted a picture of Bochnia, an important town near Krakow, famous for salt mines and ironworks. He thought back to the day he'd met the older man and his son. Busy at school, he'd forgotten about them, but the book brought back memories about the meeting and the strange conversation about his father.

He'd conceived a plan to go to Bochnia and find the mysterious man and his son. He kept their address hidden away from anyone's eyes and never told his mother.

On a Saturday in May, Ted arrived in Bochnia late in the afternoon. The orange sun was suspended above the horizon, giving a golden glow to the roofs of the town. Ted felt confident, although he worried a little about where he would spend the night if he was not welcomed at the strangers' house.

He arrived at the address in less than half an hour of walking along the main street. The town was more prosperous than Brusk, with many stores along on both sides of the street. The house he stood in front of was a red-brick, two-storey building with a small front yard. Forsythia bushes were already in full bloom.

The older man who opened the door had a welcoming smile on his face. "I thought you would never come."

"Oh, you remember me?" Ted stammered in a muted voice.

"Please, come inside the house."

"Thank you." Ted quickly recovered his confident voice.

They entered a narrow hallway that took them to a room with a view of the backyard. Two couches, a small table, and a corner lamp were the only furniture there. The sun setting beyond the horizon blazed through the window of the room, blinding Ted for a few seconds. The younger man was standing near one couch. "Please sit down."

For a while, they sat in silence, just looking at each other. Finally, the older man broke the silence. "My name is Henryk Wilk and this is my son, Joseph."

Joseph moved towards Ted and extended his hand.

Ted looked at him with questioning eyes. Joseph looked a little similar to Ted and his name was the same as his father's. Ted's heart started pounding; he was afraid that he might hear something unexpected, something that might change his life. A chill went through his body as he extended his hand to Joseph. The moment their hands met, Ted relaxed, his pulse returned to normal, and he felt a connection to the young man. He smiled. Still puzzled by the warm welcome, he looked at Henryk Wilk.

After some small talk about the travel and Ted's school, Henryk Wilk stood up. "Let's move to the dining room. My mother prepared a light supper for us."

The large dining room had a good-size table in the middle of it and six chairs around. At the end of the room was a credenza with several small sculptures made from wrought iron. Landscape paintings decorated the walls and long, white curtains covered the window. Ted had never dined in a nice dining room like this one. He smiled to himself, realising that his family didn't have a dining room; they ate in the kitchen.

After they sat at the table, an elderly woman—probably Henryk's mother—brought a plate with bread, sausages, and cheese while Joseph placed a pot of hot tea in the centre of the table.

Henryk put some food on his plate and motioned to Ted and Joseph to help themselves. "I'll be honest with you, Edward," he said.

"Please call me Ted."

Henryk's voice was suddenly filled with sadness. "Your father is my son's real father. We found out about this in October 1934 when Joseph's mother became very ill, and on her deathbed, she confessed to the affair with your father."

Ted was stunned by the words he'd heard and unable to utter any response.

Henryk told the story of many years ago. "In the summer of 1915, during the Great War, eighteen-year-old Joseph Novak arrived in Bochnia to look for a job. He came to my home, recommended by a common relative from Brusk. Joseph and I were distant cousins, but we had never met before and hadn't even known about each other. I was the owner of an ironwork shop that had several employees and a few apprentices. Business was good. As I'm sure you know, Bochnia was under Austrian occupation for more than a hundred years. When the war started in 1914, it was good for my business. We produced helmets for the Austrian soldiers, crates to carry weapons, and other hardware necessary for the army.

"I not only hired Joseph to work in my shop and learn ironwork, but I also invited him to live in the basement of my house. Joseph learned the trade and helped with the household chores. He was given room and board and earned a small salary. At the time, my wife Agata and I had one son, Roman, who was three years old.

"In 1918, at the end of the Great War when Poland regained its independence, Joseph left our household and went back to Brusk. He was well trained as an ironworker and planned to start his own shop with the help of the family. Although his departure was rather sudden, I was not surprised. Going back to my family town and starting my own business was what I would have done if I were in his shoes.

"Six months later, Agata had another baby boy that we named Joseph. Our family continued to prosper in the newly independent Poland. The country was rebuilding its industry and infrastructure and Marshall Joseph Pilsudski was creating a strong Polish Army.

"In 1920, the 'Warsaw Miracle' took place as the Polish Army stopped the advance of the Bolshevik Army into central Europe and Poland's territories expanded to the east and south-west and European countries provided financial help. Our family business doubled in size and we could afford to send Roman, our older son to study law in Krakow.

"In October 1934, when my wife Agata became very sick, she confessed that years ago she and your twenty-year-old father had an affair and she'd become pregnant. She'd felt there was no other choice but to keep the affair secret and for Joseph to leave Bochnia. I was angry and couldn't forgive my wife for this betrayal. She died soon after the confession, never regaining her cheerful nature. To this day, I can't forget my cruelty towards her, although she was always a good wife and a mother. I loved Joseph as my son, though, and believed that it was more important to raise a son than just to conceive him. I kept this a secret from both of my sons until Joseph's eighteenth birthday."

Henryk finished his long story, while Ted and Joseph sat silently.

Ted said, "I'm sorry for my father's sins and ask for your forgiveness."

"There is no need to ask for forgiveness, but it tells me that you're an honourable young man."

Ted was hoping that Henryk would talk about their strange visit to Brusk in May 1935 and his and young Joseph's inquiry about his father's death, but Henryk suddenly looked tired. He stood up and looked at both young men. "It's late, time to go to sleep. We would like you to stay at our house tonight. We will talk more tomorrow before you leave."

Ted and Joseph were left alone in the dining room.

Joseph, silent for the last four hours, stood up and with a huge grin on his face, hugged Ted. "We're half-brothers. I would like us to stay in touch."

Ted became nervous again, his mind full of questions. *Why would they want to be nice to me? What else is behind this life story?* With hesitation in his voice, he managed to say, "That would be good."

Sunday morning, after an early breakfast in the kitchen, Henryk asked Ted and Joseph to join him for a walk to the ironworks shop located three blocks away from the house. Joseph opened the heavy door leading to the shop, and Henryk motioned to Ted to go inside. It was a large area with a forge in the middle and machines that Ted had never seen in his life. He remembered his father working in the shop located in his grandparents' backyard; it had been very small with a small forge and hand tools, nothing compared to this big industrial one.

Looking at the forge, Henryk started talking. "Last year, two men came to my shop looking for a job. They had worked in France in a foundry and had a good understanding of metalwork. I hired them and during one of many conversations about their life in France, they talked about a Polish man, Joe Novak, who had been involved in an industrial accident together with another man."

"Yes, that was my father. He was called Joe in France," Ted interrupted, looking straight at Henryk.

"Here is the difficult part, Ted—they said that there was speculation that it was the Frenchman who died and that Joe Novak had assumed his identity."

Ted hesitated before he summoned his voice again. "No, it's not true. We received a letter from the company; they're paying a pension to my mother. They must have known for sure that it was my father who died."

"You're probably right. At first, we didn't think much about this, but one day the older man mentioned that Joe Novak was from Brusk near Warsaw." Henryk moved to the window and looked outside in silence.

Ted stood frozen, uncertain about wanting to know more, but Joseph's voice brought him back to the reality of his surroundings.

"It was I who insisted on travelling to your house to see if we could find out the truth." Joseph put his hand on Ted's shoulder and added, "After the visit, we believed that you were telling us the truth. If Joseph Novak was alive, he wouldn't abandon his family in Poland."

Henryk turned away from the window and looked directly into Ted's eyes. "The two men have left Bochnia since then. We think that they were just troublemakers. Perhaps you could keep an eye on any strangers coming to your house."

"I'm at school in Warsaw, learning to be a tailor. I go home only twice a month. I'll just have to hope that they never show up at my mother's home to create a problem, but I don't want to tell her about you or my visit here." Ted turned away from the forge and moved towards the door.

Rose looked intently at Ania, who was standing in the doorway of her house, panting and short of breath. "Rose," said Ania, "you have to come with me. Ted came from Warsaw and brought the most amazing book."

Rose and Ania were best friends; they were both ten years old and lived in the same neighbourhood. They were the opposite of each other; Rose was a good student, very inquisitive and full of energy, while Ania was an average student, had asthma that often left her breathless, and was happy to follow Rose's lead in almost everything. It didn't bother Rose. She liked Ania and spending time at her house. With Ted at school in Warsaw, the house seemed big with plenty of space for the girls to play.

The book was very beautiful; it was about Africa. The girls knew very little about elephants, giraffes, and big trees called baobab, and they looked at the pictures with amazement. One hour went by very quickly until Rose had to go back home.

It was the second week in a row that Rose's mother had stayed in bed, staring at the ceiling. This time was the longest Rose could remember. Her father was very impatient with his wife's moods and any free time he had, he spent in the orchard behind the house or reading a newspaper.

Rose had to take care of the family. Her older brother Franek helped her in the kitchen and with the house cleaning, but he was not willing to look after Mother or help with their young sister, Hela.

Rose got home just as Franek had finished warming the leftover soup from the previous day. She took a bowl of soup and went to the small bedroom with closed curtains. "Mom, you have to eat something. Franek made some soup."

"I don't want anything. Just leave me alone."

Rose put the bowl on the small table, sat at the edge of the bed, and touched her mother's hand gently. "Mom, you know this bad time will be gone; you need to be strong. Next week we need to bake bread. It's our turn at the bakery."

"Talk to your father. He can help with the baking."

"Oh Mother, you know that Father would rather read the newspaper than do any housework."

"Don't be angry. You have to understand him. When we got married, he had plans to build his own tack and saddle business and make good money. Unfortunately, he is struggling with getting customers, and we don't even have money to renovate the house that my grandparents gave us. He never liked to do any housework and preferred to tend to the trees in the orchard. We're lucky to have so much fruit."

"I'll never marry. I'll travel, see the world, and have a better life than you have." Rose looked at her mother and asked, "Are you sick and sad because of Father?"

After a long silence, she answered, "No, the sadness and darkness that closes around me just comes and goes. I can't control it."

"Mom, tomorrow after church, I'd like to spend some time with Ania. Ted brought this great book about Africa and I'd like to read it."

"Rose, I promise to be better tomorrow and you can go to Ania. I'm glad she is such a good friend of yours. Poor her, losing her father, and with Ted at school in Warsaw, she must be lonely." She drifted away into sleep.

On Sunday, Rose's mother felt better and the entire family went to church. Dressed in a white shirt and looking very handsome as always, her father walked ahead of the family while her mother looked old and sick behind him.

Rose could not think about anything else but her parents. *They are not a good match. I won't marry for love. I'll marry to have a better life.* She knew her father was not a hard-working man. They could have a better life if he spent more time making saddles and bridles for horses. There were always men coming to his shop, but not much business and the talks she sometimes heard were about politics, not horses. Nevertheless, she was very proud of him and liked to watch him participating in many public events. He was handsome and always well dressed. He read newspapers and could discuss politics and other world affairs better than anyone she knew. No wonder that her mother had broken her engagement to another man when she'd met Peter.

Rose, like her father, wanted to learn everything about the world. Her ambition to be the best at school sometimes put her in conflict with other students, who resented her superior attitude. When the teacher chose somebody else to read a passage from a geography book, Rose would interfere by adding facts she'd learned outside of the school. Her hand was always raised in eagerness to answer any question the teacher asked. Some of the students called her names, whispering as she walked by. She tried to ignore them and only occasionally lashed out angrily, "You'll never be as smart as I am."

Ania never displayed any jealousy and was her most faithful friend. Rose loved her not only because of her gentle and sharing personality, but also because she often helped Ania with homework, making herself feel important.

After Sunday Mass, without a word to her parents, she ran straight to Ania's home.

Ania and her mother always attended the first Mass at 8 a.m. and Rose knew that by the time she got there, they would have finished breakfast and Maria would move to the bedroom to pray in silence.

Rose and Ania were busy reading a passage about giraffes from the new book when the door opened and a serious-sounding voice startled her. "Hi girls, do you like the book?"

Rose turned around and was surprised to see Ted. She studied him for a while; he was all grown-up and serious-looking. He wore a nice blazer with a scarf wrapped around his neck. *So fashionable,* she thought and blushed. To conceal her embarrassment, she said louder than normal, "Yes, the book is great. We're reading about giraffes."

"I have a surprise for you two. In two weeks, I'm taking you to Warsaw for the day," Ted announced proudly.

Ania jumped from the table, hugged him, and whispered, "I love you, Ted."

Rose grimaced, showing sadness and hesitation. "Thank you, Ted, but I don't know if I can." She wanted to say how much she would love to go, but that her parents didn't have the money.

"If you're worried about money, I have enough to buy the train tickets for Ania and you."

Rose was shocked that Ted had read her mind. "Thank you, Ted." Not knowing how to express her gratitude, she simply said, "I'll make sandwiches to take with us for lunch."

The trip to Warsaw two weeks later was the best thing that had ever happened to Rose and Ania. Ted took them to see the Old Town and the King's Place. They rode the bus and even got ice cream. Ted knew many places and acted as if he'd lived there all his life. Rose knew that she wanted to live there one day to escape the small town, the poverty, and her sick mother. She was only ten years old but had a clear vision of herself working as a teacher in Warsaw.

At the end of the day, Ted put them back on the train and they sat there waving goodbye to him. "It was a great day," said Rose. "Your brother was so nice to us today."

"You should marry him when you're older. We could be family and always stay together." Ania was looking through the window, smiling.

"Are you crazy? He is so old and so serious," Rose said, bursting into laughter.

After the trip to Warsaw, Rose decided to study even harder. Nobody would be better than her. She started reading her father's newspapers and listened to the radio while cooking in the kitchen.

Joseph could not hide his happiness after Ted's visit. He liked his younger half-brother and hoped to see him soon in Warsaw. He wanted to study in Warsaw too, and be away from his house where he was always protected by his father and brother. His brother Roman studied law in Krakow and considered Joseph as just his little brother. He called him Joey, which was a name that stuck, much to Joseph's irritation.

"Dad, I like Ted. Do you think I could visit him in Warsaw?" Joey had a great relationship with his father and despite too much protectiveness, he hoped for permission to go. His father believed in openness and encouraged Joseph to talk about anything he wanted.

"Write to him, asking if you could visit."

"Should we tell Roman about Ted?"

"Not yet. Meet with Ted first and see what happens. I think that you would like to have a younger brother, but be careful, Ted is very serious for his age."

"Yes, I noticed that but I have a feeling that he would like to be just like other boys, only his circumstances made him very serious."

Henryk stopped working and looked at the window for a while. "It's not easy to become the man of the house at such an early age."

On the last Saturday of May 1937, Ted met Joseph at the Warsaw train station. They went to Ted's dormitory, where Joseph was staying for the weekend. After a quick lunch in the school cafeteria, they went to explore Warsaw. Although Ted was younger, he felt equal to Joseph, especially in Warsaw, where he was comfortable taking him to see important buildings, palaces, and main streets.

Anyone looking at them walking the streets of Warsaw would have thought that they were two brothers having a great time. Dressed in light jackets perfect for the nice May weather, they both felt as the world belonged to them. They were fast becoming best friends.

"Ted, I'm planning to go to military school to become a pilot."

"Lucky you, Joseph. Hope you'll never have to fly in a war." Ted was genuinely happy for Joseph. "I'm planning to establish my own tailor shop in Warsaw and will belong to a musical choir, maybe in the cathedral. I love singing and playing the saxophone. I even like to play the organ in church."

"Call me Joey. Maybe we both can live and work in Warsaw in the future, wouldn't that be great?"

Sunday afternoon came very quickly and it was hard to say goodbye when Ted took Joey to the train station. "Give my regards to your father and your grandmother."

"I'll be back soon," Joey said, hugging Ted with a feeling of genuine happiness.

At the family dinner, when Joey's older brother Roman was at home, Joey got the courage to say what had been on his mind since coming back from Warsaw. "Dad, I would like to apply to the military academy in Warsaw."

He was nervous that his father might not approve but before he finished his sentence, Roman clapped him on the shoulder and looked directly into his eyes, saying, "I support this idea. The academy in Warsaw is the best in the country."

In September 1937, Joey started his study at the academy. He was nineteen years of age and learning to become a pilot in the army was his dream come true and the promise of an adventurous life. Joey and Ted became good friends and discovered that despite having different personalities and different upbringings, they shared similar interests. They both were patriotic and loved to talk about Polish history, and they liked exploring Warsaw and visiting museums and monuments. In their spare time, they played football or walked the streets drinking soda from street vendors while looking at the fashionably dressed young women. The life here was very different from their small towns and they both planned to live in Warsaw.

Nobody other than Joey, Ted, and Henryk knew that they were half-brothers, not even Roman. Henryk had asked to keep it this way, knowing that being a lawyer, Roman would want to get everything legalised and involve Ted's mother in the process. She was still grieving her husband's death and it was better not to trouble her with the past.

On Ted's graduation day in June 1938, Joey met Ted's mother Maria and his sister Ania. Ania was twelve years old and in awe of Ted. Soon, she was even more in awe of Joey, especially his uniform. Secretly, she decided to marry him when she was old enough.

Joey continued to attend the academy during the summer. Most of his time was dedicated to learning to fly small military aircraft. His favourite was the PZL P.11, designed during the early 1930s by aircraft manufacturers in Warsaw. It had an all-metal structure and high-mounted gull wing and was considered the most advanced fighter aircraft of its kind.

The gull wing provided the pilot with great visual range. Flying the aircraft, Joey admired the panoramic view of Warsaw and the countryside. Occasionally, he would fly over Brusk, which was only a half-hour flight from the military airbase. He was a quick study and excelled in the ability to fly at various altitudes. He was also getting ready to learn to parachute jump in the fall.

During summer weekends, Ted was training at the military academy as a civilian radio operator and occasionally was assigned to communicate with Joey during his flights.

It was a great summer for both Joey and Ted. Joey knew that Ted worked during the week to support his family and save some money for his further education. One day he got the courage to ask if he could visit him and his family in Brusk. During one such visit, Maria looked at Ted and Joey with studying eyes. "The two of you could be brothers; you look similar and have comparable mannerisms. I'm happy that you met in Warsaw."

Joey looked up in the sky, thinking, *Hope Maria will never find out that we're half-brothers.*

"Mom, I'm happy that I met Joey at military school." Ted hoped that saying this would emphasise their chance meeting and stop any further discussion.

Ania was standing nearby watching the young men, thinking that the two of them were the best in the world—one was her brother and the other her future husband.

On an early morning in the spring of 1939, Jean was fretting in the chair during a meeting with Michel. Finally, he got the courage and looked up at him. "Could I ask what was done with all the information I gathered from Marc's network?"

"All in due time. Be patient, Jean. It isn't about incriminating some of the men that believe in their right to an independent Alsace."

The answer brought slight confusion to Jean's chain of thoughts. "I hope that all the risk I've been taking isn't wasted and the information is valuable?"

"Yes, it is, but there is more to it."

"What else do you need?"

"Hitler is a very aggressive politician. He has built an army that is more modern than any other in Europe. France has built the Maginot Line fortifications and it is strongly believed that it will deter Germany from invading us. But Hitler is unpredictable and we cannot allow ourselves to relax. We must step up our information gathering. We have a new mission for you."

"Emilie is getting upset with me for the frequent travelling and spending so many evenings outside of the house."

"You have to find a way to make her feel comfortable. It won't be any easier in the near future." Michel moved towards the window and looked out for a long while before he turned his attention back to Jean. "Your next mission is to travel to Berlin and meet with our contact in the German Army. His father is a cooper like you, and we set up an appointment with him under the pretence of opening trade between you and his father's company. We pay him well for his information, and you'll deliver money to him as well as some good French wine."

"Why do you think I'm the right person for the mission?"

"I'll be honest with you. There are more skilled spies, but you have the best cover. Your knowledge of the cooperage business and wine and beer industry is important in this mission. It could be your best alibi if you were questioned by the Germans."

Jean travelled to Berlin by train under a false identity. His passport indicated he was Marcell Veerborg, born in Strasbourg.

Berlin was a magnificent city with big buildings and wide streets. It was also a modern city, busy with traffic, people walking the streets with purpose, and many soldiers in crisp uniforms. Despite its world-class-city prominence, there was something sinister about Berlin, in silent ways confirming the news about the repression of Jews, Gypsies, and other minorities. Jean didn't see any of them on the streets of Berlin, making him uncomfortable, even afraid for his own life.

The meeting with Jean's contact went well; money was exchanged for a thick, sealed envelope that Jean placed in the hidden compartment of his suitcase.

"The envelope contains plan B for the possible invasion of France and must be considered," said his contact. "Some high-ranking officers are advocating for it." The conversation was short and Jean left the meeting feeling even more uncomfortable.

Jean stayed in a hotel in the centre of Berlin close to the train station. He was very nervous when he arrived at the hotel and sleep evaded him, so he decided to read his Bible. Late in the evening, a loud noise erupted in the square next to the hotel. He made sure that all the lights were out in his room before he looked through the window. A group of young men in brown uniforms were dragging a man and a woman covered in blood. The scene was dreadful to look at and Jean closed the shutters. He didn't want to go back to Berlin again.

The next morning, sitting on the train back to France, his resolve to prevent the Germans from invading France was very strong.

He delivered the envelope to Michel in a very sombre mood.

Michel appeared very concerned about Jean. "Is everything fine? You don't look well."

Although they had known each other for a long time, they had not become friends and never went for a drink or met outside the office.

"The mission went well, but I saw terrible things in Berlin. I hope I don't have to go there again."

A few days later, Michel and Jean met again. "Jean, that information you brought back from Berlin was very valuable, but my superiors think that it could be a diversion, purposely planted to avert part of our forces away from the Maginot Line. According to Plan B, Germany may consider invading France via Belgium and Holland, with the main attack to be launched through the Ardennes. Such plans are not plausible, as an army with tanks and artillery couldn't travel through the heavily forested mountains."

"The contact was adamant that many top-ranked militaries close to Hitler advocated for this plan. They know we have the Maginot Line. Why would they want to engage their army there?"

"Jean, you must travel to Berlin again and meet with the contact to obtain more information."

Between May and August 1939, Jean travelled to Berlin three times. Each time he brought more information about the German plans, but most of them involved expansion to the east.

On Friday, June 23, 1939, it was a rainy day in Dresden for Erik's graduation ceremony from the military academy. He and the other young graduates gathered in the main hall, organised in columns in alphabetical order. Parents and family members sat in chairs arranged in a semi-circle, facing a wall with German flags and Hitler's portrait with his hand raised in a well-recognised salute. A Wagner symphony was played by an orchestra located in the upper level of the hall. The happy chatter among the many parents was a clear sign of pride, not only for their sons' achievements, but for Germany under Nazi rule.

After the formality, parents and graduates socialised before going to a lunch served in the school cafeteria. Otto Hermann was beaming with self-importance as he walked next to his son.

Otto was a high-ranking city administrator in Gdańsk and a strong supporter of the Nazi Party. Having a son who had graduated as a top student in his class, recognised in front of everybody for his academic achievements, was very important to Otto and he was talking to other parents and school officials about Erik and his bright future. Rita Hermann stood quietly next to her husband and son. Her only show of emotion was a light kiss on Erik's cheek and a squeeze of his hand. Erik wasn't sure if she was happy for him.

After the ceremony was over, Erik and his parents travelled to Gdańsk to spent time with his family. He was granted a two-week leave before joining the German Army and starting further training towards becoming an officer.

After a few days at home, his mother asked Erik to travel with her to see his Polish grandmother, who was in ill health and possibly might not survive the summer.

Rita's voice was very strong. "Erik, remember you're half Polish and it should not change because you went to German military school."

"Mother, please understand that I love the Polish side of me, but believing in a strong Germany under Hitler's Nazi party is the right thing to do."

Rita's voice suddenly became very weak. "What will you do if Hitler starts a war?"

"Oh Mom, Hitler does not want war; he wants justice for Germany after the unfair Versailles Treaty."

On the way to his uncle's house where his grandmother had lived since the death of her husband, Erik and his mother talked about his youth, his divided loyalty, and he even expressed a little sadness for losing close contact with his Polish side of the family.

Soon after they arrived at the house, Erik's frail grandmother touched his face gently. "Erik, you're my oldest grandson. You always made me proud. Please continue to be an honourable man."

"I will, Grandmother." At that moment, Erik strongly believed in his words.

The few days they spent with the family went by very quickly. During many discussions with his uncle, Erik was able to fully recover his Polish language skills and listen to the Polish side of the current affairs in Europe. He disagreed with his uncle but didn't express his opinion openly.

The Assumption of Mary holiday was celebrated together with the anniversary of the Battle of Warsaw, fought from August 12–25 in 1920. The Polish Army had stopped the advance of the Bolshevik Army into central Europe, blocking the spread of communism on the continent.

The battle, called the "Warsaw Miracle," was celebrated every year, but on Tuesday, August 15, 1939, it was celebrated with a show of strength by the Polish Army and patriotic manifestations in every city and town in Poland.

After completing his schooling the year before, Ted had been placed in a very reputable tailoring shop for his apprenticeship. He learned the traditional as well as the latest fashions in menswear. He was given room and board and earned some money, which he saved most of, hoping to open his shop in Warsaw. He had plans to expand into womenswear and to hire a qualified woman to do the sewing. He was a bit nervous about the future of Poland after Hitler's rise to power, but for now, he kept on dreaming and indulging in being the big brother.

On Tuesday morning, Ted took Ania and Rose to Warsaw to see the military parade. "Girls, Poland is facing uncertain times. I think that our military isn't able to face the German Army if they invade us."

"The war won't happen. We have the assurance of France and England to support Poland against any aggression." Rose was proud to say something of great importance.

"Rose, you've been reading your father's newspapers, but you don't know the truth. You're only twelve years old and don't understand the politics."

Rose was ready to argue with Ted, but Ania asked if they could walk closer to the central stage to see the president of Poland, Władysław Raczkiewicz. Rose was actually relieved with Ania's interference as she didn't want to talk more about politics, afraid that Ted might be right and the war might happen despite all the non-aggression treaties signed by all the politicians.

Rose thoughts were dark while they watched the parade. *I'm only a twelve-year-old girl reading Father's newspapers. He doesn't even want to seriously discuss anything with me.* She was silent for the rest of the day.

While at home, Rose often talked to Ania about the articles she read in the newspaper and voiced her own opinion about world affairs. She believed in what she read and was always very optimistic.

"We're too young to understand what is happening in the world. Isn't it better just to be a good girl, a good daughter, and a good wife one day?" Ania would often say.

"Don't listen to your mother about being a good girl. You have to be strong and make choices for yourself. Learn from your brother."

Ania loved her brother—he was her hero. He was the best young man in town, studying in Warsaw, helping the family, and playing music, but she didn't want to be like him. "I would like to find a husband like Ted. I think I already know him."

Rose looked at her with surprise. "Don't talk nonsense. We should see the world first before we think about husbands."

Part Two

← WAR →

September 1939

B illy graduated from military school and was enlisted in the Royal Air Force and stationed in Blackpool.

At the end of August 1939, he was on a leave of absence in London, spending some time with his family and his hopefully soon-to-be fiancée, Eloise Kerr. He was planning to propose to Eloise on September 1st, with the hope that they could get married soon. He was only twenty-two, but he knew that Eloise was his love for life. They had met two years ago during a party at his friend's house. She was nineteen and very mature. They spent a lot of time together whenever Billy visited London. He was sure that his family would approve of the engagement and hoped that her mother would be fine with it as well.

Billy and Eloise were planning to meet at the café near her mother's flat in the early afternoon of September 1st, and then meet her mother for a late supper.

Early that morning, his father awakened him with a strong tug on his arm. "Billy, get up. Germany invaded Poland." The expression on his face was of shock and disbelief.

"Dad, what are you saying? That isn't possible …" Billy didn't get to finish his sentence because his father interrupted.

"Yes, yes, we know that Chamberlain signed the non-aggression pact with Hitler, but it means nothing right now. Get up. The British Army is asking all servicemen to go back to their stations immediately."

Billy dressed in his uniform and packed his duffel bag. Breakfast was already set on the table and the family sat waiting for him. His sister Jennie was crying as she sat next to Billy.

"Don't cry, Jennie," her mother said. "Hitler only invaded the barbaric Poles. He doesn't want war with England or the other European countries."

"Mom, please don't say anything else. We may not be the most important people in the world." Billy was surprised at his own words, as deep inside of himself, he did feel superior to others in the world. He said goodbye to each of the family members and hugged Jennie the longest. She was so brave, all her life in a wheelchair, never giving up on doing things that others took for granted. He remembered the vacations they had spent by the sea at their aunt's house, the sandcastles and airplanes built together. "I'll be back very soon and we'll go to the beach again." He gently kissed his sister on the cheek and left the house.

He took the Tube to the café where he'd arranged to meet with Eloise. Her face was swollen from crying as she entered the café. "Billy, I know that you have to cut your stay short in London and go back to Blackpool. I heard the news on the radio." Tears started to well up in her eyes again.

"Darling, I'm sure that the European governments will resolve this issue very soon. Nobody wants war."

Everybody in the café was on edge. The talk was mostly about a possible war with Germany. He knew that most customers were glancing at him, noticing his RAF uniform.

He hesitated for a moment, looked around the café, and knelt in front of Eloise. "Will you marry me?"

It was so unexpected, leaving her speechless. Everybody in the café heard Billy's proposal and looked at the young couple with anticipation. Eloise recovered from her shock, took Billy's face in her hands, and with a serious look at him, simply said, "Yes." Everybody cheered for them, wished them a happy life, and expressed the hope that war wouldn't come to other parts of Europe.

"It happened! The bastards invaded Poland!" Ted screamed as he listened to the early morning news on the small radio he kept on the bedside table. He jumped out of bed and ran to his mother's room. "Mother, Germany invaded Poland this morning."

She was already out of bed, and like every day, on her knees, praying in front of the picture of Mary, Mother of Jesus. She turned her head towards him with a bewildered look on her face.

"Pray for all of us. September 1, 1939, could be the end of our nation."

"Didn't the British prime minister sign a non-aggression pact with

Hitler earlier this year?"

"Oh Mother, he did, but you know that the pact was not taken seriously by most countries. It allowed the British and French to keep their heads in the sand."

Ted's anxious voice woke up Ania, who soon stood in the door of her mother's bedroom. "What is happening, Ted?"

Ted took her in his arms in a protective gesture. She had asthma and any anxiety could provoke an attack. "Let's sit down and I'll tell you and Mother what I heard on the news this morning."

They sat at the kitchen table and Ted prepared some tea as he started to explain with trepidation in his voice. "Yesterday, late afternoon, Germans SS troops wearing Polish uniforms staged a phoney invasion of Germany by Poland, damaging minor installations on the German side of the border."

Maria looked straight into Ted's eyes. "It may not be the beginning of the war. We have allies that wouldn't allow the invasion of our country."

"Mother, listen to me, the Germans began bombing the Polish military base in Westerplatte, Gdańsk."

"Perhaps they just want to take over the free city of Gdańsk."

"It's a war, and I have to get ready to join the Reserve Army. The order may come soon."

Maria and Ania started to cry; they could not bear to think about Ted leaving them.

"No, you're not going to join the army. You're not eighteen years of age yet." Maria's weeping seemed out of control.

"Don't cry. Nobody will ask about my age unless you're going to tell them. I received some basic training at school and I must join. This is what Father would like." He never invoked his father to make a point and it felt good, almost as his father was standing nearby, giving him extra strength.

Ted's military training had been rudimentary at first but intensified after German expansion began with the annexation of Austria and then the occupation of the Sudetenland, part of Czechoslovakia.

Maria tried to use arguments straight from the newspaper. "Don't you remember, when Germany took Czechoslovakia, our government began to call up its troops, but Britain and France persuaded Poland to postpone general mobilisation in an effort to dissuade Germany from war."

"The effort was futile. We have to stop Hitler's aggression toward Poland. Every able-bodied person must join the army and I'm prepared for it."

Ania was short of breath. "What will happen to us?"

"Britain and France won't allow further occupation of Poland. They must declare war on Hitler. We must fight now until the Allies join us."

Ted knew that the best way to join the fight was by going to Warsaw and contacting his school's principal. He was sure there would be more volunteers like him. While he was getting ready to go to Warsaw, the politicians were busy issuing warning and ultimatums.

On September 2, Britain and France demanded that Germany withdraw from Poland by September 3 or face war. At 11 p.m. on September 3, the British ultimatum expired and minutes later, Britain's Prime Minister Neville Chamberlain went on national radio to announce that Britain was at war with Germany. At 5 p.m. the next day, France declared war on Germany.

Ted's spirits rose in hopes of a quick resolution, and leaving his mother and sister alone in the house was easier than he initially imagined.

On September 5, Ted was assigned to an auxiliary unit with many of his fellow students. They were stationed in the school dormitory, waiting for an order to join the army in Warsaw.

"Ted, did you listen to the radio?" Ted's friend looked at him bewildered. "The Germans are advancing towards Warsaw with an unthinkable speed."

"We heard about it, but nobody wanted to believe that the German forces will use the military strategy known as the *blitzkrieg* or 'lightning war.'" Ted knew he was showing off with his knowledge of recent politics but he felt older, more mature than his friends.

Armoured divisions smashed through Polish defence lines, isolating them into many segments with their motorised infantry, while the Panzer tanks moved forward. Meanwhile, the German Air Force, the Luftwaffe, destroyed Polish air defences and discriminately bombed the cities to terrorise the people.

By September 8, the German Army had reached the outskirts of

Warsaw, having advanced 230 km in the first week of the invasion.

Ted and the auxiliary groups were never called to action and on September 18, after the Russian Army invaded Poland from the east, they were sent home.

"There is still hope," Ted said to his family and a few friends who gathered at his house after he arrived back from Warsaw.

Father Karol spoke with anger and everybody looked at him. "The Germans and Russians signed a non-aggression pact back in August and nobody knew about it."

Somebody in the room challenged Ted. "Ted, can you look at the cross on Father Karol's chest and honestly say that there's hope?"

Ted was desperate to give a positive answer even though he didn't actually have much hope himself. "The British and French have declared war on Germany; they'll start the offensive very soon."

But despite the declaration of war, Britain and France did little militarily to help Poland to fight the German advancement, and on September 28, Warsaw surrendered to the relentless German siege by land and air.

The Polish government and military leaders had fled the country a few days earlier, cruelly leaving messages on the radio encouraging the Polish people to fight the advancing German Army.

During the next few months, most people in Poland, including Ted, knew that Britain and France were engaged in a "phoney war" because, except for a few dramatic British-German clashes at sea, no major military action was taken.

Darkness enveloped the Polish nation and it became very clear that the invasion of Poland was a part of Hitler's plan to enslave the Slavic people and bring *Lebensraum*, living space for the German people. The Germans considered themselves racially superior and immediately started detaining Polish intelligentsia. Terror spread across the country.

Every day, Jean listened to the radio, growing more and more concerned with the unfolding events. The invasion of Poland on September 1, 1939, the non-aggression pact with Stalin, and France and Britain's declaration of war, all happened very quickly, leaving many in disbelief.

Adolf Hitler claimed that the massive invasion in the east was a defence action, but France and Britain were not convinced, and after declaring war, they worked closely as allies to be ready for a possible German invasion.

Both countries planned to fight using updated World War I tactics. The frontal attacks during the Great War had inflicted massive casualties on the French Army. This time, the army was going to remain on the defensive, believing that the Maginot Line was impenetrable. Meanwhile, they would mobilise their military force and start the offensive in around two years.

Michel met with Jean to discuss possible actions that might involve more covert work in the Alsace-Lorraine area. They needed to discover not only what Marc and his co-conspirators were doing but also other possible spying networks.

When they met at the military base, Michel didn't waste any time in informing Jean about his new assignment. "Your coopering business and the metalwork provide many opportunities to travel, meet people, and create a network of spies working for you."

"I don't want to bring any of this to my business and my shop; it would be too dangerous for my family. My children are only eight and seven years old, and I want them to have a safe life." Jean knew that his arguments were pointless but he had to try. He desperately didn't want to be involved in the spy games any longer.

"There is no other way but to bring the action close to your home. There are some Polish men working in your shop, and we know they would want to be involved in the fight against Germany in whatever way they can."

Jean sounded defeated. "What do you suggest?"

"A Polish superintendent is working for you. What do you know about him?"

"Not a lot. We don't have the opportunity to talk much, other than business conversations."

"The aggression against Poland is an opportunity to get closer to him and recruit him to work for us. Get to know him and let me know in a month what you think of him."

Andreas, the Polish superintendent, agreed to work with Jean and organise other Polish people in the region. There were a good number of them working in Thionville and the surrounding area.

The attack on Holland and Belgium and the unexpected advance of the German Army into France through the forested Ardennes left the Maginot Line without any involvement in the war. On May 13, 1940, the first German forces emerged from the Ardennes, and on June 13, the occupation of Paris started as the French government fled to Bordeaux.

The collapse of France just six weeks after Hitler's initial assault was devastating and humiliating for France.

On the first day of September 1939, Rose Podolski got up early, dressed in her school uniform, and left her house without even thinking about breakfast. She wanted to be the first one at school. After a summer dominated by the news of a possible war, she was longing for normalcy in her life. She loved school and was good at every subject, but history and geography were her passion. She was starting seventh grade already thinking about going to high school next year. There was one in Brusk, but she was dreaming about going to school in Warsaw.

"Good morning, class," Mr. Bieniak, said startling Rose from her dreams.

A multitude of voices responded in an even greeting. "Good morning."

Mr. Bieniak was her history and geography teacher and she was in love with him. She looked at him with awe and admiration. He knew everything about the world, teaching them about different countries, different people, and the history of civilisation, which was more than six thousand years old.

He cleared his voice and with an unusually stoic voice, said, "The German Army invaded Poland this morning."

Children started asking questions with fear in their voices. "What will happen to us?"

"For now, the school will be closed until we receive new directions."

Silence spread through the class and some students started to cry.

"Please ask your parents to come to a meeting this afternoon where we will provide more information. Now, please go home." Tears were glistening in the corners of his eyes.

Later, waiting for her father to come home from the school meeting, Rose was full of anguish.

"The authorities ordered the closure of all schools," Rose's father Stan said as he entered the house.

"Dad, they can't do it!" Rose started arguing, in hopes that he would say something positive.

"Rose, they can do whatever they need to, it's a war,"

The house was very quiet in the evening and everybody went to bed earlier than usual, as if sleep would erase the gloom spreading over Poland.

A week passed. Many people packed belongings and evacuated the towns to the south, away from the main road leading to Warsaw.

Early in the morning, Stan and his son Franek loaded clothes, blankets, and food on the wagon and hitched up their horse. By the time they finished, Stan's wife Renata, Rose, and her younger sister Hela had gotten up and they quickly got ready. The windows and main door had been boarded up the previous evening, and a few wood planks were on the floor ready to board up the side entrance.

They all dressed warmly despite the nice weather and quietly left the house.

Rose tugged on her mother's hand. "Where are we going?"

Renata sounded defeated. "My uncle lives in Radom. We'll go there."

"Let's go to Krakow." Rose was thinking about the Wawel Castle that she could see there.

"We're going away from Warsaw but not that far," said Stan. "The Germans will be defeated soon and we can come back home." Her father's voice was strong but Rose could detect some fear in it.

As they rode in their wagon, Rose saw many people in horse-drawn wagons, some walking with heavy loads on their shoulders, some on bicycles, and some even in cars.

Many people camped at night along the road and moved during the day; others preferred to move at night under cover of darkness.

Curled on a thin mattress and staring at the stars, Rose thought about her friend Ania. Ania and her mother had not evacuated. Ted was in a cadet camp near Warsaw, and Maria wanted to stay in the house in case he came back home or sent a letter with his whereabouts. At least half of the town had not evacuated, taking their chances on facing the Germans. What would happen to them? Rose tried to imagine an army of merciless Germans marching into town with their arms raised in a "Heil Hitler" salute. It was the image of German soldiers she remembered from short information movies they had watched at the school.

Three days into the family's journey, they settled for the night in a small hamlet. Everybody was asleep except Rose. She was not afraid or disturbed by the exodus of thousands of people; after all, they were escaping to safety. It was the first time she'd been on a journey to some unknown destination, and she was dreaming about the big world. She remembered her geography and history lessons full of the wonder of unknown countries, foreign languages, and different races of people.

Thinking about the world, she finally fell asleep. Her dream took her to Africa and she was feeling the hot sun on her face when her mother awakened her abruptly. The hot sun of Africa turned out to be a ray of sunshine beaming through a gap in the wooden planks of the roof of the barn where Rose and her family slept.

"Get up, we're going back home," Rose heard when her mother tried to awaken her.

"Why? I want to see Africa," she murmured, half asleep and disoriented between her dream and reality.

"The Germans are already on the road near Radom." Hearing her father's strict voice, Rose became more alert.

Soon, everybody was awake and talking to each other in panic-stricken voices.

Stan Podolski addressed the crowd of people gathered close to his wagon. "Everybody, listen, please. I just spoke to some people who came from the other direction." He looked around as everybody waited for him to continue. "It is true. The Germans are on the road south of here. There is nowhere to go for us. We should all go back home."

Everybody appeared to be happier on the way back. The caravan of people was full of chatter and kids ran around between wagons. Even Rose cheered up, thinking about seeing Ania again. They pushed as hard as they could, stopping only to give the horses some rest, and they were home on the morning of the second day.

Their house with its boarded-up doors and windows waited for them intact, but some trees in the orchard had broken branches and much less fruit than before they'd left.

Ania's house had dark blankets hanging in the windows. They were slightly parted to allow some daylight to enter the kitchen as Rose stepped in. "What's that?" she asked.

Maria's voice was hushed but clear. "It was announced on the radio that everybody must cover the windows so the German planes won't see the cities, towns, and villages at night."

Both girls hugged each other for a long time, happy to be together again. Maria looked at Rose. "Why are you back?"

"The Germans were on the road near Radom. Everybody turned back."

"God help us." Maria crossed herself.

Joey's career in the Polish Air Force came to a halt on September 28, 1939, when the Warsaw garrison surrendered to a relentless German siege.

Since the beginning of September, he had taken part in the dogfights with the Luftwaffe over the Polish skies and had watched some of his friends perish in their small planes, which were not a match for the sophisticated Messerschmitts.

Joey's and his friends' morale had started dwindling after Poland's government and military leaders left the country following the Soviet invasion from the east on September 17th, but despite diminishing hope, they continued to fight until there was no hope left.

Soon after the surrender, in October 1939, he and other military servicemen were ordered to leave Poland. They made their way to the Polish Air Force camp at Lyon, France, where they were organised under French command. Everything was chaotic in the camp. Waiting for orders from the French Army Command, their frustration growing, many pilots drowned their sorrow in wine and any vodka they could find. Soon, gatherings with local people became very popular and most men were eager to take part in the entertainment.

Joey liked wine and women, but the lack of any action weighed heavily on him. He wanted to fight, to kill the Germans, but other than daily exercise and meetings, nothing much was happening. Winter came and went, and all of the Polish pilots and other servicemen hoped that in the spring, the fight would start. The exiled Polish government, situated in Angers, near Paris, seemed paralysed with inaction. Joey and his companions were at a loss to understand why the declared support of the French and British Armies had been delayed for such a long time.

After the capitulation of France, in June 1940, Joey and other servicemen were evacuated to the United Kingdom and officially joined the Royal Air Force under British command in August 1940. He was stationed at RAF Blackpool.

A British officer entered the barracks where Polish pilots were housed. "Good morning. This is Flight Lieutenant William Leavitt. From now on, you're under his command." He pointed to the young officer who followed in his footsteps.

"Joseph Wilk, please step out." Leavitt's voice was strong, with a hint of dislike for his assignment.

Joey stepped forward from the group of pilots.

"According to our documents, you speak English."

"Yes, I do, sir."

"From now on, you'll work as my translator until the others learn the language."

"Yes, sir."

"Please see me in one hour in barrack number 25."

The door had not even closed when all the pilots started talking at the same time.

"Maybe something will start happening. Maybe we can fight. Joey, you need to be close to him."

Joey looked around, pleased with himself and his new status. "Listen up, guys, I'll do my best to get Leavitt on our side and speed up the training so we can fly the Hurricanes and Spitfires."

An hour later, after a breakfast of porridge and lukewarm tea, Joey reported to barrack number 25.

"Everybody, go to the orchard and pick the fruit from the trees—all of it." Stan's orders to his family didn't allow for any excuses, even from little Hela.

Franek, Rose's older brother, sounded surprised. "Some apples are not ripe yet."

"We need to collect them all. We will sell some and hide the rest from the Germans."

Franek looked smugly at his father. "Do you think the Germans are stupid and won't check the cellar?"

"We will dig a deep hole behind the shed and cover it with tree branches. Don't waste any more of my time with stupid questions." Stan was angry. He didn't like anyone to question his authority, especially his son.

Franek worked with a neighbour, digging the hole, while Rose and her mother and sister started collecting the fruit. In three days, the hole was ready. Franek and Rose went down the ladder to the bottom of it. It was deep, twice the height of Rose, and dark and cold. They used branches and hay to cover the bottom and sides.

Franek wanted to scare Rose. "It's like a grave."

"Don't say stuff like that." Rose bravely looked around but her heart was pounding as if in anticipation of something bad that might happen in the depths of the hole.

She continued to work, but chills were trembling in her body and she could not shake off the dark thoughts of death.

The work was hard for the next two days, as from dawn to dusk, they stored the fruit and covered it with blankets and branches. There was enough for the family and some for the neighbour who worked alongside them.

For a few days, Rose's body was aching and she stayed in bed despite the nice weather. It wasn't only the pain that kept her in bed; she didn't want to admit to anyone that she was scared of the reality that had descended upon them.

When she finally emerged from her miserable state, she decided to visit Ania.

"Why are you here, Ted?" Rose was shocked to see him in the house.

Ted's face was pained. "I never got to join the army. We were sent home from the camp outside of Warsaw."

Maria scolded them in a stern voice. "Kids, don't speak loudly; we don't know who's listening."

"Mom, don't panic. England and France declared war on Germany. It will be over soon," Ted said.

Rose looked at Ted, wondering if he truly believed his own words. Then she tried to divert the conversation. "Have you heard that the schools were closed?"

"Once the war is over, everything will be back to normal."

Ted was trying to sound confident but Rose had her doubts.

Ted and two other men were in the crypt of the local church, assembling new radio equipment they'd received from an anonymous ex-military official, who had been part of the underground movement from the beginning of its existence.

It was July 1940 when George had contacted Ted, quizzing him about his participation in the September campaign fighting the invading German Army and his radio communication training. Ted remembered the first meeting with George in full detail—the excitement of being part of the resistance and the hope that the war could be over soon. He almost lost hope when France was defeated and the Polish government relocated to London. Waiting for any new directions from London was hard, and Ted imagined the worst possible scenario for the Polish people.

As he unpacked the boxes of radio equipment, his mind drifted to the beginning of the mobilisation. When the Command of the Union for Armed Struggle relocated to London, England, after the fall of France, it started mobilisation of the Polish people in centres of national resistance, with the aim being to rebuild the nation after a demoralising defeat by the Nazis.

George nudged him with his elbow. "Ted, start moving. You were lost in your thoughts for a while."

"Sorry, just so much uncertainty with the government moving farther and farther away." Ted could not hide the cynicism.

"Don't think about the unknown future. We have work to do here."

Bolek, the other man in the crypt, looked at Ted with pity. "We need to move the skeletons from the three coffins to the largest one. Ted, you can start doing it."

Ted felt sweat dripping down his back as he proceeded to open the coffins. *No person has looked inside them since they were sealed,* he thought, as he touched the dust-covered wood, the copper cross covered with a patina of half a millennium. Ted had been brave and calm for most of his life, but moving the bones that had rested in the crypt for five hundred years was unnerving.

"Only the three of us know about this radio station we're setting up. It must remain secret; it's an order." George sounded authoritative.

"When can we use it?" Ted touched the radio.

"I'll let you know."

They spoke with hushed voices not only to avoid any attention from the outside but out of respect for the remains of the founders of the church whose bones were now being disturbed.

"As of Sunday, Bolek will work as the church custodian."

"Is the priest fine with this?" asked Ted.

"The priest can be trusted."

"I know him very well. He allows me to play the church organ." Ted was happy to mention this.

"We know. You may have to play the organ when we radio-contact London."

"Don't worry, Ted, I'll be working around the church, making sure that we know when the Germans are close by." Bolek sounded a bit smug.

That night, Ted pushed away his food on the table without even trying it. He couldn't eat. The smell of the crypt and the rattle of the moving bones had been too much for him that day. He went outside, sat on the bench at the back of the house, removed a hand-rolled cigarette, and had a smoke.

The Battle of Britain was very fierce, with many casualties every day. Many experienced British pilots were killed, wounded, or simply exhausted. The Luftwaffe was very strong and relentless in attacking Britain. As a sergeant, Billy Leavitt took part in many raids and was losing hope of defending his country against this strong aggressor.

Billy wasn't pleased when, in August 1940, he was assigned to train the newly arrived Polish pilots stationed at RAF Station Blackpool. The RAF pilots had expected the Poles' arrival and most of them talked condescendingly about their ability to fight. Some of the Englishmen even used a slur while talking about the Poles. Billy had a low opinion about Polish people in general and especially their armed forces after their defeat in just a few days of war.

The British aircraft were new to the Polish pilots and their training had to be fast and intense. During their introduction, Billy observed that the pilots were very eager to learn and to join the RAF pilots in the war against the Luftwaffe. "Maybe their eagerness will overcome their lack of knowledge," he muttered to himself as he left the introduction meeting.

Hour later Lieutenant Leavitt and Joey went to the meeting room. "Pilot Officer Wilk, this is the training room where you and your fellow countrymen will meet every morning at seven sharp."

"Yes, sir." Joey was in a happy state of mind and didn't notice the arrogant tone of Lieutenant Leavitt's voice.

"Your assignment as a translator starts now. I hope your English is proficient and you know the military lingo."

"I hope so. I had good English language training in the Polish Military Academy."

"Here is a good dictionary; learn all the required military vocabulary. I expect precise translations. I hope you understand the gravity of your responsibility." With a nod of his head, Leavitt indicated that Joey should leave the room.

Such an abrupt dismissal didn't bother Joey. He knew about the superiority the Brits displayed towards not only the Polish but all foreign pilots, marines, and cavalrymen who had flocked to England to join the British Army to fight and defeat the Nazis.

Allowing oneself to be disturbed by this attitude was pointless as the goal was to learn and to get into the fight in the shortest possible time.

The training went relatively well and in the second half of August 1940, Joey and other Polish pilots were allowed to fight against the Luftwaffe. By the end of October, the Battle of Britain was won.

"Officer Wilk, the contribution of the Polish pilots will be respectfully recognised by the Command of the RAF during the official dinner planned for this Saturday. I wanted to be the first one to tell you this," said Billy.

"Thank you, sir. It was an honour to serve under you."

"Without the Polish pilots, Britain would have lost the battle." There was an uncomfortable smile on Billy's face. Admitting that others could do an equal or even better job than the British Army men was demeaning and painful.

"We hope to continue to serve Britain and Poland until the monstrous Nazis are destroyed. I would wish to stay under your command."

"I'll see what can be done about it." Billy looked at the saluting pilot and left the room.

Michel was in a foul mood when Jean met with him in the local café. The spring of 1940 had dealt a devastating blow to the French defence strategy. The Germans were not in Thionville yet, but it was a matter of few days before they spread everywhere, like weeds growing out of nowhere, destroying anything in their way. "On June 15, the French Army will start its withdrawal from the Alsace and Lorraine area," he told Jean.

"What the hell happened that we allowed the Germans to capture Paris and most of France in such a short time?" Jean didn't want to sound sarcastic, but it was difficult to accept the events of the last three months.

"Do you remember the Plan B you brought from Berlin? It should have been looked at by the generals, not just swept under the carpet as something only a lunatic could come up with," Michel said, looking down on the floor, embarrassed.

"It's too late to fret about it," said Jean. "We should just learn for the future. You asked me to recruit some Polish people in the area to work for you. Andreas enlisted around twenty of them. What should they do next?"

"Jean, you and the Poles are on your own. I'm in the last group to evacuate. We will sabotage all equipment and weapons in the Maginot fortifications."

Jean bent over the table and asked quietly, "Could we take some of the weapons? I'm sure that Andreas will find a way to store them somewhere."

"My orders were to sabotage all," Michel said, looking straight into Jean's eyes. "It will take us a few days and we will work mostly during the daytime. You know the fortification very well. I'm sure that in the chaos, we won't be able to account for everything."

Jean lowered his voice to a whisper. "Is the security the same as always?"

"It is chaotic there. Send Andreas and a few other men tomorrow night. A load of weapons will be stored for them outside the gate in the ditch. They must have transportation."

"I hope you won't get in trouble." Jean was truly concerned.

"We're all in deep shit. I can handle that kind of trouble. I wanted to say goodbye to you, Jean. I don't know what will happen to the French Army and us after the evacuation. God only knows."

"Good luck to you, Michel." Jean had tears in his eyes, not knowing if he would see him again.

Most of the French Army was able to evacuate, but by the 17th of June, the Thionville sector had been enveloped by the Germans and retreat was impossible for the fortress troops.

After sporadic actions, mostly by the French in firing off ammunition in order to destroy as much as they could, they surrendered on July 2nd. Alsace and Lorraine were incorporated into the Third Reich.

"Emilie, Marie-Ann, Jean-Marc, the Germans issued a decree that the German language was obligatory from now on," Jean announced as they finished their supper.

"I hate the German language," young Marie-Ann piped in. She was eight years old and acting like a teenager. She was smart and rebellious, but it was only now that Jean saw these characteristics clearly. She was just his little girl and Jean had not expected her to respond this way. In some deep part of himself, he was proud of her.

"Marie-Ann, you and Jean-Marc learned German at school. Mother and I speak only a local dialect and from now on, you must help us to learn German."

"I'll teach you," their son Jean-Marc responded without hesitation. He was a very serious ten-year-old boy, who most of the time preferred books instead of playing games with others.

"At home, we can continue to speak French, but in public, it is dangerous." Emilie's sadness was contagious.

They sat in silence—even the children understood the gravity of her words.

"How long will the Germans be here?" asked Marie-Ann.

"We don't know. We're French and we will continue to cultivate our language and culture; we just have to do it quietly at home."

France was divided into the Free Zone in the southern part, governed by General Petain, with a newly established capital in the small town of Vichy. The northern part was the Occupied Zone.

Jean pondered leaving Thionville, but after intense discussions with Emilie, considering either the northern Occupied Zone where her family lived or Vichy, France, where Jean came from, they decided to stay in their home, hoping for a quick end to the war.

Numerous young people from Alsace and Lorraine were conscripted into the German Army; some fled to Switzerland or joined the resistance, but many stayed in town working for local factories that now supplied the German Army.

The wine industry didn't suffer from the occupation. Germans liked wine, as did the French, and Jean's cooperage business continued to do well as a lot of wine was sent to Germany and to the German troops on various fronts.

At his office, Jean spoke to Andreas. "We got new orders for wine barrels. I worry that we may not be able to produce enough unless we reorganise the business."

"I agree with you. Some of the Polish workers left Thionville to join the Polish Army in Bordeaux and many young Frenchmen have been conscripted into the German Army, making it difficult to find new labour."

"Before the Germans realise that we could produce some hardware for them, I'll close this part of the business and move the workers to the cooperage department."

Andreas loved being in charge and any action fuelled his energy. "I'll organise this immediately. I think that we should hide most of the iron-work equipment before the Germans seize it. I'll take care of that."

At the age of fourteen, Rose's life without school was mundane, spent between house chores, looking after her younger sister, and visiting Ania. She secretly kept some of her books in the attic in a box under some old clothes. Radios and schoolbooks were not allowed and the Germans con-fiscated most of them. She knew it was dangerous keeping her books, but she could not part with them. In the first year of the war, Rose was never brave enough to even look at them. She was more afraid of her father than the Germans, as he became very strict, trying to protect his family from the dangers of war.

Stan continued to make horse harnesses and reins and traded them for food with farmers in the surrounding area. In the summer, the orchard was full of fruit that Renata and Rose sold at the market.

At the beginning of September 1940, Rose was sitting in front of a basket of apples at the market when she was startled by a familiar voice.

"Hello, Rose." An older man was standing in front of her.

She looked at the man, who had grey hair, a beard, and a big moustache. "Are you Mr. Bieniak?"

"Yes, Rose, it is me, but keep it quiet, please."

"What happened? Your hair is so grey."

"I'm getting old," he said with a smile. "Come to the six o'clock Mass with your father."

He quickly moved to another stall at the market.

Rose could not hide her excitement as she searched the market with her eyes, hoping to see him.

The days were getting shorter but at 6 p.m. it was still bright and sunny when Rose went to the church with her father.

When the Mass was done, Rose, her father, and a few other parents and teenagers stayed in the pews. The priest came into the church again, and behind him was Mr. Bieniak, Rose's favourite teacher.

The priest pointed his hand towards the teacher as everybody waited in silence. "Good evening, some of you remember Mr. Bieniak. We have spoken to your parents and they've all agreed that we could start schooling you again."

Mr. Bieniak looked slowly at each teenager. "We decided to talk to the best students only."

"It is forbidden by the Germans to teach; therefore, you all must be very quiet about it." The priest put his pointer finger on his mouth in a symbolic gesture of silence.

"We would like to continue to teach you the seventh-grade curriculum, so when the war is over, hopefully soon, you can go to a high school." Mr. Bieniak concluded the meeting.

It was agreed that the five teenagers present at the meeting would come to the church twice a week in the morning and once a week to the dance hall, where Mr. Bieniak and another teacher would teach them literature, math, science, history, and geography. It was a limited curriculum but enough to get them into a high school later on. To camouflage their studying activities, they would bring brooms and rags to clean the church and the dance hall.

Rose's happiness was exploding inside her, even with the limited scope of learning. There was only one dark cloud hanging over her happiness; she could not share the news with anyone, not even her best friend Ania, who was not included in the secret school. Rose wasn't even sure if Franek and Mother knew about it. She would have to find ways to do her homework without others noticing it. Father would help her to find the right time and place to study. She was almost sure of it.

On November 1, 1940, George ordered Ted to be in the crypt at midnight. Every November 1, Polish people observed All Saints' Day. After attending

Mass, they took part in a procession to the local cemetery to pay homage to their deceased forefathers, relatives, and friends. Everybody lit candles on the graves, met with out-of-town relatives, and enjoyed a late supper.

After the visiting relatives left his house, Ted rested for a while and shortly before midnight left quietly through the back door.

Bolek was already in the church waiting for him. "Did anyone seen you coming here?"

"No, the town is quiet. Only the candles on the graves are still burning."

George startled Ted in the dark church. "Like our hope burning among the ruins. We will contact the Polish Armed Forces in Britain. Our pilots are fighting as part of the RAF forces, giving us hope that the war might be over soon." George's voice was stoic as always.

Bolek signalled to Ted and George. "Shush, I heard some noise."

They quickly dispersed, hiding behind the altars in each nave of the church. Ted's heart pounded as he noticed two shadows emerging from the side door of the church that had been left unlocked. *Who are they?* he wondered. *I must see them closer. They have no right to be here at this time. Did they follow one of us? Do they know about our radio station?* His thoughts were racing as he removed his shoes and crawled out from behind the altar. Like a fox, he moved quietly toward the two men still standing in the shadow of the side entrance. His mind worked quickly. *I must draw them closer to see their faces.*

He found a candle in his pocket, which he must have forgotten to put on the grave. He threw it at the cross hanging from the ceiling. The candle hit the cross and made a loud noise in the darkness. The two men looked up at the cross, which was suddenly lit by the moonlight entering through the stained-glass window. Ted looked up and saw one of the men's face. He recognised him as someone who served in the Polish Blue Police under German command. He didn't see the other man's face as the two left the church in a hurry.

After five minutes of silence, Bolek came out from behind the altar and went outside. A few minutes later he came back with relief on his face. "They're gone, something must have frightened them."

Ted laughed quietly. "Yeah, the piece of a candle I threw at the cross.

Remember, it's All Saints' Day and it's easy to scare anyone. The ghosts might be around."

"I saw you crawling on the floor. Did you recognise either of them?"

"Yes, I know one of them; he serves in the Blue Police."

"You'll have to find out why they were here. Bolek and I'll go to the crypt. Ted, you follow the policemen." George didn't expect any protest from Ted.

"Following them could be fruitless. We need to know who spied for them." Ted quickly conceived a plan that would involve being captured by the police. Once he was in a local jail, he could learn more.

Running in the dark, he quickly went to his house, which was across from the church, took a shot of vodka and ran to the cemetery. Candles were still burning on most graves and some people were still praying and talking. Ted took one of the candles and lit a pile of dry leaves near the gate. A few people ran towards him, pushing him away. Ted, pretending to be drunk, started a fight with two men, shouting obscenities at them. The fire was forgotten and it quickly spread to the next pile of leaves. The two policemen from the church appeared at the gate of the cemetery; Ted's plan was working so far. Ted pretended to run away but stumbled and fell down. The policemen leapt on top of him while the other people put out the fire.

They took Ted to the police station and locked him in a cell next to the main room. Very soon, Ted appeared to be asleep.

"What a crazy night," said one policeman.

Ted listened without opening his eyes. The cell had an opening with bars in it and he could hear everything.

"You got scared in the church, didn't you?" Ted heard laughter.

Ted knew one of them very well; his name was Kris and they had been classmates before the war.

"I think it was a sign that we shouldn't go to the church at night." Kris sounded serious and a bit scared.

"What about the suspicious activities there?"

Kris sounded uncomfortable with the conversation. "I think that the man who told us about it was just bluffing. I know him; Bob Jaro is a drunkard and often tells unrealistic stories."

The other policeman kept pressing. "The German commander asked us to investigate this rumour. I think Bob is their spy. What are we going to report tomorrow? That the cross started swinging but nobody was there?"

"We just have to tell them that we checked the church and there were no suspicious activities there." Kris went silent for a while. "We live in dangerous times; I just want to survive the war. I'm going out for a cigarette."

"Ted, did you hear what happened to Bob Jaro?" Maria called to her son after coming back home from her round to the farms.

"No, I haven't heard anything." Ted didn't lift his head from the stove and kept himself busy starting the fire in the woodstove.

"He was badly beaten. Nobody knows by whom. He may never walk again. You must be careful and don't act stupid like the night you were arrested." Mother started to unload the cheeses and eggs she'd brought home.

Ted's hands were trembling and he dropped a log of wood on the floor. He bent down, hoping to avoid further conversation. He had ordered the beating of Bob, but he had not expected it to be so bad. He knew that it had to be done to stop Bob from delivering messages to the Germans or the Blue Police. Many others could die if the snitching didn't stop. He started preparing tea for his mother. "Maybe the Germans did it. I hope the war will end soon."

Life in Brusk was relatively quiet during the first year and a half of war. The German Army set up its headquarters outside of Brusk on the other side of the river. They patrolled the town and the surrounding area every day and they often came to the market to purchase fruit. Rose was a quick study, and soon she was able to speak basic German. The soldiers, mostly from the *Feldgendarmerie*, were young men and occasionally talked to some young locals. Rose used the opportunity to practice her limited German and impress her teacher.

In May 1941, Rose came early to the class in the church, hoping to talk to Mr. Bieniak. She wanted to tell him about the books she had hidden at the beginning of the war.

Sitting at the back of the church, she heard some scratching noises coming from the left nave. A little frightened, she looked towards its direction. A stone floor tile moved and a head appeared from inside the floor. Frightened, she remained motionless in her pew. In the next few seconds, she recognised Ted emerging from the floor. She quickly lowered her body, hiding at the bottom of the pew. A second man came out from the floor and then they pushed the tile back into its place and left the church without talking.

What was that? Rose thought as she lifted herself up to her seat.

She was still frightened when Mr. Bieniak entered the church.

"Rose, why are you here so early?" He looked at her with astute eyes.

"I need to talk to you about books."

For the next few days, she could not stop thinking about Ted's head emerging from the floor. She couldn't concentrate during her classes as her eyes constantly drifted towards the spot where she'd seen him and the stranger. She was burning with curiosity and needed to talk to Ted.

After Sunday Mass, she stopped at his house under the pretence of visiting Ania, who had not been feeling well in the last few days.

"Ted, can I talk to you outside?" Rose asked after she finished talking to Ania.

He appeared surprised. "Fine."

They left the house through the back door and walked into Maria's Garden.

"Last week, I was in the church when I saw you and another man coming from the hole in the floor."

For a moment, Ted was silent, and then he whispered, "Rose, we all have secrets. Swear that you won't tell anyone about what you saw, and I won't tell Ania about you attending classes in the church and the dancing hall."

"You know about the school?" She looked behind her back to make sure Ania was nowhere nearby.

"This conversation is over. Remember to keep the secret and it's best if you forget about it." Ted turned and walked towards the house.

In the summer of 1941, Erik travelled to the eastern part of Poland to work with a *Feldgendarmerie* unit in the city of Lublin. On June 22, 1941, Germany broke the Molotov–Ribbentrop Pact signed on August 23, 1939, and attacked Russia. History was often cruel to Poland and ironically their former aggressor became Poland's ally in the fight with Germany as the polish territories occupied by the Russian Army since 1939 fell to the Germans. Erik's assignment was a difficult one. He needed to infiltrate the Polish people to learn about their cooperation with Russia.

As part of the *Feldgendarmerie* unit, he performed occupation duties in territories directly under the control of the *Wehrmacht*. This involved policing the areas behind the front lines, ranging from traffic and population control, to suppression and execution of partisans and collaborators with the Russians.

"Heil Hitler." He saluted as he entered the office of the captain.

"Sergeant Hermann, you were sent here because of your ability to speak Polish."

"Yes, sir."

"I have an assignment for you. I want you to infiltrate the local population to find out about the Polish underground organizations and their cooperation with the Soviets and their exiled government in London. First Lieutenant Hans will bring you up to speed."

"Yes, sir."

On the way to his barracks, Erik wondered when he had become such a "Yes" man. He supported the German occupation of Europe and their latest invasion of Russia. He liked the army discipline, the clear orders, yet something bothered him. The inability to voice his opinion not only to the higher-ranking officers but also among his fellow soldiers was something that he occasionally struggled with. Erik remembered his grandfather, Fred Pasiak, who had taught him to be an independent thinker, fiercely patriotic, and a proud Polish man.

That was a long time ago, a different world. I'm German and I need to follow commands for the greatness of the Third Reich. The thought restored his confidence in himself as he entered the barracks.

Erik liked his first important assignment. Among the Polish people, he not only felt powerful but he could use their language to befriend both man and women.

Soon he had started an affair with a widow who had lost her husband, a young Polish officer, during the Soviet invasion.

"Hello, Eva," Erik greeted the young woman as he entered her small apartment.

"Would you like a drink?" she asked flirtatiously.

Since the death of her husband at the hands of the Soviet Army, Eva had hated the Russians and often said that she liked the strong, handsome German officers.

A month after their affair started, Erik sensed that she was in love with him. She was a good choice for his assignment. Having experience in married life, she was comfortable and very promiscuous with men. She was his first woman, and Erik enjoyed their relationship. He learned to flirt with women, to fulfil their desires, to make them feel comfortable in his presence. It was a skill that would be very helpful in his future assignments. He met other people in her apartment and was accepted as a half Pole, half German who was forced to serve in the German Army against his liking.

He brought good cognacs to Eva's place and soon his circle of casual friends expanded. Polish men liked his cognac and after a few drinks, their conversations were less guarded, allowing Erik to get useful information. Most of them hated the Russian occupiers and easily shared information about their movements and the people collaborating with them. Erik never killed anyone personally, but his ability to infiltrate the local population and get useful information led to several arrests and the death of many people.

After a year of service, Erik was promoted to sergeant major in the *Feldgendarmerie*. With the promotion came more responsibility and a transfer to a different assignment.

It was a beautiful June evening when Erik went to see Eva for the last time. He was very tense and attempted to relax with a few drinks.

"Is something wrong? You're drinking more than usual." Her eyes were beautiful when she took his hand into hers and looked at him with radiating love.

"Everything is fine. I just received a letter from my mother. I miss her a little."

He had received a letter but not from his mother; it was a letter with instructions about his new assignment. He had mixed emotions. He was anxious to work on a different assignment but sad to leave Eva and the easy life he lived here.

Their lovemaking that night was passionate, almost violent. It transformed their bodies into one being. Feeling each other's movements and moving in the same direction, they were lost in their pleasure. They stayed in bed, gently embracing for a long time. When Eva fell into a gentle sleep, Erik got up from the bed, went to the bathroom, and splashed cold water on his face. He could not bring himself to tell Eva about leaving. He was trained to be a spy, to control his emotions, and to cut off any contacts he made, but training was different from reality. It was hard to leave Eva and his romance with her. He dressed quickly and left the apartment without looking back at his lover.

Ted was awakened by the screeching tyres of a convoy of trucks driving through the town. He looked at the clock; it was four in the morning and still dark outside. November 1941 was a mix of warm, cold, and rainy days. The last few days were exceptionally nice, bringing a slightly peaceful feeling of hope to the town. He looked through the narrow gap in the curtains covering the window, careful not to attract any attention from the Germans. As he counted the trucks driving by his house, he had a premonition that they were heading for the Jewish quarters in town. The Jewish community in Brusk was a small one but very prominent. They owned bakeries, coffee houses, and shops known for beautiful silks brought from as far as China. Ted knew a few young Jewish men his age. Some of them played football very well and often joined the town's team when they played against other towns. He was not close friends with them, as typically, after any festivities, the Jewish young people went back to their section of town, avoiding mingling with the gentiles. Their buildings were differently built from most of the other people's in Brusk. Most of their houses were connected to each other with a wall interspersed with wooden gates leading to the courtyards behind. The entrances to the houses were from inside the courtyards and their social life happened there. The most prominent buildings were facing the street and housed the Jewish businesses. Only once had Ted been invited to enter the courtyard, when he helped his football teammate to get home after a leg injury during a game. Ted remembered feeling almost claustrophobic entering the gate that led to the courtyard surrounded by walls.

When the last truck rolled past his house, Ted quickly dressed and silently left the house. The Home Army followed the developments in Warsaw and other cities where the Germans had established ghettos for the Jewish people. Poles were expelled from their apartments to make room for the Jewish people from Warsaw and surrounding areas. The best houses vacated by the Jews were taken over by the German officers and the street names were changed to German. In November 1940, Germans closed the Warsaw Ghetto to the outside world, surrounding it with a wall topped with barbed wire.

The Jewish community in Brusk was slowly getting smaller as many people left, escaping to the east as far as Russia. Some of the young people were trafficked by the Home Army to farms in the mountains, in hopes that the Germans might not reach them there. Many of the elderly and families with children stayed in Brusk, hoping that the Nazis would never come for them.

Ted ran along the street at a safe distance from the trucks ahead. A few people stood in their doorways, looking with horror towards the trucks heading for the Jewish quarters. It was early dawn when the gates opened and the exodus of people with suitcases proceeded towards the trucks parked along the wall.

Surprisingly, it was a peaceful march, and the people helped each other to get to the trucks. Ted couldn't do anything but hope that they would survive in one of the ghettos.

A shout, "Halt, halt!" diverted his attention and he noticed a young girl running away from the trucks. The shout from the soldier made her even more scared, and she ran faster until she stopped in front of a woman standing on the other side of the street. The woman embraced the girl and they stood together, paralysed with fear.

"Let her go." The words of the German soldier echoed along the street.

The woman and the girl didn't move, just stood there like a stone statue, unable to even lift their eyes.

In the next few seconds, the unthinkable happened. The terrifying staccato of the MP 40 gunfire broke the silence and Ted watched the woman and the girl slowly collapsing to the ground.

Forgetting that at the beginning of the war, the Germans had issued a decree that any Polish person helping Jewish people would be executed, he jumped forward and knelt next to the two bodies.

The girl was already dead, but the woman had open eyes and was whispering a prayer. Ted took her hand and watched the life seeping out of her with each shallow breath.

Somebody shouted, "Ted, run away. They'll kill you too." He was frozen with hate, unable to move, and think clearly. His mind was filled with the sound of the gun. He knew the MP 40 gun; it was deadly and killed many people. Ted had captured a number of them during the Home Army night actions, mostly from German trains or storage areas.

When he recovered his senses, the Germans had already turned their attention back to the deportation of the Jews.

The Jewish quarters stood empty after their occupants were taken away. One day, a small wooden sculpture of a woman embracing a child was left near a gate leading to the empty courtyard. Sometime later, somebody moved it to the local church.

Since the invasion of France, Jean had kept a low profile and avoided any involvement in activities that could be considered illegal by the Germans. He suspected that Andreas and his colleagues were involved in some form of underground movement but never inquired about it.

It was March 1942, and he had not heard from Michel since the surrender of the Maginot Fortress; perhaps he was dead or had been sent to a POW camp. Jean hoped that he wouldn't hear from any of his past co-conspirators and wouldn't have to be actively involved in any actions against the Germans. He didn't think of himself as a heroic person and preferred to lead a quiet life. He believed that the war would end one day, and he hoped to survive the difficult times. He just wanted a peaceful life for himself and his family. Sitting in a dimmed room, he was reminiscing about the last few years of his life. He didn't notice Emilie standing in front of him.

"Jean, it's time to go to bed. Tomorrow, I need your help in the garden."

As he lay next to his wife, he continued to reflect on his life since he could remember it. Things had happened to him and he'd had to deal with them. The accident, the marriage, involvement in the spying activities, all had happened to him as he was pulled by some forces beyond his control. Perhaps, before the accident, he was a different person. Perhaps he was courageous. Perhaps he loved somebody else before Emilie. Perhaps he was a better person. All that had been erased from his memory and dwelling on the forgotten past was not useful; it made him uncertain. He was a down-to-earth man, a good businessman, and he loved his family. Staying low and waiting for better times was the best option for him. Thinking about his life and the choice he'd made to stay safe put him to sleep.

Hours later, Jean was half-awake, listening to the sound of rain tapping on the window. He had a vague memory of the strange and somewhat scary dream that had woken him up, when he realised that not only was the rain continuing its lashing on the window of their bedroom, but there was something else. Somebody was tapping on the glass with increasing force. Jean looked at Emilie as she awakened and listening to the tapping.

"What is that?" She clutched his arm.

"Go quietly to the kids' bedroom and lock the door. Don't leave the room until I go out and check."

The kids' bedroom was on the other side of the hallway, next to the storage room on one side and the stairs to the basement on the other side. Occasionally, they discussed their escape route in case of any danger—from the kids' bedroom, to the basement, through the small window hidden behind bushes, and then to the shed. There was a trap door in the shed leading to a small cellar with blankets, warm clothes, and non-perishable food. Being a practical man, Jean had prepared the escape route soon after the Germans took over Thionville.

The moment Emilie left, Jean put on his coat and went through the back door to catch the intruder.

"Marc, what are you doing here?" Jean's face twisted with worry.

"I was afraid you would never come out. Can we talk?"

"Wait for me near the shed. I'll be there in a moment. I just need to tell Emilie that it was you tapping on the window."

Marc sounded uncomfortable. "Don't tell her that I'm here."

It took a while to convince Emilie that nobody was out there and that Jean needed to go out to check for any animals eating their vegetables, which had just started sprouting from the ground.

Marc's voice was very low as they entered the shed. "Jean, I'm in trouble and need your help."

"What kind of trouble?"

"I've worked for the Germans in Berlin since the beginning of the war. My mission was to gain their support for free Alsace. As you know, I've dedicated my life to this cause and I wanted to believe that the Germans would support it." Marc's bitterness indicated that things were not as he'd expected.

Jean became irritated. "They support the Vichy government, which is just as bad as the Nazis."

"I was sent here by the Germans to contact my spy network and look for any subversive activities in the Alsace-Lorraine region."

"You think that I'm involved?" Jean's irritation grew and he was afraid to hear anything more from Marc.

"I don't want to work for the Germans anymore. I realised that they never supported our cause; they used me to get information about the Maginot Line and the Alsatian freedom movement. They didn't want to help us; they planned to crush us all and any hope for free Alsace."

Jean was still very wary about Marc's motives. "So, why are you here?"

"I need your help to put me in contact with the underground to help me to move to Spain."

"What about your wife and son? Are they safe? I haven't seen them for a while."

"I sent them to Africa before the German invasion. We have relatives that live near Cape Town. They're safe there. I hope to join them and never come back to Europe."

"I have no means of helping you to go to Spain. Even if you get there, how will you get to Cape Town?"

"I have some contacts there; they'll help me."

Jean's voice was barely audible. He didn't want to be involved in any dangerous activities. "I've lost all my contacts and wouldn't know where to look for anyone that I knew in the past."

"Let me tell you something. You have no choice but to find a way to help me. I didn't want to do this to you, but if you refuse, I'll reveal your true identity." Marc was becoming agitated.

Jean was suddenly paralysed with fear. "What do you mean, my identity?"

"You're not Jean Navarre; you're Joseph Novak, the Polish immigrant who was considered dead in the accident," Marc seethed through a clenched jaw.

"Are you out of your mind?" Jean snapped angrily.

"I know things and will use them if you don't help me."

"You're bluffing. There is no proof. There can't be! I'm Jean Navarre." Jean was ready to attack Marc with his fists.

"Maybe I'm bluffing or maybe not. Do you want to take the chance of me planting any doubt of your identity?"

Jean tried to mask the uncomfortable feeling that was spreading through his gut. "Who would believe your story?"

Marc continued to put pressure. "There are enough secrets in your life that some may believe in the rumours I can spread, and they can put fear into your life. It is better that I'm gone for good. You see, I know about the family in Poland, the widow Maria and her daughter Ania. Maybe it isn't your family, but isn't it surprising that you named your daughter Marie-Ann?"

"Why didn't you reveal this earlier if you thought it was the truth?"

"You became my good friend; I didn't want to create any trouble for you, Emilie, and the children. Throughout my life, I've always kept secret knowledge that could be used to my advantage in situations like this one."

"I don't believe in your insinuations and I want you out of my life for good."

"Then help me to go to Spain. You'll find a way. I'll be back in two days. Get to work."

Back in the house, Jean splashed some water on his face to calm down. When he looked up, Emilie was standing next to him. He put his arms around her and buried his head in her hair. She didn't ask any questions. She only kissed him gently on the cheek.

He loved her very much; she was his backbone, always giving him sound business advice and raising their children mostly on her own while running her flower and vegetable business. He put his head quietly next to hers, trying to forget the conversation with Marc. He knew that something was hiding in his past, something that he was afraid of. He felt that discovering it would make him a dishonest person and perhaps destroy his current life. He needed to get rid of Marc forever. He pondered his options. Doing nothing was not a choice he could make. He needed to either talk to Andreas or denounce Marc to the French Gendarmerie. Late that night, he made a decision.

Ted knew, without even opening his eyes, that it was time to get out of bed. He hadn't slept well, tormented by a premonition that something bad was about to happen. The rain coming down added to his foul mood.

It had been over fourteen years since his father's death, and thoughts about his life as an orphan descended on Ted, clouding his mind. He could not convince his body to move as the sadness gripped him and the headache started to throb in his temples bringing tears to his eyes. If only his father were alive, it would be easier to endure these dark times of war. Although only a boy of eight when his father had died, he had matured quickly into a serious, responsible man. Sometimes he was tired of always being the responsible one, consoling his mother in her grief and looking after his younger sister, Ania, who didn't even remember her father.

Ted was a ranking member of the Home Army, always up-to-date about new developments in the war. In February 1943, he was informed about intensified German operation to capture young people and send them to labour camps in Germany. Nobody knew the day or time of their arrival, increasing a sense of foreboding among the population. He wondered every day if the Germans were taking the young people to labour camps only.

Since the massive deportation of Jews from the Warsaw Ghetto to the German concentration camps that started in January 1943, and the resistance from many young people equipped with guns and Molotov cocktails, everybody was living on edge, in fear of what the next day might bring.

The Home Army smuggled arms to the young Jewish men in the ghetto and encouraged them to rise up against the Germans. It was better to die fighting than to be deported to the camps. It was already known that the people of the ghetto weren't being relocated east as the Germans told them; they were being sent to Auschwitz-Birkenau and other German concentration camps where big signs above the iron gates, "*Arbeit Macht Frei*" ("Work Will Set You Free") greeted them.

The Warsaw Ghetto uprising took the Nazis by surprise and lasted longer than anyone expected. Then the rage unlashed on the ghetto spilled over to the entire Polish population. The infuriated SS beasts intensified their brutal actions of capturing and sending Polish people to labour camps, spreading fear among them.

The steady drizzle that was falling on Ted's roof sounded like a German platoon marching closer and closer. Despite his heavy heart, he knew he had to get up and leave right away. He glanced at his sixteen-year-old sister, sound asleep in the next bed, and quickly gathered his thoughts. "Ania!" he whispered. "Time to get up."

"I'll be ready in a minute," she mumbled, slowly rising from her bed.

For several weeks, Ted had been organising the young people of the neighbourhood to leave their homes at 4:30 a.m. and hide in the hills surrounding the town. At first, everybody was fine leaving their homes every day but lately, some of them, too tired and cold, had lost their resolve to hide and stopped going.

"Maybe the Germans won't come here," some were arguing more frequently.

"Don't let your guard down," Ted responded over and over.

He and Ania grabbed their blankets and went to the meeting place. Ania's closest friend Rose was not there. "Not her!" Ted whispered to himself. He knocked on Rose's door. "Why aren't you ready?"

"Ted, I'm not coming today. Don't try to convince me otherwise."

He knew from the look in Rose's eyes that it was pointless to argue. He liked this stubborn and know-it-all streak in her; he liked many things about her. Reluctantly, he left the house and joined the others on the trek up into the hills. Half an hour later, German trucks arrived in the town, and soldiers went from house to house, snatching young people. Ted watched in horror from the hills, feeling powerless. He dropped his binoculars and, for the second time that morning, felt tears streaming down his face. Later, he found out that thirty people had been taken. Rose was among them.

Jean approached his superintendent early in the morning. "Andreas, I would like to talk to you."

"Yes, boss, what is it?"

They went into Jean's office. Coffee was brewing on the stove, pleasing their senses with its rich aroma.

"It must be something important." Andreas knew that coffee was a rarity, difficult to get, and that Jean was about to ask for a big favour.

"I'll get right to the point. Somebody I know is in danger and needs to be moved to Spain." Jean started pouring the coffee.

"What do you have in mind?" Andreas accepted the mug of hot coffee.

"Prior to the war, you recruited some Polish men to work with the French Army."

"Yes, I did, but Michel is gone and nothing has happened since then." Andreas started drinking his coffee, avoiding Jean's eyes.

"I don't need to know what happened since the war started. I need you to find a way to help this man."

"Do I know him?"

"No, you don't, and let's keep it that way. He is hiding from the Germans and needs to disappear very soon. Let me know what can be done."

Andreas was ready to ask more when Jean pointed towards his coffee.

"Let's drink our coffee before it gets cold."

It took a week to get new documents and plan a route for Marc's escape.

The last words Jean heard from Marc were: "Thank you, Jean. Do what's right for the people you love now and who you loved in the past."

Rose could feel every bump, every pothole in the road as the truck moved in an unknown direction. It was dark under the canvas top of the truck, only a little light coming through some holes. She recalled every second of that awful morning.

She had been tired of getting up early every day and going to the hills. It was the last day of March, the weather had turned cold, and Rose didn't want to leave her bed to go out. She'd had cold tremors all night and thought that she had reached the point of not caring if the Germans came or not. Even when Ted knocked at her door, she wouldn't change her mind. She could see that Ted was desperate to convince her to go with them, but nothing would make her change her resolve. When he'd left, she'd put the blanket over her head and tried to sleep again. Sleep was not coming but instead, her head was full of thoughts of adventure in a big world.

"Get up, Rose." Her father spoke quietly, shaking her urgently by the arm. "The Germans have arrived. Grab your dress and let's go."

In the early dawn, she followed her father to the orchard towards the "apple hole." Stan removed one branch from among many covering the hole in the ground and urged Rose to jump in. He put the branch back, closing the gap on top and she found herself in full darkness. Her heart was beating very hard as she covered herself with a blanket spread over the apples and potatoes stored at the bottom of the pit.

A frightening sound of flapping like big wings of a giant bird was coming closer and closer to her hiding spot. The same branch that Father had put back on top was lifted and the big head of a German soldier in a helmet peered down.

"I know you're there." His harsh voice boomed over her head. She understood the German language and even liked it, but this voice was vibrating with dominance underlined with hate.

She stopped breathing, hoping that he could not see her.

"I saw you jump in there. Come out or it will be your grave."

She remembered the day she had dug the hole with Franek, laughing as they called it the "apple grave." Now it could be hers. She removed the dirty blanket and started to climb. The soil was cold and wet, making it impossible for her to reach the top. She'd forgotten about the ladder stored on one side of the pit.

I'll never see the light again. No more dreams about a better future. She started to sob. Her body was convulsing and she hated the feeling of fear. She put her head down and waited for him to kill her.

"Take the end of the rifle so I can hoist you up." She was shocked to hear the booming voice above her head.

She looked up and stared into the eyes of the German soldier kneeling down and extending the stock of his rifle towards her.

Without hesitation, she grabbed it, and with his help, she lifted herself out of the hole, towards uncertain life.

When Rose emerged from her thoughts, the early sunlight was coming through the canvas holes in the roof of the truck. She strained her eyes looking around, estimating that about thirty people were seated on the floor of the truck. Two German soldiers were positioned at the back of it with rifles in their hands. They were looking down with absentminded looks on their faces. When more light started pouring into the truck, people started waking their bodies from the lethargy that had descended on them after the shock of capture. Rose looked around and recognised Ada, an older girl from the neighbourhood.

They acknowledged each other but dared not say anything. It was cold inside the truck. Rose was shivering in her light dress and a scarf that her father had tossed to her as she was marching in front of the German soldier that captured her. Ada, who wore a warm jacket, quietly moved close to Rose and covered her shoulders with one side of her jacket. They rode in silence, sharing the warmth of their bodies.

Around two hours into this miserable journey, the truck stopped. The German soldiers jumped out and started shouting orders.

"They sound like vicious, barking dogs," Ada whispered to Rose's ear.

Somebody lifted the canvas and Rose could see many people marching in one direction. Hundreds of people with their heads down and expressions of fear on their faces were walking towards a huge building.

Immediately after the Germans had driven away with trucks full of young people, Ted ran to Rose's house. Everybody was crying, even her father, Stan. Ted pulled him by the sleeve and asked him to step outside.

"I'll help to get Rose back."

"What will you do?" Stan lamented. "They are already far away from here."

"The Germans take bribes, and I can help you to get the money."

Ted met with George, who promised to look into it. Afterwards, waiting for the decision was agonising. He avoided Stan, afraid to show his despair and any hint of his feelings for Rose.

Ania cried a lot, sitting at the table and looking at the book about Africa. "Rose was dreaming about travelling the world; now she's travelling but most likely to her death."

"Don't say stupid things." Ted became agitated and left the house.

Three days later, Ted brought the money to Stan. Those three days were the most agonising that Ted could remember. It was a race against time before Rose crossed into Germany. Despite all odds, he hoped that the 200 US dollars he'd borrowed from the Home Army would bring Rose back.

When Stan left in search of Rose, Ted's adrenaline, which had kept him moving with lightning speed, now left him exhausted. His thoughts drifted to the awful morning when Rose had been captured. He realised that he was in love with her. The love surprised him, but when he thought about it, he recognised that many of the small things he did for his sister were really done with Rose in mind. He became aware that he had always looked forward to her visits and the time she spent with Ania. They provided him with opportunities to talk to her and challenge her opinions about the world. She was the opposite of him: she was a dreamer, while he was down to earth and practical; she was cheerful, while he was sombre; and she was becoming more beautiful every year.

"We are at a Warsaw prison."

The news spread quickly among the people in the truck. Rose was fighting her tears when a German soldier ordered everybody out. She'd never seen so many people in one place, not even during their travel to Radom escaping from the invading German Army at the beginning of the war.

Over three years later, the Germans were everywhere, not only in every country in Europe but also far into Russia and even her favourite continent, Africa. She didn't want to look at the people around her, the gravel under her feet, or the big prison ahead.

Is my life over? she wondered without sharing her sadness with Ada.

She was sixteen years old and didn't want to die. She tried to focus her mind and imagine the warmth of Africa, the graceful giraffes, and the fearless lionesses. Thinking of Africa often helped her to survive difficult times.

She was led by Ada among the procession of people until they stopped near the gate to the prison.

"Your name and address?" said one of the several soldiers sitting behind a long table.

"Rose Podolski."

"Gate number four." She heard the order and turned away from the table. Glancing ahead, she saw Ada heading for the same gate and she smiled for the first time. It might be easier to share the unknown future with somebody she knew.

They were given black coffee and some bread for lunch. Rose was not hungry, but the black and bitter coffee tasted surprisingly good. She extended her hand with the bread to a teenage boy sitting next to her.

He smiled at her. "Keep it. We don't know when we may eat again."

He looked younger than her, maybe fourteen years old. Rose felt sad for him to be separated from his family at such a young age. She looked around, noticing everybody in the large room. They were all young no more than twenty years old. Some were dressed in stylish coats, even hats, while others were in poor peasant jackets. The majority of them were like

Rose, somewhere in the middle between rich and poor.

After waiting all day, everybody was sent to prison cells for the night.

Rose and Ada made sure they were not separated. The young boy was walking close to them as if looking for their protection. They slept on prison beds that were stripped of any blankets. The beds were narrow and made of wood with a small support to put their heads on.

Ada and the boy were next to Rose, lying quietly. Rose started telling them about her dreams of the world and soon the stories were full of invented adventures in her favourite Africa. Her fear disappeared and she drifted into deep sleep on the hard bed.

In the morning, they were given just the black coffee and Rose shared the forgotten piece of bread from yesterday with Ada and the boy. She still didn't know his name and decided not to ask. It would be easy to become sad and fearful again if they shared their real-life stories. Her imagination could keep them hopeful, somewhat sheltered from the harsh reality.

Hundreds of people were loaded onto a cargo train without windows. Most likely, the trains had been used to transport cattle as the smell of manure was still very pungent.

They travelled through the day and night, stopping frequently for the Germans to push more prisoners into the cars. Finally, the train stopped at a busy station and everybody was ordered to disembark. They were marched to a military camp not far from the train station. Red-brick barracks had been built around the main square, which was paved with flat grey cobblestones. They were left standing in the square for many hours. After an hour that seemed like eternity, Rose felt numb and unafraid. Her mind was blank; only one thought was replaying itself over and over again. *My life cannot end here; I'm too young.*

Slowly, she recovered from her trance and looked around with defiance in her eyes. The red-brick buildings were three stories high with rows of identical, barred, rectangular windows. The barracks lined three sides of the square and the fourth side was protected by a tall, brick wall with a massive gate in the middle. Two booths were attached to the wall on each side of the gate with an armed soldier in each. On top of each building, Rose noticed machine guns, each manned by two soldiers. In the middle of the square stood a wooden tower and four soldiers were looking down at the crowd standing below. If she and Ada had any thoughts of escaping this place, they were quickly fading in the enormity of the fortress.

Still, Rose said, "Ada, we're still in Poland. Maybe we could escape from here?" She looked at her friend without any expectation of an answer.

"Maybe to Africa," Ada replied, bursting into a laugh.

Before Rose could react, they were ordered to walk into the biggest building in the camp. In the entrance, they were given a small bar of soap and directed to a change room to remove their clothes. Standing naked, Rose noticed with relief that women and men were separated into different rooms. She would have been very ashamed to be seen naked by the young men in the camp. Surprisingly, the German soldiers guarding the showers were females, dressed in uniforms. Rose had never worn trousers and tried to imagine if it was more comfortable to wear them instead of skirts. She thought she would like to try them one day.

From the shower, they were moved to a steam room and after that to a laundry room where they cleaned their clothes. When the cleaning was completed in the late afternoon, everybody was given a bowl of soup and assigned to various barracks. Rose and Ada were lucky to end up in the same one.

The next day was Sunday and all the prisoners were assembled in the main square where a simple altar with a cross was set up.

"What now, you evil monsters?" whispered Rose.

"They'll sacrifice us on the altar."

"Don't make fun of everything, Ada."

Ada smiled and gently hugged Rose. "It's the best way to survive the dark times in our lives. Don't give in to despair; this is what the heathens want you to do."

Soon, a priest appeared at the altar and performed a Catholic Mass in Polish. Everybody around Rose stood with their heads down. Many cried, while others held hands and prayed together.

Rose was in a state of disbelief as she looked around at the multitude of praying people. She hated the Germans even more now, asking God to strike them down and punish them all. They killed people and enslaved others to work on their farms and in their factories. They were oppressors, appearing to believe in God, but God was nowhere to be found and not helping the innocent ones.

"No more praying. We have to look after ourselves alone, without any hope that God may help us." Rose clenched her fists.

After the Mass, some of the prisoners spent time outside in the main square and some went back to the barracks to get away from the unhappiness around them. Nobody knew what might happen next; tension and sadness were all around despite the warm sunshine that broke through the clouds.

Rose and Ada resolved to stay strong and be resilient to anything that might happen to them. Both knew that they'd most likely be sent to different places and might never see each other again. To pass the time, they talked about their childhoods and people they knew, missing them already. Ada was not in a joking mood anymore as the realities of impending doom hung above them.

"Rose Podolski, step outside." A middle-aged German officer stepped into the barracks where Rose rested on the wooden bed. Rose was scared and after a quick hug with Ada, she stepped outside.

Several other young people were standing in the square. When Rose joined the group, they were marched towards the gate. The cobblestones under her feet were uneven and she tripped. Somebody caught her before she hit the ground.

"Oh, it's you. Thank you." Rose recognised the teenage boy she'd befriended.

"Don't thank me, maybe we're going into something worse than this place." He looked at her with a blank expression on his face.

The gate opened and the prisoners were ordered to march outside. Rose closed her eyes, expecting a firing squad. Instinctively, her thoughts turned towards God, and she said her prayers. She heard the gate closing behind them and opened her eyes. A few adults, including her father, were standing near the gates, and after a little confusion, they all ran towards each other.

"Father?"

"Rose, don't talk. Let's move quickly out of here before they change their decision." Stan took her by the arm and moved away from the gate.

They reached a horse-driven wagon waiting for them two blocks from the gate. A man unknown to Rose started driving the wagon away from the camp and the train station.

After around an hour, they stopped at a train station in a different town. Stan shook hands with the driver and together with Rose, went to the station.

"Don't talk," he cautioned his daughter. "Some Germans take bribes. You're free now, but we must be careful. I'll explain it to you when we get home."

Ted was standing outside of his house, watching Rose walking towards him. "Hi, Ted. I heard you helped my father to get the money to bribe the Germans."

"Better if we don't talk about it. Others might be upset. As you know, many people were taken to Germany. We haven't heard from them yet." Ted went inside the house and busied himself with handling some post office materials lying on the table.

For over a year Ted, with the help of his mother, operated a small post office in their house allowing him and other Home Army members to meet there without raising suspicion from the Germans.

"You're not responsible for what happened to some of us. It was our fault for going against your better judgement and staying at home that night."

Ania's head appeared from the door, smiling at the two of them. "Let's celebrate Rose's release."

"You two celebrate. I have things to do." For a brief moment, Ted stared into Rose's eyes without showing any emotion, and then he left the house.

He stopped on the other side of the street, lit a cigarette, and thought about his love for Rose. *Love in troublesome times.* His jaw clenched.

He finished his cigarette and decided to join Ania and Rose in the little celebration. After all, he wouldn't pass up a piece of his mother's cake.

Ania cut a piece for Ted and the three of them sat at the table mostly in silence. When they finished, Rose offered to clean up the table.

"You went through a lot in the past few days. Enjoy this day." Ania took the plates and started washing them in a basin.

"The old general store is in disrepair and my father is opening a new co-op store. I'm going to work there and help to repay the money." Rose looked into Ted's eyes. "I'm very grateful for your help. Ania is lucky to have a brother like you."

"Glad I could help." Ted blushed with embarrassment showing on his face.

"When I was imprisoned for those few days, I resolved to live in the present. It might sound odd but since awful things, even death, can happen any time, we need to live fully every day." She sounded unsure of her words, as if they were too big for her age and Ted might not understand her feelings.

"I have to go." Uncomfortable with such a personal conversation, he left the room.

Talking to Rose, he'd realised that it was difficult to keep his love suppressed and not to show his true feelings for her. Her talking about "living for today" made him feel awkward. He was not a romantic person and talking about feelings was out of his character. He decided to avoid her as much as possible; he didn't want to burden her with his love. His priorities were to serve the Home Army, fighting the Nazis, and his life was in constant danger. He could not share it with anyone, not even the girl he loved. Despite this testing moment, he was glad that Rose was his sister's best friend. Rose was the adventuresome one, always encouraging Ania to achieve more. In a way, Rose was like an older sister, looking out for the best interests of his sister, and that was good enough for now.

The location for the new store had to be approved by the German *Feldgendarmerie* stationed across the river. The local priest, Father Karol, had been planning to go with Rose's father, Stan, and one of the Blue Policeman to the German camp, but he became sick with a severe cold and had to excuse himself from this mission. Stan was uncomfortable going with the Nazi-collaborating policeman, but he didn't want to wait any longer for the approval. The policeman was new to the area and Stan didn't know his name and preferred it that way. The town needed a new store and Stan wanted to be its proprietor. He needed money to repay the debt for Rose's freedom, and he liked to be part of a group of people with influence. Organising and running the co-op store would make him more prominent in the town. So, going to the German base alone with the policemen was a choice he made in order to speed up the approval of the store, even if he was uncomfortable with it.

Walking in silence behind the policeman, his thoughts drifted to his youth. His family had been poor when he was young, and after completing primary school, he had to move to Silesia to work in a coal mine. He hated his job; it was hard and dirty. His only consolation was the companionship of other men, some of them educated. They would discuss current events and the future of Poland, and he could read newspapers that some of the workers brought to the cafeteria.

After four years of hard work, he finally decided to visit his parents in Brusk. He'd never had a loving relationship with his family, blaming them for being poor and sending him to work in the mines instead of going to a high school.

On his first visit back home, he met Renata during a dance party at a local hall. She was older than him and her family was wealthy, but unfortunately, she was engaged to a man from another town.

He decided to break up her engagement and marry her. The challenge of making her fall for him was difficult at first, but he used his good looks and charmed her with the worldliness and charisma that he'd acquired while working away from his family. He didn't care about love; he wanted money and status.

Thinking about his past, he arrived at German headquarters, where a young officer waited for them in the office. The policeman did most of the talking and the approval was granted an hour after Stan submitted all the required documentation.

"That was easy."

"Only because I was with you," the policeman stated with authority.

"Thank you."

"When the store opens, I want a twenty per cent cut of the profits. There are no negotiations; these are orders from the Germans. A small part is for me and most of it is for them. In case you don't know my name, it is Stefan Mara. Remember me, as I'll visit your store to collect the share."

They continued to walk back to town in silence.

The approved building for the store was a closed library in the centre of town. Soon after the invasion, the Germans had closed it, and it stood abandoned with boarded-up windows and locked doors. Nobody knew what had happened to the books and other cultural items collected since 1918.

Stan entered the store with three other men. "Rose, you have done a great job cleaning the building and getting it ready for the counter and shelf installation."

Rose spoke before her father even closed the door behind him. "How quickly can you do your job?"

One of the men looked at Rose with a patronising smirk on his face. "We will install everything in one week."

"Good, because the merchandise and non-perishables will arrive next week."

Stan looked at her and smiled. He knew that she liked to be in charge, organising the store, planning the orders, and interviewing young women to hire as salesgirls. The memories of the March week in captivity appeared to be fading away as she immersed herself in work. She was like him. She wanted to be important, wanted to use her knowledge and quick mind in public. The store was a perfect opportunity for her to shine. Being the smartest girl among her friends was not enough; she wanted others in town to see her talents and her leadership.

"Mr. Joey Wilk, I would like to meet with you in London," were the first words of a letter Joey received in May 1943. The letter was from Billy's fiancée, Eloise Kerr. It was puzzling, as it didn't provide any clarification as to the nature of the meeting, only the name and the address of the café where they were to meet.

Joey was stationed at RAF Station Northolt, located close to London. Getting there by train was easy once he obtained permission to leave the base. He and the other Polish pilots continued to fight alongside the British pilots with renewed dedication after they'd been officially recognised for their achievements during the Battle of Britain. They were respected not only by the RAF command and pilots but also by the people of Britain.

Joey arrived early for the meeting and decided to do some sightseeing. He had visited London in the past and each time discovered interesting buildings that stood among the ruins inflicted by the Luftwaffe. The café was located near Tower Bridge. Since the bridge was such a landmark in London, Joey spent some time admiring it without paying attention to the time. When he checked his watch, it was already late.

As he entered the café, a young woman in a white blouse waved at him from the table near the window. Her cup of tea was almost empty.

He formally extended his hand. "I'm sorry for being late. You must be Billy's fiancée. I'm Joey Wilk."

"Hi, Joey. I'm Eloise. Please sit down."

Sitting across from her, he scanned the café for a waiter. Some people at other tables were looking at him and smiling. Some even waved.

"Do you know these people?" Eloise looked a little uncomfortable with such attention.

"No, I don't know any of them. I suppose they recognise my RAF uniform with the Poland badge on the sleeve."

"I heard about the Polish contribution to the victory over the Luftwaffe and the hero-worship attitude towards the Polish pilots, but I didn't expect it in this small café."

"Don't pay attention to this. Would you like another tea?"

Before Eloise could answer, a waiter appeared in front of them with two cups of tea and two glasses of liqueur.

"On the house." The waiter put the cups and glasses on the table and secretly saluted Joey.

Eloise looked at the waiter and Joey, showing anticipation that some explanation would be forthcoming.

Once the waiter was gone, Joey turned to her and smiled. "Many restaurants pay for our drinks and occasionally for our food."

"Wow." She was speechless and looked at Joey with astonishment.

"Please, tell me why we are meeting here," he said.

"Billy asked me to meet with you."

"Why wouldn't he meet me directly?" His face became tense with an expectation of bad news.

"Billy's Hurricane was shot during one of his combat missions and the plane barely made it back to RAF Base Rufforth. The plane crashed on the runway and Billy and his crew were injured."

As she continued to talk, Joey noticed a certain efficiency about her, not only the way she was dressed in a simple white shirt and a navy skirt but the words she used to describe the accident. She was plain-looking and soft-spoken but her poise and charm mesmerised Joey.

"I'd like to see him. Could I go with you next time?"

"I just came back from a leave of absence, visiting Billy in a hospital in Leeds that houses injured soldiers from Rufforth. I may not be able to see him for a while. We are very busy serving our country."

"Are you in the armed forces?"

"WAAF," she answered simply.

"Women's Auxiliary Air Force." He stated the obvious just to buy some time before he could ask her more questions. "Where are you stationed?"

"I'm in London on a temporary assignment working as a telephone operator at The Royal Artillery at Woolwich. I was working at Broadway Press when the printing company diversified and I was delegated to sewing parachutes."

"War is changing the way we all live. What were your plans before the war?"

"I was supposed to study millinery. My family owned a millinery business. I spent many days in the design department and created some of my own hats. I guess I continued in the textile industry for a while." She giggled at her own words.

Joey was enjoying the conversation but could not read her; in some moments, she appeared to be friendly, even charming, but most of the time, she was very serious and official. She wasn't like many young women he'd met, willing to flirt, drink, and have sex with the gallant Polish pilots. She intrigued Joey.

When he was about to ask more questions, Eloise stood up, ready to leave. "I can't go, but Billy would be happy to see you if you can get there." She extended her hand to him and left the café.

Two weeks later, he travelled on the train to Leeds.

"Hello, Billy." Joey sounded cheerful as he entered the hospital room. Billy was alone in the room and appeared to be sleeping, so Joey decided to wait for a while instead of waking him. He looked around the room and at his sleeping friend.

Billy's head was covered in bandages. His leg, in a white plaster cast, was elevated on a wooden block covered with a soft blanket. The room was small but clean with a window allowing the afternoon sun to wash it with a golden luminosity. There was another bed closer to the entrance and two chairs. A small table on the side of Billy's bed had some medicine bottles and a cup of cold tea.

Joey sat in one of the chairs and his thoughts drifted back to the Battle of Britain and the friendship with Billy christened with the blood of friends that had fought alongside them.

Prior to this, most of the British pilots and especially the RAF command didn't regard the Polish pilots as worthy of their place among them. Joey often heard the sniggering behind his back about how the Polish Air Force had lasted only a few days before being crushed by the Luftwaffe.

Their attitudes changed after the Poles helped to defeat the Luftwaffe, but some of the pilots continued to disrespect them.

At first, Billy was like the others, condescending and disheartened by his assignment, but he never openly made jokes about their ability to fly and fight, often walking a fine line between the camaraderie with his countrymen and the somewhat unruly newcomers. He was responsible for the Poles' training and Joey was his right-hand man, translating all commands. Their relationship was formal at first but with time, became friendly enough to share an occasional beer at a local pub. Without realising, they became close friends, bound by war.

Although the Poles considered their training disgraceful and believed they were purposely being kept behind the line of fire, they persevered and continued to call Britain "The Island of the Last Hope."

Billy brought Joey back into reality with his booming voice. "Joey, you're here."

In a flash, Joey went to Billy's bed and grabbed him by the shoulders. "What are you doing in the hospital, my friend? Getting some rest?" They both started to laugh.

"How did you get here so quickly?"

"Eloise told me about your accident, and the captain gave me a few days off." Joey bent to embrace Billy.

"I hope to get transferred to one of the bases near London, close to Eloise and you, my friend."

They spent the afternoon talking about the Battle of Britain, about the unexpectedly long war, and about their plans for the future. Joey had not thought much about the future; he lived for today and was happy to fight the Germans.

"I'm planning to get married; Eloise and I are engaged and I want to make her happy before the war ends." Billy drifted into sleep.

Later in the afternoon, Joey took a local train to the base in Rufforth and went to Billy's room. It was a good-sized room sparsely furnished without any personal effects on display except for a framed picture of Eloise in a sundress with sea waves in the background. She looked different from the girl Joey had met in the café. Sexy and vivacious, she flaunted the confident look of somebody who lived a good life. He dropped his bag on the floor and slouched on the narrow bed. His thoughts drifted back to the meeting with Eloise. She fascinated him with her mysterious personality and lack of interest in the flashy life of the Polish pilots. Billy was lucky to be engaged to her.

In the middle of the night, he woke up, still in his clothes. His body was aching from the long trip on the train. "Billy, you must have vodka or gin somewhere in the room," Joey said to himself as he changed into his army-issued pyjamas. He found brandy in the desk drawer and took a mouthful directly from the bottle.

When he woke up the next time, grey light was coming through the window. It was early morning and he could hear the rain pounding on the roof. Before going to the mess for breakfast, he went for a walk through the military base. The base was new, built in 1942 by the US Army's Aviation Engineer Battalion. Although it was "war duration only," it looked well organised, with comfortable living arrangements. Joey saw a lot of soldiers of various ranks rushing in and out of buildings with many women among them. He noticed the difference between the British and the American servicemen, with the latter appearing more relaxed and louder, as if the war was a big adventure in a foreign land.

After breakfast, he went back to the room, put the unfinished bottle of brandy into the drawer, and got a ride to the hospital.

"Sorry to interrupt." Joey startled the nurse, who appeared to be changing Billy's bandages. The scene was a little unusual; Billy's eyes were closed and the nurse's hands were moving up and down under the light blanket.

"I'll be back in a while," Joey said and he quickly left the room. It was mid-morning and too early for a drink in a local pub. He sat on a bench outside the hospital, glad that the rain had stopped earlier in the morning. Half an hour later, he was back in Billy's room, where his friend waited for him with a smile on his face.

"I'm glad you're finally back. Don't think much about what you saw. It is war, after all." Billy laughed, adding, "They'll remove the plaster from my leg this afternoon and I'm starting rehabilitation right away."

"I think you already started." They both erupted into a hearty laugh.

"I need anything to help me to recover as quickly as possible."

"I'll do my part." Joey looked mischievous.

"I'll be back tomorrow afternoon. Make sure you're allowed to leave the hospital for a few hours, under my care. We need to check out some pubs here."

Joey was back on his base in Northolt on Friday evening. It was unusually quiet, not like a typical Friday evening with the drinking and dancing that often ended up in the private quarters of the pilots.

Women in the army were liberated, serving as analysts, telephone operators, even flight mechanics. They earned money, were independent, and expected death anytime. That gave them the power to be as free as the male soldiers and to live life on their terms. Like many men, they too wanted to enjoy every moment of life.

Joey went straight to the mess where some Polish pilots were still sitting at the tables.

"Why is it so quiet here?"

"Two of the first lieutenants were killed during a reconnaissance flight over Germany."

"That may bring changes to our battalion. We might not stay together any longer." Joey became pensive, thinking that he might be moved farther away from London. He hoped it would not happen.

After Joey's visit, Billy felt energised, expecting full recovery soon. Although he was yearning to be in combat again, he didn't mind being in the hospital. Cora, the nurse looking after him, was very attentive while performing daily routines of changing the bandages, administering medicine, and helping him lifting his body to a more comfortable position.

Billy had felt uncomfortable the first time she removed his underwear to wash his body.

"Don't be silly, Billy. We see many men here in the hospital." She tried to dispel his embarrassment.

"But you see me in broad daylight."

"I can see you in the dark too, if you want."

They both burst into laughter and her hand stayed a bit longer under his shoulder.

The initial daily routines were soon affected by their mutual attraction and physical desire. Billy discovered that Cora was very liberal with her attitude towards sex and skilled in giving and taking pleasure despite the bandages and Billy's restricted movements.

On the fourth weekend of his hospitalisation, Eloise came to visit him. Sitting on the chair by the side of his bed, she talked about London, her work in the military services, and the small rations of food.

"Everybody is starving. Many children were sent to the country to stay safe and the suffering is showing on people's faces. How long can we endure the war?"

He summoned his strength and asked, "Could you lie down next to me?"

Eloise didn't hesitate and gently sat on his bed.

Billy took her arm and was about to pull her down when Cora entered the room. Everybody froze as if something indescribable and prohibited was happening.

"Sorry, it must be the wrong room." Cora turned and closed the door behind her.

"Please lie down," said Billy to Eloise.

They stayed in silence, their arms intertwined and both lost in their thoughts.

"Billy, I won't be able to come in two weeks, I'm very busy at work. When I see you next time, you might be fully recovered."

The next day a different nurse came to change the bandages and Billy became anxious about not seeing Cora. "Where is my regular nurse?"

"She was called to an emergency but will be back soon."

The next two days were a torment for Billy. He desired Cora but loved Eloise and needed to clear the air.

When Cora finally returned, she said, "Don't worry about anything. I'm used to seeing soldiers come and go."

Billy could see that she was trying to be strong and hide her feelings. He said, "I should have told you from the beginning that I was engaged."

Cora finished washing him and looked at him with longing in her eyes. "It is war and we all have our secrets."

Dressed in his uniform, Joey met with Eloise in the same café in London on Sunday. She looked less formal than the first time; her lips, brushed with red lipstick, matched her scarf and she looked alluring.

"Let's go for a walk," Joey invited her after they finished their tea.

Outside, she struggled with her jacket and turned towards Joey.

"Let me help you." Joey reached for the collar of her jacket, which was turned inside-out at the back. As he straightened the collar, touching her skin, a warm feeling overtook him and without thinking, he kissed her on the lips.

She didn't move as if she'd been expecting it and even wanted more. Looking into his eyes, she took his hand and they walked for a long time together talking about everything...except for Billy.

After an hour of walking, they stopped at the front entrance to her apartment. Eloise opened the door and without hesitation invited Joey inside.

"Are you living here alone?"

"My roommate is away this weekend visiting her family." She looked at him with an anticipation that puzzled and excited Joey at the same time. She made two cups of tea, put some biscuits on a small plate, and left the room. In five minutes, she came back in red lingerie, drew the curtains, sat on Joey's lap, and kissed him for a long time. Kissing her, Joey frantically removed his clothes, lifted her in his arms, and took her to the couch in the corner of the small room.

He was not surprised that she was still a virgin. He wanted this to be a great experience for her; he was gentle while exploring her body and reacting to her every emotion with tender attentiveness.

They stayed on the couch fully embraced without speaking a word. When it was time for Joey to leave, he dressed slowly, looking at her resting with one arm under her head. She was beautiful, he thought, but she belonged to Billy. It was wrong to be with her, but he knew they would meet again, defying her engagement and his friendship with Billy.

Ted walked twenty-two kilometres to a town located halfway between Brusk and Warsaw. The printing shop was located in the basement of an industrial bakery on the outskirts of the town. Twice a week, the newspapers were ready for distribution and a few men came to the shop to pick up their bundle. It was a very dangerous mission and he had to walk at night both ways to minimise the chance of being spotted by German patrols.

Ted used the password that was required each time he was there. "Do you need fresh wood for your bread ovens?"

The middle-aged man in dark overalls with a grey apron covered in flour nodded at Ted. "Let's check the pile."

They went to the back of the bakery. The people Ted always met there didn't know his real name. They all used pseudonyms. Ted was known as Korsak and his contact as Bor.

When they were at the back of the bakery's main room, Bor stepped into a small, dark room where a trap door leading to the basement was opened.

"Korsak, we're behind with the printing tonight; you'll have to wait for around two hours until the newspapers are ready." Bor shrugged his shoulders as an expression of apology for the problem.

"Is the problem with the printer serious?" Ted became anxious, thinking about the delay.

"The printer is getting old, but we have somebody who makes the parts for us to keep us going."

"Do you expect more issues with the equipment?"

"You're asking too many questions; papers will be ready as always, just two hours late." Bor looked at Ted through his glasses. "Wait outside."

It was 4 a.m. when the newspapers were finally ready. Ted rolled them into two tubes and stuffed them in the inside pockets of his trousers.

In May, the sun rose early and Ted would have to walk most of his way at dawn. It could be dangerous as the German *Feldgendarmerie* started their patrols early in the morning. Ted always avoided walking near any roads, sticking to his paths through the forest. Unfortunately, due to the delay with the printing, he had no choice but to walk the shorter route that took him closer to the road. He needed to be at the post office in the morning as the couriers picking up the newspaper for distribution always came early.

Ted was around five kilometres from Brusk when he spotted a patrol of three German soldiers. He quickly turned away from the road into the forest and started running. He had a bad feeling that the Germans had spotted him and might chase after him. At least he had an advantage over them; he knew the forest and some hiding spots created by the partisans. His worst feelings were confirmed as he heard the Germans following his tracks in the forest. He turned around and saw the shadows of the three soldiers. Fear enclosed him like a vulture that landed on his head, pecking on his brain.

"Control your emotions the way you were trained," he whispered to himself.

He racked his memory to locate the closest hiding spot while checking that the cyanide pill was still in the little compartment in the collar of his shirt.

It was standard procedure that when captured by the Germans during any action of sabotage or distributing papers, the person had to bite the end of the collar containing the cyanide and die before any interrogation. Ted always thought he was prepared to die, but thinking about biting into the cyanide that morning frightened him. His whole life flashed before his eyes. Although it was full of unhappy moments, there were good times as well: camaraderie with his friends, kissing girls, secret dances, and even occasional theatre play. Ted loved music and acting, especially the comedies of Polish playwright, Fredro. Rose was a good performer and Ted liked to look at her acting from behind the stage. Thinking of Rose injected new strength into his body as he ran towards the hiding spot. Located under big spruce with low branches providing cover all year, it was a deep hole in the ground covered with a thick layer of tree branches.

On September 6, 1939, Krakow had surrendered to the German Armed Forces without a fight, and six days later, it was declared the capital of the general government of the newly proclaimed German territory under Nazi occupation.

When Erik arrived in Krakow on the last day of June 1943, he was surprised to see a beautiful city without signs of destruction. Governor-General Hans Frank had no interest in destroying the city's infrastructure as the Germans used it as a supply base for agriculture and light industry for the Third Reich.

Erik's new official assignment, as a commander of a *Feldgendarmerie* unit in the southern part of the territory, was surveillance of all roads leading from the city to the Tatra Mountains. His real assignment was an infiltration of local underground networks. It was believed that a strong Home Army sector operated in the mountain region with main communications channels leading through Krakow.

"Sergeant Major Hermann, you speak Polish, don't you?" Lieutenant Colonel Mueller addressed Erik as he entered the office.

"Yes, I do."

"Here are the addresses of twin sisters. One is suspected of working with the underground, and the other could be easily persuaded to work with us. We need information about the communication channels operating in southern Poland. You have six months to penetrate the underground."

This operation required a different approach from Erik's previous ones. In the past, he would identify his target people, befriend them, and use them as informants. This time, the order was very specific and the people he needed to infiltrate were already identified. Erik knew the urgency of the order but thought that six months might not be enough to complete his assignment. Although he worried about the short time for the mission, his desire to succeed overcame his doubts and a scheme began formulating in his mind.

After dinner the next day, Erik changed into civilian clothes, left his garrison, and walked to Krakow's main square. He stood at the end of the main street, taking in the view of the square. It was enclosed by elegant, historic townhouses, Medieval palaces, and churches. The centre of the square was dominated by the Cloth Hall, which was in the Renaissance style. On the opposite side, a magnificent church with two differently sized towers and a big, arched door with carvings and stained-glass windows attracted his eyes. The doors were closed and Erik made a mental note to ask for permission to see the inside of the church. To his left, a tall Town Hall tower stood proudly, looking over the city like a guardian angel.

The Cloth Hall and the Town Hall were draped in Nazi flags with swastikas, partially covering the facades of the buildings. Erik walked to the centre of the square and only then he noticed a large plaque on the Town Hall, which read, "Adolf Hitler Platz." He was proud of the name and the display of German might.

Finally, he moved closer to the Cloth Hall, remembering that his reason for being there was to become familiar with the daily activities in the square where commerce was conducted during the day and restaurants, including small diners, that were opened until the curfew at 10 p.m. Observing a few nice restaurants in the square, Erik noticed that most of the customers were German officers, young women dressed in the latest fashions, and a few civilian men who appeared friendly with the Germans. The patrons of the small diners and bars were local people working in the market or small shops during the day. He decided to visit some of the diners to look for any activities that could be useful to his plan.

"Could I have a plate of pierogis?" Erik asked the middle-aged woman who approached his table.

"We're out of pierogis, but we have a beet soup with home-made bread available."

Eating slowly, he observed the few people in the diner. Men were dressed in shabby jackets and women in dresses from the pre-war times. He could see that some clothes were too big; most likely, people had lost weight with the small portions of food available to them.

The woman who served his soup startled him as she appeared near his table. "Are you alone?"

Although he didn't want to carry on a conversation, he decided to give her the answer that had just come to his mind. "Yes ma'am, I'm in Krakow for one night." He looked up, eager for her to go away.

"What brings you here, young man?"

"I'm a train machinist. My train is leaving for Warsaw in the morning. I would like to pay for the dinner as I need to leave soon." Erik was sure that he passed as an average Polish worker.

Waiting for the bill, he lazily looked around to see if anyone was looking at him. A young woman came out of the kitchen to collect empty dishes. She was pretty but dressed in a grey dress with an apron covering her figure. She appeared unremarkable. She briefly looked at him with unusually green eyes, took the empty dishes, and moved to another table. Nobody looked in his direction, but the conversation with the woman serving his soup had been a little unnerving.

He was very careful when he left the diner, making sure that nobody followed him. He didn't want to have any complications at the start of his mission.

Within a week, he knew well the activities in the old town, during the day and evening. Traffic and population control had earlier been a part of his duties in the army and he was well trained to see everything around him.

Within days, he observed that one of the twin sisters frequented fine restaurants, accompanied by the same man. They were friendly with many German officers and their companions. The other sister appeared to be quiet, and Erik spotted her in the market several times, buying potatoes, carrots, and eggs. Something was familiar about her, but Erik could not think what it could be. He never came close to her for fear of being noticed. On each occasion, she talked to a man who had a shoe repair stall at the market. The man was young and handsome and Erik thought that perhaps they were romantically involved.

Although very different, either sister could be involved with the underground. He knew that often what seemed obvious was not the answer.

On Saturday, he reported to his superior all his observations and stated that he had a plan of action.

Erik looked very handsome in his army uniform as he entered the elegant restaurant on Saturday evening. His companion, an older officer, talked to the waiter in German and soon they were seated near the entrance where Erik could observe the people coming in and out. He was introduced to the Germans attending the restaurant that knew most of the Polish patrons. In the next few weeks, he visited the three most popular restaurants and became acquainted with the regularly attending guests.

One night, Erik approached the glamorous twin sister entering the restaurant. "Good evening. Are you alone tonight?"

She didn't answer his question but responded with the same question. "Are you alone tonight?"

"My name is Erik Hermann. Would you like to join me at my table?"

"I'm Marlene, and yes, I would like to join you for dinner." She looked straight into his eyes without any inhibitions.

Erik felt a jolt of uneasy excitement. Could it be because she was beautiful and confident or because she was there to use him as her contact? He needed to consider any possibilities. "Marlene isn't your name, is it?"

"Yes, it is. My mother was half Austrian, half Polish, and liked German names. What about you? What part of Germany are you from?"

Erik had his standard answers about his fictional hometown near Potsdam, his father serving in the army, and his mother looking after his older brother's two kids. His story had to be credible and not too offensive to the Poles he befriended. He did not reveal that he was half Polish.

Their conversation was light and lively and they started to meet once a week in a restaurant frequented by German officers.

Erik knew that on other evenings Marlene visited restaurants with the handsome man he'd seen on the first day he'd laid eyes on her. She followed the same routine, going to different restaurants on different days.

"Good evening, Frau Marlene." Erik startled her as she stepped outside of a restaurant with the handsome man and a German officer on her arms.

For a second, he saw panic in her eyes, but it was gone quickly and beautiful, flirtatious green eyes were looking straight at him. She didn't respond. She just smiled at him as the trio left the restaurant and walked to the other side of the main square. Suddenly, Eric remembered the green eyes of the girl in the apron cleaning the tables in the diner. He'd never connected the girl from the diner with the other sister he observed in the market.

Two identical sisters but so different in appearance and mannerisms. Which one is the ringleader? The revelation hit him like a lightning strike, making him stumble on the stairs of the restaurant. He had to steady himself against the doorframe while raking his memory for details from the evening he'd seen the other twin sister for the first time. In the first week of his assignment, he had seen her frequently in the market but never realised that she worked in the kitchen of the diner.

Thoughts ran through his mind, making him angry for being so careless. *How could I have missed that? Why did she come out of the kitchen to collect the dirty dishes and look at me? She must work for the underground and Marlene could be the key to getting information from her twin sister.* A new plan was forming in his head.

Two weeks later, after dinner followed by a few drinks, Marlene invited Erik to her apartment. It was located in an area where most of the German administration lived, and seeing a woman with German officers was not a rare occurrence.

When they were lying in bed after passionate sex, Erik lit a cigarette. "Who is the young man who comes to the restaurant with you?" he asked. Everything was going as per his plan, but talking about the young, handsome man, made Erik uncomfortable—even a little jealous.

"He is my friend from school. We've known each other since we were children."

"Are you in love with him?"

Marlene looked at Erik with surprised eyes and smiled. "Erik, don't you realise that my friend Tom and the German officer are in love? I'm their cover."

Erik's head was spinning, not only from the alcohol, but also from the realisation that the situation was getting more complicated than he'd envisioned. He smiled and kissed her hard, drawing some blood from her lips. It tasted salty and he didn't like it. He thought that it could be a bad omen of something dangerous happening to his or Marlene's life.

Erik knew the German officer who was in love with the Polish man. His name was Peter Umlin and he served in the governor's administration. He held the rank of sergeant major, as did Erik.

The game was becoming more complicated and dangerous, and the stakes were higher. If Marlene, Tom, and Peter Umlin worked together and he played the game well, he was sure of a promotion after the exposure of not only the Polish underground network but also possibly Germans spying for them.

Within a month, Erik and Peter became friends and often had dinner together with Marlene and Tom. Tom paid for most of the dinners and often bestowed luxurious gifts on Erik and Peter. By now, Erik was sure that Peter was delivering secret information to Tom and suspected that he was paid for it in US dollars. Erik's plan was to win the trust of Tom and Peter, using Marlene as the key contact person.

Ted listened to Ania's tapping on the window in his tailor shop in unison with the drops of rain tapping on the other side. It was light June rain, much needed for the farms and Maria's garden. Ania's tapping was annoying at first, and he wanted her out of his shop but didn't want to upset her. The rain was about to stop and hopefully she would go to work in the garden. Some vegetables were ready to harvest, among them Ted's favourite red radishes and he planned to enjoy some of them before going to the cemetery.

Ted's friend had asked him for help cutting down the dead branches of an acacia tree overlooking the gravestone of a long-dead relative. When they finished cutting, his friend left to get some ropes to bundle the branches together.

"Hi, Ted." George appeared from behind an old oak spreading its mighty branches in the corner of the cemetery.

"George, did something happen? My friend will be back any minute and it's better …" Ted stopped in mid-sentence as another man he'd never met before appeared next to George.

"Korsak, we heard that you were asking many questions during one of your visits to the printing shop." The stranger came closer to Ted.

"Questions?" Ted appeared bewildered by his words.

"As you know, the printing shop was raided by the Germans last week. The two men in the shop and the baker were arrested by the Gestapo."

George sounded more conciliatory. "Ted, you have to lay low for a while. Some believe that you might be the German informant."

"This is ridiculous. I would rather die than help the Germans." Ted's rising voice echoed between the gravestones.

George kept his voice low. "Control your temper, Ted. It isn't the time to get angry."

"George, you know me. I could never …"

George raised his hand to stop Ted mid-sentence.

Ted was still seething with anger but his voice was quiet. "How can I prove my innocence?"

"We've never had any reason to doubt your loyalty. It is just a precaution that we must take. I'm sure you understand." George hesitated for a moment and added, "There won't be any distribution of papers for a while. Your usual contacts were informed about the printing shop raid and won't be coming to your post office."

George and the stranger left the cemetery through different gates. Ted, still angry and confused, started gathering the branches into piles. He needed to keep busy to prevent his anger from taking over his mind. Soon his friend came back and they finished their job in silence.

The rest of June was full of torment for Ted. He had done everything he could to fight the Germans since he'd joined the Home Army. He remembered being one of the first ones to join the organisation and to take the oath. *How could they suspect me?* he wondered. *Who was the stranger that came with George?*

Late at night, unable to sleep, he recited the oath over and over again.

Before God Almighty
and Mary the Blessed Virgin,
Queen of the Polish Crown,
I pledge allegiance to my Motherland,
The Republic of Poland.
I pledge to steadfastly guard Her honour
And to fight for Her liberation
with all my strength
even to the extent of sacrificing my own life.
I pledge unconditional obedience
to the President of Poland,
to the Commander-in-Chief
and the Home Army Commander
whom he appointed.
And to resolutely keep secret
whatever may happen to me.
So, help me God.

Tears flooded his face. "It will pass. George will prove that I'm innocent," he whispered to himself, burying his face in the pillow.

That night, Ted resolved to not be bitter about the suspicion that had fallen on him. He thought of others who had taken the oath and pledged "to fight for Poland's liberation." The Home Army command could not take any risks and any suspicious behaviour had to be investigated. He fell asleep thinking about his life being full of challenges since he was six years old, and about his responsibility for his family and his country. He thought about Joey. They'd lost contact soon after the capitulation of Poland and the exodus of the Polish Army to France. He missed his friend and their carefree life before the war.

Joey's life was turned upside down by his unexpected love for Eloise. He'd never had a girlfriend and the state of elation filled every part of his being. He could not hide the happiness from his fellow pilots, even when he tried to act as nothing had changed in his life.

"Find your cloud nine, lovebird," was a frequent shout when he was boarding his plane.

It wasn't easy to find the time to meet with Eloise, but they managed to be together at least once a week. Joey was hoping, despite all odds, that something might happen to free Eloise of her engagement to Billy. After all, there was the nurse he'd briefly met in Billy's hospital room. He blocked any thought of his friend, allowing himself to love freely without any remorse. Summer 1943 was the best time in his life, despite the war and constant danger of being killed in a battle.

"Joey, Billy is coming to London next week." Eloise averted her eyes, looking uncomfortable.

"I knew that sooner or later it might happen. What are we going to say?"

"I won't talk to him about us. I love you, Joey, but please understand that it isn't the right time to tell Billy about us."

"Where will he stay?"

"With his parents. If you worry about Billy and my staying together, please don't. I didn't have sex with him before I met you, and it will continue that way."

"He may want to see me during his visit. What should I do?" Joey was on the border of panic.

"He is coming for three days only. I'll make sure that between visiting his family and time with me, he won't have time to do anything else."

By August, their romance was at its zenith, and Eloise appeared more beautiful, more vivacious, even curvier.

Could she be pregnant? thought Joey, but he didn't dare to ask.

At the end of June, George came to the post office and approached Ted, who was standing behind the counter.

"Are my breeches ready for pick up?" George spoke the agreed upon password.

"Wait a moment, I'll check." Ted turned around and moved to the back of the post office. He was trembling with fear and leaned against a wall to calm down. "Blessed Virgin, please send me good news today."

They stepped into a small dark room and Ted turned on a kerosene lamp that spread some light on shelves with supplies for the post office, mostly boxes with blank papers, stationery, stamps, and pencils.

"Ted, the investigation is done. You're free of any suspicion."

"I'm glad to hear this." Ted embraced George.

"It was the baker who collaborated with the Germans. We got suspicious when he was released in a week's time while the other two men were sent to another jail."

"Do I know them?"

"One of them was Batory and the other a courier from another region. There were other people at the shop but they managed to escape. You were lucky it was not your day to be there; you could be in the Gestapo jail right now."

"When will you call me into action again?"

"Come to the crypt on Friday evening. New orders from England will be dispatched."

Ted was ecstatic to take part in the underground movement again. As he entered the crypt, he noticed new and smaller radio station equipment than they had operated before his temporary banishment.

George pointed to the new equipment. "We received the radio equipment from Krakow. It's part of an action to step up the resistance."

"Ted, you missed a few things in the last month, but we will bring you up to speed very quickly." Bolek's voice was very reassuring, making Ted feeling welcomed.

"I'm happy to serve again. What would you want me to do?" Ted's voice revealed eagerness and anticipation of new activities.

George sounded upbeat. "First, you must learn to operate the new radio. Bolek will arrange this with you in the next few days. Today we must rearrange the coffins again and empty one for storage of money and medicines that will start coming from England."

Ted removed the crowbar from the hole behind a stone in the wall and opened three coffins full of skeletons. It was not any easier than the first time, when they had rearranged them from five coffins to three. Involuntarily, Ted crossed himself, asking the dead forefathers for forgiveness.

"We will have to disassemble the skeletons and pack the bones tightly in two coffins." He forced himself to sound neutral.

"Let's think that they are happy to defend Poland and wouldn't mind staying close to each other." Bolek always found some humour in many strange situations.

The rearranging was done in one hour, respectfully taking care of every bone. There was something supernatural about being in the presence of the remains of the founders of a church that had been built in the sixteenth century. So much had happened in Poland since the time they'd build the church. Ted remembered his father taking him for a walk and telling him about the history of Poland and especially the region of Brusk. Despite the many upheavals that had plagued Poland through centuries, the Polish people continued to strive and never lost their identity.

Ted's heart was bursting with pride; he was happy to be back in action and to fight for his beloved country. His father would be proud of him for fighting until the Germans were defeated.

The orders from the exiled government were dispatched to all parts of Poland. Members of the Home Army, which included many women, were ordered to train for a future general uprising. The active defence would step up, including sabotage of all German activities that hurt the lives of the Polish people.

In the next weeks after the communication, large number of *Cichociemny*, Silent Unseen soldiers, were sent from England to main resistance centres in occupied Poland. They were specialists in various military and civilian functions and were to train the members of the Home Army as per a plan created between the Polish resistance command and the exiled government.

Soon after the plan was implemented, various activities started to take place. Ted was part of the ten-man team taking part in receiving parachute drops delivered by airplanes at night. Weapons, medicine, and money from England were moved quickly under cover of night to the local church and old tombs in the nearby cemetery. In the church, the weapons were stored in the attic and behind the altar. Medication and money, mostly US dollars, were hidden in the empty coffin in the crypt.

A secret training centre was created in the basement of the fire hall. Two captains of the Silent Unseen group were assigned to train young cadets and non-military personnel. Ted, who had received good training before the war, was promoted to the rank of sergeant and chosen to assist in the training of recruits from the area.

In the basement of the fire hall, they learned the handling, dismantling, and cleaning of various weapons as well as theoretical lessons in ground operations, movement behind enemy lines, and sabotage of bridges and railroads. Ted was involved in the practical training that was often carried out at dawn in the hills outside the town. He knew the hills very well from the times that he'd led the young people to safety from potential German capture. Sometimes he had flashbacks to the awful morning in March when Rose and the others were taken and driven away in trucks. These flashbacks made him more determined to train the cadets, instilling in them determination and the willpower to fight even in the face of death.

Each morning that Ted met with the cadets, he started with the same words. They were like an oath that needed to be repeated every day to keep the flames of passion for the fight alive and growing. "Today, I pledge to love our country even more than yesterday. I pledge to fight the enemy until we're free. Free on Earth or in Heaven." He recited this, looking at each person with his dark, determined eyes. After a few days, all the cadets said the words in unison with Ted. They were happy moments, full of promise for a better future. Fighting the enemy was like an addictive drug to Ted. He lived for it every moment of his life.

It was a sunny late afternoon on the last day of August 1943 when Eloise quietly entered Billy's room. He looked up from the table with surprise showing on his face. He was drinking tea and reading a newspaper, not expecting her visit for another two weeks.

"Eloise, what are you doing here?" he exclaimed a little too loudly.

"Hi, Billy, aren't you happy to see me?"

"Of course, I am … you just surprised me."

He took her in his arms, gently kissing her lips as his hand drifted from her back to her hips. At first, her body tensed and she just stood there, allowing Billy to kiss her. With each passing second, her body relaxed and she returned his kiss with a passion, probing his mouth with her burning tongue. Pressing her body against his, she gently pushed him towards the bed. Their movement was gentle and slow, both moving in harmony, like the wings of a butterfly landing on a flower with the expectation of an exhilarating drink of the sweet nectar to quench the hunger and satisfy all senses.

One by one, she undid the buttons on his shirt and kissed his chest while removing her blouse. Full and warm breasts spilled out from her lacy lingerie and pressed against his chest. Billy's head was spinning with the desire to make love to her. In the depths of his mind, thoughts were lingering to stop the desire before it could get too far. Confusion descended on him and he allowed Eloise to lead him. She gently slipped her hand inside his pants and firmly moved her fingers along the shaft of his erect penis.

"Billy, I love you and want to be your wife." Whispering sweetly into his ears, she removed her panties and climbed on top of him. She started moving gently, climbing to the top of his swollen penis and lowering herself deep down, almost swallowing his inflamed flesh. They made love hungrily, pressing harder and faster until both reached the crescendo of their desire.

In the next few minutes, Billy was softly snoring, while Eloise rested her head on his chest.

They made love again when Billy woke up, exploring each other's bodies, learning the small pleasures of kissing each part of them.

"You're very sexy, Eloise. I never would have guessed the passion inside you."

"Let's get married now. It's been four years since you proposed," Eloise asked without any hesitancy.

"Your breasts are so soft and gentle. I want to touch them all my life." Billy kept talking without hearing what Eloise said.

"There's a chapel here in the village. I heard that during the war, marriages happen very frequently as nobody knows what the next day may bring," she whispered in his ear.

Two days later, on Saturday afternoon, they got married. A few of Billy's friends from the RAF station attended the wedding.

"Too bad Joey wasn't here, he would be happy for us," Billy said while Eloise distracted herself with picking up the half-empty glass of champagne.

Joey was restless when Eloise went to Rufforth for a few days at the end of August. He was hoping that she would break off the engagement with Billy and decide to be with him. Was it too much to dream for? Sometimes he despised himself for betraying Billy, but the love for Eloise was stronger than any other feelings.

Eloise looked tired and distracted when they met after her return from the base and he loved her even more, wanting to protect her from the darkness of the war. She looked down at her hands resting in her lap. "Joey, we need to talk. Billy and I got married last Sunday."

"You did what?" Joey gasped for air.

"I couldn't continue to see you anymore. You knew I was engaged to Billy."

"I was hoping that our love would be stronger." He wanted to say more but Eloise stopped him. "Joey, you're not English—being with you would be considered a mésalliance, and my family wouldn't accept this. Billy is from a good English family, and if we survive the war, my life with him will be good and stable. My mother approved of him and we planned our lives together even before the war started. You were just a dream, a stranger that came and went away. Part of my heart will always love you, but it was never meant to be forever."

"Eloise." His weak voice died on his lips, looking at her stern face.

"Hush, we won't see each other again, and never mention anything to Billy. He loves you like a brother; it would break his heart to learn that we both betrayed him."

"Eloise, please …" He was about to beg her to stay, but her eyes were looking through him. "You stay here and finish your tea," he said. "I'll leave now."

Eloise visited Billy in Rufforth more frequently during September and October. She volunteered for a lot of overtime work, allowing her to take time off to visit Billy twice a month.

"Billy, I'm pregnant." It was a beautiful October Sunday, and they were still in bed folded in each other's arms. It took Billy a long moment to respond, making Eloise a little nervous.

"I love you, Eloise. I'll ask to be reassigned to a different mission away from direct combat. The baby has to have two parents when the war is over."

"I'm very happy. The times are difficult but our love can conquer everything."

"You must tell Joey about the baby. I would like him to be the godfather." Billy embraced Eloise tightly, feeling her uncontrollable tremor.

Erik was sipping cognac on the couch in Marlene's apartment, waiting for her to return from the kitchen.

"I'm planning to leave Europe after the war," he said in Polish.

The words left her speechless and staring at him for a long time.

Erik watched her recovering from the shock of him speaking in perfect Polish. Before she could respond, he said, "Since the Americans are part of the Allied forces and are arming the Russian Army, Hitler won't be able to continue his domination."

144

She slowly recovered from her shock. "Who are you?"

"My mother is Polish and my father German. I was sent to German military school and dedicated my service to the Third Reich, believing in the order they planned to bring to Europe."

He closed his eyes and they both sat silently for a few seconds, which seemed like an eternity.

"I'll be frank with you, Marlene. I would like to earn US dollars as Peter Umlin does."

"I don't know what you're talking about." Her voice was strangely raspy. Coughing, she turned away from him and poured more cognac into their glasses.

"We won't talk about any of this tonight. It's all too much for me. Perhaps you should leave."

A few days later, Marlene asked Erik to come to her apartment later than usual. She opened the door and gestured him in.

"Bruno, please meet Erik." Without saying another word, she left the living room.

When she came back half an hour later with a plate of cheese, Bruno stood up, kissed her on the cheek, and left the apartment.

By the end of October, with the agreement of his superior, Erik started meeting Bruno at Marlene's apartment, delivering information that was carefully planned with his commander. The information was mostly correct but not important to the German operation in Krakow and southern Poland.

The relationship with Marlene changed subtly and was not as enjoyable as in the past. When he asked her about it, she was elusive in giving him a straight answer.

One evening as they entered the apartment, Erik noticed a slight movement of the dark curtain in the window. Marlene spoke unusually loudly when she asked if he wanted his usual cognac. He walked quickly to the window and moved the curtain. He was shocked to see her twin sister behind it.

Looking back and forth between the two women, he said, "Which one of you is Marlene?"

"Erik, my name is Laura." The twin sister stepped from behind the curtain as Marlene left the apartment.

"The last few times it was you who slept with me, wasn't it? This is why Marlene was acting a bit strange each time we met in the restaurant?"

"Yes, it was me. Sorry about it, but the bed is the best place to get to know a man and his intentions. I never went out with you; I just slipped into the bed when you'd had few drinks and could not easily notice any differences."

"I can't believe Marlene would do this to me."

"Marlene isn't involved in the underground; we mainly use her charm to lure German officers to her apartment."

Erik appeared to be hurt. "Was it all lie; she didn't care for me?"

Although it was his plan to infiltrate the Polish network and use Marlene as his contact, he had unwillingly become romantically involved with her.

"Sometimes things get complicated; she cares for you and it was not the plan." Laura poured some cognac into a crystal glass and drank it in one shot.

"Where is she?" Erik was visibly hurt.

"She is at her friend's and will see you next week."

"Strange turn of events." He was ready to leave but she stepped in front of him.

"Tomorrow, please come to this building, but go to the apartment above this one. We have a new assignment for you."

He could not believe that it had been Laura and not Marlene in bed with him the last few times. Now, it was obvious to him that the timid sister from the kitchen of the diner was the dominant twin, and Marlene would do whatever she was asked to do by Laura.

Erik considered informing his superiors about the meeting with the underground, but with all the new developments, he decided to go alone. He had to be sure that the Poles accepted him as a spy. When he entered the apartment above Marlene's, Laura, Bruno, and a young man introduced as Marek were sitting around the table. The meeting was quick.

"Erik, we need information about the upcoming meeting of high-ranking German officers with Governor Frank." Bruno spoke with utmost seriousness in his voice.

"What do you need to know?"

"Names, itinerary, time of their tour of the Wawel Castle, anything you can get."

The meeting was very short, and in the end, Erik was asked to go to the apartment below. Marlene was not there. Not sure of the next steps, he poured himself a drink and sat on the sofa thinking about the latest developments and formulating a plan of action. He had to act quickly and come up with a plan to deliver something to the Poles. Lost in his thoughts, he was startled when Laura entered the apartment.

"Marlene isn't coming here today. Tell me about your childhood growing as half Polish/ half German." Laura sat at the table as Erik told her some stories from his childhood. He hoped this would improve his credibility as a disillusioned German officer even more. It was good for his assignment as a spy.

"Good work," said Lieutenant Colonel Mueller when Erik suggested his plan of action. "I'll let you know when we're ready. Now you're dismissed."

Erik left the office pleased with the positive response to his plan. He would receive some less important information mixed with fake plans and itinerary for the meeting with Governor Frank. The next week he would meet with the same three people, deliver an envelope with the fabricated information, and go to Marlene's apartment. In order for everything to appear normal, Erik needed to be seen with Marlene in the restaurant at least once prior to the day of the meeting.

Marlene looked at him through her glass of wine. "Erik, when we met, it was supposed to be just a casual relationship as per my sister's request."

"Look at me, Marlene. How can I even know if it's you?"

"Remember the night when the glass broke and I cut my finger? I still have the scar." Marlene extended her hand.

He took it in his and squeezed it gently.

"We don't mutilate ourselves to have the same scars. There are other marks that I don't share with Laura. I'll show them to you tonight."

"Let's not talk about anything involving your sister. It's just you and me, tonight."

They made love for a long time. Erik kissed Marlene tenderly, trying to forget the devious role he was playing in this relationship. He cared for her but hoped that he didn't love her. It was good that the end to this action was coming soon, as he realised that he had the tendency to care too much for the women he used as spies.

It was a cold evening on the last Wednesday of November. Erik went to the meeting with Bruno and his people to deliver the envelope.

Marek opened it and looked at the papers. "I see the names of the officials visiting but I don't see any dates." He looked carefully at Erik.

"The dates were changed and we don't have the final schedule yet." Erik tried to look relaxed, suspecting that they might never fully trust him.

"Do you know the reason for the change?" Laura asked, looking at the documents.

"I'm not high enough in the ranks to have access to such information. I heard that Governor-General Hans Frank needs to go to Berlin in the next few days. Perhaps that's the reason for the delay."

"Fine, when you have the information, let us know. Bring a new bottle of cognac to Marlene's apartment. It will be a signal that we need to meet the next day."

The meeting was short and Erik went to the apartment below. Marlene was waiting for him. A small cake and champagne were on the table.

"What are we celebrating?" Erik tried to suppress a little shaking in his voice.

"It's my birthday today, and we should have a good time." She kissed him on the lips.

A cold shiver went through his body as he thought about the next few minutes. He went to the window and lit a cigarette while Marlene went to the kitchen.

"Darling, can you open the bottle?" She glided gently towards him.

At that moment, the door to the apartment opened and Marek ran in with a gun in his hand. "You betrayed us!" he shouted at Erik as he fired his gun.

"What are you doing, Marek?" Marlene's scream became hysterical as two German soldiers followed Marek into the apartment. Before he had a chance to turn, they fired at him.

Erik was injured but conscious when he turned towards the soldiers who'd entered. "She isn't involved. You've got the others. Leave her alone."

Marlene stood in the middle of the room like a statue, unable to move. She looked at Erik with sadness and resignation. "Who are you?"

He turned away when one of the soldiers put a gun to her head and led her away from the apartment. The other one helped Erik to his feet and escorted him to the car waiting on the street.

Surgery was done the same evening and the bullet was removed from Erik's shoulder.

In a few days, he was released from the hospital and was called to Major Urlik Ubentrop's office. Ubentrop was new to the Krakow post and Erik had met him only once before.

"Good work. We captured the people in the apartment and three others watching the building."

"What about Marlene? She was not involved."

"She is still in our prison. If she is innocent, she will be released soon."

Erik didn't move as he waited for more information.

"I signed the papers for your release from the unit in Krakow. It is dangerous for you to stay here."

"Where am I transferred?" Erik expected good news.

"There is no transfer yet. Right now, go back home to recover."

Lying in his bed in his parents' apartment, he felt bitterness and disappointment. He might never know what happened to Marlene, and the way he was being treated by his superiors was very unsettling. He had expected promotion and transfer to the *Wehrmacht*, not just sick leave.

The fall of 1943 dragged slowly, even though Joey signed up for every flying mission, both the reconnaissance and fighting the enemy. Frequently, while flying over the North Sea, he wished he would die in a battle. It would be an honourable death, better than living his miserable life.

In the middle of December, he received the Medal for Long Service and Good Conduct and was assigned back to RAF Station Blackpool, the place where his RAF service had begun.

The Polish pilots and a few Polish young women serving in the army organised a Christmas Eve supper. Joey knew some of the pilots who had fought in the Battle of Britain but the women at the table were new to the air force.

"Merry Christmas. My name is Vera." A young woman approached him to share the traditional thin wafer called *oplatek* with him.

"I'm Joey Wilk," he said without much enthusiasm.

Rita Hermann tried her best to prepare a nice Christmas. She even got a little spruce tree that Erik helped her to decorate. They didn't talk much. She didn't want to know about her son's actions during the war and he could not tell her anything anyway.

Father was at home, released from the German Army after losing his leg and one eye during a battle on the Eastern Front. He was bitter and stayed mostly in his room.

When they sat at the table to share the Christmas Eve supper, the conversation was very strained.

"I got a bottle of schnapps. Please bring it, Rita. Let us share a drink." Erik's father was no longer the confident Nazi supporter; he looked old, injured, and defeated.

The schnapps made the conversation easier.

Father was a little drunk and raised his voice. "Erik, you don't say much, but I can guess that you're disappointed with the results of your service and loyalty to the Third Reich."

"Let's not talk about it," interrupted Rita.

"It's fine, Mom. Let's talk. Father, please say what's on your mind."

"I thought that sending you to the military school and raising you as a good German boy would erase the fact that you were half Polish."

Mother tried to stop further conversation. "Otto, we don't have to talk."

"I was more tolerant when I was young, and I loved your mother very much. Unfortunately, I allowed myself to be influenced by Hitler's politics and believed that Germany should rule the world." Otto lifted another glass to his lips.

"I believe in a strong Germany as well." Erik looked at his father and raised a glass to him.

"You see, my son, I realised that because you are not pureblood German, you can be a low-ranking officer and do their dirty work, but they'll never promote you to the high ranks." The bitterness in Otto's voice was painful to hear. He continued after a few moments of silence.

"Germany isn't winning and Hitler's strategy is failing. I know that you have to continue to serve, but be careful, try to survive this war and come back to us when it's all over."

"Your father and I talked about the war and we agree that it brought only misery to this world." Mother looked down at the plate in front of her and absentmindedly pushed it away.

"I know, Mother, you were against me joining the army, but you knew very well that there was no other choice. I wanted to be on the winning side and bring German order to the world." Erik took her hand and kissed it gently.

"Look at you and your father, both injured in the war. I'm happy that you're still alive when so many people have died."

When the supper ended, Erik went to his room. He found his old book about Captain Nemo and started leafing through it and his mind drifted to his childhood. He fell asleep dreaming about travelling the world when there was no war.

In January, a notice came ordering Erik to report to the German head-quarters in Gdańsk. There, he received a transfer to a small town outside of Warsaw.

The transfer letter was addressed to Sergeant major of *Feldgendarmerie*, Erik Hermann.

Disappointment and bitterness spread through him like poison. His father was right. The promotion was not forthcoming.

Part Three

← LOVE AND BETRAYAL →

January 1944

After a quiet time during Christmas 1943, Ted welcomed the full schedule of activities at the secret training centre. That was his calling, to train others in the techniques of sabotage, fighting the enemy, and preparing for the final push to destroy the Nazis.

The scale of the war was shifting in favour of the Allies and the typically quiet town of Brusk was bustling with activities. A new, larger *Feldgendarmerie* contingent arrived at the German base in the old castle on the other side of the river. Soon after, they started the demolition of the Jewish quarters, which had been abandoned for over a year. Special equipment was brought to Brusk and German engineers established their headquarters in one of the most prominent abandoned buildings not far from the general store. The news spread around that a hospital and a convalescent centre for German soldiers from the Eastern Front would be built there.

Ted's tailor shop was frequently used for repairs of the tattered uniforms of the soldiers who were already arriving from the Eastern Front. Tired and injured soldiers were stationed in many houses, including the homes of some of Ted's friends.

Everything was changing very fast. Although, due to the high German traffic in town, it was more dangerous to continue the Home Army's activities, the opportunities for spying and learning about enemy plans and the war on the Eastern Front were plenty.

In January 1944, a large load of officers' uniforms was brought to Ted's shop. Checking every uniform carefully for the required repairs, Ted sensed a piece of paper sewn into the bottom of a long coat. He could not risk removing the paper during the daytime, so he put the coat at the bottom of the pile, planning to look at it after the curfew hour. Any action he took in the shop could put his mother and sister in danger, and he was very careful not to bring any suspicious activities to the attention of the Germans.

Late in the evening, he took the coat to the cellar, where he lit a small carbide lamp, casting some light in the room. The shadows danced on the walls and the ceiling, making him shiver. He'd never liked the cellar. Ever since he'd been six years old, Ted was always being sent down to it to bring up vegetables, potatoes, or other items requested by his mother. He could open the trap door without even looking at it and quietly walk down the ladder. He knew every step and the layout of the cellar, yet he hated it and always felt a bloodcurdling sensation down there, even as an adult. Each time he went down, Ted tried very hard to eliminate any thought of his father, but the cellar was like a grave with his father's ghost lurking somewhere behind the shelves.

Clearing his mind of thoughts about his father and the fatal accident in France, Ted carefully opened up the bottom of the coat and removed the envelope. He was disappointed, seeing only a letter addressed to "Dear Hilda." It was written in very neat handwriting and although Ted's German was rudimentary, he understood the essence of it.

The German army was suffering a big loss on the Eastern Front and morale was dwindling. Many soldiers didn't believe in winning the war any longer, but the SS officers were everywhere to make sure that they fought to the last drop of blood. The winter was very cold, their uniforms were tattered, and food rations were smaller, often leaving them hungry and cold.

Although the letter had not contained any plans or strategies, it was good information about the dwindling morale among the German Army, the losses they'd suffered, and the feeling of imminently losing the war. The battle of Stalingrad, which ended almost a year ago in February 1943, defeating the German Army, brought a strong possibility of the end of the war, but Hitler had not given up sending more troops to the east.

Ted closed the letter and placed it back in the lining of the coat. He smiled, looking defiantly at the shadows dancing in the cellar.

"There is hope."

January 1944 was cold with the easterly wind blowing relentlessly over central Poland. Erik had been in a foul mood since he'd arrived at the military base near Brusk. To his surprize he was promoted to the rank of second lieutenant and commanded two squadrons of *Feldgendarmerie*, but his aspiration to join the *Abwehr*, the German military intelligence service for the *Wehrmacht*, dissolved into thin air after the operation in Krakow. He could not fathom that his career was practically over and he would never go to Berlin to work with the best. He was highly educated, achieved great results in the espionage capacity, and had always shown the greatest loyalty to the Third Reich, but perhaps it was as simple as having a Polish mother that blocked his promotion. He often had a dark thought, hating both the Germans for denying him his dream career and the Poles for diluting his pure blood.

He visited the town of Brusk once after his arrival, in order to get an understanding of the scope of his duties, and he decided that when possible, he would command his squadrons from his headquarters on the other side of the town's river. The duties were mostly mundane administration and enforcement responsibilities, servicing the activities related to building the hospital and convalescent centre for the soldiers coming from the Eastern Front.

His squadrons were busy lodging the exhausted soldiers in private houses, procuring clothing, food, and basic necessities for them. Erik didn't want to see the soldiers arriving from the east. It was depressing to see the wounded, hungry and demoralised soldiers. After the battle of Stalingrad, the German Army was mostly in defeat, but talking openly about it was dangerous and could lead to being sent to the Eastern Front. Everybody feared the front and the Russians. The Red Army was formidable and nothing could stop them. Despite thousands upon thousands of casualties, they kept pushing out the German Army from the eastern territories.

Most of the soldiers convalescing in Brusk were young and scared. They knew that after a short break, they would go back to fight the war that was already lost.

In February, Erik had to visit Brusk on a regular basis, but it was almost always for a meeting in the headquarters of the engineers in charge of the demolition and building of the hospital.

"Lieutenant Hermann." Erik heard his name being called, but the scene on the street kept him captivated. It was a group of German soldiers disembarking from a few trucks. They were all in ragged, dirty uniforms or strange coats that Erik assumed had been taken from some Russian soldiers. They could barely stand at attention as an SS officer shouted orders to them.

"Lieutenant Hermann!" The elevated voice pierced through Erik's ears like a bullet. He turned around and found himself standing right in front of a captain who'd entered the room.

"Sorry, sir, I just watched the new contingent of soldiers …"

He didn't finish before the captain spoke again. "My name is Hans Herbert." He extended his hand to Erik. "This is one of the reasons you're here today. Your men are doing a good job with the housing of the soldiers, but we need to speed up the building of the hospital. Unfortunately, we're dealing with some sabotage or perhaps just vandalism, and some of our equipment on the site has been damaged. It could be happening here or in transportation." Colonel Herbert cleared his throat as if he was somewhat scared to talk about it.

"What do you expect of my squadron?"

"You need to assign some of your people to guard the area day and night as well as inspecting the equipment on a daily basis."

Erik sounded surprised. "Isn't the equipment being used regularly?"

"There are some delays with the approval of the final plans for the hospital, and despite the urgent need, we don't have the decision yet. It is expected very soon and when we get it, we cannot afford any delays due to damaged equipment. Start dispatching your men immediately."

Without any more explanation, Captain Herbert left the room.

Erik's spirit was lifted a little. Perhaps, there would be more productive activities very soon. Dealing with the poor and demoralised soldiers was depressing to him and to his men as well. Involvement with the building of the hospital could bring new opportunities, new people to work with. Maybe the German situation was not as bad as he'd heard. Building a convalescent centre meant that Germany was still strong—maybe he could prove his worth and get moved out of *Feldgendarmerie* to *Wehrmacht*.

By the end of April, Erik's hopes for any change were gone. The hospital construction had been cancelled. His people had to supervise the removal of the equipment and continue to guard the empty site. The mundane work of housing the exhausted soldiers was unbearable, making Erik angry all the time. Since his assignment to the town of Brusk, he had the worst feeling he'd ever had. The year 1944 so far was bad. The latest developments were the final confirmation that his life was going down.

A letter from his mother arrived on a day when his thoughts were the darkest since he could remember. It was the usual information about his father's health, smaller rations of food, and lack of medication. The last words in her letter were somewhat ambiguous, but he knew the meaning of them.

"The victory is coming. Stay strong, stay alive, and follow your heart. I'm waiting for you." She knew that the war was lost for Germany and was urging Erik to be careful. It wasn't much but the letter brought some positive feelings to his heart, and for the first time, he decided to go to the town and just look around. Perhaps, he could even be friendlier to the young soldiers coming from the Eastern Front.

"Good morning." A strong voice brought Billy back from his thoughts.

He'd arrived at RAF Medmenham, where the Central Interpretation Unit (CIU) of the Royal Air Force was secretly located. He'd kept his promise to Eloise and asked to be transferred to a non-combat mission, and he'd been assigned to be trained in interpretation and analysis of photographs taken by so-called "spies in the sky."

It was his first day of training. He was in the company of men and women in blue navy uniforms, air force uniforms, infantry khakis, and some civilian clothes.

"Today, we would like to welcome five new members to our team." The man with a booming voice continued talking to the group.

Billy looked around, trying to recognise who the new members were. He noticed one young woman sitting at the end of the third row of chairs with a sad face. He made a mental note to talk to her to find out more about the roles of women in the CIU.

"Let me introduce to you the man who made it possible for our pilots to fly and take photographs of the enemy positions—Sidney Cotton." Everybody looked towards the opened door where a man in his late forties appeared in a pilot's uniform.

Billy had heard this name before but listening to his story was breathtaking. Sidney Cotton was an Australian industrialist, entrepreneur, inventor, and first of all, pilot. He wore an outdated pilot's uniform and everybody looked at him with awe when he started to tell his story.

After coming from Australia to England at the age of fifteen, he quickly became passionate about flying and upon completing college in Cheltenham, he joined the Royal Naval Air Force and trained as a pilot.

"You all are probably wondering why I came here dressed in this old uniform." Everybody chuckled and nodded towards each other.

"This is the very first uniform of this kind, which I designed before the Great War." He looked at his audience and looked pleased with himself.

Billy smiled, recognising the showman in Sidney. He was like a breath of fresh air and his presentation was fascinating. The uniform that Billy wore while flying was more modern and comfortable and it was all thanks to Sidney.

"While training as a pilot, I quickly noticed that when I flew in a mechanic's one-piece uniform, I was much more comfortable and warmer than flying in the standard two-piece uniform. It took me a while and my own money to design it and convince the air force to implement it."

Billy listened to the presentation that now focused on explaining how Sidney had improved the photography-taking that contributed to the fundamentals of aerial espionage and his accomplishments as the "spy in the sky", especially flying over Germany before and during the first years of the war. He no longer was in active service but continued to work on new inventions that could improve the chances of winning the war.

Billy's fascination with Sidney Cotton turned into dissatisfaction with his own achievements. He quickly took account of his war experience: Battle of Britain, becoming lieutenant in charge of a battalion of pilots, and then the accident that put him out of flying for a while and the promise to Eloise to stay away from combat. Nothing much compared to the achievements of Sidney Cotton.

During the lunch break, Billy spoke to a few people, mostly the senior analysts, and he forgot about the young woman with the sad face.

At the end of the first day of training, he was in a brooding mood, thinking about his life, when he almost ran into the young woman, who was walking alone towards the barracks.

"I'm sorry! Oh, it's you." Billy smiled as he recognised the woman from the training room. "I'm Billy Leavitt; we were in the same training today."

"So were many other people." Her demeanour was unfriendly towards him.

"Sorry if I crossed any boundaries of your privacy," he said.

"Don't be sorry. I'm not in good spirits to talk to people right now. My brother is missing in action after his battleship went down before Christmas."

Billy stood speechless, slowly processing the magnitude of her words in his mind.

"Good night." She moved away from him and changed the direction of her walk, making it clear that she was not in a mood for any casual conversation.

He looked in her direction for a while; she'd spoken English with a slight accent that reminded him of Joey. Sudden longing for the good times he'd had with Joey came rushing through his head. Slowly, he turned towards his barracks, thinking of contacting his Polish friend.

The cold winter of 1944 spread through large parts of England, making any outdoor activities dreadful. Staying indoors most of the time was a change that Billy welcomed. The photographs-interpretation training went well and all the new recruits were already busy looking for details showing any new movements of the German Army as well as details of the Allies' advances towards the final destination, Berlin. The Nazis were losing the war but Hitler and his command wouldn't allow themselves to admit the defeat, and were regrouping the troops to strengthen their power. As of September 1941 the Photographing Development Unit (PIU) had been consolidated with the CIU and moved from Wembley to RAF Medmenham. This unit had been created in cooperation with a

British company, the Aircraft Operating Company that owned Wild A5 Stereoplotter, which was able to enlarge pictures nine times. Based on the pictures taken from an altitude of 10,000 metres, skilled operators created detailed maps enabling the British military and its allies to fight the Nazis.

On rare occasions, Billy spoke to Vera, but he never mentioned his friendship with Joey. It never crossed his mind that they might know each other. He observed that Vera and many other women were more detail-oriented and their interpretation of the photographs was more accurate. Although pleased with the role of women at Medmenham, he was harbouring a little resentment for their interpretation ability and the recognition that came with it. Filled with some bitterness, he came to the realisation that the stationary life in the office was not his calling. By the middle of February, he was ready to change his life, and he asked for a transfer to active service.

"First Lieutenant Leavitt," Billy introduced himself as he entered the office of the major in charge of the interpretation unit.

"Please sit down. I would like to discuss your new assignment."

Billy moved so quickly towards the chair that he almost tripped over it. He was relieved that the major was not looking at him and he recovered his balance quickly. That could have jeopardised whatever new assignment waited for Billy.

"You're transferred from the office to the mobile interpretation unit." Billy knew of the mobile units and occasionally had assisted in moving the material from them to the building for detailed analysis.

"When do I start my new duties?"

"Tomorrow at 8 a.m."

Billy's feelings about his new assignment were mixed. He was happy to be assigned to the mobile operation unit, but he was longing for the actual flying and maybe even to be a pilot in one of the photograph-taking planes.

Since Billy's first day at Medmenham, Sidney Cotton had been his hero. Cotton's bravery and his unorthodox approach to implementing progress not only in the area of photography but also in aviation as a whole impressed Billy and he often looked for any opportunity to speak to Sidney.

The next day Billy was travelling in the mobile unit towards the designated location for the reconnaissance flights, the Benson airport. To his amazement, the vehicle was a blue Super Snipe.

Billy loved two things in life: planes and cars. He'd never owned a car but knew a lot about them. The Super Snipe had been introduced in October 1938, by using the four-litre inline six-cylinder engine from the larger Humber Pullman of the Humber Snipe, normally powered by a three-litre engine. The result was a car of enhanced performance and a top speed of 127 km/h. Billy loved this car and could not believe that it was being used as the mobile interpretation unit. He was greatly looking forward to his new responsibilities. On the first day, his duties were to observe others performing their jobs to be ready to do them the next day.

The moment the photography plane landed at the landing strip, technicians removed the cassettes with films and moved them to the cars, which immediately transported the materials to the base where the photographs were developed and a team of interpreters would analyse them. It took one hour from the landing of the plane to the first interpretation.

Was the ship still in the port? Was the factory destroyed during yesterday's bombing? Were the tanks on the move? Every day, these and many other questions were answered and the information was sent to the RAF command via phone. The materials were then directly transferred to Medmenham, where large groups of experts pored over them looking for details. The speed of action was adrenaline-charged and the knowledge that they were first to deliver first-hand observations was very fulfilling.

After the Christmas celebrations, Joey was assigned to a group of Polish pilots with a mission to fly over Poland to deliver weapons, medicine, and training materials. He underwent short training in flying in darkness and recognising the arrow of lights set up by the Home Army, indicating the direction of the parachute drop. It was a dangerous mission and many pilots had died in 1943. Joey's enthusiasm and tremendous dedication to his new duties were fuelled by his new feelings for Vera and her bravery.

During the few days of Christmas, he'd spent a considerable amount of time with her. They shared stories about their lives before and during the war, and with each hour of their conversation, Joey's admiration for her grew more and more.

Between assignments, he thought about their short time together and particularly her confession about wartime life in Russia and her journey to the RAF. He recalled the evening when he'd gone to the women's barracks to meet with Vera for dinner in the mess. Although they'd known each other only just a few days, he already saw Vera's various moods, from happy, to indifferent, to dark and emanating a sense of foreboding.

Although a dark mood occasionally enclosed her and it was best to leave her alone, her mysterious past intrigued Joey and he wanted to understand more about her.

He had never gone to her room without prior arrangements; she was not spontaneous and liked everything to be preplanned. That evening, instead of meeting her in the mess, with a bottle of vodka and a bouquet of fresh spruce branches, he decided to surprise her in her room, hoping to find out more about her while she was unprepared and perhaps less guarded.

"Hello, Vera." He sounded confident but his heart was pounding, not knowing what her reaction would be.

"Oh, hello, why are you here?" She was sitting at a small table reading a letter, her face painted with sadness.

"Some girls said that you weren't coming to dinner tonight. Is something bothering you?" Joey's face showed genuine concern.

She looked up; tears were glistening in her eyes. "I got a confirmation that my brother died on the battleship in December. I hoped that he survived and was taken prisoner." Her voice was barely audible. "We lived through a lot together and he is gone now."

Joey put the spruce on the table and poured two small glasses of vodka. "Would you like to tell me about him?"

She inhaled the fresh winter smell of the spruce and drank the shot of vodka all at once. "Before the war, we lived in a small town in eastern Poland," she said, looking at the floor and gathering her courage to talk about her family. "Soon after the Germans and Russians invaded Poland, my family and many people from the town were evicted from their houses and marched into a train station.

"Where did they take you?" Joey touched Vera's trembling shoulder and she folded her body into his arms. Her monologue in a soft voice filled the room with its gravity.

On the 10th of February 1940, Vera and her family had been arrested along with many Polish families in the Eastern Poland, the Borderlands. The winter was very bad, with the temperatures around minus 40 C. Approximately 250,000 people were sent to Siberia on 110 cattle trains.

The family ended up in a settlement in the Chelyabinsk province, close to the border with Kazakhstan. Everybody except for young children worked in iron, copper and coal mines.

A large number of newly and hastily built wooden huts were erected very close together to accommodate the deportees. The camps were called "corrective labour camps" and the people were classified as counter-revolutionaries and therefore not protected by the Geneva Convention.

The hut had two rooms separated by a corridor. Vera's family of six lived in one room and another family of four in the other room. Her family slept on one large bed and a cot with straw as a mattress. The washroom for the camp was communal, although there was a main washroom with showers at the mine they could use. Everyone over the age of fourteen had to work. Vera worked twelve-hour shifts down an iron mine. She and others worked there in cold, wet, and dangerous conditions.

Her job was to pick up the rocks removed by miners and load them onto a trolley. They were poorly dressed and had no gloves. The food the families ate was black, hard bread, salt, and hot water. Occasionally, a watery soup was served to the workers in the mines.

"I don't know how we survived."

Joey recalled that her simple statement didn't reflect any resentment, just surprise at being alive.

Following Operation Barbarossa, the German attack on the Soviet Union on June 22, Polish-Soviet diplomatic relations were re-established. The military agreement signed in August 1941 allowed a Polish land force led by General Władysław Anders to be formed in the Soviet Union, commonly known as "Anders' Army." The Polish prisoners were free to leave the Gulags.

Vera and her family boarded a train and crossed the border into Kazakhstan. After a two-day journey, they left the train, and to survive they had to look for jobs on local farms. For several months they worked from dawn to dusk, paid with a few potatoes and a little flour, just enough to keep them barely one step from starvation. But it wasn't enough. Their father got sick and couldn't work.

Working on the farm, although it was dangerous, Vera and her sisters and brother tied strings to the bottoms of their pants and often pushed some of the wheat, barley, and even potatoes up into the legs. They cooked and ate it secretly and shared some with the little children of their neighbours. At the farm, they met two men who came to buy eggs. When the men heard the girls spoke Polish, they introduced themselves as Polish soldiers from a Polish Army Unit stationed not far from the farm. It was in a town called Czok-Pak.

Soon after the visit of the two soldiers, Vera's family and other Polish people in the area went to the camp. Shortly after, around 45,000 people were transported to British and Polish bases in Pahlevi and Kazvin in Iran. In Pahlevi, teenage girls and boys were offered the chance of going to Palestine to continue their schooling and to serve their country at a later date. Vera joined the Polish Young Women Soldiers' School in Quastina and her brother enlisted in the navy.

In November 1943, Vera completed school as a Flight Mechanic and enlisted in the Polish Auxiliary Services in Palestine. She was transferred to the Polish Air Force under British command. Her first posting was at RAF Blackpool in December 1943. Her brother served on the battleship *Orkan*, which was destroyed in the North Sea in the fall of 1943.

"What about your family?" asked Joey.

"I lost contact with them after I left the camp in Iran. I hope they are safe somewhere and we will find each other." Vera's story was full of misery, bravery, and hope for a better future. The hope was what sustained her through the ordeal.

Joey lifted her face towards his and gently kissed her on the lips. He wanted to be part of her future and perhaps build happiness together when the times were better, though not yet.

"Vera, I'm starting a new mission flying over Poland."

"Be safe."

"I will. You made me want to survive the war."

In the next three months, Joey flew over Poland many times. Most of his missions were over Warsaw and the area around. He often wondered what had happened to Ted. Was he still in his town and alive? Sometimes he had the aspiration to become one of the Silent Unseen, the group of specially trained people who parachuted over Poland with a mission to train the Home Army recruits in the skills of sabotage and prepare them for the final battle with the German Army. Joey often imagined landing in Brusk and finding out about Ted. Being Silent Unseen required assuming a different name and staying in hiding, with only very few people aware of their true identity. Meeting Ted was improbable.

The notion of the secret mission was brave, dangerous, and also very romantic in the way only Polish people would feel. For generations, the people in occupied Poland had fought the occupiers, kept up their language and education, and always dreamed about freedom.

Often at night was when he thought about becoming one of the Silent Unseen and getting sent on a mission to Poland, but thoughts of Vera and the feelings that had developed between them during the winter stopped him from making such a decision. His love for Eloise had faded away with the winter days, and he didn't even think about the baby she was expecting in May.

February 1944 brought grim changes to Rose's life. Three German soldiers were stationed in her small family house. The whole family of five had to move to one bedroom while the living room was converted to housing for the soldiers who arrived from the Eastern Front. They were young men under twenty years of age, skinny, and exhausted, with their wounds wrapped in bloodied bandages. Misery and low morale were written all over their faces. They knew that once they recuperate, they'd be sent back to the front again.

Rose was younger than they were, but she thought she was more mature than them. She was sorry for the young soldiers and hated herself for these feelings. Every night she prayed that the next morning, she would hate them, but she didn't.

To escape this predicament, she left the house early every morning and went to the store. With the arrival of many Germans in town, the store was very busy. The soldiers had their mess set up in the school, but they frequently came to the store for minor items such as cigarettes, stationery, and occasionally vodka.

New routines dictated life in Brusk. People kept their heads down to avoid any possible confrontation with the Germans. They stayed in their houses more and prayed every Sunday in a local church that the war would end soon and the Russian Army would avoid their town.

On Easter Monday, many young people gathered together after Mass and as was customary, buckets of water appeared and splashing with water began. Young men were in charge of the buckets of water and girls giggled while the water splashed their faces. It was time for fun, sending away winter and welcoming spring and a new beginning.

"Quiet everybody!" A loud voice dominated the others in the group. They all stopped and looked toward a group of men walking the main street.

Several young German soldiers dressed in clean uniforms were walking toward the square. Rose recognised some of them. They were stationed in her house and the houses of her friends.

Walter, a handsome young soldier, waved his hand and smiled with a friendly expression on his face. "Can we celebrate your Easter tradition with you?" He had approached Rose's brother Franek, who looked confused and unsure of himself, but almost instantly others waved at the Germans and asked them to join.

Franek recovered his voice and approached Walter. "It could be dangerous for us to play with you."

"It isn't dangerous; all the high-ranking officers left to spend Easter with their families. The others are in the officer's mess, celebrating and drinking."

Everybody started to chat with each other in broken Polish and

German. They were all young and eager to live fully, and both sides hoped for the end of the war.

"Hitler Kaput," was the most common expression from the mouths of the young Germans.

"Rose, we're going back to the *Ostfront* this week." Walter's eyes fluttered as he fought tears coming to his eyes.

"Oh." Rose didn't want to show any emotion, either sadness or relief.

"There is a new group of battered soldiers from the Eastern Front and most likely some of them will be stationed in your house again."

"Will this ever end?" Rose looked with boldness into Walter's eyes.

"It is ending, but Hitler and his officers keep sending more young men to the front. Some of them are just sixteen years of age."

"Young or old, you're all Nazis; you brought this tragedy to the world."

"Not all of us wanted the war, but we had no choice."

"Don't say anything more. Now that the end is closer, you all want to be the good ones. Maybe you were good people before the war, but most of you didn't do a thing to stop the killings, destruction, and fear of each other."

Rose turned away and left the group. She was not as angry as she appeared, and as she walked toward her house, she felt sorry for Walter and the other soldiers. Going back to the Eastern Front, they faced a very high probability of dying there.

She became upset with herself for having been unpleasant to Walter. For all she knew, it might have been his last conversation with a young woman before his death. Why did she always have to take the high ground—to be righteous and hard-nosed? She was seventeen years old and wanted to be free of fear and hate. She wanted to love and be loved.

Will such times ever come, or is my generation lost forever to a normal life? Dark thoughts troubled her mind; she needed to go anyplace away from other people.

The orchard was awakening from the winter, and fruit trees were already showing the first buds. Rose looked at the big apple tree, put her cheek against the fresh buds and tears slowly rolled down her face. *It has to get better,* she thought.

"Jean, what is wrong with you?"

Emilie was losing her patience once again. Since the beginning of winter, her husband had become very reclusive and spent most of his time in the workshop. Even Christmas, his favourite holiday, was not much better.

Jean forced a smile, looking up at Emily. He loved her very much. Looking at her face, he recognised that he must snap out of his dark thoughts and be a father and husband again.

"I'll be fine, I promise. Must be the winter and the long war that's affecting me."

"I'm going to the town right now. Check on the children; they're playing in the bedroom." Emilie put her hand on Jean's head, kissed him gently on the lips, and left.

Jean wasn't sure if he could be normal again, but he knew that he must hide his thoughts about his unclear past and make an effort to return to his daily routines. Since Marc had left, he'd known that his past was not as straightforward as he wanted it to be. His dreams about unknown people in his past life were becoming more frequent, often keeping him awake at night. He was afraid to think about the deeper meaning of his dreams. Often there was a woman and a boy and a young girl. The boy in his dreams always had his head down, stubbornly looking at the ground.

Could I be somebody else, as Marc suggested, or is it just my imagination playing tricks in my troubled mind? During the sleepless nights, afraid, he analysed his dreams. The fact that they were about a woman and two children could simply be related to the fact he had a wife and two children and about his concern for them. His brain had sustained some damage during the accident in the foundry and that had possibly affected some of its functions. The more he thought about his dreams and the unknown past, the more frequently he was up at night.

It cannot continue this way. Most likely, Marc just wanted to scare me with the story about my past in order to force me to arrange his escape. He stood up and looked defiantly into the mirror. "Whoever you were in the past, you're now Jean Navarre, husband of Emilie and father of two children."

He stood there for a while until he felt the love for his wife and his children filled his heart. He didn't want any uncertainties in his life.

In the middle of the night, ten men prepared the landing field for another parachute drop from England. In the spring of 1944, the drops, mostly of weapons, medicine, and money, were coming every week.

Ted was among seven younger men lying in the grass in the shape of an arrow. Each held a flashlight on his chest. When the signal came, they flashed the lights for ten seconds, making the arrow visible to the approaching plane. Then they'd hide in the bushes nearby. It was a beautiful, warm March night, so different from that March night over a year ago. Ted shivered, thinking about the time when the Germans had taken Rose. His thought drifted back to events from last year.

He had not expected the anguish that overcame him that March night in 1943 and the realisation that he was in love with Rose. Until the night she was gone, he'd only thought of her as his little sister's best friend.

He closed his eyes and visualised her beautiful face and her slightly curvaceous body, but more than her beauty, he loved how captivated he was by her wit and her knowledge about the world and politics.

He was imagining telling her about his love for her, when he was roused from his thoughts by an order to flash the lights, pick up what had been dropped from the plane, and run into the bushes. He heard one quick command: "Ted, bury the parachute." The Germans had been spotted not far from the drop site. Only an immediate action would save the drop and possibly the men. While others took away the supplies, Ted buried the parachute.

In a few days, a meeting of the Home Army unit was called at Ted's house, where he'd set up the post office and tailor's shop in the early days of the war. It was the designated place for meetings, distribution of underground newspapers, and planning of actions. Although people were coming in and out of his house, strict precautions were taken at all times, and passwords had to be used. The possibility of spies operating in their area was a real threat. They used four different zones for the parachute drops and it was not a coincidence that the Germans had gotten so close to the action. "There is a new contingent of *Feldgendarmerie* stationed in the castle on the other side of the river," said George.

"Yes, I saw them in the store the other day," said one of the men in the room, and he added, "I heard some of the Germans speaking Polish with Rose, who works in the store." "Perhaps Rose could help us. Ted, you know her, can we trust her?" asked George. "Yes, we can trust her. She speaks some German and could get some valuable information from them. I'll talk to her," said Ted.

He was unhappy about getting Rose involved, but she was a fighter and after her capture a year ago, she would be glad to help to defeat the Nazis. He prepared himself to talk to her as soon as she came to see Ania.

"Rose, can I ask you to do something?"

"Yes, what is it, Ted?" she asked.

"Can you talk to the Germans coming to the store and get any information about their plans, movement, anything at all?"

He was looking straight into her eyes, making her shiver under the intensity of his gaze.

Rose didn't know that Ted was in love with her, and his intense gaze faded away before she had a chance to smile at him. *He is nice but so serious and unapproachable—too bad.* She smiled to herself with a little sadness.

The war and Ted's deep involvement with the underground were the priorities for him. Frequent actions of sabotage put him in constant danger, and he could not burden her with his love. It was better for all that he kept his feelings hidden deep inside his heart.

It was becoming more difficult to receive parachute drops from England due to the increased activities of the German Army in the town and surrounding area. The Home Army had to move farther into the fields, away from the town and constantly changed the areas. It was exhausting, not only getting to these farther distances on foot, but also having to find new ways to hide the weapons. Between the drops, the medicine and money were cautiously transferred to their hiding spots in the church. The weapons were moved from temporary storage in the fields to the attic of the church and tombs in the cemetery. Ted was tired from lack of sleep and working all the time in his shop, making customer orders but mostly repairing German uniforms. Because the Germans needed him to repair the uniforms, he was not forced to work on the demolition site.

He watched as others were made to demolish the vacated Jewish houses and start preparations for the building of a hospital and convalescent facility for soldiers from the Eastern Front. Ted and his men were given the order to sabotage the construction zone, especially the equipment brought for the demolition. It was a dangerous operation but Ted and his friends were trained well by the Silent Unseen sent from England. Trained to detect any movement on the part of the enemy, they moved like shadows, without any noise. They didn't visibly damage the equipment. Rather, they removed small but important parts, put a nail in a tire, or even did something as simple as jamming an exhaust pipe with dirt.

On the last day of February 1944, Billy waited on the tarmac for the last plane coming back from the mission. Looking towards the horizon, he was startled by a voice behind him.

"William Leavitt?"

Billy turned slowly and looked at a man close to his age dressed in a wrinkled pilot's uniform. It took him a while to recognise his friend from school.

"Paul Walker?" He was as stunned as if he'd seen a ghost. They'd lost track of each other shortly after school and their paths had never crossed since then. He smiled and shook his friend's hand. "Can we get together later tonight? I have to get to work right now. The plane is just landing."

"See you at the mess." Paul walked away towards the barracks in the distance.

It was late evening when Billy finally was able to join his school friend in the mess. Paul was one of the pilots flying the photographic planes over Europe. Before taking on the new mission, he had been a Spitfire pilot and had taken part in the Battle of Britain. Sitting at the table drinking beer, the young men reminisced about their times at school and the war that had taken so many of their friends.

Billy was fascinated with Paul's stories about flying the single-man planes, taking photographs from high altitudes. He understood about the risk taken by these pilots each time they flew the planes. He had a good knowledge of the airplanes and the photographic equipment, but hearing stories from Paul was a turning point for him in deciding to return to active duty as a pilot. He would have to keep his decision a secret from Eloise, knowing that she would plead with him to reconsider. Despite the danger and the strong possibility of dying and leaving Eloise widowed and his unborn child orphaned, he could not resist the temptation of flying again to serve his country the best way he could.

By mid-March, Billy was assigned to a reserve list of pilots. He attended a fast-track training of flying the stripped-to-bare-frame planes and operating the photographic equipment. His first flight was a short one over the English Channel. It was a different experience than flying a regular Spitfire with all its comforts. The cold temperature inside the plane sharpened his senses. He had to fly at a high altitude but check the conditions all the time to prevent water vapours from the exhaust system from creating a line of condensation that would leave a visible white cloud behind, a clear sign to the enemy. Billy learned to check the temperature, speed of the wind, and cloud formations, to make sure he was not flying outside of his altitude.

It was shortly before dawn. The sky above him was dark blue and the red sun looked like a fireball hanging low above the distant horizon. The supernatural view distracted Billy for a second, but he quickly recovered his bearings and returned his attention to the task at hand. To take good photographs, he had to tilt the plane to the left and then to the right. This allowed for a greater area to be covered by the cameras.

It was a short flight but he was happy when it was over. He had many questions to get ready for a long flight over Europe, and he was determined to do his new job with excellent results.

His trainer John was on the tarmac, waving at Billy. "How was your first flight?"

"Let's talk. I have many questions." He took a cigarette from John and inhaled it with delight on his face.

It wasn't until the end of March when Billy mustered the courage to tell Eloise about his new mission.

"How could you do this?" Eloise raised her voice. "You never even asked my opinion."

Eloise's sobs went on for a while. Billy wasn't sure how to comfort her. He loved her very much but felt that things had changed since her pregnancy. They had seen each other every other week, but her mood swings were creating some distance between them. He tried to understand that pregnancy was not easy on a woman, but something was different about her connection with him and her frequent moments of silence created some discomfort. Sometimes, at the end of a visit, he was happy to go back to the base.

April brought some ease to Rose's gloomy feelings. She spent most of the time in the store, greeting customers and taking their orders. Organising the merchandise on the shelves, and taking inventory in the evenings. She welcomed the early morning hours and fought any tiredness to get out of bed and go to the store.

Her breakfasts were meagre, mostly yesterday's potato soup or a piece of often stale bread. Spring was especially bad as the vegetables and fruit stored for the winter were mostly gone and the new ones would not be ready until June. Rose was luckier than many of her friends. She was making a small salary and could afford to buy an egg or a bit of cottage cheese to eat in the store. Often, she would buy a little more to bring to her family. She liked attending to the customers, keeping busy at the store, and staying away from her house, where everything disturbed her: their poverty, a mother suffering from depression, a younger sister who wanted to play, a brother who was too obedient, and a father who should have provided a better life for the family. She tried to think about something else, instead of her father. Lately, her feelings towards him were conflicted. Sometimes she had hate inside her heart, blaming him for their poverty and unhappiness; other times, she was proud of him and felt the love he had for her.

In the store, she was in charge. People liked her and her way of engaging many of them in a short conversation. She was beautiful and smart. She had graduated from her underground school last year with the highest marks, full of dreams about continuing her studies when the war was over.

It was a warm, sunny May day when Erik came to the general store in Brusk. Behind the counter was a young woman helping the few customers that were there. He stood in line and quietly observed the people in the store. But he could not concentrate and his eyes frequently turned to the young woman behind the counter.

"Good afternoon," he said with a strong voice when his turn came to order some groceries.

"Hi there," she answered, looking straight into his eyes with a big smile on her face.

She was not timid like many girls facing German soldiers.

He ordered some cigarettes, forgetting the other items he needed to buy. Their hands touched when he handed the money to her. Looking into each other's eyes, they stood on the opposite sides of the counter, hands still touching. His thoughts took him back in time—she reminded him very much of his mother.

He remembered his mother's beautiful eyes full of sparkle, always laughing and teasing everybody around. They were the good times, before the war. A lot had changed since then and somehow, Erik had lost half of his soul—the Polish half.

He allowed himself to think of himself as the "better one," a member of the Aryan race, as told at school, Sunday Masses, and by his officers. He aspired to be the *Wehrmacht* senior officer and possibly to work for the *Abwehr*. He believed that the Third Reich would dominate the world and wanted to be on the side of the winner. It had not happened as he planned.

Erik left the store with mixed feelings rushing through his mind. He was mesmerised by the girl but desperately wanted to forget her. He reached the banks of the river, sat down under a tree after making sure that nobody could see him, and closed his eyes.

His thoughts were irrational, filled with hate for the world, for the girl, for himself. He slowly calmed down and thought about the origins of his hate. He knew that it had been in him for a while, since his assignment in Krakow had been followed by a clear message that he wouldn't be promoted and moved to the *Wehrmacht* stationed in Berlin. He blamed the Polish side of him that made him less of a German in their eyes. He hated the Germans for rejecting him, for not appreciating his devotion to the Third Reich and the work he had done for German glory.

The hate was depressing and he knew that he could not go on like this forever. His mother was waiting for him in Gdańsk and the girl behind the counter was prettier and livelier than anyone he knew. His mind drifted to a different dimension, different times, dreams of adventure, travel, and perhaps love.

He was roused from his dream by the laughter of approaching men. They were soldiers coming back to the base from the town. Their demeanour suggested that they accepted the daily life here and most likely hadn't thought much about their predicament and the eventual outcome of the war. Two of them were half Polish like himself and used this to their advantage, making some acquaintances and flirting with some girls. Erik thought that their relaxed attitude and lack of ambition were far better than his stressful and full-of-hate life. Slowly he got up and followed his fellow soldiers to the base.

All night he tried hard to eradicate her from his memory, but she was inserting herself there and he sensed that she was close to him in spirit. He could not free himself from the spell she cast on him. Thinking about the girl with the blue eyes behind the counter, his belief in the superiority of the Aryan race started to crumble. He felt that his humanity was cracking and his only escape that night was thoughts about his mother.

"Rose, can you take my order?" A female voice brought Rose back from her dream-like state.

She was still staring at her hand, which touched the young German officer. The shivers shaking her body were not of fear or hate; they were a display of her sudden elation with a new feeling of wonder, of something that vaguely promised happiness and change in her life.

When the last customer left, she closed the store without her usual attention to details and left in a hurry. It was late afternoon and the sun was still very high. She went to her new sanctuary, the orchard. There, she always found peace and escape from her mundane life.

Her favourite apple tree, spreading its branches high and wide, was already in bloom. She kept a plank of wood and an old blanket under the tree, and she sat on it facing the hills. She never looked towards her house. She had never liked it, always dreaming about a different life and a different world.

She closed her eyes and the image of the young German from the store materialised in her mind. Afraid that the image would disappear forever and with it the young soldier, she kept her eyes shut. She wanted desperately to see him again despite the danger of it, and for now, she just wanted to keep his image inside her and fantasise about love.

The days dragged on forever, waiting for the soldier to come to the store again. Every day she took extra care to look her best. The May days were warmer and she could wear the few summer dresses she had in her wardrobe. They weren't much but they were colourful and emphasised her nice figure. Her brown hair was long and wavy and she always set it in a full French bun, making her look older than her age. Her hair was the envy of other girls and Rose knew how to take advantage of it. She was not a flirtatious woman, but her smarts, confidence, and hair often attracted young men's attention. She never allowed herself to be involved with anyone local, always dreaming about the outside world and a better life. Maybe she had been missing some happiness, but she remained true to her resolution of avoiding the mistake of her mother.

Five days later, he came back to the store. Nobody was around and she had already put away most of the remaining supplies in the back room. She was struck by his presence, and to avoid her embarrassment, she turned around and reached for the cigarettes.

She recovered her composure and even laughed. "I guess you need a new supply."

"Thank you. My name is Erik Hoffman." He extended his hand. Rose hesitated for a moment, looking at his hand. Slowly she extended hers and introduced herself.

"Rose—beautiful name." He was still holding her hand.

Rose became uncomfortable looking at his hand, the hand of an enemy, but she could not move her hand and separate from him. She knew she was doomed and didn't care. When she finally removed her hand, she turned the uncomfortable situation into a lighthearted one. "You must smoke a lot. You bought some recently." She looked at him with a mischievous smile.

Erik blushed and after a moment of silence, they both burst into laughter. He looked into her eyes and for a moment, they forgot that they were on the opposite sides of the war.

"Rose, you're like a beautiful flower among the ruins and devastation of the war."

She stared at him with embarrassment on her face, not because he was the enemy complimenting her, but because suddenly she'd lost her train of thought, taken aback by the beautiful words spoken in Polish.

"You speak our language well."

"My mother was Polish and I spoke it with her most of the time."

"There are others like you, half Polish and serving the Nazi army." She regretted saying this the moment she finished her sentence.

"Often, we had no choice, especially having German fathers. I guess we believed in the new order in the world. How wrong we were."

"Never mind what I said. Come back again. I have more cigarettes."

Rose looked down at the counter, afraid to look after the soldier who was closing the door behind him.

The first days of March 1944 brought some relief from the winter days. Jean bought a few tulips at the market on the way back from the mechanic who serviced his car. The Germans had allowed him to keep it, recognising that he was part of the supply chain to the wine industry. They loved their Alsatian wine, considering it part of the German heritage in this region.

Jean was fortunate to keep his car. He loved it. It was a black Peugeot

Eclipse with beautiful, curvaceous lines. The interior was impressive, with light-beige leather seats and a black console. It was a six-year-old car kept in mint condition and used only for special occasions when the weather was nice or when they went visiting. Emilie and the children loved riding in the car on the rare occasions that they took trips outside of the town to visit some close-by wineries.

Driving back from the market with the tulips on the passenger seat and deep in his thoughts about Emilie, Jean missed the turn to his house. He realised his mistake right away but decided to travel a little distance and take the back road running behind his property, close to the forested area. From a distance, he noticed the quick movement of two men running towards the trees. Jean slowed down the car and looked around carefully. He wasn't sure but thought that he saw some bushes on the side of his property moving. It could not be the wind as the trees in the forest were standing still like guardians of something secretive happening behind their facade. His body shivered and he sped up the car. Should he investigate what was happening or expunge it from his memory? Lately, he'd been good at disregarding any other thoughts and forcing his mind to focus on daily tasks and his family. After parking the car at the back of the house, he almost forgot to take the tulips for his wife.

"Let's have some wine, my love. Such nice spring weather today." He presented the tulips to Emilie and hugged her with renewed passion.

She kissed him briefly on the lips. "You're in good spirits today, any particular reason?"

"No reason—just wanted to be close to you and the children to make sure you're safe." He sipped the wine that Emilie had brought from the cellar along with a little cheese. "Did anyone come to the house today?"

"It was quiet, except for the children looking for spring flowers in the backyard."

Jean looked a little worried. "They're not children anymore. Jean-Marc is almost thirteen years old and very mature. Hope he isn't up to any mischief."

The next morning, Emilie was busy preparing a breakfast of fried potatoes when Jean went out to the back and walked towards the end of his property. He was driven by curiosity and worry from the day before.

"Good morning, boss." The strong voice of his superintendent, Andreas, stopped him in his tracks. He turned briskly towards Andreas and looked at him in silence.

"You look tired, Jean. Is everything fine?"

"Yes, it is, but what are you doing here so early in the morning?"

Andreas looked briefly toward the fence that was a little distance from the two men. Appearing bothered by this encounter, he shrugged his shoulders.

"Answer me. Why are you at work so early?"

"I would suggest that you don't inquire anymore and for your peace of mind, don't walk to the fence."

"It's too late now. I did see some men running from the fence to the forest yesterday afternoon, and I wanted to check for any damage to the property. Do you know anything about it?"

"It would be better that you didn't know anything, but the cat is out of the bag, so perhaps you need some explanation."

Jean immediately regretted asking for an explanation. He had tried to live through the war with little involvement in any dangerous actions. His involvement prior to the war and the recent help for Marc had made a serious impact on him. Although he tried to live a peaceful life, some demands were placed on him and he always accepted them with reluctance. He was afraid that this time he would get involved in something dangerous.

All day at work, Jean avoided Andreas, hoping that the impending nightmare would vanish. They arranged to meet after work in the warehouse half full of barrels waiting for delivery in the summer. The wine business was relatively good, but everybody involved in it had to reduce their profits drastically. The Germans paid severely reduced prices to the winemakers and this affected the entire supply chain in this industry. But it was still much better than being unemployed or forced to labour at German sites.

All the employees had gone home when Andreas took Jean to the back of the warehouse. He moved a few barrels away from the wall, bent down, and opened a trap door in the floor. Using a steep ladder, he led Jean down to a small bunker.

Jean looked around the small dark space. "Who built this and when?"

"Your wife's garden benefited from the dirt we dug out last year. We have done a good job if you didn't notice."

"But there is nothing here, not even any necessities hidden here. I assume you built it to take shelter in case it was necessary."

"Wait, Jean, there's more." Andreas pushed a small wall and a concealed door opened to a bigger room lit with carbide lamps.

Two men were in the room, looking at Jean with anticipation. After a moment of silence, Andreas introduced them.

Zenon, a young Polish man, skinny and no more than twenty years old, nodded, while Pierre introduced himself in fluent French, extending his hand to Jean.

The room was furnished with a small table, two folding chairs, and a mattress propped against the wall. A piece of equipment unknown to Jean was on the table, along with papers and other materials. In the corner stood a small radio transmitter with headphones next to it.

"We're helping the French Resistance to smuggle some people to various destinations."

Jean looked scared, absorbing the words and looking carefully around. "You're endangering my family. You had no right to start this operation on my property." He started to get angry but stopped himself before the others could notice.

"Sorry about this, but your place was the least dangerous to set up this type of undertaking."

In the next half hour, Jean learned that the men were experts in preparing false documents and operating the radio station. Pierre was in charge of the cell and Andreas was the main contact man with the network on the ground.

They were responsible for moving military personnel from other countries to England. Most of the people they assisted were underground soldiers that had spent time in other countries, training their people in combat and sabotage in preparation for the final rise up against the Nazis. Some of the soldiers had been recalled back to England with the help of cells like the one in Jean's warehouse.

"I understand your dedication and admire it, but the danger to my family is great."

"Your cooperage business is valuable to Germans. They know you and you have many privileges to stay in business."

Jean felt trapped in this unexpected situation and remained silent for a long while. Pierre gave him a glass of water. "Listen, we're here and you have to accept it. Don't enquire about it anymore, and ask your wife and children to stay out of this part of the property."

"That sounds like an order."

"Yes, it is. Some people don't like your prosperity and believe that you're too friendly with the Germans."

"I'm doing what many others in the wine industry are doing." Jean was suddenly scared. He'd never thought about this aspect of his business.

"Let's go." Andreas pulled Jean by the sleeve and they left the bunker. "I have something else to show you."

They went to the fence and Jean noticed fresh earth piled up against some bushes. He looked at Andreas questioningly.

"We're digging a narrow tunnel leading to the forested area ahead. We're taking every precaution possible. Go about your business, and have an excuse to avoid this end of your property, pretend that your leg is bothering you more."

"I'll see you at work tomorrow." Jean walked slowly towards his house with a noticeable limp.

Jean didn't have to pretend. Whenever he was under stress, the leg pain intensified and the limp worsened. He wondered if Emilie had noticed his exaggerated limp lately. He was under a lot of stress and hoped that his wife and children were spared the anxiety of him being unwell.

In May, all activities around the demolition site suddenly came to a halt. Just as they had every morning, the Polish men forced to work there came to the site at 6 a.m., only to find caution tape around the entrance with a sign affixed to a post: "Don't enter."

The news of the closure of the demolition site spread quickly. Rumours started mushrooming within the first hours after the engineers left the town. Two opposite views were dividing people that gathered in the main square.

"The Germans have lost the war and the Russians are coming," some argued.

"The Germans are regrouping and mounting a massive attack on the Eastern Front," others said, with fear in their voices.

Ted needed to know what was going on. Some of the German uniforms were still in his workshop, and that gave him the idea of taking them to the German headquarters across the river to gather as much information as he could. As he approached the German headquarters in the castle, he noticed increased activities there. Two soldiers stood guard at the entrance and motioned to him to stop.

Ted said, "These uniforms belong to Germans officers that were stationed in town. I went there to deliver them but the building as well as the demolition site were closed. Perhaps the officers are here and would like their uniforms back." He didn't expect any answer from the guards but to his surprise, one of them spoke.

"Some of them arrived here last night. You may go inside and deliver the uniforms,"

After a brisk pat-down, Ted was allowed to go inside. He walked along the wall toward the centre of the courtyard. He took his time walking, stopping from time to time to rearrange the uniforms hanging on his left arm. Observing the area, he noticed that many Germans were gathered in the centre, their voices loud. Carefully he approached the highest-ranking officer and pointed at the uniforms.

"I need to deliver them to the officers who were stationed in Brusk. I was told some of them were here."

Again, to his surprise, he was directed to a tent erected on one side of the courtyard. "The officers are there. Drop the uniforms inside."

Ted carefully entered the tent and looked around. Five men were standing in front of a big map with clearly marked lines running along the river. Ted studied the map quickly; the lines could only indicate possible trenches to be built on the west side of the river.

He coughed to get their attention. "These uniforms were left in my workshop for repairs; they're ready and clean."

A young officer motioned towards a table near the entrance. "Leave them on the table."

Back in the courtyard, Ted spotted two Polish policemen he knew well. "Good morning, Olek," he said. "Is the digging of the trenches going to start soon?" He took a gamble that the news about the trenches was already known in town and they wouldn't suspect that he was spying.

"Yes, the work will start at full speed immediately. Tomorrow, we will start gathering people from town to work on the trenches." Olek's voice was low, as if he was tired of the servitude to the Germans he'd chosen at the beginning of the war.

"Who is going to build the hospital?" Ted persisted.

"They are moving the hospital to the existing facilities west of Warsaw."

Ted left with some solid information and a big question about the relaxed security at the headquarters.

Late in the afternoon, during a meeting of the Home Army, Ted reported the news about the digging of trenches along the river.

"Each of you needs to do some reconnaissance and report your findings." George removed a pack of cigarettes and gave it to Ted. "This isn't an ordinary packet of cigarettes. It is a hidden miniature camera that you can use to take some pictures of the German activities on the trenches. Within a month, I need full documentation of the length of the trenches, the terrain, and any possible heavy artillery brought there."

It was early morning when a loud knock woke Ted up from a deep sleep. His mother was already at the door, opening it to two German soldiers with rifles slung on their shoulders.

"All of you, get ready and gather in the main square in fifteen minutes." The soldiers left right away, moving to another house.

The people who soon gathered in the square were divided into subgroups. Young men, including Ted, were assigned to use heavy picks to move the earth. Young women and older man were in a group that would remove the earth and pile it up on the east side. Others were in a group, moving logs to reinforce the trenches. Some women were assigned to the field kitchen to prepare meals for the supervising Germans and one meal a day for the workers. Ted's mother, Maria, was assigned to the kitchen.

Ted was glad about the assignment to dig the trenches. He knew some of the Germans and the policemen and soon was assigned to a small reconnaissance group, responsible for staking the ground as per plans for the layout of the trenches. It was a perfect opportunity to evaluate the extent of the operation and to use his camera to take pictures for his report to George.

The frequency of Billy's flights increased to a few per week. The Allies were gathering their armies in the south of England, ready for the biggest and bravest attack on the Nazis in Europe. British, American, French, Canadian, and Polish forces were amassing their people, weapons, trucks, and tanks, and the ports were full of an armada of ships. Multiple daily reconnaissance flights and new spy plane photographs were ensuring that a sudden attack on British soil wouldn't destroy the Allies' plans of winning the war.

On the last day of April, Billy was on an assignment to fly over northern France to photograph the Maginot Line in the Northern Lorraine area. He left the base at four-thirty in the morning, intending to be over the Maginot Line at sunrise.

The Spitfire he flew was a newer version of the plane and had been outfitted for the mission. It was stripped of everything inside, leaving just the bare shell of the plane equipped with cameras, an oxygen mask, and enough fuel to get him back to England.

It was very cold in the cabin, making Billy's body ache all over. The oxygen mask covering his nose and mouth created additional discomfort, and the feeling of loneliness spread over him. He missed flying the Spitfire in a formation with other planes while communicating with other pilots and the adrenaline of heading into a battle.

He looked at the camera-operating box in front of him, mounted in the place where the gunsight was originally located. Then he glanced at the maps spread in his lap to confirm his location. Billy was flying at nine thousand metres altitude when the weather below him changed suddenly. The clouds were gathering and the possibility of taking good pictures from that height diminished.

There was no communication between him and the base; he knew the decision was his. He considered turning back and flying to the base but his hesitation was only momentary. A lot depended on this flight and his photographs. Based on his training, he understood the task from both sides: the pilot and the photographic interpreter. He recalled analysing pictures obscured by some clouds that had still provided important information about the recently bombed train trucks that the Germans were rebuilding.

"I'm not going back." He spoke aloud to give himself some encouragement, his voice muffled by the oxygen mask.

Based on the maps and the equipment reading, he estimated that he was minutes away from his destination. Although it was dangerous, he decided to lower his altitude and dive down below the blanket of the clouds.

The town of Thionville was to his left and the fortifications almost below him. He started taking pictures of the area. His swift, tilting movements from left to right were dizzying but there was no other way but to do it fast and turn around.

He was on his way back when an explosion ripped the tail of his plane and he started diving down. With no parachute to rescue him, he tried to lift the front of the plane, hoping to glide towards the earth and survive. His last thoughts were of Eloise, the unborn baby, and Joey.

Jean looked out the window towards the warehouse to the left of his factory. It was almost dawn; the sky was shrouded in clouds and he could sense a heavy rain drenching the town. It had been almost a year since he'd gotten into the habit of looking through the window towards the factory. He had not questioned Andreas about the forbidden activities conducted on his property. He knew that a tunnel to the end of his property was completed. He judged this by the amount of dirt spread in the garden and by the wood and even barrels disappearing from the factory. It wasn't a lot, so he decided not to make a fuss about it. He often wondered why Emilie hadn't noticed the fresh dirt in the garden. Perhaps she was too preoccupied with providing food and basic necessities for the family, paying no attention to such trivial things.

Looking toward the warehouse, Jean noticed Andreas walking toward the gate in his usual energetic manner. Suddenly, Andreas stopped and looked towards the western horizon. Jean turned his head in the same direction, noticing with surprise a small plane emerging from the blanket of clouds.

"What the heck …" He hadn't finished his thought when the tail of the plane burst into flames and it started losing altitude. In a few seconds, the plane levelled off and glided toward the forest behind his property.

The plane didn't explode but a small trail of smoke indicated the location of the crash. Fear paralysed Jean momentarily and he lost sight of Andreas. He dressed quickly, despite his stiff leg, and went outside the house toward the warehouse.

Nothing out of the ordinary was happening there, and he decided to walk toward the fence where the entrance to the hidden tunnel was camouflaged between the budding bushes and evergreen trees growing well above the height of the fence. He decided to look into the tunnel. Since his accident in the foundry, he'd been afraid of small, dark spaces and had never attempted to go inside. To his surprise, he noticed that the tunnel went both ways—to the warehouse and to the other side of the fence. He hesitated for a while, considering going back to the house, but he knew he would hate himself for such cowardliness.

He closed his eyes, and touching the sides of the tunnel, he went inside. He realized that the walls and the low ceiling were heavily reinforced with wooden planks. For a moment, he was pleased with this discovery; it meant the tunnel was strong, preventing any road caving from above. Once the wood supports were less frequent, he opened his eyes, hoping that the end of the tunnel was near. When he emerged from underground, he was disoriented. It took him a while to get his bearings and orientate himself towards the plane crash. After five minutes of walking, he noticed the flames and stopped in horror.

He had almost turned away when somebody grabbed his arm and pulled him in the plane's direction.

"We need your help, since you're already here." Andreas looked at Jean and whispered, "Thank you for staying out of the way until now."

A sudden thunder tore through the air and heavy rain lashed at them and everything around.

"God is on our side." Andreas looked up and crossed himself.

Two other men were already on the plane crash site, removing the pilot, who was covered in blood.

Pierre was giving orders to the men at the scene. "The flames are almost gone; we need to see what can be salvaged from the plane."

Jean went to the pilot, hoping to find a sign of life. He had almost died once and only the quick help of his former coworkers had saved his life. He looked for the pilot's pulse. It was very weak, but the man's heart was still beating. "He's alive. We need to take him to a safe area." Jean was astonished by his own words. Was he too quick to offer his opinion?

"The Germans will find the plane and will wonder about the missing pilot." A man Jean didn't recognise emerged from the wreckage with a heavy box in his arms.

"You get him inside the bunker. I'll check with the morgue to see if any recently deceased men are there," said Pierre as Jean looked at him with horror.

An hour later, the pilot, stripped of his uniform, was hidden safely in the bunker below the warehouse. Pierre and the other man dressed the body of a dead immigrant worker in the pilot's uniform and placed it in the wreckage.

"Please forgive us," said Pierre as they burned the corpse's face and broke his legs.

The next few days were a nightmare for Jean. The full realisation of the underground operation in his cooperage warehouse, the existence of the tunnel, the people from his factory involved, and outsiders coming in and out in the dark of the night were pressing on his consciousness. Knowing that the pilot was hiding in the bunker brought mixed feelings of fear for his family and strangely, the satisfaction that even though he hadn't planned it, he was involved again in fighting the Nazis.

Lying sleeplessly next to Emilie, he thought about ways to protect her and the children. Summer was coming soon and he needed to prevent Marie-Ann and Jean-Marc from going to the end of the property to play or pick wildflowers. He decided to erect a fence halfway along the property on the pretence that his business needed to expand and construction might start there. His children were obedient and he felt that it might be a sufficient deterrent for them.

Emilie was on his mind for the next few days. The fence wouldn't stop her from checking the entire property. He could not tell her to avoid the area as it would raise her suspicions right away. Her garden close to the house was already in bloom and she had been talking earlier about expanding her vegetable plot closer to the back fence. His nightly torment didn't produce any ideas on how to keep Emilie away from the "forbidden zone" as he named it. He might have to ask Andreas for some suggestions. Days passed and other than sending Emilie to do some mundane chores outside of the house, he had not come up with anything credible for her to accept.

Jean entered the kitchen, summoned by the nice aroma of cooked vegetables. "What are you cooking? We already had dinner today."

"Just a soup for tomorrow. I might be busy all day; the market stall needs some repairs and I might do that." She turned towards Jean and kissed him on the lips.

"You think the market might be busy this spring?"

"Everybody needs food, even the Germans. They need our vegetables in addition to the crops they always confiscate from the farmers."

"I hope you're safe working there," Jean said sheepishly.

"We're in the fourth year of the war; I know what I'm doing." She became a little impatient and turned towards the stove.

Jean left the kitchen angry at himself for not being able to come up with any ideas and the fact that Emilie always seemed to be full of energy, going about her business and even his requests with remarkable resilience.

After the kids went to bed, Jean took his Bible from the side table and looked at it with hope. The Bible had both the Old and New Testaments together. Bound in thick, black leather covers with a cross in the middle, it always gave him some comfort, and he felt the power coming from inside the scriptures. He opened it randomly to reveal the 25th Psalm of David.

To you, O Lord, I lift up my soul.
O my God, in you I trust;
let me not be put to shame;
let not my enemies exult over me.

Reading the psalm, he found peace flowing through him. Thinking about the meaning of his reading, he glanced through the window. A shadow resembling Emilie was moving towards the warehouse. He put the Bible down, left the house, and quietly walked to the warehouse. He saw Emilie's shadow entering the hidden door behind the barrels. The sight of her there paralysed him and he hid behind a stash of freshly cleaned and charred barrels. It was half an hour later when she emerged from the bunker. She passed without noticing him and a moment later, Jean opened the secret door for the first time since the plane crash.

The pilot was sleeping on the narrow bed when Jean entered the room. A glass of water was standing on the stool next to the bed. Jean lifted the glass and sat down, looking at the young man. Not knowing what else to do, he took his handkerchief, moistened it with water, and touched the pilot's forehead. He sat there for a while, thinking about Emilie, realising that he didn't really know everything about her. They loved each other and she was a great mother and wife, always busy in the house and the market, and she seemed happy with the life they'd built together. How could he not have realised that she was leading a secret life? Was the life of a wife of a prosperous man not enough for her? Why did she involve herself in dangerous activities? With his head in his hands, he rocked back and forth on the stool. The moon was high in the sky when he left the warehouse.

"Jean, where have you been?" Emilie was sitting at the table reading the Bible he left there.

"I went to see the pilot." He looked at her with an ashen face.

"There are no secrets between us anymore then. It is better this way." She looked at him and smiled.

"It is dangerous. Why did you get involved?"

"Oh Jean, I'm a nurse. How could I not get involved?"

"But you don't work as a nurse anymore."

"In these dark times, people such as me are needed."

"But the danger to our family and the employees …?" He stopped talking when he saw her resolute face.

"Jean, I never questioned your involvement in working with the French Army before the war. I never asked any questions. It was my choice to help my country in the best way I could by being a nurse when needed."

"Mother, you cannot steal potatoes from the German kitchen. They may catch you one day." Ted looked at the bowl full of freshly boiled potatoes with a little bacon on top.

Maria smiled and touched his hand. "I'm careful—I learned it from you. Eat when we have them."

"Mom, what do you mean you learned from me?"

"I wear your pants under my dress, the ones you used to smuggle food to Warsaw."

Ted looked bewildered at her.

"They're baggy and have secret pockets. You made them well, my son."

"But Mom, I would never expect you to be so courageous. It's dangerous."

"I like potatoes, not only to eat but to touch them, to feel the texture to get them ready for the plate. I've worked with them since I was a little girl, since my father died."

"You've never told me anything about your childhood. Since Father died, you stopped even talking to me except for daily small talk and pleading with me to stay safe."

"Perhaps tonight I could tell you and Ania about my life."

Ted was intrigued by his mother's love for potatoes and how it might be related to her childhood. He'd never asked about her past, assuming that her life was unremarkable until she married his father. He noticed Ania in the backyard and quickly stepped outside.

"Ania, have you ever talked to Mom about her life?"

"No. You know the way she is, doesn't talk much."

"Should we ask Uncle? Maybe he could tell us something about her."

"She is older than him. He probably doesn't remember much. Let's wait until she tells us her story."

Maria had only been four years old when her father went to work in the coal mines of Silesia. He made good money and she and her siblings had a good life under the stern but loving care of their mother. She completed two classes of primary school, where she learned some math and to read and write in Polish. Further schooling was not available in Brusk, but she was never too keen on more education. Her knowledge was sufficient to write letters to her father and read the ones received from him. He visited them every Christmas, Easter, and a week in the summer, and they were the best days of her life.

In the spring of 1910, her father came to visit his family. There was an epidemic of typhus in the area and despite being warned against visiting, he came to see them and especially Maria, his favourite daughter. He was strong and healthy, and yet he succumbed to the illness and died within a few days. Many people died that year but in Maria's family, it was only her father. Soon the family was facing starvation as the money stopped coming and they owned only a small plot of land that could grow potatoes and vegetables but they could not afford to buy even a sack of potatoes to plant a new crop. Their life was very hard. Almost a year later, in early spring, Maria's mother begged a seasonal-workers recruiter to take Maria as a domestic help to a landowner in the west part of Poland, which was under German administration. Despite objections, due to her young age, the recruiter took pity on the whole family and Maria was accepted.

The landowner was very good to her, and she was assigned to the kitchen, where her main responsibility was to peel potatoes. She was paid the same wages as the other workers and soon was able to send money to her mother, not only to buy food, but also potatoes to plant for the fall crop. Maria did this for ten years, until she met Joseph and married him.

Maria told her children this story, sitting on the chair with Ted and Ania looking at her with wonder. "That is enough for tonight," she said.

"Mom, I never knew about your life. I love you very much." Ted knelt and kissed her hands.

"Mom, was it there that you became so elegant, acting like a lady? Nobody in town is as elegant as you are." Ania walked through the kitchen, keeping her head up, imitating her mother.

"The owners were good to me and gave me some of their used clothes that were much better than anything I owned." Maria stopped talking and closed her eyes.

Darkness was all around him when he opened his eyes. Billy thought that it was the afterlife or that maybe he'd woken up buried deep in the dirt. He gathered his thoughts. If it was the afterlife, there should be light and not darkness as in some accounts of people claiming to have come back from death. If he wasn't dead, then he must be buried alive. Panic shuddered his body but he could not move his arms or legs to feel anything around him. He opened his mouth to shout but his throat constricted and he could hardly gasp some air. Suddenly, a sharp pain paralysed his body and he screamed. He closed his eyes and started to pray.

With his eyelids shut, he sensed some dim light hovering above him. That scared him even more and he squeezed the eyes shut even harder.

"Are you awake?" a voice in accented English asked close to his ear.

"Am I alive or is it just a trick that my dying brain is playing on me?" Billy whispered to himself.

"You're alive and in a safe place, but your injuries are extensive."

"Where am I?"

"In France. We're waiting for a doctor to come to see you, but the Germans are on alert after your plane crashed, and we need to take all possible precautions."

Billy vaguely remembered flying through the clouds … and then there was darkness all around him. When he woke up the next time, more light was around him and a man with a stethoscope was looking at him with concern.

"Your ribs and leg were broken, but the men here did a good job immobilising it. You should be fine, but it will take time."

"Will I walk again?" Billy asked in a faint voice.

"I'll set your leg; you may not be perfect but you should walk again. We don't have anaesthetics, but a strong vodka will help you with this pain."

Billy drank from a cup and his body and hands were fastened to the table with belts. He drifted into blackness again.

It was dark when he woke up and he had less pain in his leg and body. He was stretched out on a mattress and smelled damp earth around him.

"Where the hell am I?" He thought he was screaming but his voice was barely audible. There was no answer this time.

For the next few hours, he drifted in and out of consciousness. Finally, someone came to the room with a carbide lamp in his hand. An hour later, Billy learned what had happened to him.

"Thank you for saving me," he said.

The days in June were long and the weather beautiful. A lot had changed since the building of trenches started. The town was empty of young people since they had to work digging and cutting trees in the nearby forest to use them for reinforcement. Erik wanted to keep Rose away from the work in the trenches but she refused. She didn't want to be seen as protected by him, and the store was allowed to open three days per week, giving her a break from the back-breaking trench digging.

Erik and Rose fell into a weekly routine of meeting after the store closed and walking by the river that ran lazily between Rose's town and the German camp.

"I look at the river and I don't see it as a division between us," said Rose, "Even if you're on the other side, we see the same water, water that washes away the grief, blood, and hate into this world."

Erik took Rose's hand and led her to the river. "Wash the sins of my past," he said. "I'm in love with you and ask for your forgiveness."

Rose pulled him underwater, their bodies touched, and they kissed for a long time. The kiss took them away from real life and for a long moment, they were free of war, hate, and lack of hope. Lying on the grass later, Erik talked to her about his pre-war life: the daily routines of his unit, the towns and villages he visited as part of his policing duties. He hoped that Rose would absolve him of the wrongdoing of his past, and that their love would survive the war. They both dreamed about the future together, a future where all the bad memories were swept away by time and the river of life would bring only happiness. It was a sweet dream.

Often, Erik suspected that Rose worked for the underground Home Army and his information was being passed to them. He didn't care if she was a spy. Maybe his information would help to end the war. Maybe it was better to die redeemed than to wait for the impending defeat of Germany and remain guilty forever. He decided to carefully pass on more information to her without endangering her.

Most of all they liked to talk about their future. Rose told him that she wanted to escape the small town, and lack of opportunities. She knew she could do better, and being part of the bigger world was her childhood dream.

One afternoon, Erik was in the store waiting for Rose to finish organising the meagre supplies on the shelves when a young man with dark hair slicked back from his wide forehead entered and went straight to the counter. "Hello, Rose, do you have coffee?" he asked.

"Wait a moment, I'll check. Ted, meet Erik, from the *Feldgendarmerie*."

She turned towards the shelf to look for coffee. It wasn't real coffee anymore. This was a coffee-like beverage made from wheat and chicory, but it tasted fine with some milk and saccharine.

Ted looked up and fixed his eyes on Erik. They stared at each other for a moment like two rivals, ready to fight for her. The few seconds seemed like an eternity.

When Erik resurfaced from his thoughts, Ted was gone.

Rose walked briskly to the house hoping to be there before dinner. With each step, she took she felt light, empowered, and exultant. She was not worried about the consequences of her forbidden love; she was too happy to even think about it. She slowed her steps as she analysed everything about Erik. He represented all that she dreamed about; handsome, educated, charming, and worldly.

She suddenly stopped in her tracks. *He is also the enemy.* The thought of it exploded with pain in her head. She stopped and sat on the grass along the narrow path. She needed to calm down before going back home.

She had spent a longer time than usual with Erik, folded in his strong arms and talking. They'd found a secluded place by the river, away from prying eyes and met there as often as they could. Since they had seen each other for the first time, both were consumed by their forbidden love.

She thought about Ted asking her to get any useful information from Erik and tried to justify her time spent with him as a patriotic duty, but she knew very well that it was the love, not the duty, that thrust her to him.

Her father stood outside of the house. "Rose, you're late."

"I'm not a child anymore; I can do what I want." Rose was defiant because she expected him to confront her about Erik.

"Girl, it is wrong what you're doing. He is German."

"Oh Dad, you know he's half Polish and was forced to join the army."

Her father's eyes were filled with anger. Rose was his favourite child, and she knew that he considered this a betrayal of his love for her.

"You must stop this nonsense right now; it is dangerous and it is wrong."

"I love him and we will never stop loving each other."

"Don't you see that you're just a German whore? Such a shame to me."

"Oh, you only worry about yourself and your reputation. You're nothing, just a poor man."

Her head spun around when he slapped her face. She saw regret on his face, but could not stop herself from adding more hurtful words. "I'll have a better life than you ever gave us." She turned around and ran away from him.

She was in the middle of the cemetery when she stopped. She needed to hide somewhere away from people.

She crossed the cemetery towards a small gate on the other side. It was quiet there and she sat down on the ground, pressing her back to the old stone wall. Tears started to blur her vision as she suppressed the cries that shook her to the core. The feeling of somebody close to her forced her to open her eyes.

Slowly she lifted her head and gazed at Ted standing above her. "What are you doing here?" she asked.

"I was walking nearby when I saw you here. What happened? Why are you crying?" Ted asked gently.

"I had an argument with my father. He was right; my life is a mess and

I can't help it." Rose started crying again.

"You don't have to say anything. Some things are beyond our control." Ted sat next to her. His arm extended around her shoulder brought her some comfort.

Walking through the forest to the new printing shop, Ted still felt the warmth of Rose's body leaning against his. He loved her and the pain of knowing that she loved somebody else was unbearable. He didn't care that it was a German soldier, only that it was somebody else, not him. His thoughts drifted to his father and his father's troubled life—the reckless behaviour that had almost destroyed another family, the son that he'd never known, and his death, which had almost destroyed his own family. Ted had learned to live with pain and constant longing for a male figure in his life. Rose's love for somebody else was just another defeat, another pain that he had to deal with.

He switched his thoughts to the mission at hand. The messages the Home Army was receiving from England were about an uprising against the Germans. Ted was delegated to a group of young people that might be involved with weapons supply to Warsaw. Since 1943, his cell in Brusk had received rifles, ammunition, grenades, dynamite, and other items that were stored in the church or in old tombs in the cemetery.

Thinking about the uprising cleared Ted's mind of Rose and his father. He had developed the ability to concentrate on anything he was involved in, and he delivered results. Since his short expulsion from the Home Army a year ago, he had proved that he could be trusted at the highest level of the organisation. He was looking forward to today's meeting and planning the most important action since the beginning of the war.

Two days later, he met with George and two other men in the church's crypt.

"Ted, what was decided during your meeting at the printing shop?" George asked without any formal greeting.

"I'll start making bags for carrying small weapons and grenades. I'll need fabric to do so."

"We will give you some. It will be the silk from some of the parachutes. Make sure the Germans don't discover this."

"My mother is braver than I thought. I'll ask her to keep watch while I'm making the bags."

"The Russians are advancing towards Poland, and more German soldiers from the Eastern Front will be stationed here. They may put up a strong fight in the trenches."

"Did you get the message from Rose that the SS may put some land mines in the trenches?"

"We're looking into it. Could she find out more?"

"Yes, the German may tell her the markings that they use to identify the mines." Ted could not bring himself to even utter Erik's name. He always referred to him as "The German."

"Let's meet in three days at Ted's shop." George dismissed the meeting.

Green weeds and colourful wildflowers grew in abundance where the hospital was supposed to have been built. It was cordoned off by barbed wire and guarded by two German guards. Nobody dared to go there, afraid of the Germans and the ghosts of the dead people. In the first week of June, the guards disappeared, leaving behind a sign that said it was forbidden to enter the area. It didn't take long for the kids to find an easy passage and start playing hide and seek and treasure hunt.

Rose was looking after some customers in the store when an explosion shook the area. She and others ran outside of the store, confused and looking for answers. Some people were tearing away the barbed wire not far from the store. Rose heard a cry from the demolition area. She saw some children had been playing near the cordoned-off zone and now she expected the worst, hoping that she was wrong and her young sister was not among them. She felt paralysed, unable to make any move because whatever had happened there was going to affect her life. Slowly she regained her wits, closed the door of the store, and walked towards the crowd gathering in front of the already torn-down wire. Covered in dirt from the explosion and waving their hands, a few children ran towards the crowd of people.

"There are more kids there," an older boy shouted and collapsed into somebody's arms.

Rose and two men started to walk carefully towards the crater left by mine. She didn't think about the danger of another explosion; she was propelled to walk by a fear that it was her tragedy.

Her younger sister Hela was lying on the ground. Hela's face was buried in the dirt and blood was splattered over her dirty dress. Rose slowly turned Hela onto her back, begging her to wake up.

After a few seconds, Hela's body twitched and she opened her eyes. "My arm hurts," she whispered to Rosa's ear.

It was a horrific sight. Hela's forearm was mangled flesh and bone and barely attached to her elbow.

"Don't close your eyes. I'll take you home now."

Hela was light as a feather, skinny for her age, with bright-red hair that hung down over Rose's arms. Rose fixed her gaze on the red hair, avoiding looking at the injured arm as she walked to the house.

The news spread like lightning, and Franek was already on the street running towards his two sisters. A bed sheet was torn into strips and Hela's arm was bandaged by her mother. Nobody said a word, as if they all felt responsible for the accident. Hela was a bundle of energy and always had a carefree attitude. At the age of twelve, she was the youngest of the three children, often left alone to do house chores and play with other children in the neighbourhood.

War was a terrible time for the youngest. With no school to attend, and parents and older siblings working to bring some food to the table or in forced labour for the Germans, they were growing up without guidance or normalcy.

Looking at Hela lying in the bed, Rose felt anger towards the whole world. Her head was pounding with one word screaming inside: *Why? Why? Why?*

In the afternoon, she left the house and went to the secluded area where she often met with Erik.

She barely opened her mouth. "What are you doing here?"

"I heard about the explosion, and I went to the store but it was closed." He looked at Rose, his face pale.

Her dress was stained with blood and her hair was in disarray.

She looked at him with an emptiness in her eyes. "It's your fault," she hissed.

"Rose, tell me what happened?"

He took her into his arms, and she didn't resist. She was too unhappy to fight, to hate, or even to cry.

When she finished talking about the accident, Erik stood up rapidly. "Wait here for me. I'll bring my first-aid kit."

Waiting for Erik to come back, Rose recalled every day since she'd met him. It had been a difficult but happy time for her.

Her thoughts drifted to Erik and their weekly dates, to their favourite spot, where dreaming about a better life was easy. They had watched nature change around them, the trees covered with a shroud of green, the riverbanks filling with grass and wildflowers, the red poppies and blue cornflowers oblivious to the war and devastation all around. She would have stayed there forever, her eyes closed, and dreaming about the world floating above her. Erik came back in less than an hour with a small canvas bag hanging over his shoulder.

"Take this for your sister. We have a young doctor on the base who believes in his oath to serve the sick. He gave me some penicillin that your Polish doctor could use if necessary."

Rose rushed back to the house, holding the bag in her arms, afraid it might disappear and Hela would die.

She heard voices in the room adjacent to the kitchen, the only decent room in the house. She gently opened the door and froze in fear.

Hela was lying on the table while the doctor was bandaging her arm. It was just a stump above the elbow. Rose almost screamed when she noticed her father looking at her with furious eyes. Before he could say anything, she lifted the canvas bag.

"I have first-aid supplies and also some penicillin."

The doctor turned towards her. "Please open it, remove the items, and place them on the bench near the window."

She followed his instructions carefully.

The doctor looked at the medical treasures in front of him. "Good, we have a tube of antibacterial ointment. I'll use some of it right now to cover the wounds."

"What about the rest?" Rose looked at him with anticipation.

"I'll use one of the penicillin injections as well. Nothing else can be done right now. You'll have to watch her through the night and put a cold towel on her forehead. Hopefully, she won't develop an infection or a high fever."

"Thank you, Doctor." Rose was instantaneously strong again, ready to fight for Hela's life.

The next week was very difficult for the entire family. Mother suddenly succumbed to her depression, Franek had to go to the trenches, and Father was silently walking in and out of the house.

Rose took charge of the household and divided her responsibility between looking after Hela and running the store. She learned quickly to remove the bandages, look after the wounds, and use the supplies from Erik.

After one week, the doctor finally smiled. "The worst is over; the medication you brought, Rose, saved your sister's life."

Later that day, Rose went to the orchard and sat under her favourite apple trees. Some apples were ready to eat and she took one and relished the sweetness of it. The sun was low on the horizon when she woke up under the tree with her apple half-finished. Her father was sitting next to her.

"Rose, I'm sorry for being angry with you. I guess Erik is a good man."

After the accident on the abandoned construction site, Erik waited for a week before attempting to contact Rose.

When they met in the store, the conversation was very short.

"Can we meet in the usual place by the river?" He wasn't sure if she would even want to talk to him. He knew that Hela was in stable condition, but two boys had died in the accident and the town was mourning their deaths.

"Father is looking after my sister; I think I can meet you today."

Erik was sitting with his back to the big oak spreading its branches high to the sky, as if telling the people around to draw strength from its vitality, from its renewal each spring after the cold winter stripped it of its majestic foliage.

He watched Rose walking briskly towards him. She was always so purposeful, adamant to achieve what she wanted. He loved her for her determination, for the dreams they shared together, giving him a new purpose to his life.

They sat quietly for a while, holding hands.

"My father sends his gratitude for the medical supplies. They saved Hela's life."

He didn't respond. He was glad that he'd acted so quickly and got her the first-aid kit, but the guilt of creating such grief in the first place was wearing heavy on him. "Rose, I didn't know that mines had been planted on the construction site."

She didn't respond, only looked to the sky and opened her mouth to take a deeper breath.

He wanted to kiss her, press his body against hers and give her some faith in the future. But he didn't move, afraid that it was too early and she might reject him.

"In the next two weeks, the trenches will be completed and the work will be moved farther west." He stopped talking and waited for her reaction. The silence on her part was deafening and he closed his eyes and prayed. He felt a gentle kiss on his lips and opened his eyes. She was ready to stand up and leave.

"Stay a little longer," he whispered to her.

She put her head on his shoulder and spoke. "I want to scream, I want to hate you, but I can't. I love you."

He stroked her hair, getting some strength from the gentle move, the feel of her silky hair that smelled with a faint fragrance of plain soap, the only one available to the people.

"Rose, now listen to me carefully. I think that the German Army won't establish the front line here. They keep the *Feldgendarmerie* in the dark, but something is different about the SS soldiers' demeanour. They are planning to plant landmines in the trenches before they leave. I'll try to get some information about their plans."

"That would be helpful. We wouldn't want anything to happen, anything like the explosion at the hospital construction site." Rose looked towards the river and a convulsion shook her body.

Erik pulled her towards him. "I'll get the information so when the army is gone, people are careful and avoid going there."

They sat in silence for a while, unable to find words to talk about the explosion and Rose's sister. Finally, she took his face in her hands and kissed him for a long time. "Thank you. I must go now."

July was full of bad news for the Germans. The Russian Army was already in Polish territory and winning many battles. The town of Brusk was again full of injured and fatigued German soldiers recuperating before marching to join the new battles. The *Feldgendarmerie* was busy keeping order among the soldiers, providing necessary supplies to speed up their recovery, and assigning them to new locations on the Eastern Front. Erik hated his job but was secretly relieved that he didn't have to join the fighting army.

Meetings with Rose kept his spirit alive, and he hoped for an end to the war. It was not easy to find out about the land mines in the trenches. He knew they were concealed there but without help, he could not find out their locations. He decided to ask for help from one of his soldiers, who like him, was half Polish.

Erik approached the soldier he planned to talk to. "Hugo, can you spare one cigarette?" He took the cigarette, lit it, and inhaled without looking at Hugo.

They both looked towards the river, lost in their own thoughts.

"The war may end this year," said Erik, slowly releasing the smoke in a long breath.

"Dangerous to talk about it," muttered Hugo under his nose.

"Everything is dangerous right now. It was not supposed to be this way."

Hugo remained silent, looking at the river.

"Why did you join the *Feldgendarmerie*?" Erik kept up the conversation while appearing not to be much interested in it.

"I escaped the poverty." A long moment passed before he continued.

"We lived in Silesia. My father was German and my mother Polish. He died in a mining accident when I was ten years old. I had three sisters younger than me. After my father died, we were very poor. My mother's family had disowned her for marrying my father, and she wouldn't dare to ask for help from my German grandparents. They didn't like us anyway as we were the lower class to them. I was eighteen when Germans started recruiting men to serve in the army. It was my opportunity, so I joined."

"Was it a good decision?"

"It didn't really matter. You know that all half-German men had to join the army sooner or later."

"Like yours, my father was German and my mother Polish. I was raised equally in both cultures. After my Polish grandfather died, I lost close contact with that side of my family, and after Hitler's rise to power, my father became his strong supporter. I was sent to a military school and like my father, believed in the Third Reich."

"Do you believe in it right now?" Hugo didn't look at Erik; his sarcastic tone was that of a man who felt superior because his motives to join the war had been void of any moral stand or judgement of other people.

"Let's say that I'm not willing to die for the Reich anymore."

"Who would?" Hugo slowly exhaled the grey smoke of his cigarette.

"Have you heard that the SS mined the trenches?" asked Erik.

Hugo looked at him in disbelief. "Everybody knows that."

"They may ask us to protect the trenches. It would be terrible to die of our own mines."

"I know most of their locations. You and your ranks sometimes act like you're from a different world."

Erik faked surprise. "How so?"

"I can show you the markings so you don't have to worry about your life. Besides, you're a good lieutenant, so I can do that for you. We can take a walk right now." Hugo started walking towards the trenches.

For a week, Billy battled a high fever, drifting out of consciousness several times a day. Quiet voices around him whispered in a language he could not understand. He wanted to talk to them, to make sure they were real, but his throat was constricted and the voice wouldn't come out. In his moments of consciousness, he felt that his life was coming to an end. His mind drifted to the day he and his family went to visit his aunt and he saw the small plane. He knew right there that flying was his destination. He regretted that he had not been able to see his younger sister before she died from the influenza last winter. If he'd only known she was sick, he could have brought good medication from the Medmenham centre. He remembered her crippled body in the coffin, the funeral attended by the closest family only. She had been brave, always cheerful despite being bound to the wheelchair.

Jennie, are you coming for me? The thought formulated in his head, but he was afraid to say it out loud. *Jennie, I'll be a father soon. Don't take me yet. The baby needs me.*

The next time he woke up, a man with a scarred face covered in greying beard was spooning some water into his mouth.

"The worst is over," the man said in accented English. "Somebody will be here to help you with some food." He stood up and left the dim room.

After a little warm soup with bread, Billy felt stronger and more hopeful.

The woman tending to him was smiling as she touched his forehead. "Your fever is down; we'll take you out to get some air when it's dark."

"It's dark here all the time. Are you real or an angel?" Billy looked at her with a grin on his face.

The fresh air was exhilarating and Billy's strength doubled with each deep breath. The sky above him was clear and the first stars started to appear on the horizon. He looked up towards Heaven. *Thank you, Jenny, for giving me another chance at life.*

Two weeks after the plane crash, Billy was able to stay outside after dark, using crudely made crutches.

"We contacted the RAF in England and confirmed your identity. Until they can extract you from here, we may use your help in interpreting some maps and pictures."

"Anything you ask. I would love to help."

"Just remember that you can't come out of hiding until somebody takes you out every evening."

By the end of May, Billy's morale was high. Although he was still in some pain, the involvement in the underground activities lifted his spirit, and his admiration for the few men and one woman involved in caring for him and fighting the Germans was immense. Although he was a military man and had been fighting for his country since the beginning of the war, his actions seemed much less heroic in comparison to the daily danger these people were subjected to in order to save the Billys of the world, smuggle messengers across the country, and spy on Nazis and the Vichy soldiers cooperating with them.

"The Germans took most of your plane, but they left some pieces behind. I brought some for you to remember your beautiful Spitfire." A young man who had been in the room at least twice before dropped some pieces on the desk.

"My name is Billy. What's yours?"

"You can call me Jack."

"Jack it is. Could you bring me a small knife? Maybe I could carve something from the pieces you brought."

"Jean, the man with the limp, is a good carver. He can help you, but don't ask him many questions. He keeps to himself."

There were not many fragments of the plane and Jean started giving Billy carving lessons with pieces of wood. Soon Billy knew that metalwork was Jean's calling and carving was his favourite pastime. They developed a strange relationship, sort of father and son, and Billy sensed that having an opportunity to teach somebody and share his passion was a welcome addition to Jean's existence.

"Billy, what would you like to carve from the plane pieces? I think you're ready to do it."

"My wife is expecting our baby around this time. I would like to give her a brooch."

Billy observed Jean taking each piece of the smoke-covered metal and acrylic glass and putting them in different arrangements on the table.

"I think you can do it," said Jean. "But first you should draw the brooch. You could choose some colours and I might find some paint that you could use."

"I'll do that right away. Could I go out in the daytime? It would help me to draw the most beautiful brooch for my wife," Billy pleaded with Jean.

"I'm not the one in charge here. Let me check with the Andreas."

The first days of June were like a dream for Billy. After a month without seeing the sun and feeling its warmth on his face, Billy was exhilarated. Tucked behind the warehouse on a log of wood, he could hear a symphony of singing birds all around him. A plethora of colours assaulted his eyes and the gentle, warm breeze on his face was intoxicating.

He looked at the blue sky, which reminded him of the sea in Eastbourne when they had visited his aunt. The turquoise water and the occasional whitecap created an image of the brooch for Eloise. He sketched it carefully on a piece of paper and coloured it with the crayons Jean gave him.

It was an arduous and slow process to create the brooch.

Jean gave him some metalwork tools that could cut into the metal and acrylic glass from the Spitfire. After the rough shape was created, Billy, guided by his teacher, used very fine tools to create the final design, resembling the sea. The brooch was made from acrylic glass with a little sailing boat made from the metal piece and placed in the centre. The clasp of the brooch was an old one that Jean found in a box that had once contained beautiful pieces of jewellery.

"You asked for just a turquoise and white paint, but I brought you a red one as well. Perhaps you can use it in your design; it would be a good memory of your stay here in France."

"The colours of your flag, aren't they?"

"Let me tell you the history of the flag, as it resembles your turmoiled life somewhat." Jean closed his eyes and waited for a while before he spoke again.

"The history of the French flag reflects the turbulence of the country's past. Before the French Revolution, the country had settled on a Royal Coat of Arms in gold with a blue shield set on a white background. During the French Revolution, the Paris militia wore red and blue hats made of coloured ribbons, called cockades. They were the city's traditional colours. When the militia developed into the national guard, its first general, Gilbert Du Motier, Marquis de Lafayette, added white to the Parisian colours to create a tricolour national cockade. The cockade was incorporated into the uniform of the national guard. The flag adopted in 1790 was based on this national guard cockade and modified in 1794. During the 1815–1830 Bourbon rules, they used a royal white flag, but after the July revolution in 1830, the tricolour was brought back and has been in use ever since."

"Hello, Joey." Eloise was standing on the other side of the table in the small restaurant where they'd often met in the past.

She was rather small in her pregnancy. The blue sweater hung loosely over her body, hiding the full belly from the outside world. Her face was swollen and her eyes were red, looking at him from behind puffy eyelids.

At first, Joey had been annoyed by the invitation to meet, but looking across the table, he felt sorry for her, sensing that life was not easy being pregnant during these difficult times.

"How are you, Eloise?" he said after a long silence.

"Billy is missing in action." Tears flooded her eyes and a loud sobbing filled the space between them.

In the next half an hour, she told Joey about Billy's broken promise to stay away from flying, his new mission of taking the aerial photographs, and how he'd disappeared over France near the Maginot Line.

"Joey, the RAF is considering sending a rescue mission. They know his current location. He's hiding with the French underground."

Suddenly, Joey felt sick to his stomach, not only because of Billy's state but because of the fact that he'd avoided any contact with Billy in the last several months, betraying their friendship. Looking at Eloise in anticipation of more grim news, he took a sip of water.

"I would like to ask you to volunteer for the rescue mission," she said quietly, looking down at her hands folded on top of her abdomen.

Joey was speechless. Unexpected emotions started to rush through his body and he had the sensation of Billy looking at him, awaiting an answer.

"I'll do it," he said decisively and reached for her hand.

The planning for the rescue mission started two weeks later. They couldn't do much until Billy's leg and ribs were healed and he could walk on his own.

"He is in a good hiding spot. We're in contact with the French underground people who rescued him. One of them is Polish and you, Sergeant Wilk, are the best person to go there," the rescue mission coordinator said as he concluded the planning meeting.

It was the end of June 1944 when Joey was on the plane with a parachute on his back. He was carrying basic food and sanitary supplies as well as money to pay their way back to England. It was a dangerous mission and his life depended on the weather, the people on the ground, and many other factors that had been considered but were not possible to fully predict. They flew at night to have the best chance of avoiding the Germans spotting the plane. Joey thought about missing the opportunity to take part in Operation Overlord and the progress of the Allied Army into Normandy. The Germans were fighting fiercely, but the famous D-Day was being hailed as the beginning of the end of WWII. The RAF forces aiding the infantry had been crucial to the success of the operation. He wished he had been part of it, but at the same time, he was glad to save Billy and repay his debt to him.

His thoughts drifted to Vera. He had waited until their last meeting to tell her about the meeting with Eloise and about Billy accident and his rescue mission.

Vera was always very stoic and hid her emotions most of the time. It wasn't any different when he told her about the assignment until he mentioned Billy's name. "What is the last name of your friend?" she asked with unusual interest.

"Leavitt. William Leavitt," he answered before he realised that it was better to keep any names out of this conversation.

"I know him. We were together at the Medmenham training centre. We spoke a few times; he was always polite and never asked many questions. He never mentioned you, and I never thought that you two might know each other. Such a small world."

"He became a father last month and I was asked to be a godfather of their son." He was uncomfortable with the conversation. There were so many secrets in his life and he hoped they would never resurface for the sake of all involved. He'd seen the baby just a few days ago, a healthy blond boy with blue eyes. Joey thought that the baby resembled him more than Eloise or Billy. He got chills thinking about it and had put his head down when the pilot brought him back from his thoughts.

"Ten minutes to our destination. It's still dark outside. The sky is without any clouds— good conditions for landing. You'll be able to see the terrain and navigate your parachute. God be with you, Joey."

Speeding towards the earth, Joey felt free of his sins and his dark moods. It was a good feeling and he wanted to stay this way forever. A ray of sunshine caught his eye, awakening him from his ghostly state. He opened his parachute at the last moment before it was too late.

He saw forested landscape to the left of him. His landing spot was on the other side of the hill, far enough from the town to minimise the possibility of being spotted by the Germans or even the townspeople. He was well trained in navigating with the parachute, but a forest was always a difficult obstacle. Looking desperately for a place to land, he spotted a little clearing between the trees. He wasn't sure if it was a natural clearing or man-made. Anything man-made was more dangerous, due to the possibility of people's activities, but he had no other choice than to land. He landed smoothly on soft, wet ground.

After a moment of hesitation, Joey folded his parachute and ran toward the forest. The load was heavy, but leaving any trace of his presence in the open could lead to his capture and jeopardise the mission. His thoughts were totally on his assignment to bring Billy back home. In two minutes, he was in the shelter of the forest, his uniform wet and his shoes full of water. He sat under the leafy canopy of a big tree to take a breath. With a small spade, he dug a hole in the soft ground and hid his parachute there. From his knapsack, he removed a civilian jacket and a cap and placed them on the ground in front of him. He was halfway through removing his warm canvas jacket when a distant rustle of leaves alerted him to some movement. He quickly changed the jackets and covered the hole with a layer of dirt. The moment he moved to the other side of the tree trunk, a dog appeared in the clearing. Joey observed it as it sniffed the ground and slowly moved towards the tree. Expecting German soldiers coming into the clearing, he removed his pistol and waited. Although he was trained for combat and ready to fight to the death, he was scared and momentarily regretted taking on this mission. The dog came closer and sat in front of the tree.

"Shoo, shoo!" Joey frantically waved his hand at the dog.

To his surprise, the dog moved away and went back into the forest.

Joey quickly covered the fresh dirt with leaves and started moving deeper into the woods. After a while, not hearing any movement, he studied his crude map of the area, looking for the meeting place coordinates. He needed to go to higher ground to get there. With a compass in one hand and a pistol in the other, he moved silently between the trees. As he reached the top and looked up, a tremor shook his body. The same dog was already there and a tall, middle-aged man was looking at him.

"You're safe. Follow me."

After five days in a safe house, Joey was informed that he would be taken to the hiding place of Billy Leavitt. He dressed in grey trousers, a blue shirt, and a grey pullover provided by the man he'd met in the forest.

He never met anyone else in the safe house, although he could hear whispers in the late evening hours.

He looked at his reflection in the mirror and slowly put his head against the cold glass. His happiness to meet Billy vanished with the cold of the mirror's touch. He felt ashamed of being such a hypocrite, coming to save Billy when he'd already killed the friendship with him. The prospect of facing Billy while forcing himself to conceal all the lies and betrayal was suddenly unbearable. Would he be able to face the man he'd once loved and admired and pretend that nothing had happened between them? Billy was not aware of Joey's romance with Eloise and he hadn't suspected any betrayal on Joey's part. Should he come clean and tell Billy about Eloise and the child that was most likely Joey's? It would be honest and could clear Joey's heart, but what would it do to his friend's life and the life of the little child waiting for his father? His legs buckled and he sat down and wiped his forehead, suddenly covered with perspiration.

"Billy, somebody from the Royal Air Force is coming to meet with you." Andreas helped him to come out of the room and sit behind the warehouse.

"Who did you say is coming?"

"The only thing I can tell you for now is that he is from the RAF."

"But you must know why this person is coming."

"It is a rescue mission to take you back to England. I'll let you know when he will come to meet you."

Billy was in a state of disbelief. He was helping Andreas and Pierre communicate with the French organisation in London and other underground networks throughout Europe. With his drawing skills, he even helped to prepare some documents for people in hiding but never expected that a rescue mission could be organised to find him. He missed Eloise and often thought about his child, but he was not lonely here and was resigned to staying in France until the end of the war. Sometimes, when he closed his eyes and turned his face to the hot sun, he imagined himself and his family living here. He was learning the French language and had read some books by French writers. The Lorraine and Alsatian regions were full of sunshine, wine, and good cheese, things that were scarce in England, and Billy loved all of it. The information about the rescue mission had given him a little blow to his dreams. He wasn't sure if going back to England at this time was what he wanted the most. Although he still loved flying and being a pilot was his purpose in life, he questioned this destiny. Eloise wanted him to stop flying, but he had no other training that would allow him to make a good living outside of the military. After the two crashes that he'd luckily survived, he was losing his faith that he would survive the third one if it happened. He watched the setting sun for a long time and willed himself to be hopeful in his future and to take a day at a time and maybe, to come back here again.

The next day morning, he shaved and dressed early, ready to meet his rescuer. Since his substantial health improvement and better mobility, he'd been allowed to sleep in the warehouse behind the barrels. He practiced a quick retreat to his bunker after clearing his bedding and placing it in an empty barrel. He was able to complete his disappearance in under five minutes, enough time before any unwelcome person could discover him.

"Good morning, Billy. I brought you some breakfast." It was the young man who had earlier introduced himself as Jack. Billy's disappointment must have shown on his face because Jack looked at him with a puzzled look.

"You don't like what I brought you?"

"No, it's not that. I was expecting somebody else, the Englishman."

"I don't know about anyone from England," Jack replied quickly and he left the breakfast on the top of the barrel that had been set as a night table.

Left alone, Billy was staring at the food when Andreas came in. "Billy, you're a trained military man, don't ask dangerous questions of people other than myself."

Billy slowly recovered his bearings and looking up, he shook his head. "Sorry, I was prepared to meet the RAF person this morning and didn't think straight when Jack came here with the breakfast."

"I should have told you yesterday that it will be at least a week before you meet the man. We need to take every precaution to prevent the Germans or any possible collaborator from discovering our cell. He is in a safe house until we know that nobody was alerted to his arrival."

The days were dragging as if there was no end to them. Billy wrapped and unwrapped the brooch many times to calm his nerves. Holding the brooch in his hands gave him a feeling of calm and resignation to the fact that the future wasn't in his hands anymore.

When the day came, Billy was less prepared mentally than he had been earlier in the week. Waiting was making him unsure of anything that was about to happen.

"You'll meet him this evening." Andreas shook his shoulder. "Be prepared."

"What is his name?"

"You will find out soon."

The meeting was arranged in the warehouse close to the main entrance. All the employees were gone at that time of the day and all safety precautions were taken by the few people involved.

A man with a cheerful voice stood in the entrance. "Good evening, Billy."

"Joey! I can't believe it!" Billy froze in half step as Joey ran to him. Both men embraced for a long time while Andreas looked surprised and confused by the scene.

After a long talk about their lives, particularly about Eloise and the baby, Billy and Joey finally went to sleep in the hidden corner of the warehouse. Lying on the mattress, Joey felt relieved and assured that keeping the biggest secret of his life to himself was the right decision. His feeling of betrayal and lies vanished and he could concentrate on his secret undertaking. To accomplish it, he needed the help of a local person. The next day, both friends spent the afternoon at the back of the warehouse. Joey met Andreas and Jack but they kept their distance and later left the premises.

"Billy, who is the most trusted man here?"

"They all are, including the wife of the owner. Hope you can meet her; she is a nurse and she saved my life."

"What about the owner of this place? Is he a part of the cell?"

"He only learned about its existence when I arrived here. Somehow, they managed to run it under his nose without his awareness."

"But you said his wife was involved."

"Most likely she was able to keep him away from it, and he never suspected that she was involved. The less we know, the better."

"Maybe she would be able to help me." Joey was whispering more to himself than Billy.

"Help you with what?"

"It's a long story and only three people know about it."

"You've got me intrigued. You must tell me before I suggest the best person to help you."

It was already dark when Joey finished telling the story about the father he'd never met.

"You think he was really in Thionville and was buried here in town?" Billy was fascinated with the story of Joey's father and the friendship with his half-brother.

"I haven't thought about my father for a long time, but when Eloise asked me to volunteer for the rescue mission, I remembered the story about his death here."

"What would you like to do about it?" asked Billy reaching for Joey's hand.

"I would like to find his grave if anyone could take me to the cemetery."

"We can ask the man in charge here".

The Germans were losing many of their battles on the Eastern Front. The Russian Army offensive operation code-named Bagration inflicted the biggest losses in German military history. But Hitler was still claiming some victories against the Russians and many troops from other fronts were being moved to the east.

"Erik, I'm glad you brought the information about the mines, but I beg you to be careful." Rose was pleading with him while nestled in his arms.

"My dearest, nobody is safe right now. Let's not talk about it."

They sat for a long time, looking at the horizon and the orange sun slowly coming down. Like the Third Reich, it had been glowing and powerful not long ago, but now it was already on its way to darkness. Erik's thoughts were neither happy nor unhappy. He had stopped expecting much for himself; he only wanted to protect Rose and allow her to dream about the future, maybe even with him.

Next day, a young officer approached Erik. "Lieutenant Hermann, you're requested to report to the Gestapo office right now. Please follow me."

Erik entered an office that had been previously occupied by the *Wehrmacht* officer. Nothing had changed since the Gestapo took over. There were only more maps on the table.

"Heil Hitler," he said reluctantly, knowing that refusing to use this greeting could mean a sentence to the Eastern Front.

"Heil Hitler. It was brought to our attention that some of your people might be delivering information to the Polish underground. We caught one sneaking around the trenches. We're not wasting time to interrogate him, but as a punishment, he will be sent to the Eastern Front immediately."

"Who is the soldier?" Erik asked, dreading the answer.

216

"Hugo Lemrik."

"I need every man to police the area and provide order to the troops recovering from the front." Erik knew that this plea was useless but he had to try.

"You'll work with your remaining men and make sure you do a better job of controlling them."

Late at night, Erik was tormented by the fact of sending another man to his imminent death. He looked back at his life, wondering at what point he'd become the man he now despised. Was it when his grandfather died and he was plunged into a life of discipline, order, and duty? Was it when he joined the military school where he was subjected to blind obedience and fear of questioning anything? Was it when he joined the German Army and started believing in the superiority of his race and its right to rule the world? Or even worse, was it when he started his assignments of infiltrating the underground networks, sending men and women to their deaths because that could elevate his standing in German Army?

Erik could not grasp the true nature of his personality. It could be full of compassion when returned to its basic instinct, but when serving his ideals, it was calculated and devoid of any human feeling towards others.

He looked back at the recent history of the rise of the Nazis, clearly seeing that it was people like him who had allowed evil to spread and dominate the world. When Hitler had come to power, it was obvious that measures had to be taken to channel the tensions among the people arising from the feeling of unjust treatment by the Treaty of Versailles, which had created the high unemployment and maybe even the lack of prospects for a better future. Hitler brought a solution that promised prosperity to the masses and they accepted it without question. He made it right to blame others for their misfortunes, to replace reason with total obedience. Now Erik could see the evil that had spread from one possessed man to a group of his closest backers, to party members, and to the majority of the German people. The evil that told them they didn't have to think, that it was their right to take from others and claim as their own. The ones that questioned were robbed of freedom, their property damaged and possessions looted. The evil had spread its dark forces and people felt superior under the spread of the protective wings of the Nazi domination.

Desperately, Erik wanted to find an explanation for his shameful life, and grabbing onto the notion of an all-powerful evil almost brought him some relief. But thoughts of Rose disintegrated the elusive relief. He clearly realised that the blame for his actions was with him.

Any explanations that ran through his mind were only meagre excuses to avoid looking directly into his soul, the substance of his existence. He could no longer escape the moral obligation to recognise wrong from right and had to accept the shame coming from this realisation. He decided to save Hugo by accepting the blame for spying.

But the next morning, when he woke up in his warm bed, thinking about the relative safety of his current situation, he pushed from his mind the thoughts of personal responsibility and decided against any action on his part, justifying it with the ugliness of the war. He knew that the chances of saving Hugo were close to none, and if he tried to save his soldier, the Gestapo could send him to the Eastern Front as well. He didn't want to die; he chose to stay alive and deal with his blemished honour for the rest of his life. It was just one more merciless act in the reservoir of many in his past few years.

Jean turned to the Bible to find inner peace almost every day. After the accident followed by amnesia, he could not recall the faith he was raised in and assumed that like most French, he was a Catholic. It was an assumption of convenience to be aligned with Emilie's Catholic upbringing.

Over the centuries, many people in Lorraine and Alsace had turned away from the Catholic religion forced upon them by the French and turned to the Protestant faith that was practiced by many of their ancestors long before the St. Bartholomew's Day massacre of the Huguenots in Paris in August 1572.

Tonight's reading brought some calm and reflection to Jean's life. "Create in me a clean heart, O God, and renew a right spirit within me." He repeated the passage several times, hoping to be guided by it every day. The events of the last two months had been stressful, especially learning of his wife's involvement in the underground movement.

Late in the evening, Emilie sat next to Jean and took his hand in hers, interrupting his silent reading. "Darling, I have something to say, but I need you to stay calm."

Jean could not grasp her words at first. "Calm? What do you mean?" His voice was low with a touch of panic.

"Nothing bad, just memories that may upset you." She squeezed his hand and continued. "The pilot who came on the rescue mission to take Billy back to England is Polish. He said that his father worked here in the foundry."

"Many immigrants worked in the foundry. What is your point?"

"He said that his father died in an accident here, and that his name was Joseph Novak."

"Joe, my friend that lived here with me?"

"Yes, my darling. It is him."

Sitting with closed eyes, Jean was silent for a long time. Emilie waited patiently to allow him to calm the nerves that always were on edge whenever his thoughts went back to that terrible day.

"The pilot asked for help in finding his father's grave."

Jean recovered his composure. "Does he know that we were friends?"

"No, not yet."

"What are we going to do about it?"

"We must tell him the truth about your friendship with Joseph and take him to the grave."

"Can you take the children to the market tomorrow? I'd like to meet the pilot in person in the house."

Jean brought the Bible to his heart, looking for strength and inspiration to face the son of his deceased friend.

The next morning, he slowly limped towards the kitchen door after he heard the loud knock.

"Good morning, Mr. Navarre." A young man dressed in Jean's old trousers and sweater stood on the other side of the door. He was taller than average and had a muscular torso and a friendly face. The blue eyes and dark blond hair made him look Slavic, similar to but more refined than some of the Polish men who at times worked in his cooperage shop.

"Please come in." Jean was conscious of his limited English but comfortable enough to have this conversation. In the last two months, his spoken English had improved considerably as a result of the many conversations he'd had with Billy.

"My name is Joey Wilk, Joseph like my father."

Jean motioned to Joey to follow him to the living room, where a plate of cheese and two cups of tea were set on the small table near the window. He spoke slowly, choosing the correct words. "I heard that you were inquiring about the grave of your father, who worked here in Thionville and died in an accident."

"Yes, sir. That is true."

"Tell me about your father."

"I never knew him."

"I'm confused. What do you mean, you never knew your father?"

"I learned about him when I was eighteen years old."

In the next half hour, Joey told Jean about his family, his mother's early death, learning about his biological father, meeting Ted, Joseph's son from his legitimate marriage, and Joseph's death here in Thionville.

"That is a sad story." Jean sighed and took a sip of already cold tea.

"Oh, not so sad. My father who raised me was the best father I could have. Ted, my half-brother, became my good friend. Even my father liked Ted."

"I have some information for you. Maybe Andreas told you that I had an accident and lost my memory."

"No sir, he didn't tell me that. I just inquired about finding my father's grave."

"What I'm going to tell you next is the knowledge that I gained from others."

When Jean finished his story about his friendship with Joseph, it was already past noon and the sun was high on the horizon.

Joey sat silently looking past Jean with unfocused eyes. The surprise painted on his face changed to bewilderment and then sadness. "My father lived here in this house and sat at this table many times. The coincidence of me sitting at the same table is unbelievable."

"Life chooses strange paths for us people. Sometimes I'm glad I lost my memory; it's easier this way."

"I have to go now." Joey stood, ready to leave.

"Wait a moment. I have something that was left behind by Joseph. Would you be fine if I gave it to you?"

Joey didn't answer; his face was blank because he was almost not ready to absorb more.

Jean removed a little box from the windowsill close to the table. "Here are some letters from his wife in Poland, a small photograph of her and their two children, and a small carving of a cross."

"Thank you. I won't know what to do with it."

"It is yours now, young man, and you can do whatever you wish. In the next few days, you'll be taken to your father's grave."

Joey came back to the shelter in the warehouse and sat at the desk cluttered with papers and various small tools. The box in his hand was unopened when Billy came inside.

"You were in the house for a long time. What did you learn?"

"Here are some things that belonged to my father. Jean and he were friends once, and he lived here in this house."

"That is spooky. What on earth put us here in this part of the world? Maybe there is a path designed for all of us." Seeing Joey's face full of pain rather than the joy of the discovery, Billy was trying to be lighthearted.

"Maybe Andreas will let me go through the tunnel to the forest. I need to be alone to absorb all this. It's more than I ever imagined."

"Maybe I can go with you," Billy offered.

"No, I need time to myself before I can go to see his grave."

"I'll check with Andreas for you." Billy left the shelter.

Later in the day, Andreas came to the back of the warehouse where Joey and Billy sat on a bench.

"Sorry, we cannot allow you to go to the forest. Our operation here cannot be jeopardised by any unnecessary movements. I'm sure you understand that."

"Yes, I do. By the way, my name is Joey Wilk."

"We prefer to avoid using names as much as possible. Better for everybody's safety."

"Of course, I'm not thinking straight right now."

"We will let you know about the grave." Andreas disappeared inside Jean's house.

"How can they live here in such secrecy?" Joey asked and immediately regretted the question.

"Joey, in England, we fight the Germans from afar, flying our planes. We know the danger of the war, but we don't experience it every day. Here it's different. Their underground actions have to be undertaken under the noses of the Germans. Every movement has to be calculated and plans for every possibility have to be in place as much as possible."

"Yes. I should have thought about it before asking."

"When we're out of here, I'll tell you about my rescue here. Most bizarre—I could write a book about it."

"That's an idea, maybe we will do it together, about yours and my experience here." Joey smiled for the first time since he'd come back from the meeting with Jean.

After Billy left the shelter, Joey removed the cross from the box and looked at the beautiful carving. It was made of dark wood, most likely mahogany, with insets of metal creating the letters IHS. Joey knew the letters were a Christogram symbolising the name of Jesus Christ. Until now, his thoughts about Joseph had had a negative undertone, but looking at the cross, he realised that life wasn't as simple as black and white. His father must have been a religious man, living his complicated life in the only way he knew was possible. It dawned on Joey that he was repeating the mistakes of his father. He took the small picture and looked at Maria, Ania, and Ted. Closing his eyes, he wondered, *How many stepbrothers and sisters will my son have? Will he ever learn the truth about his biological father?* His thoughts drifted to the father who had raised him. He missed him very much. Slowly, he opened his eyes and thought of Billy with the hope that his friend would be a great father to the little boy. He decided to read the letters later and if possible, bury them at the gravesite. They belonged to Joseph and no one else.

Three days later, in the late afternoon, Emilie took Joey to the cemetery. They entered through a massive iron gate with one side opened during daytime. The sight of the cemetery took Joey's breath away. A vast city of catacombs and monuments spread out in front of him. Most were built from grey stones with surfaces covered in moss and dark smudges that had embraced the graves throughout the centuries. Most of the crosses were carved from the same stone, but the tangle of them was broken up by some graves with iron crosses and fences around them. It was June and the trees and bushes between the resting places were in bloom, making the cemetery more like a mysterious garden, not a place of sorrow and reflection.

There were subtly visible influences of German and French culture. Emilie pointed out the few Germanic graves, which were more austere in design and some looked abandoned.

Emilie looked sadly at the abandoned graves. "Even after death, the people are divided as was the land of Alsace and Lorraine."

They walked in silence, not wanting to disturb the quiet of the place until they reached a newer part of the cemetery.

His father's grave had a simple stone and an iron cross with a plate bearing his name and the date of his death. Joey noticed that the grass was freshly cut around the grave and some fresh flowers had been placed on the stone. Was it done just for his visit or had somebody cared for the grave all the time, he wondered. He removed a piece of cloth from his pocket, unfolded it carefully, and scattered the ashes stored there. The day before, he had burned the letters after reading them carefully and memorising some passages. Maybe one day he would be able to see Ted and tell him about this place.

"The cross was made by Joseph's coworkers from the foundry," whispered Emilie.

"Did you know my father?"

"I never met him. He was a close friend of Jean's."

Joey lifted his head and looked straight into her eyes. "Back in Poland, we heard some stories that he hadn't died."

"I'm certain that Joseph died. He was in the same accident as Jean. It was the quick action of the people at the foundry that saved Jean. There was nothing they could do to save your father. I'm sorry." Emilie looked carefully at Joey, who turned his head towards the cross. Looking at his profile with the short beard he grew in the last few days, he reminded her of Jean from the early days of their marriage. Her mind drifted to the days in the hospital when she'd looked after Jean and nursed him back to health, to the days when he wouldn't open his eyes although she knew that he was conscious. She recalled the morning when he finally opened his one eye and smiled upon hearing the name of Jean Navarre. The tension on his half-burned face had disappeared as he squeezed her hand.

Looking back at Joey, a horrifying thought crossed her mind, but she rejected it right away. She looked at the grave and forced herself to be assured that the man inside was the Polish worker, Joseph Novak. The thought kept pressing on her temples. Joe Novak, Jean Navarre—the names could sound similar to somebody who'd just recovered from a coma but could not remember anything else. She willed herself to look back at Joey and this time, she didn't see the resemblance.

"Joey, time to go back," she said.

"Thank you for taking the risk of bringing me here." He took her hand, raised it to his mouth and kissed it.

A shiver shook her body as she realised that Jean would kiss her hand regularly.

"Is this something that Polish men do?" She stepped back in a rapid, nervous way and walked towards the entrance of the cemetery.

Two weeks had gone by since the two pilots had left Thionville. Jean waited for news from Andreas about their safe passage to England. In the last three months, Jean had learned to trust his foreman to conduct their underground work with the fullest secrecy and all possible precautions to minimise the danger to his family. They built the fence separating the shop and warehouse from his private property to discourage his children from wandering near the warehouse. His son was over fourteen years of age and as tall as Jean. He loved to study and had not shown any interest in the business. His passion was languages and mathematics and he was hoping to go to university one day. Jean didn't remember his passions as a young boy and sometimes regretted with sadness that whatever he had learned as a young man was erased from his life. Whatever he had liked in his youth was gone, but his skills in wrought-iron design and his love for carving had stayed. Often, looking at his son Jean-Marc with pride, he could see the strong resemblance to Emilie with the same dark eyes and wavy hair. He was happy that Jean-Marc took after his mother. Emilie was a formidable woman, positive and supportive. She was good at everything she decided to do and Jean hoped that his son would be a great man one day.

His daughter Marie-Ann was the sparkle of his life. At twelve years of age, she wanted to be like her mother. She loved gardening and helping Emilie at the market. She had a great imagination and a talent for crafts. Her drawings of flowers and birds were hung all over her bedroom and two had been framed by Jean and were hanging in the living room. She had blue eyes like him and brown hair, cut very short. She resembled Jean but he could see that she was changing every year and the resemblance was fading. He imagined her taking over the cooperage business and being one of the few women that could run a business on her own.

"Jean, are you awake?" he heard Emilie whispering from the other side of the bed.

"Yes, I'm thinking about Marie-Ann taking over the business one day. I think she will be good at it, like you with your garden and market."

She didn't respond to his words but moved closer to him and took his hand in hers. "Jean, do you remember anything from your past?"

His body tensed and he could hear his own heavy breathing in the silence of the night.

"When I took the Polish pilot to his father's grave, the sun came onto one side of him, illuminating his face, and he looked like you."

"What are you saying, Emilie?"

"For a short while, I thought that perhaps there had been a mix-up and you're not Jean Navarre but Joseph Novak."

Jean remained silent for a moment, looking into the darkness. "Why would you ask about this? There were witnesses during the accident." His breathing was calmer now than a few minutes ago.

"I love you, Jean and I don't really care about your past, but what if you're Joseph and you have family in Poland?" Her whisper was almost inaudible.

"I don't remember anything prior to the accident. I'm sure that the witnesses were right. I'm Jean Navarre."

"It's all very strange. The young man who never knew his father came to your house to rescue his friend. It's too much of a coincidence. It's almost as if God wanted him to come here."

"I think we should sleep now."

Jean paced back and forth between two garden chairs in the backyard, his face pallid despite his summer suntan. The grey in his otherwise dark beard emphasised his lack of grooming in the last few days. He saw Emilie going to the attic and suspected that she was looking through a box with old items that had been put away after the accident in the foundry. He had never wanted to look at the contents of the box until recently, when he'd removed the few items of Joseph's to give them to his son. Since then, the box had an unsettling hold on him, filling his heart with dread that something sinister was hidden inside it. He was almost sure that Emilie sensed his uneasiness and had decided to confront it by going through the box. The words had not been spoken between them but Jean knew that she wanted to find something to ease his suffering.

Afraid that his nervous pacing might attract the attention of his children or the workers, he went in the direction of the warehouse. He almost collided with Andreas, who was walking from the shop to the warehouse pushing a cart with barrel lids.

"Good afternoon, boss." Andreas stopped to allow Jean to go first. Although the two men were more like friends, Andreas always treated Jean as a superior, showing the respect demanded by his status as the business owner.

"It's late. Why are you still here?" Jean said absentmindedly.

"Have nothing to do at my small apartment; it's easier to keep busy working."

"Have you heard from the young men?" Jean didn't look at Andreas when he asked about Billy and Joey.

"Ah, you miss them too. We all do. The three months with Billy were very intense but left many good memories."

"I think about the two of them frequently. Perhaps they would want to come back here one day, maybe even stay," said Jean looking towards the back of the warehouse.

"Billy was talking about coming back here with his wife and son to work at your cooperage or maybe even to start something of his own."

"I guess the weather and the wine could convince anyone to move here permanently. What about you, Andreas?"

"I'm just living day by day, waiting for the end of the war. Don't want to make any plans until it's over."

"Yes, of course."

Seeing Emilie standing on the porch in front of the house, Jean lost interest in the conversation. He dreaded approaching his wife as if something unexplainable was hanging in the air. The feeling transfixed him and he thought of escape as the only way out of facing her. Since their conversation at night about Joseph, he was fearful of any confrontation with Emilie that would involve the accident. He stopped, waiting for the dread to disappear. After a while, he looked at Emilie still standing on the porch and moved towards her.

"I found this." She extended a small sepia picture towards Jean.

He didn't take it from her. Instead, he looked at her with a bewildered expression.

"The back of it states that this picture is of Joseph Novak. It was taken in September 1929."

He stood silent, lost in his inability to remember anything clearly. There were places, people, even church bells, but all of it was in a far distance, covered with dense fog and it dissolved before he could even see it.

"Jean, the picture could be of you. Do you remember anything from your past?"

There was only blackness in his mind and he started to tremble. "Joseph lived here with me, and the picture must have been put away with some of his belongings that were not sent to his wife."

She looked at him with tenderness in her eyes. "Whatever happened on that day, remember that I love you; you're my husband, the father of our children. You're Jean to me."

He didn't permit himself to understand the full meaning of her words.

"He is dead," was his only response. He looked straight into her eyes and what he saw deep inside them was acceptance.

The news coming from the East was full of hope and despair. At times, Ted would refuse to believe that the Bolsheviks might be as dangerous as the Nazis. They were fighting the same enemy as Ted was. They were supported by the Allies and had sacrificed so many lives to free the world from darkness. It was difficult to comprehend that they were as evil as the Home Army command portrayed them to be.

He wanted some clarification to his nagging question about what happened after the operation called *Ostra Brama* July 7 – 14 when the Home Army fighters pushed out the Germans from Vilnius, declaring it a great Polish victory. Was it true that the next day the Soviet Army entered the city and arrested Polish officers and forced the Polish fighters to join the Polish People's Army (PPA) that was organised by the communist and left-wing parties?

With more information trickling in to Brusk about the approaching Russian Army, Ted considered the possible influence of the Polish People's Army on the outcome of the liberation of Poland. What would a possible life under the communists look like? The Home Army's portrayal of the PPA was one of evil, and Ted's command demanded that they must fight the Nazis and the Bolsheviks equally.

On July 23, Ted was ordered to an unexpected meeting in the crypt.

"Yesterday, Radio Moscow broadcasted the Polish Committee of National Liberation's Manifesto," George announced with a sombre face.

"What does it mean?" Ted appeared subdued.

"The committee was formed together with the main Polish communist organisations. As you know, since 1940, the Polish communists supported by Stalin have been slowly growing in power and the Polish Workers' Party has already established a conspiratorial State National Council, which they declare to be the wartime national parliament in Warsaw."

"But they were never recognised and accepted by the Polish people or the exiled government." Ted kept pressing for more news.

"We don't know the details of the manifesto yet. The Radio Moscow broadcast was vague and sounded more like something that was not finalised yet."

"What is London advising us to do?"

"You, Bolek, and I will meet in the crypt every day at 5 a.m. We hope that a clear action will be decided very soon. After the message from London, we will meet with the Peasant Battalions command to form a plan."

Soon the news they expected gave them new hope. The Lviv uprising of the Home Army started with full force as part of a secret plan to launch the countrywide, all-national uprising ahead of the Soviet advance on the Eastern Front.

The preparations for the general uprising intensified as a new wave of young, wounded, and exhausted German soldiers from the Eastern Front arrived in Brusk and were stationed in many houses. Their presence hampered the Home Army actions and extra precautions had to be taken all the time. There was a vast contrast between the morale of the arriving soldiers and their command. The soldiers were deflated, hoping for the end of the war and afraid of going back to the front. The command, especially the SS, were vicious, not only towards the Polish people but also towards the young soldiers, and they spread fear and propaganda about winning the war.

Under the darkness of night, Ted, promoted to the rank of sergeant, led his squadron with the delivery of bags full of weapons and medical supplies to the cell operating in the forest ten kilometres away from Brusk. From there, another cell picked up the supplies and delivered them to designated hiding spots in the near vicinity of Warsaw. In addition to the weapons and medical supplies, some bags contained a Polish flag and arm bandanas made feverishly quickly by Rose and Ania in Ted's shop.

July 1944 was an anxious time for Erik. Nazi propaganda from Berlin spewed exaggerated stories about victories and a renewal of German domination of the world. In Brusk, the tension among the young Polish people was rising and Erik felt that the acceptance of him that he'd gained in the last few months was evaporating quickly. A letter from his mother informed him that his father's health was failing and they were thinking about moving to Grandfather's farm. Erik asked for three days of leave to visit his family and to his surprise, one was granted to him. The day before his leave, he met with Rose in their secluded spot by the river.

"Darling, I'm going to visit my parents for a few days."

Rose was silent for a while before she looked at him. "Don't stay in Warsaw and don't ask me why."

"Why did I fall in love with you during such troubled times? I'm only bringing hardship to your life." Erik was talking more to himself than Rose.

"You roused me from a life that had no hope for a better future. Yes, the war is awful but it will end soon, and together we will see the world and live our lives to their full potential. I was just a child when the war started and it did take my hope away from me. Young people want to be happy and loved even in such difficult times. You gave me both the love and happiness. I'll always love you. Promise that you'll be back in a a few days."

Erik turned towards her as they lay on the grass and tilted her face towards his. "I promise." Soon, exhausted but exhilarated from making love, they rested on the grass, looking at the blue sky.

Erik took the train to Warsaw where he had a two-hour wait for a connection to Gdańsk. The local train didn't have a first class but the first two cars were reserved strictly for the Germans. There were very few soldiers on the train, and Erik was relieved that he didn't have to talk to anyone. Waiting at the train station in Warsaw, he sensed a tension among the travellers. People were walking quickly and with a purpose showing on their faces and suddenly he remembered Rose's warning to avoid Warsaw. He didn't know the city well but the train station was very familiar to him as he had changed trains there on many occasions. He didn't want to remember those occasions; they were mostly in his past: Lublin, Krakow, Gdańsk, Berlin. Each time in the past, he had felt superior dressed in his smart officer's uniform, looking down at local passengers. But on that late July day of 1944, he didn't have any feeling of superiority, just the opposite. He sensed that the city and the people in it were like a ticking bomb ready to explode and oust the occupiers. There was no fear and submission in their eyes or their bodies. They walked like proud victors that had already taken what was theirs. He thought about the Russian Army fighting to the east and approaching Warsaw. That could not be the source of their triumphant attitude. The Polish people hated and feared the Bolsheviks as much as the Nazis. There must have been something else they were experiencing, but what?

The train to Gdańsk arrived and Erik boarded together with a few other Germans. He didn't want to talk to anyone and after a short while, he moved to the restaurant car and sat at the small table farthest away from the bar. He ordered some food and a glass of schnapps and thought about his strange feeling at the Warsaw station. He concluded that influenced by Rose's warning, he must have imagined the defiance and proudness of the people. After two hours in the restaurant, he returned to his train compartment and immediately pretended to be asleep. He was not in a mood to talk to any soldiers that might sit next to him.

It was early evening when he arrived in Gdańsk. Although tempted to walk the streets of his childhood city, he decided to take a taxi to get home before his parents went to sleep. A few days earlier, he had telephoned to inform them about his arrival. He was longing to see the joy on his mother's face and hopefully some on his father's as well. It was his father who opened the door.

"Welcome home, my son."

They embraced but after an awkward few seconds, his father removed himself from Erik's arms and called his wife.

She came out of the bedroom, dressed in a beautiful summer dress, her hair done in a French roll, and lipstick freshly applied to look the best she could, to greet her son. After a long embrace, she took his jacket and hung it on the rack near the entrance. "We shall celebrate your arrival with some food and drink."

They sat at the table and shared their meal of sausage and potatoes with a fresh cucumber salad on the side. The conversation was light and to Erik's surprise, his father didn't talk at all about the Germans losing or winning the war. He was quieter than in the past and Erik could see that his illness had taken a considerable vitality from him.

During the next few days, they talked about moving to the west to stay with Father's parents on the farm. Father acknowledged that the war was coming to its end and a small village would be a safer place to be than Gdańsk.

On the last day of his visit, Erik's father gave him a little package that contained a miniature silver cross and a ring with the family insignia. "The cross and the signet have belonged to our family for many generations. It's always the first son who receives them after the death of his father. I'm not dead yet, but my days are numbered and I want you to have these little mementos." Otto Hermann stood from his chair and father and son embraced for a long time.

"I'll wear the cross and the signet with pride."

Later, when his father had retired to bed, Erik helped his mother with the dishes and after that, they sat for a long time, speaking quietly in Polish.

On the morning of his departure from home, Erik's mother pressed a small box into his hand, saying, "May God keep you in his care."

On July 27th, dreadful news arrived from Lviv. The Home Army had defeated the Germans, but the Soviets then entered the city and disarmed the Polish troops. Soldiers were merged into the Polish People's Army and the ones who refused were sent to the Gulag camps. It was such a dark reminder of the uprising of Vilnius. Two Polish cities that had been occupied by the Nazis were now in the hands of the Bolsheviks. Ted hoped against all hope that the information received through the underground network and the radio communication with London had been misinterpreted. The Polish Army was fighting alongside the Russian Army and they were fighting to free Poland not to send people to Gulags. That was the news Ted wanted to believe; otherwise, his belief in free Poland would crumble.

"Mother, I would like you to bless me." Ted knelt in front of her.

"So, the time came." She put her hand on his head.

"My squadron is leaving at night to march to Warsaw. We should be there in three days."

A nearly inaudible sob jerked Ted's head towards the door of the bedroom. Ania was standing there with her apron raised to her eyes. She tried to suppress the cry, but it turned into a convulsion of her shoulders and an animal-like sound of panic.

Ted arose from the kneeling position and gently took her in his strong arms. "I promise I'll be back." He left the house in the dark of the night.

Erik was back at his base on July 29th and was immediately dispatched to control the roads and train station in Brusk and look for unusual movement of people. He was not given a clear reason for this order and sensed that there was a lot of uncertainty on the base and even a silent undercurrent of unexplained fear. Early on the morning of July 30th, he left the base with his men. He assigned five of them to control the train station and divided the rest of them into three groups to patrol the roads leading to Warsaw. A young driver rode the motorcycle while Erik sat in the sidecar with a map open in his lap. All day they cruised between his men, getting updates. The train station was busier than on other days, mostly with people coming from Warsaw. Although the train station was a small one, it was a hub for local commuters going to various towns south of Brusk.

"Have you questioned any of the people?" Erik asked one of the men he'd assigned to the station.

"Yes, they said they were going to visit families to spend a few days of summer outside of Warsaw," the soldier in charge reported to Erik.

"Anything suspicious?"

"Nothing, mostly mothers with children."

The roads were also busier than normal, but Erik's people didn't find anything suspicious. They searched a few cars and found only families with personal possessions. Erik remembered Rose's warning to avoid Warsaw and this increased traffic made him suspicious that something was about to happen, but since nothing suspicious was found, he kept any thought to himself. Next day, he learned that the Russian Army had arrived near

Warsaw and built camps on the east bank of the Vistula River. It was not surprising to Erik; he knew about the Soviets progressing towards Warsaw, but it nevertheless gave him a chill. They were only fifty kilometres apart and despite the trenches built along the small river with good fortifications, Erik knew that it was not enough to defend against the Soviets.

On August 1, Erik was informed that the people of Warsaw had taken up arms against the German Army stationed in the city. As the members of the *Feldgendarmerie*, he and his people were not involved in direct battle. But the order he received to stand by and wait for further instructions was perturbing him. In the next few days, the news of the uprising was the main talk on the base. The Gestapo unit was in full readiness to leave the base and was waiting for the final order. They were equipped with flamethrowers, ready to kill anyone in their way. It was disturbing to even think that he could be sent to fight alongside them.

Ted and his men were on the second night of the march when it was halted around twenty kilometres outside of Warsaw. Ted was called to a meeting with a few other men of his rank. They waited for almost an hour in total silence before an officer in a battered, pre-war uniform of the Polish Army joined their circle.

"The Soviet Army arrived in Praga, a district of Warsaw on the east bank of the Vistula River." His voice was filled with anxiety, indicating rather bad news.

Ted knew that he should wait for more information from the officer, but his impatience took over. "The uprising is scheduled for tomorrow, August 1st. Will the Soviets help to fight the Germans?"

"There is the Polish People's Army alongside the Russians and they are eager to enter Warsaw tonight. Our command is in discussions with the Russians, but we don't have a clear answer yet."

"What about us? We're very close."

"You're to wait until new orders come from London."

The rumours were already rampant in the camp. They heard that the Russian Army had refused to enter Warsaw, that many of the Polish

People's Army who'd arrived with the Russians had defied their orders and crossed the river to join the fighters.

The most terrifying news spread like wildfire on August 7th. Around 40,000 men, women, and children had been murdered by the Germans during massacres in one district of Warsaw. The absence of clear direction from the Home Army command was unbearable and some partisans decided to march towards Warsaw, hoping to enter the city.

The morale amongst Ted's men was very low and it took all his energy to keep order in his camp while waiting for orders. Serving in the Home Army since its inception had instilled in Ted respect for orders and suppression of any actions that were not directly issued by the command.

After a few days of waiting and watching in horror as fires sprouted above the Warsaw skyline, the waiting men were dismissed and ordered to march back home.

Two long weeks passed before Erik was able to get permission to leave the base. He was perturbed when he didn't find Rose in the store, and he decided to go to her house. Since the accident, and Hela's injury, Erik had been allowed to visit Rose in the house but only if Rose invited him. Going to her house without her knowledge could be unsafe for the entire family if other people were there. Erik suspected that most of the people in Poland were conspiring against the Germans, although nothing obvious could be noticed. He decided to go to the orchard first with a faint hope that Rose might be there. He knew her favourite apple tree and went towards it. The tree with big branches hanging down under the load of apples was a magnificent sight. *It must have been the first tree planted in this orchard generations ago*, thought Erik. Nobody was around but he found baskets of apples under the tree and a ladder leaning against its trunk. He took an apple and sat under the branches, waiting.

A few minutes later, Rose spooked him as he was eating the apple with his eyes closed, thinking about his childhood at his Opa's farm. He had been so young then and oblivious to the fact that the Germans and the Poles, although living close to each other, led different lives. His parents were the rare exception of a mixed marriage, making Erik blind to the differences until he was older and sent by his father to the German military school.

"Erik." She hesitated and added, "You're here. I thought you'd never come back."

She looked at him with sadness in her eyes. "I thought you were sent to Warsaw."

He stood up and took her in his arms. "I hope I will not be sent."

"Let's go out of here. Father and other people are coming in a minute to continue picking the apples."

They moved towards the hills where Rose had hidden many nights in the spring of 1943. Erik knew the story of her capture and her interrupted journey towards slavery.

"Rose, I was thinking about the unusual turn of events in your life, from being captured by Germans to loving one of them. I hope our love will last forever."

He knelt in front of her, took her hand and looked straight into her eyes. "Rose, will you marry me?" As she stood there speechless, he removed the little box that Mother gave him from his pocket, opened it slowly, and removed a modest ring with a blue stone in it.

"I will."

Instead of making her life happier, the ring was like a stigma, making her afraid to wear it. She could not share the news with anyone and would put on the ring only when she met Erik. Whenever they met, the conversation was more awkward than in the past, as both of them were afraid to talk about their engagement or the end of the war.

Rose finally got the courage to start the conversation on a beautiful Sunday in September while they were in their secluded place. "Erik, what will happen to us when the war is over?"

"If I survive, I'll come for you, my love."

"Don't talk about dying. But when the war ends, where will you go? To your parents in Gdańsk or to Germany?"

He didn't answer but looked beyond the river at German headquarters in the rundown castle where his home had been for the last several months.

"I'll be back for you. Let's not talk about it right now."

"Billy, tell us more about France and your rescue." Billy's sister Lynn looked at him with eyes full of wonder and admiration.

It was two weeks since Billy and Joey had made it safely to England. Soon after reporting to his RAF station and completing detailed report of his accident, Billy was granted a ten-day leave to spend with family. After a few days with Eloise and the baby boy, he went to visit his parents.

He liked repeating the story of his rescue in France and the way back home. His family had met Joey only briefly after the Battle of Britain and had never asked about him again. Now grateful to the Polish pilot whom they'd disregarded, they tried to rethink their attitude towards the foreigner they had considered less than them. Being British was their badge of honour, their right to be superior. They wanted to hold onto this feeling of supremacy even though the war was breaking the old paradigms and putting Britain at the mercy of other powers.

Billy closed his eyes and for a moment, he thought about the changing times, about his family's struggle to see others as equal, and about what kind of person his sister had evolved into during the war.

He looked at Lynn and started telling his story again, each time remembering more details and interesting anecdotes.

The travel through France went mostly as planned by Andreas and his people. The underground network, working efficiently to move people to their destinations, did it right under the noses of the Germans. Many French peasants along the route had provided places to sleep and offered food and transportation in a silent understanding that it was part of the war effort against the evil that had spread through the world. Halfway through his monologue, Billy remembered a new detail that had happened near Caen in Normandy. With their French scout, they had walked into a forest where a large contingent of Canadian soldiers was stationed under an open sky. It was always the understanding that only the scout would talk if they met any people on their way. This time they must have taken a wrong turn because even the scout was shocked to see the soldiers. Billy and Joey remained silent while their guide tried to communicate with some soldiers in his poor English.

Soon a young private appeared in front of them and speaking French, asked for their identification. An hour later, sitting at a table in the soldiers' mess, they talked about the war, about freeing Normandy and the French Army marching to Paris. Billy and Joey talked about flying the Hurricanes and Spitfires and the Battle of Britain in 1940. Both pilots were tempted to join the Canadians in the Anglo-Canadian-American offensive that had started on the beaches of Normandy. The Canadians contacted their command but were informed that the two pilots must return to England.

"Who was this Canadian who spoke French?" asked Lynn.

"He was from Quebec, where the primary language is French. His family were descendants of the first pioneers who arrived in the new world and they were from Normandy. He was happy to be back in the land of his ancestors and defend it on behalf of Canada."

"It is so romantic to be from the new country but still love the one of his forefathers." Lynn looked dreamily at Billy.

"Where's Joey now?" asked Billy's mother.

"He's back in Blackpool, ready to fly again."

"Perhaps he could join us one day for dinner." Mother's voice was hesitant and she looked at her husband, who nodded his head in agreement.

"I'll ask him."

After dinner, they all moved to the living room to enjoy tea and some cookies that Billy had brought from his mess. Lynn put on the gramophone and the music of Mozart filled the room. They were sitting in silence listening to the music when the sudden sound of sirens blasted through the windows of the flat. They all jumped from their chairs, ready to grab their bags with necessary supplies, when they suddenly realised that Billy was putting on his uniform and heading out to the door. "I must get to Eloise and the baby. Is the Tube running during the bombing?"

"Take my motorcycle. It will be dangerous but faster." Father grabbed the keys and ran outside.

Billy followed his father while the others ran to the shelter. He remembered the motorcycle and the trips he'd taken on it with his father all over London. Although it was his father's treasured toy, he'd occasionally allowed Billy to ride it. It was such a long time ago. Billy's thought drifted to the time before the war as his father was removing the cover and checking the gas in the tank. "It's full. Ride safely."

Billy was stunned by the strength of his father's embrace. He had never been comfortable showing his affection and this hug came as a sign of love and unspoken fear for Billy's safety as he embarked on the ride among the falling bombs.

Billy released himself from his father's embrace and started the motorcycle. There was no time to cherish the kick of the pedal, the swing of his leg over the seat, the turning of the gas supply to hear the roaring sound of the engine. His mind was running through possible routes to Eloise and his son. He knew the location of their designated shelter, and he focussed on reaching it before the bombs obstructed his way.

August 2nd was the day when the Germans launched V-1 flying bombs in one of their last attempts to destroy London. Not many of them reached the city centre, but the damage created by the bombs was extensive, smashing many houses and shattering glass in most of the buildings.

From a distance, Billy saw heavy smoke coming from the vicinity of the shelter. "God, please don't let it be the shelter!" he screamed as he swivelled the bike between the falling debris. He lowered his body to almost hug the bike and turned the gas to its limit. He felt stones hitting his body, cutting through his skin and covering his hands in blood. He was not thinking anymore; he and the bike became one being, almost flying through the streets with one aim: the shelter.

People were scrambling from inside the shelter, which was located in the tunnel of the underground train. Billy jumped from the bike, leaving it flat on the sidewalk and ran towards the Tube. Fighting the crowd coming out of there and going deeper inside, he stopped for a moment and asked everyone the same question. Mostly the same people were taking shelter in the designated places and Billy hoped that they knew his wife and the child. "Have you seen Eloise and a small baby?"

An old woman pointed towards the tunnel. "The farther part was hit the hardest. First responders are removing the debris and helping the injured."

Soon Billy was removing the debris faster than anyone around. Some of the responders looked at him with astonished faces; it was most likely his RAF uniform that surprised them. Dead bodies covered in blood were among the debris. Billy pushed them aside, digging farther. Soon he could hear voices coming from the area behind the debris. The next ten minutes were the longest in his life, longer than his descent from the French sky in the damaged Spitfire. The agony that ravaged his soul gave him the strength of a giant to dig deeper without recognising the pain of every muscle of his body, of every blood-covered cut on his hands, as tears of anguish streaming down his face mixed with the dust created a ghostlike image. They reached an opening in the fallen concrete and Billy crawled inside without any thought of the danger of the rubble collapsing on him.

He glanced at the surroundings; a few people were lying on the ground while a few others were removing the debris from their bodies. At the far end of the opening, a woman lay on the floor, half-covered by a flat concrete slab. He crawled towards without looking around anymore.

"Eloise, can you hear me?"

Her face had been cleaned of debris and blood, and next to her was a bassinet covered with a blanket. Billy lifted the blanket and small blue eyes looked back at him without an understanding of any danger around. He hastily kissed his son's forehead and turned towards Eloise.

Her eyes were open and a faint smile appeared on her face. "Billy." She closed her eyes again.

"Keep your eyes open. I'll talk to you while we remove the slab from you." He turned toward the other people and two rescuers who had just entered the space. "Help me to lift the concrete slab."

"We tried, but it's too heavy," said the man coming towards him.

"This is my wife. Please help me."

"We tried and could not do it. If we try again, it may cause other parts of the ceiling to collapse on all of us."

"You're a soldier and understand the danger. Please wait until we clear the area and get some equipment here," one of the rescuers said softly but with a firmness in his voice.

Billy lifted his son from the cradle, took Eloise's hand, and placed it on the little bald head. A loud baby cry filled the space and Eloise opened her eyes.

"Stay awake. Help is coming. You'll be fine."

"My baby." She smiled and looked at Billy.

"I'm sorry I wasn't at home."

"Don't feel bad. It is a war, and unexpected things happen often."

"When you're rescued, we'll go to my parents' flat to stay there until the end of this war."

"Billy, I may not survive. I must tell you the truth." Eloise closed her eyes and Billy didn't dare to urge her to open them again.

"When you were stationed at the Rufforth base, I had a relationship with Joey." She opened her eyes and looked straight into Billy's. The resolve he saw in her frightened him.

"The baby is Joey's. I wanted it to be yours, but I'm certain it's his." She closed her eyes again.

A tremor went through Billy's body as he slowly looked at his son's face. In the few days since his return, his love for the baby had grown stronger every minute he saw him. To accept what Eloise had just told him was beyond his comprehension and a growing pain was filling his heart.

"Billy, I'm sorry, but I needed to tell you the truth before I die."

"Eloise, you must live. The baby needs you."

"Now that you know the truth, you must do what is right for little Joey." She closed her eyes, her hand resting on her son's head.

Sitting close to Eloise, his body refusing to move, his mind unable to think clearly, Billy stared at the sleeping boy, wishing that the moment would disappear and he didn't have to make any decisions.

"Billy, please remove the brooch from my blouse."

"It's yours. What do you want me to do with it?"

"It belongs to my son now. Perhaps, one day he'll learn about our love gone wrong during these trying years."

Minutes later, which seemed like an eternity to Billy, the first responders came to rescue the wounded people in the underground.

"Sir, please step aside. We need to evaluate the woman and the boy."

Billy stood up and looked with blank eyes at the young man and woman bending over Eloise.

"Sir, are you related to them?" the young woman asked with a voice that was a mixture of maturity and exuberant young goodness.

He stared at her, thinking about his sister Jenny, that if Jenny had been able to move without the wheelchair, she would have been like this young woman, full of life and serious, taking on enormous responsibilities while still seeing life from a teenager's perspective. It was a perspective that was full of hope and readiness to accept any challenges, expecting the challenges to deliver only a good experience.

"Are you OK?" The young woman took his hand and shook it energetically. He looked at her and remembered that Jenny was dead. This realisation brought back his mind to the present situation. "Yes, I'm fine. This is my wife. Is she alive?"

"Rob here is going to examine her and we will take her to the hospital."

The sudden cry of the baby filled the space, bringing smiles to the rescuers and some of the survivors still waiting to be evacuated. Billy thought that babies had a happy effect on people—innocence, love, and hope—but he felt only despair.

"Sir, please hold your son. We need to lift the slab and remove your wife from under it and get her on the stretcher."

Four men lifted the slab on one side and two responders slowly pulled Eloise out.

Billy was unable to move and for a long awkward moment, the young woman held the baby boy in her arms and stood looking at him. "Sir, your wife is safe now. Go to her. I'll stay with the baby." She pulled his arm to bring him back from his stupor.

"What is your baby's name?" she asked, looking at him with bewilderment, not understanding his reaction.

"He is a boy." Billy could not bring himself to say his name. He turned towards Eloise being placed on the stretcher by Rob and another volunteer, and tears started to fog his glassy eyes. Slowly, he realised the awkwardness of the situation and took the boy into his arms.

Billy needed to find a place for the boy and to go to the hospital where Eloise was being taken. He sat outside the damaged entrance to the Tube, looking at the devastation around him and feeding the boy with a bottle full of milk he'd found in the bassinet.

With cold calculation, he considered his situation and the next steps for the boy. He thought about taking him to his parents, where his sister Lynn would be thrilled to help with the boy, but the fact that he was not the father was stopping him from bringing the child to his family. He thought about Eloise's mother as the best person to look after the child for now. A sudden chill went through his body. *Is she even alive?*

Eloise's mother sat in an armchair, holding Joey in her arms. She had just stopped crying after the news about her daughter being crushed under the concrete ceiling of the tunnel. Sitting on the sofa matching the armchair, Billy looked around the room. The apartment looked worn-out, but everything was clean and some decorations brought warmth to the small area. Pictures of Eloise and other family members were displayed on the credenza among some candlesticks with partly burned candles.

Billy kept looking at the display of pictures, which resembled an altar with long-gone saints. He imagined everybody lifting themselves from the frames and floating towards him. It sent a shiver through his body and he stood up. "I have to go to the hospital. Will you take care of the boy for a while?"

Eloise, covered by a blue blanket, and motionless with eyes closed, looked like a ghostlike figure devoid of any colour on her face. Faint, slow breathing was the only sign of life and it was barely there. Billy sat on the edge of the bed with her limp hand pressed against his heart. The hospital room was very small, with three other injured persons sleeping in their beds. The smell of disinfectant was making him nauseous and he wondered if it was harmful to the wellbeing of the patients. He had brought some flowers and put them on a small table alongside some bandages and a glass of water.

"Eloise, I don't know what's best for the boy," he whispered, looking at her for some sign of recognition of his voice. "Was it my constant absence that pushed you into Joey's arms, or was he the one who wooed you and tarnished your innocence?"

Billy thought about the day when Eloise had come to visit him at Rufforth base and after a passionate night had convinced him to get married on the base. He wondered if she was already pregnant at that time and had simply run into his arms for safety and a reassurance of normalcy and stability in her life.

What was Joey's involvement in her life; was he a predator or an accidental lover? Joey was his best friend, somebody who had stood by Billy during his miserable days after the crash, somebody who took an enormous risk to come to France to save him. Was Joey already sleeping with Eloise and pretending to be his friend while visiting him in the hospital?

"Why did you do it? Why did you ruin our life together and my friendship with Joey? Were you that selfish and didn't care about our feelings?" His voice was rising and it woke up an elderly man with his head covered in bandages.

"Hush, don't get angry. Whatever it is, it will pass. Life is short and we don't know what may happen in the next hour or day."

"Sorry." Billy stood up and left the room.

Riding his father's motorcycle to RAF Andrews Field, Joey's new base, Billy's anger grew with each kilometre passed. He left before dawn, hoping to arrive at the base early enough to catch Joey before his daily duties. His friendship forgotten, Billy concentrated on his hate, not only for Joey but for the war, for the miserable lives all around him. His desire for revenge consumed his ability to think clearly. He could not even devise a plan of dealing with Joey, as each time he started thinking about it, his mind drifted into blackness.

He managed to appear calm when he arrived at the gate to the military base. After checking his documents the guard pointed out Joey's barracks and allowed him to enter without further questions.

It was six in the morning and the base was waking up to its daily routines. Billy stood close to the entrance of Joey's barracks, waiting for him to come out. The moment he spotted Joey exiting the door, he jumped in front of him and smashed his head with his bare fist.

"You fucking Polack! She even named the boy after you." Billy kept pounding on Joey's head and chest, screaming, "Fight me, you bastard."

Joey didn't respond; he only tried to cover his head with his arms.

Soon his back was against the wall of the building, bracing himself for more blows. Other soldiers gathered around, cheering and encouraging Joey to fight back. Blood started streaming from his nose, but he just stood passively, bombarded by the angry Billy's fists.

"The boss is coming," somebody shouted.

As abruptly as he started the fight, Billy stopped and looked around. The soldiers around them tried to block the view of the fight and one of them handed cigarettes to Billy and Joey.

"What was that about? Aren't you guys friends?" asked the soldier closest to the fight. Billy recognised him as one of the Polish pilots he'd trained in 1940.

"Nobody's business. Please leave us alone." Billy looked at Joey standing silently in front of him, and the feeling of anger started to subside. "Can we talk?" he said. "Eloise was badly injured."

With his head down, Joey was able to say, "I'm sorry, Billy."

They ate breakfast in the mess and Billy talked about the V-1 rocket attack on London, the collapse of the train tunnel, and the rescue of Eloise and little Joey.

"I'm sorry about Eloise." Joey was truly shaken by the events in London.

"She's in a coma and may not survive. I left the boy with her mother and he's fine for now."

The silence that followed the conversation was deafening as neither one of them wanted to face a future without Eloise.

Billy's posture changed and he appeared to shrink in front of Joey. "I don't know if I can raise the boy without Eloise."

"I'm flying to Poland on a mission that may take a few months. When I'm back, we'll discuss best options for the child," Joey said with certainty in his voice.

"Eloise just asked me to do what's best for the baby. She didn't say what she meant by it."

Joey spoke sadly. "Let's hope that she survives, and it should be her decision to make about the future of her son."

"And if she doesn't survive?"

"The two of us will figure it out. I can raise my son if that is what we decide."

"Eloise's mother will need to be part of the decision."

Lying in Vera's bed with her head snuggled in his shoulder, Joey thought about the fight with Billy, about his lack of remorse, about the feelings that were indescribable because he had no regrets about the events of his past.

As Vera's body moved next to him, he had the sensation of the warmth of the French sun on his body. Like Billy, he thought that he could live there and raise his family.

Something else, other than the sun and the beauty of France, was pulling him to that place. Jean was like a father figure to him and Billy. Although not actively involved with the underground, he had become close to them, sharing his talent of woodworking and wrought-iron smithery. In some moments, it felt like being at home in Poland and helping Father in his shop. Perhaps, his childhood memories and the smells and sounds of a shop somewhat similar to his father's, were the pull for the Thionville area. Or was it something else? Could it be that Joseph had survived the accident and through some mishap, assumed the persona of Jean Navarre? Emilie must have known something that even Jean was not aware of. Could her unusual conduct at the cemetery held some secret to the past? He was glad that she'd avoided him until his departure. What would he do if he learned a possible truth about Joseph?

What future was destined for little Joey? Who would be the father raising him, loving him, and teaching him the ways of life? Joey thought about life and the irony of colliding paths such as his and his father's.

"Darling, I must go." He took Vera's face gently and looked into her sleepy eyes.

"Joey, what is troubling you?" She soothingly touched the bruises on his face.

"There are secrets that I harbour. I can't share them with you now."

"Will they separate us?" Vera's voice, calm with no sign of emotion, was an expression of her difficult life, the expectancy that something bad might happen at every turn of life.

"It will be your decision when you know the truth."

"That's a heavy burden that you may place on my shoulders."

"I'm sorry, sometimes I forget about your life journey and the decisions you had to make since you were a child."

"I'm in a good place now, just waiting for the end of the war."

"I love you." He hugged her.

Soon after their massacre of civilians, the Germans started the deportation of the citizens of Warsaw. While the fighting in different pockets of the city continued, an exodus of people on a massive scale begun.

Ted and a very few sworn men organised an operation to smuggle people from the transit camp outside of Warsaw and relocate them to towns and farms as far away as possible. The majority of the people left in the transit camps were relocated by the Germans to forced labour or concentration camps.

"Ted, a young woman is waiting for you outside," whispered Ania as she entered Ted's shop.

"Do we know her?"

"She said that she's met you."

A woman in a stylish summer dress was standing outside Ted's house. She was smiling at him as he stepped towards her. She was in her late twenties with a graceful figure and blonde hair. Despite her smile, her face showed signs of exhaustion and perhaps hunger.

"Are you looking for me?"

"You don't remember me, do you?" She seemed to be trying to be assertive but her voice was trembling and her eyes were pleading.

"Are you from Warsaw?"

"Yes, you saved me from the camp. I heard that you're a tailor."

"Yes. What would you like to be made?"

"I'm a seamstress. I had my shop in Warsaw. I thought I could work in your shop."

"There isn't much work. I don't know what I could offer to you."

"I can do any sewing and maybe you could benefit from my fashionable designs. I'm sure there are young women that would like to remake their old dresses into newer fashions."

"I can't pay you, but I could provide shelter and food. When can you start?"

"Right away. I have all my belongings with me." She pointed at a small suitcase standing near the wall of the house.

Brusk was flooded with people who had left Warsaw avoiding capture by the SS soldiers and put themselves at the mercy of small towns and villages. The Germans sent reinforcement to fight the uprising and the stories of their brutal, systematic killing of underground fighters, civilians, and children were quietly told by the many evacuees.

Rose continued to see Erik despite increased danger for both of them. Their love was more intense than before, desperate in the understanding that it was going to end and the future was unknown.

By September, the uprising in Warsaw continued but was reduced to desperate fighting in isolated pockets of the city. The Russian Red Army was already in Polish territory, pushing the Germans farther west. The uprising had stopped the advance of the Red Army, but everybody knew that it was just a politically motivated halt.

"Erik, why is your army still fighting and killing people?" Rose asked him, searching for some understanding.

"Do you know the story *The Emperor Without Clothes*?"

"It's a children's story." Rose looked at Erik, searching for more.

"It looks to me like the people surrounding the emperor, the officers close to Hitler, don't want to tell him that Germany has essentially lost the war, so he goes on mobilising the young men and sending them to war."

"But a child eventually told the emperor he had no clothes. Can't somebody in the army do that?"

Rose was looking into a distant horizon, remembering the children's tale. She'd never liked children's tales, preferring books about the world and adventure. The reason she knew some of them was because of her younger sister Hela. Rose had often read to Hela from a tattered book by Hans Christian Andersen. Occasionally, she created stories using her imagination too; they were the best, even Hela liked them.

"After so many years of indoctrination and war, the people in Germany have lost their understanding of good and evil. They'll blindly continue to fight."

"Even knowing that Paris was liberated in the last few days?"

"Most likely many of them don't know about it." Erik put down his head on the grass and looked at the blue sky. It was a difficult conversation and he had to admit to himself that to continue the war was pointless, yet he was part of it and continued to follow orders. He was one of the thousands of deniers who were not able to break away from the madness created by the Third Reich.

"Erik, you're not one of them. You're good and loving. There must be more like you."

"Let's not talk about it," Erik snapped at Rose.

"Listen to what I want to say. With so many strangers in towns and villages, you could hide among them and pretend to be one of them."

"No, I could not. It would be a desertion, ending with the death penalty. If I didn't desert earlier, doing it now would be cowardice." He looked at Rose with a smile that was a reflection of sad resignation.

Rose persisted. "I have a suggestion to help you to escape. Please do it for me and our love."

"What is it?" Erik didn't show much interest but continued to listen anyway.

"Put your uniform on the banks of the river near the castle with a note that you committed suicide by drowning. I'll bring you my brother's clothes that you could use to escape."

He didn't answer. He just squeezed her hand and looked at the sky.

Billy's second week of leave from the base was mostly spent at the hospital. Sitting at Eloise's bedside, he thought about his wartime life. Up to now, he hadn't thought much about sleeping with other women while Eloise was in London. In his mind, it was fine for the men, especially the soldiers, to flirt and romance with many women but not for women to do so. He realised the paradox of such a belief. Maybe the nurse in Leeds had a boyfriend as well but swayed by Billie's charm and a moment of weakness had become Billy's lover. He was becoming more and more obsessed, trying to figure out what was moral and what was not. He felt as there were two men inside him, one questioning societal norms and the other justifying them as a God-given right to decide the lives of women.

He didn't realise that he had started a conversation with himself. Like a madman, he whispered quietly. "For generations, men worked and made the decisions, including women's rights. But was it right?—Eloise is smarter than many men, why should she be subjected to male domination?—Societies' were built on men's domination, creating powerful empires for centuries.—But the norms started changing at the beginning of the twentieth century and women won many rights in many countries.—But look at your family. Your mother is quiet and listens to your father.—They are the older generation. Shouldn't I see the world differently?—Would you like a world where women's emancipation makes them equal to men?—Maybe, but I would have to accept Eloise's right to make a choice and a decision to keep Joey's child.—Then, what about Joey having the same morals as you and having an affair with Eloise?—That's different, he was my good friend. It is a double betrayal."

Billy could not stop having this endless conversation with himself, and he realised that he might go mad if he continued. He stood up and left the room still whispering to himself.

"Billy, are you all right?" He was brought back to reality.

"Oh, Mrs. Kerr, same as yesterday."

"But Billy, you're looking disoriented. What happened?"

"Perhaps we need to talk. See your daughter now. May I come to your apartment in the evening?"

Billy stayed with his parents as his and Eloise's apartment had been partially destroyed during the bombing. Half of the building had collapsed when the bomb landed on the street, creating a deep crater that diverted all traffic in the area. Despite logic, Billy climbed to the first floor and into his apartment. He recovered some clothes, blankets, the boy's crib, and a small box with Eloise's jewellery. He left all this with Mrs. Kerr except for a small pendant that he'd given to his wife last Christmas. He put it on the gold chain with a cross that he always wore.

It was barely dark when he walked to Mrs. Kerr's apartment, but very few people were on the streets. Most tried to be at home close to the family and ready to run to the shelters when the sirens blasted in the air.

Billy loved London, the city he was born in. It was where he'd gone to school and where he'd met Eloise at a friend's party. It seemed such a long time ago. Life was promising then and he and Eloise, being from the prosperous middle class, could only see a happy life ahead. All was gone; their dreams had vanished not only with the war, but with Eloise's betrayal. He was perplexed by his thoughts, and even angry at himself for blaming his wife more than Joey for the disloyalty.

He knocked at the heavy door and moments later Mrs. Kerr, with Joey in her arms, opened the door. The conversation was one-sided. As Mrs. Kerr listened without a word, Billy told her about his last conversation with Eloise, about her confession and that she had asked that Billy made the right decision for the boy.

"Mrs. Kerr, I cannot raise the boy. He reminds me of the disloyalty of the two people I loved."

"I'll raise my grandson." They were the only words she said.

The next day he was at the hospital early in the morning, feeling uneasy about his decision to abandon the boy. As he walked through the hallway, a nurse he had seen before approached him. "Please come quickly. Your wife has regained consciousness."

They both ran to the room Eloise shared with other patients.

Billy knelt by her bedside and took her hand. It was paper-white and cold. He kissed it as she opened her eyes.

"Billy, where am I?" Eloise tried to lift her head but could not.

"Shush, don't move. You were injured in a bomb attack; you'll be fine."

She closed her eyes again. Billy squeezed her hand and whispered, "Open your eyes, my love. I'll take you home."

"My brother is coming to see me."

"Your brother ..." Billy stopped himself from talking.

Her brother had been dead for a long time. He was ten years older and had died in a freak accident at the university after drinking with other freshmen students. The accident was never investigated properly, tainting the family with bitter anger that had left it shattered. Soon after, Eloise's father had left and they'd only received one letter that he was in the United States. He never contacted them again.

"Robert is coming. I see him."

Billy kissed her hand again. She was dead when he lifted his head. Unable to move, he knelt for a long time until the nurse touched his shoulder and asked him to leave the room. He stepped into the hallway and took out a cigarette. When he finished smoking, he left the hospital without looking back. That was the last time he saw Eloise. He tried to remove the image of her sunken face from his mind, and his thoughts drifted to the day when they'd made love for the first time.

Looking back at the day when Eloise had surprised him with the visit and marriage proposal, he wondered again if she was already pregnant and if all the love and marriage had been just a charade. By the time he reached his parents apartment, his feeling for Eloise seemed to vanish, and his only desire was to go back to his RAF station and immerse himself in the war.

After the funeral, Billy and his sister Lynn walked away from the cemetery, leaving Eloise's mother to watch the coffin being lowered into the ground. Lynn put her arm inside Billy's, resting her head on his shoulder. It was a cloudy day with a sporadic drizzle that battered their faces as they walked in silence.

"Are you going to leave Joey with Mrs. Kerr?" asked Lynn as they stopped in front of a small bakery.

Billy pulled her through the door. "Let's go inside."

They ate a fresh piece of bread with a cup of tea, sitting at a small table in the corner of the bakery. Their hands wrapped around the hot cups as they inhaled the aroma of tea and warm bread. Afraid to lock eyes with each other, they looked through the window.

Finally, Lynn broke the silence. "I would like to be part of his life. I could help Mrs. Kerr until you take him back."

"Lynn, the boy isn't my son." Billy's face was devoid of any emotion.

She looked at him in shock, recognising that he was telling the truth. "Do you know who the father is?" she asked calmly.

Billy tilted back his chair and his face momentarily flared with anger. A long while passed before he responded.

"No, I don't know."

The September evenings were getting cooler every day. The days were beautiful and the fresh, cooler breeze of the evenings was a small relief to Ted's feelings of failure. The sky was full of stars and the moon was getting bigger every day, but sitting on a bench in front of the shed, Ted was oblivious to this beauty of nature. Today was a particularly bad day for no other reason than the constant anger that was boiling to the brim inside him, filling his heart with a sense of worthlessness.

He heard quiet steps approaching the shed. Laura was walking lightly towards him and he was pleased to see her glide through the evening. She was a very elegant woman—even in a burlap bag, she would have looked different from the women of his town. Her walk was gentle but full of the confidence of a sophisticated and mature woman. Her blonde hair was loosely hanging and the breeze was blowing it in different directions. She was not beautiful, but Ted liked the bigger nose and the blue eyes that seemed to observe everything around her. He didn't know much about her past life in Warsaw other than the story he'd overheard about her fashion shop and the dress she'd made for some German wife. He didn't want to hear any stories about life in Warsaw before the uprising and only talked to her about the work he assigned to her. He was pleased, though, that she blended in well with Ania and Rose.

His thoughts stopped abruptly and he wanted desperately to remove his sudden longing for Rose. It was difficult to see her almost every evening, knowing that her relationship with Erik continued despite the awful circumstances of the endless war. His love, similar to hers, was desperate and without expectations of a fairy-tale ending. He knew that he could not stop loving her, and she could not stop loving Erik. They both were doomed and maybe destined to live a miserable life after the war.

"Hello, Ted."

He stared at Laura for a while and then asked her to sit down next to him.

"You shouldn't torment yourself for not joining the uprising," she said quietly.

His face tensed as he looked in the direction of Warsaw. Always very intense, Ted had changed since the failed attempt to join the uprising. Laura was correct to guess that he was tormented, but she could only know the obvious, the suffering of not fighting. There was more to it and he hoped nobody would ever know. The obvious he could partially compensate for by actions of sabotage, delivery of weapons, and assisting civilians fleeing the battered city. But the deep darkness in his heart, his unwanted love, was his other torment. And perhaps the biggest anguish was his battle with himself to squash the desire to kill Erik.

"There is no torment; it's just my life since I was a six-year-old." Ted turned his head slowly towards her.

"Ania told me about your father's death."

"I'm used to this void in my life. Sometimes I just accept my fate and believe that things happen for no particular reason."

"Perhaps, it is easier to believe in the randomness of events in this world; otherwise, one might as well stop feeling, stop breathing, stop being." Laura took Ted's hand in hers and gently caressed it.

Ted's body tensed and he put in every effort not to acknowledge the unexpected feeling of pleasure her touch gave him.

"You don't talk about your father or your feelings with anyone." Her hand kept squeezing his hand with tenderness.

"I always had to be the strong one, for my mother, my sister, for my friends. It's expected of me and I don't know any other way."

"Ted, you can talk to me. I'll be gone one day and will take all your secrets with me."

Ted was surprised at the feeling of comfort this gave him and at his desire to talk to her. How would he even start to talk about anything personal in his life, things he wouldn't even acknowledge in his darkest moments?

"It is hard to open up. Start by telling me about your memories of your father."

After a moment of silence, he told her everything he remembered until the day his father left. He felt the relief as his life's burden started to slowly fade away. He wanted to tell her more, to feel the lightness spreading over his body, to be just a young man without the care of the world.

When he finished, they sat silently for a while as if waiting for something to happen. Not looking at Ted, Laura unbuttoned the front of her dress and gently placed Ted's hand inside her brassiere. He froze, unable to do anything, and his mind became blank as he waited for her next move. She turned toward him and gently kissed his mouth while pressing her body against his. The desire that exploded inside Ted was like a force greater than any before known to him. She guided his hand down to her inner thighs while she reached down to touch his most secret parts. Ted's experience with intimacy was very minimal, making her daring approach excruciatingly exciting. He pulled her down to the ground behind the bench and impatiently lifted her dress with one hand while pulling down his trousers with the other. Their mouths didn't separate, as if they were fused into each other, and the blood started to flow between their lips. He was inside her, feeling the heat of her body melting away the darkness of his life. He wanted this moment to last for a lifetime. When it was over, he put his head on her soft bosom and tears started to roll down his face.

Rose's days were very busy with helping Hela to get ready for the day, working at the store, seeing Erik, and spending evenings with Ania and Laura. Laura was ten years older than Rose and Ania, but despite the age difference, they became friends instantly. All three of them spent evenings sewing and chatting at Ania's house. There were many people from Warsaw escaping the carnage there and finding refuge with families throughout Poland. Some had families in other areas and moved there as quickly as they could. Some, like Laura, had to seek refuge with strangers.

Rose was fascinated by her new friend, though in her usual way, she pretended to be more worldly than she was. But she was secretly glad that Ania was openly fascinated and asked for stories about life in Warsaw.

"Do you know that Ted went to school in Warsaw for two years?" Ania was beaming with pride.

"What school?"

"He studied at the Salesians' school. He planned to open his shop in Warsaw but the war changed everything," Ania said sadly.

"Ted took us to Warsaw a few times before the war. It was great." Rose chimed in.

Laura smiled. "Life in Warsaw was full of energy and excitement; new businesses were opening everywhere. I'm sure that Ted would have been very successful there." She put down the fabric that she was stitching and looked absentmindedly at the window. "You should see Warsaw now. Almost everything has been destroyed by the Germans."

"Ted went there many times. He was selling food that he had to smuggle to Warsaw and with the money, he bought fabrics and accessories for his tailoring," said Ania.

"The devastation that is happening right now is unimaginable. You had to be there to see it." Laura blinked her eyes to stop the tears.

"Will you tell us about your life there?" Rose and Ania said simultaneously.

"Another time. Let's finish this dress right now. Ania, you know your brother. He does not allow any slacking." Laura laughed and both girls followed.

Rose loved the friendship with Laura. Like Erik, Laura was a part of the bigger world, a world of opportunities and a better life. Late at night, Rose would analyse every aspect of Laura's stories. Some seemed far-fetched, some ordinary, some sad, but they all were about people who had interesting lives. She would think about her own life, which on the surface, was a good life. She'd had her share of experiences, such as the capture by Germans, the underground school, responsibility for the store, saving

Hela's life, and the biggest one, the love of Erik.

Why do I always want more, something different than I have? She could never answer this question, but it was always nagging her and often making her unhappy. She was dreaming that after the war, she and Erik could live in Warsaw or perhaps in America. She fantasised that nobody would know that Erik had served in the German Army and they could have a good life together. Often, she had contradictory dreams that clouded her vision of the future. Although confident, in moments like these, she would become unsure of herself and she'd walk to the orchard to sit under the large apple tree.

One evening, Laura said, "Girls, I want to show you something."

Rose and Ania were busy removing seems from an old jacket that the customer wanted redone with a thick layer of lining, ready for the cold autumn days. Laura removed a picture from her pocket. They looked at the small picture of a young woman standing in front of a big house with trees in bloom on one side. It looked rich and like nothing they'd seen in their lives.

"Who is it?" As always Ania was the one to ask the first question.

"It is the wife of a German major who was stationed in Warsaw. I made a few dresses for her."

"How was that possible?" Rose sounded more accusing than she intended to be.

"Rose, you're not the one to judge me." Laura looked at Rose with tension on her face that quickly changed into a smile. "Would you like to know more?"

After a moment of silence, Rose said, "Please."

"As you know, my shop was located in Warsaw's Old Town. My family owned the building and I inherited the shop after my mother developed arthritis and couldn't keep needles in her hands. She was a great and well-known seamstress, and I learned from her the love for making beautiful clothes. At the beginning of the war, business was slow and we often had no food to put on the table. My beautiful dresses were worn by many young women on the streets of Warsaw, and soon the Germans learned about my shop. I accepted them as customers and most of their orders were for their wives or girlfriends in Germany. They brought beautiful fabrics, usually from Italy, and they paid relatively well. One day, a handsome major came into my store, followed by a private carrying a big package. The major gave me a picture of his wife and asked me to design and make two dresses for her. You see, all the high-ranking German officers wanted to be stationed in Paris and sending something beautiful from Warsaw was like an exoneration for their failure of not making it to France. When the dresses were made, he forgot to ask for the picture and I kept it."

"Why would you want to keep it?" Ania asked in shock.

"Look at the back of it." There were the name and the address of the major's wife, Ester Von Shultz.

"When the war is over, I'll write a letter telling her about the misery her husband and thousands like him brought into the world. I'll ask her if she noticed broken swastikas stitched inside the pockets and I'll tell her to go to hell and burn there forever."

She lifted her eyes, full of anger, and noticed Ted leaning against the door frame. In a split second, he vanished.

"Are you having an affair with Ted?" Rose asked Laura as they were sitting under her favourite apple tree.

"No point in lying. Yes, I make his life a little happier."

"What do you mean? Isn't he happy just to be the guy responsible for the world, involved in his underground war?" Rose sounded a little hurt.

"Everybody needs love even if it is one that is not meant for eternity."

The silence between them lasted for a long while before Rose turned towards Laura. "Are you suggesting that Erik's love for me is just a wartime sentiment, and once the war is over, I won't see him again?"

"I don't know, but he is here only temporarily and unfortunately for you, he is the enemy."

"He promised." Rose's expression looked cold as ice. Not even one muscle was moving. She was willing herself to stop thinking about what Laura said.

"Don't be upset, Rose. I heard from Ania that he was a nice and honest man. Perhaps, there are Germans who are nice. I wish you happiness after the war."

Laura steered their conversation toward fashion and books she'd read before the war. Listening to Laura, Rose's mind drifted to her imaginary future with Erik and their happy life somewhere away.

But there was a nagging feeling of wrongdoing inside her.

Ted's romance with Laura came upon him like a hurricane, leaving him bewildered by the explosiveness of it and the energy that it drained from him. Each meeting full of passion and physical desire left Ted with mixed feelings of fulfilment of his youth and guilt at betraying Rose.

"Ted, enjoy the moment; we don't know what the next day may bring." Laura was lying with her head on his chest, looking at the dark sky hanging low above their heads.

"I'm enjoying being with you. You're my first girlfriend." Ted considered her his girlfriend despite keeping the romance secret. He always believed himself to be very mature and responsible, but with Laura, he was vulnerable and he felt that she could read his mind.

"It's very obvious that you're in love with Rose. Only she and Ania don't see this."

"No, I'm not …"

"Don't say anything." She stopped him from further denying the obvious.

After a moment of silence, Ted turned his head toward Laura and with boyish honesty, he said, "I try not to love her. She doesn't deserve my love. She betrayed the country."

"Be careful what you're saying. She is young and Erik is handsome, kind to her, and represents the big world. She wants to escape from this small town, from her dominating father and a mother who is obedient to her husband."

"Who told you this?" Ted asked with slight anger in his voice.

"We talk—women like to talk to each other about their dreams, even Rose."

"But he is German."

"War brings different challenges to people. Whatever he did in the past, Rose forgave him. At the end of the war, he will leave with his army and she will never see him again."

"That isn't a consolation for me." Ted got angrier, stood up quickly and looked at Laura. "I want to leave this small town as much as she wants to. I already had plans to establish my tailoring business in Warsaw. I had a friend there." Ted stopped suddenly thinking about Joey.

"Tell me about this friend."

"It was a young man a few years older than me. He was a pilot and I trained with him to operate radio stations to communicate with pilots. We were going to fight the Germans together and win glorious victory. How naïve we were. I don't even know what happened to him since the capitulation. I never heard from him again."

"Is he alive?" Laura pulled Ted back down to sit on the ground.

"I spoke to his father soon after we lost the war. He heard that Joey had left for France with the Polish Army. I never went to see his father again."

"It sounds like you two were close friends."

"More than that. Can you keep a secret? One that nobody can ever learn?"

Laura nodded and after a long pause, Ted continued. "Joey was my half-brother. Only he, his father, and I knew about it. Joey's mother confessed to her husband on her deathbed about her romance with a young man who later became my father."

In the next half hour, Ted told Laura everything about his life with his half-brother.

When he finished, his eyes were still closed, remembering each moment spent with Joey.

"Not even Ania knows Joey's identity?" asked Laura.

"She does not and the trouble is that she was falling in love with him. She was only twelve years old, but she couldn't stop talking about him, even professing that she would marry him one day."

"Good that he's gone. Four years is a long time in a young girl's life. Hopefully, she has forgotten about him." Laura was smiling at the idea of little Ania in love with the twenty-year-old pilot. "I'm sure it was very romantic for her to imagine Joey as her man."

Ted chuckled sarcastically. "The war robbed us all of dreams, opportunities, and even imagining a normal life. Some even went the wrong way with their love."

"You're a good man, Ted. Don't judge Rose harshly. Rose knows this. Be good to her the way you always have been and she will love you one day. I see it in her eyes, the way she looks at you, as if regretting that it isn't you that she loves. She told me that you were very serious and unapproachable, always having one reason or another not to get involved with girls. She thinks that your only mission in life is to serve the country and get involved in big stuff, whatever it is."

"That's strange. She always comes across as opinionated and, on a mission, to be better than others."

"The way I see it is that the two of you are meant to be together, ambitious and always setting goals for yourselves." Laura pressed her body against Ted, "But right now, you're here with me and let's enjoy our time together."

The decision to become the Silent Unseen was easy after Joey came back from France. He couldn't just fight as part of the RAF forces anymore; he needed to face the German and Russian enemies and help his and Vera's homeland in a way that could make a difference. Perhaps he wanted to do it for his son as well, to atone for his sins and be worthy of little Joey's love. On the plane to Poland, he remembered every word of his last conversation with Vera. She had accepted his confession without any judgement.

"It was your preordained destiny. Your life's experiences will allow you to make the right decisions. Your son and your father will take their rightful places in your heart."

"I don't know the right decision yet."

"I'll always love you and stand by you, whatever you do."

"The mission to Poland is dangerous. I may die there. I wrote a letter with my wishes regarding my son. Open it only in the case of my death."

Joey remembered her sad eyes after he spoke about the letter. Up to that moment, she had been holding on to the belief that potential death was not part of the mission, but his mention of the letter suddenly changed the mood of their meeting, as if death was inevitable.

Joey had asked to be sent outside of the town of Brusk. His mission required him to infiltrate the Polish People's Army associated with the Bolsheviks and evaluate their growing influence in the territories liberated by the Russians. Privately, though, his mission was also about finding Ted and learning about his family in Bochnia. He had not heard from them since he arrived in England.

Inside the plane, surrounded by darkness and the humming sound of the engines, Joey thought about his life. The fight with Billy, or rather his submission to being punched and kicked, made him feel like a failure in life. He wanted to restore the good parts of his life into his being, to show his father and Ted that he was an honest person, proud of his accomplishments. But the thoughts about failing Billy were pressing down on him. Unaware of Eloise's death, Joey thought about the bombing and the tragedy that had put her into a coma with an uncertain future. And he thought about baby Joey, now being cared for by his grandmother, who might never know his mother. One day, little Joey might realise that not only was his mother not a part of his life but that his real father was absent from it as well.

"Joey, half an hour before the drop," the pilot informed him.

Still dazed from his unhappy thoughts, Joey muttered, "I'm not a failure." He needed to snap out of his negative mindset before he landed in Poland. Focussing on the positive thinking exercises he'd learned during his early days in the RAF, he closed his eyes and concentrated on deep breathing and purging negativity from his mind. *Clarity and concentration are the essence of my mission.* He remembered the oath that he'd taken to serve in the Home Army and started reciting it. It calmed him and now he was ready to face new challenges.

With lights turned off, the airplane started to lower its altitude. The clear sky and the stars above were beautiful but created a feeling of supernatural existence as something abnormal was all around them. They noticed fires raging in the distance and the few men on the plane could not stop staring at the distant inferno.

The pilot, who had made this trip many times, said, almost too casually, "It's Warsaw burning. The uprising continues but most likely not for long."

"Are we going close to Warsaw?" asked Joey.

"Around fifty kilometres southeast from it."

Silence descended on the few men and the tension became almost unbearable.

Soon, the pilot nodded down toward the earth. "Joey, can you see the lights below in the shape of an arrow? Look carefully, as this is your point of contact. The lights will go out in a minute and after that, it is your instinct that must take you there. They'll flash once more when you're in the air. Pay attention."

The other two men on the plane checked the big wooden box attached to a parachute. It contained weapons and medicine. "The box goes first, then you jump. We're ready in two minutes."

The plane was flying low and Joey could see the terrain below. In the next moment, the door opened and the box was pushed out with its cord pulled to open the parachute. Shortly after, Joey was speeding down to his destination. He felt the sharp pull as his parachute opened and he looked down. The lights came on momentarily, giving him the exact location of his landing.

"God, keep me safe."

Lying on the grass at night, Ted and the other young men turned the flashlights on to signal their location. Another drop was coming from England. One was a box of weapons and medicine; the other was a Silent Unseen agent. Ted was becoming increasingly angry at the Home Army command in London. He couldn't question their orders, but silently he didn't want to see another agent coming to tell them what they must do. Sending more weapons for the final battle would be much better.

He watched the two parachutes coming down and concentrated on the man manoeuvring his parachute in an attempt to land close to the centre of the field. It was Ted's responsibility to take care of this Silent Unseen, known only by the code name Oriole. *Silly code name*, thought Ted. He was proud of his own pseudonym, Korsak. He always thought of it as a sailor's name, a name that meant adventure, bravery, and winning at all costs.

Ted's sarcasm turned to contempt for Oriole, a bird that migrates to other countries for the winter, thus escaping a hard life for the comforts of an easier life. It's never rooted in one place to know the full richness of that place or the strong connection to the roots of all the forefathers who fought for the freedom of Poland.

For no other reason than his own anger, Ted didn't like the stranger floating down towards him. When the pilot touched down on the ground, Ted, with face smeared with soot, moved toward him. His first task at hand was to fold the parachute, place it in the bag, and only then ask the stranger to follow him.

"Before we move, cover your face with soot and put this jacket and cap on." Ted's voice was low and purposely unfriendly.

They needed to move quickly in the dark of the night to a village on the other side of the forest. That was their first hiding place, and from there, the Silent Unseen was assigned to a safe place for at least a week or longer. Some of the Silent Unseen had come for a short assignment and some had come to Poland in 1942 to help organise the Home Army and had stayed until now. Two brothers who had come in 1942 were high-ranking officers whose family was from a neighbouring area. Before the war, their family had been landowners and lived on a beautiful estate in a centuries-old house that had now been converted by the Germans into a warehouse. Before the war, Ted and they would never have met as they were from different social classes, but the war made everybody more equal and the two brothers were very unpretentious and became good friends with Ted.

"How far do we have to go?" asked Oriole.

"Half an hour. Don't talk. It might be dangerous." Ted was tired and wanted to get to the safe place as quickly as possible and then go back home to get some sleep.

They stopped not far from the village, close to the first house on the outskirts of the forest.

"The bird landed in its nest," Ted said the password in a low voice.

"The nest was repaired today." A stocky man appeared from behind a tree and motioned to Ted and the pilot.

They followed him into the house, where a small carbide lamp was casting some light in the room.

Two other men were sitting at the table, which had food on it. One of them spoke. "Oriole, my name is Falcon. You already met Korsak. The others are Gornik and Fox."

An older woman came in with a bowl of warm water. "First, wash your faces."

As Joey started to clean himself up, Ted left the house to be a lookout as required. The first half hour was critical in an operation like this one, to make sure that they were not followed by Germans.

It was almost half-past midnight when Ted heard the screeching tyres of a truck. "The Germans are coming."

A trapdoor in the floor was lifted by Fox and everybody quickly moved to the hidden cellar. They heard a piece of furniture moved over the trapdoor and soon after, heavy boots pounding on the floor above.

One strong voice was heard directly above the trapdoor to the cellar, giving commands to the soldiers. Ted vaguely recognised the German's voice and anger grew inside him. He was almost certain that it was Erik.

Ted moved to the upper steps of the ladder to the cellar and kept his ear to the trapdoor to get as much understanding of the commands as his knowledge of German would allow. He never looked down at the three men below him, but he removed the cyanide pill and placed it in his mouth. He knew that the others would do the same, but Oriole was not yet oriented on the safety procedure and, if captured, would be tortured and confess to his mission.

The fifteen minutes of deafening silence in the cellar dragged endlessly, but the Germans finally left. In the next hour, the men in the basement sat silently, waiting for Falcon to open the hatch. The Germans were checking other houses and they had to wait until they left the village. Ted was still sitting on the top step, dozing off from time to time, when Fox whispered into his ear to remove the pill from his mouth. Ted had almost forgotten about the cyanide and a shiver went through his body when he thought about accidentally biting on it. He was prepared to die for his country but not while hiding in a cellar.

It was two hours before the door was opened and Falcon motioned to the men to come up from the cellar. Ted and Falcon immediately went outside to discuss the events of the night.

"Somebody must have told the Germans about the drop. They were looking for the pilot." Falcon looked back into the house where Oriole and Fox were talking quietly.

"Good thing the collaborators didn't know about this house. We could all be dead, including your mother. They should stop sending more Silent Unseen. We need weapons, not instructors," Ted said angrily.

"It isn't our decision, Ted, and remember that you're responsible for this one."

"Who was the German giving orders very loudly? Was it Erik Hermann?" Ted cringed when he mentioned his name.

"Yes, it was and he saved us. When you guys went down to the cellar, we didn't cover the trap door fully and he noticed it. He moved quickly and put his foot on the exposed corner. He didn't move until the other soldiers checked the entire house and left."

Ted looked at Falcon with mixed emotions. He hated Erik, but he knew that Rose was getting good information from him, most likely given to her voluntarily. For the first time, Ted had to admit that Rose might be right about Erik's changed attitude towards the war and serving the German Army. But he hated the idea that Erik could be a good person and turned quickly to the entrance of the house. He stopped suddenly when he looked at the pilot and Fox standing near the window. The pilot's profile was familiar and swept Ted's mind with memories of good times and friendship.

"Oriole? I mean, Joey, is that you?"

Joey looked at Ted, and his jaw dropped in disbelief. "Ted, is it really you?" Joey opened his arms and both men hugged for a long time while the others were stunned by this unexpected scene.

After their astonishing meeting in the safe house, Joey and Ted spent time together whenever it was possible. One week had already passed since Joey had been moved to a long-term safe house outside of Brusk. He told Ted about his mission to find out about the influence and popularity of the Polish People's Army among the Polish people. "My orders are to infiltrate the army and learn about their plans for Poland. I need to move to the east soon. Do you know anyone who could help me to infiltrate the PPA?"

"George knew about your mission before you left England. We're working with the underground network to move you safely to Lublin." Ted was sad to separate from his friend again, but he knew the importance of the mission and his role was to assist Joey in accomplishing it.

"The Home Army and the exiled government in London are worried about the political landscape of Poland after the war."

"In our area, the Home Army is very strong but in eastern Poland, the PPA is getting stronger. Many of us living here worry about the future after the war," Ted said grimly.

"Ted, before I leave, could you invite me to your house? It would be nice to see your mother and Ania again."

"OK, I've hesitated so far because of Ania. The last time she saw you she was just twelve years old and since then she frequently talks about you. It seems that she's in love with you."

Joey laughed. "That was such a long time ago. She was just a shy girl."

"She glorifies you and talks about you as the prince that will come on a white horse to marry her. I'm afraid that this time she could fall in love with you, not just the memory of the dashing pilot."

"I have a fiancée in England—perhaps you could convince Ania that it was just a young girl's fantasy. I'm her half-brother."

"At times, I've wanted to tell her about our father, but I never got the courage to disclose the secret. Perhaps it's time to do it."

"I'll leave it up to you."

When Ted left, Joey thought about France and Jean—Jean, who could be Joseph, their father. His motive in going to Ted's house was to look at any photograph of Joseph that might be in the house. He wasn't sure exactly what he was hoping to discover, but at least he wanted to see a picture and compare it to Jean. So far, he hadn't told Ted about Thionville, their father's grave, or Jean. When he'd talked about saving Billy, he hadn't mentioned the specific place in France.

Two days later, Ted invited Joey for supper at his house.

"How is Ania?" Joey was uncomfortable asking.

"She was disappointed that you were engaged but mostly happy that you were alive."

"Did you tell her about our father?"

"There's no point in her knowing. He's dead. It's better that she and Mother remember him as an honest, loving man without a dark past."

"Sometimes unexpected things in life just happen, don't judge him harshly."

"I don't think much about him anymore."

"I would like to tell you something about me. I have a son with a married woman. She is Billy's wife."

"Your best friend?" Ted exclaimed.

"It's a long story. We were in love, but she decided to marry Billy without telling me about the child. She was injured during the London bombing and confessed the truth to Billy. She was in a coma when I left England, and Billy was very confused and not ready to raise the boy. When I'm back in England, we will decide on little Joey. It all depends on whether Eloise survives."

"What happens if she doesn't survive?"

"Vera and I may raise him and stay in England for the sake of the boy. I would want to be part of his life as a father or at least as a good uncle."

"Joseph, Joseph Junior, nickname Joey, Joey Junior. That sounds more like a curse that was cast on all of you. Sons fathered by interlopers bearing the same name."

"Don't judge us. I had a good life and will make sure Joey Jr. does as well."

"Sorry, Joey. I don't know much about fatherhood." Ted stood up and added, "I'll come for you tomorrow afternoon. Mother is making pierogis for dinner. Hope you like them."

Joey's new documents were in the name of Jan Walus. Although Ted's family knew his real name, for the safety of everybody, they were asked to call him Jan. The dinner was a happy occasion to talk about the pre-war times in Warsaw, and Joey asked many questions about their everyday life in Brusk. After dinner, Ted removed a bottle of home-made wine made from rosehip and apples.

"I shouldn't ask, but maybe you could tell us about your life," Ania could not resist asking.

"I'll stay outside of the house to make sure nobody's listening." Ted took his cigarettes and went outside.

Quietly, Joey told them about his service as a pilot, about the battles he'd fought, about Vera and her journey from the Borderlands to England, and about his friend Billy. Finally, he stood up and said, "I need to stretch my legs; do you mind if I look at some of your family pictures there on the shelf?"

"I'll bring a beautiful picture of my mom and father from their wedding." Ania rushed to the bedroom and in a few seconds, she returned with a framed photo of a young couple on their wedding day.

"Beautiful picture. Sorry about the tragedy of losing your husband, Mrs. Novak. He was a handsome man."

"Ania, can you bring the picture of your father that he sent from France shortly before his death?" Maria's voice was shaking at the mere mention of this tragic event of the past.

Joey stared at the photograph of Joseph Novak taken fifteen years ago. He wanted to remember every detail of it, not only because it was a photo of his father but also to compare it with his memory of Jean Navarre.

Ted stood in the door smoking a cigarette. He didn't like smoking but did it to justify standing outside of the house. Laura was approaching. She liked to spend time with Rose and the other young women. Usually, they met in Rose's orchard, where apples were plenty and tasting them was a delight.

Ted spooked her coming out of the shadow of the door. "How was the girls' party tonight?"

"Same as always. They're so hungry to listen to my stories from life in Warsaw. Franek joined us tonight. Rose is very protective of him."

"Mr. Podolski favours Rose and is unfairly harsh towards his son. Sometimes I wonder how my father would have behaved during the war."

"Do you miss him?"

"Only when I search for some sense in this world. Perhaps he would have helped me to understand it and ease the pain a little. It doesn't happen often. For the most part, I'm glad he isn't here anymore."

"The lives we live—so much pain, so much unknown."

Ted estimated that Joey had finished talking about his life in England, and it was time to take him back to the safe house.

He didn't want Laura to know about Joey's visit and needed to take her away from the entrance. "I missed you," he said. "Can we go to your room for a few minutes?"

Her room was just a corner of the storage area where Ted kept his supplies for the tailor shop. They sat on the bed and he kissed her gently on the lips.

"You're somewhat different today," she observed. "Tense and wary."

"I have to go now. Don't ask anything, and please don't leave your room." Ted looked at her with pleading eyes.

"I'm going straight to bed. I'm tired tonight." Laura kissed him on the forehead like a mother sending her son away.

Ted went outside to check for any suspect activities on the street. Everything was quiet, so he went back to the house to get Joey and take him to the safe house. They moved like shadows through the town. When they entered the cemetery to take a shortcut, Joey stopped and whispered, "Ted, I need to tell you something."

"Is it important? I need to be back home before midnight and we have a long way ahead of us."

"It is important. Can we sit for a while? Do you know a safe spot here?"

Ted knew all the safe spots in a large area around Brusk. There were at least three in the cemetery.

After they sat on the steps of an old crypt, Joey looked straight into Ted's eyes. "I was in Thionville and visited the grave of our father."

Ted gasped for air. Just a few minutes ago, he had spoken about his father with Laura, and now Joey was talking about him. It felt unreal, as if he were in another dimension where ghosts were surrounding him closer and closer.

"Ted, did you hear me?" Joey pulled Ted's arm to bring him back to reality.

"Our father, you said."

"Yes, it was Thionville where I went to rescue Billy. Billy and I stayed in the house of a close friend of our father's. He had been injured during the same accident but survived."

"You went to see Father's grave. Does anyone remember him there?"

"Ted, I may not see you after I go east on my mission. I may not even survive. There's something else that I would like to share with you."

Ted looked at Joey, unsure if he wanted to hear more. Unexpectedly, the memories of his father became very painful and he searched his pocket for a cigarette. He could not find any and he swore under his breath.

Joey handed him a cigarette and waited a while for him to calm down before he continued. "I have a suspicion that our father is alive and lives under the assumed name of his friend, Jean Navarre."

"How could that be? The company sent us a letter about Father's death, compensation money, and most of his belongings."

"Everybody believes that, but there were some rumours …"

"Are you telling me about rumours? How dare you tarnish my father's name?"

"Calm down. He was my father too. One man died, his body crushed by a heavy load of lime and the other was badly injured with half of his face maimed and his limbs broken. This man lost his memory, and it was assumed by everybody that he was Jean. They buried the dead man as Joseph Novak and Jean never recovered his memory. He has a wife and two children. Marie-Ann and Jean-Marc.

"Names of my mother and sister combined."

"When I was there, I learned that Jean is an honourable man. He established a cooperage business and worked for the French Army before the war. During the war, a safe house and a rescue sanctuary have been established on his property. His real passion is wrought-iron works, just like our father. I sensed that his wife Emilie also might suspect that her husband was actually Joseph."

Ted stood up. "This is just innuendo and fantasy."

"Perhaps. One of the reasons I wanted to come to your house was to see pictures of our father. I looked at the picture of Father that he sent just before the accident—he looks like Jean. Emilie said that they were very close friends and even looked alike."

Ted started moving away from the crypt. "Time to go."

"Ted, I wanted you to know. There is nobody else that I could talk to about this and in case of my death, the knowledge will carry on with you."

"I'm not angry, my brother, just another burden to carry."

"Ted, I'm planning to see my father in Bochnia. I hope that he does know that I'm in Poland, we sent a message to the contact person in Krakow. Can you go with me and talk to him before I enter the house?"

Two days later, Ted and Joey were on the train to Krakow. Unshaved and poorly dressed, both men melted easily into the travelling crowd. Ted had a lot of experience travelling by train, and he observed the platform at every station to check on the German soldiers entering and leaving the train. He was aware of the number of them and the cars they entered. He knew from experience that if the soldiers didn't move from one car to another at every station that the travel was relatively safe and the passengers would not be searched.

The train moved lazily among the fields of rye and cabbage already harvested. Most of it had to be given to the Germans but small quantities were safely stored in the farmers' barns. Some fields were golden with the stubble of straw shining in the sun after the rye was harvested, and some were still partially green with the leaves of cabbages left on the ground. People were walking the fields with sacks hanging from their shoulders, frequently bending to collect any edible parts of the grains and leaves that were left. In the distance, cows grazed on the grass separating each farmer's field. It was typical for the small farms to define their boundaries with narrow paths of grass and bushes. The grass was abundantly thick this fall, and the grazing cows looked healthy.

"The farmers try to raise two cows as they have to give one to the Germans. The other will be butchered and part of it sold, with some meat saved for the families." Ted was looking at the beautiful landscape so typical of Poland. Small narrow fields, houses often covered with roofs made of straw, and flowers behind the white picket fences.

"What about the big farms owned by the rich landowners?"

"The Germans repossessed them and assigned administrators to run them. They hire seasonal workers, who work for board and food." Ted looked through the window at the passing landscape and pondered on the future of Poland after the war. "I heard that the Polish People's Army is talking about partitioning the big farms among the poor seasonal workers. Many people like the idea of owning a piece of land."

Their voices were soft, disappearing into the loud noise of the turning wheels slowly making their eyes close. Ted was the first to realise that the train was not moving. He looked through the window and recognised that they had arrived at the Krakow station. They quickly jumped off of the train and disappeared into the crowd.

Joey crouched behind a big tree obscured by the overgrown bushes near the shed. It was almost dark when he and Ted had gotten to Bochnia. Ted went to the front door while Joey found a broken fence at the back and crawled into the backyard. Nostalgia overtook him as he looked at the house. Not much had changed since he'd left, but the house, washed by the fading daylight, appeared older, covered with a layer of dust, and lacking a caring hand to make it appear lived in. His childhood memories flooded through him, and he had to fight tears by pressing on his eyelids.

His memories were filled with love, safety, and the pride of being young Joseph Wilk. Looking at the house, he had a premonition that it was the last time he'd see it. A tremor went through his body and he closed his eyes.

He was alerted by the door opening at the back of the house. It was his father standing on the porch, looking towards the fence.

Joey ran to the house and embraced his astonished father. They stood in a loving embrace for a long time while Ted and Joey's grandmother stood in the door.

"Joey, come inside. Only Grandma and I are here." Father turned toward the house.

"Grandma, it is so good to see you and Father again." Joey felt like a young kid coming back from a playground.

Food appeared on the table and soon the conversation was in full swing. Late into the night, Grandma went to her room and the three men whispered about Joey's assignment.

"Your brother is coming home tomorrow; I hope you can wait until he's here."

"We contacted the Home Army cell in Krakow to arrange safe passage for Joey. He has to be in Lublin next week." Ted became serious and looked at Mr. Wilk, expecting his full approval.

"I understand. We won't take much of Joey's time."

The next morning, Joey's older brother Roman arrived as the family sat down to breakfast.

"Roman, so many years …" Joey ran from the table to his brother.

"Let me look at you, Joey. You're such a grown-up now." They looked at each other for a long time.

Roman, six years older than Joey, was a tall, handsome man who took his looks from his father. His dark hair was thinning and his temples were peppered with grey. He looked much older than Joey remembered, aged not only by time but also by the burden of war and survival in an occupied country where every day could bring death or even worse: prison and torture.

"There is so much to talk about. I hope you can stay until tomorrow."

"I will." They embraced again until their father cleared his throat and invited them to the table.

"This is my friend Ted. Maybe you remember him from before the war. We were together in Warsaw."

"Hello, Ted." Roman looked directly into his eyes and said nonchalantly. "Korsak, isn't it?"

"Pilot?" Ted said his code name quietly, staring back at Roman.

The two men looked at each other and started laughing.

"What is it?" But immediately after he'd asked the question, Joey understood the situation.

"Joey, I was the person that Korsak contacted to arrange for your passage to Lublin." Roman looked at his younger brother with a smile and after a while, he added, "I had no idea that it was my little brother. It makes it harder to send you into this dangerous mission."

"Life is full of surprises. I made a promise to my girlfriend that I'll see her again and I will."

Ted left after breakfast. Both Joey and Ted were emotional, knowing that it might be the last time they saw each other. War had made them understand that they could only hope for the best, but any day death could strike without announcement.

The conversation around the table continued past breakfast late into the afternoon. Joey spoke about his friendship with Billy, about his mission to France to bring Billy back to England, about his Vera from the Borderlands, and after hesitating, he talked about his son, Joey Jr. He didn't mention that it was Billy's wife who was the mother of his son or the fallout from his friendship with Billy after her confession.

He avoided many details and both his father and Roman didn't ask questions, sensing that the answers could be difficult.

"I told you a lot about me. What about you, Roman?"

"I'm still living in Krakow, working in a factory and secretly practicing law as my part of contributing to the Home Army."

"How do you practice underground law?"

"Many documents are coming from the government in exile; they require my legal interpretation. Lately, we're busy documenting ownership of land, houses, and businesses that were confiscated by the Germans. And very important, we're documenting the stolen treasures from the Wawel Castle, museums, and private collections."

"How do you do this?"

"It isn't complete, but we're doing our best to keep records of what we know. Once the war is over, law and order must return to Poland."

"One of the serious worries of the government in exile is the influence of the Bolsheviks and the spread of communism to Poland, this is why I was sent to get more information from the parts already liberated by the Russian Army." He looked at his father and with concern in his voice, asked, "Would you consider leaving Poland if the communists take over?"

"Roman and I have discussed such a possibility, but we hope for the best."

Joey's mission went mostly uneventfully, but the message he was taking back to London was a grim one. Along with the Russian Army, the Polish communists were working to spread the propaganda of a free Poland with land for the poor and the equality of all classes. They were gaining popularity, but the government in London and the Home Army could still tip the scale in their favour by negotiating the fate of Poland with the Allies and getting their support to keep Poland out of the reach of communist Russia.

His safe passage back to England was reminiscent of his escape from Poland after the defeat in 1939. He was in the free part of France, which had been liberated in the summer of 1944 and was stationed with the Allied forces in Normandy, waiting for transport to England. The jubilation in France was exhilarating. Everybody was celebrating and telling stories about the D-Day victory in June and the liberation of Paris in August.

Joey considered visiting Thionville. He was almost sure that Jean was his and Ted's father. The two men must have been mistakenly identified and Joseph's amnesia had made it easier to accept that version of events. It would be a dangerous trip, as Lorraine and Alsace were still in the hands of the Germans, and the Allies had slowed down their advances due to various logistical issues.

At the end of the day, he decided that going to Thionville was not the best choice and instead, he wrote a letter to Jean, sitting long into the night, calculating every word he put on the paper.

Dear Jean,

Greetings to you and your family. The last two months I spent in my home country and I'm now on the way back to my place where my fiancée awaits my arrival. My friend Billy and I are very grateful for your past hospitality. Billy's wife has been badly injured and left in a coma. I don't have any news about her current condition. During my travels, I met Joseph's family, his wife Maria, son Ted, and daughter Ania. After the letter from the Rhine Foundry informing her about the death of her husband, Maria turned for help to the local priest, Father Karol. He helped Ted to go to school to be trained as a tailor. Ted finished the house that Joseph and Maria had started to build and established his tailor's shop in one wing of the house. He is a very serious man, responsible for his mother and sister. He is serving his county with all his heart and looking forward to a brighter future. He seldom smiles and sometimes can be caught looking toward France as if he wants to connect with his absent father.

As you know, Ted and I are half-brothers and we both feel the absence of Joseph. We talked about meeting in Thionville one day to see the places that our father walked. He deeply misses him but does not want to acknowledge this, as it would upset his mother. She is a very devout Catholic and her prayers help her in everyday life. Joseph sent her a replica of a famous painting of Saint Mary by Bartolome Murillo and she kneels in front of it every day, praying for Joseph's rightful place in the afterlife. The painting is very special to her as a large copy of it is hanging in the church where she and Joseph got married. Ania does not remember her father; she was only two years old when he left. In her mind, Ted is the head of the family and she admires him for his courage and wisdom. She had to stop her education when the war started but would love to go back to school one day.

I was invited for supper at their house and saw a picture of Maria and Joseph's wedding as well as the picture of Joseph that he sent them just before the accident. He was a handsome man. Sometimes I'm sad that I never met my father, but I was raised by a great man and I consider him my true, loving father. I try not to be angry at Joseph for never acknowledging that I was his son. I don't want to think of him as a coward for leaving my mother pregnant, but I was told that he was a very young man when it happened and he thought it was best to disappear from her life.

I'm sending best regards to you and your family.
Joey.

Ps. One day Ted and I will meet with you to listen to some stories about Joseph.

Joey looked at the letter, written on a slightly crumpled piece of paper, and he hesitated to fold it and put it in the envelope. He felt some guilt in writing it, knowing deep inside his heart that the purpose of his words was for Jean to recover some of his lost memory and perhaps reach out to his first family and him as well. He knew that this might bring some upheaval to Jean's current life, but he was sure that Emilie already knew Jean's true identity. Slowly, he folded the letter, put it in a brown envelope, and sealed it. His hand trembled as he wrote the address, but once it was done, a peaceful feeling spread over him. He knew that it was the right decision.

After the liberation of Paris, most people in the Lorraine-Alsace area were hopeful that the end of the war would come soon. Jean, his family, and his employees became more vigilant as it was known that some locals who preferred for the Germans to win the war were collaborating with them, enabling the German Army to score some unexpected wins. Some villages were evacuated by the American troops to allow the advancement of the Third Army under General George Patton. Many older people flocked to Thionville while young Mosselans were enlisted into the German military service.

Jean's well-established position in the area and the tolerance of his business by the Germans, who benefited from his service to the wine industry, was not secure anymore. Together with Andreas, he established an around-the-clock watch on the premises but didn't cease the operation of the cell.

Emilie wouldn't give in to her husband's pleas. "Jean, more than ever, we need to continue to operate."

"The war is almost over. Why would we endanger our children?"

"We did it for over three years, don't bring your children to this equation now. If something happens, Andreas has agreed to take the fault and there is no evidence that we were involved. I made sure there is nothing incriminating in the house."

Further appeals didn't make any inroads in changing her mind.

Soon his mind was preoccupied with a letter he'd received from Joey. Late at night, listening to Emilie's light snoring, he got enough courage to get up and read it. When it had arrived earlier that day, his reaction had been puzzling even to him. The letter was like a living thing, making his body react to it with trembling, as an icy-cold feeling spread through his veins. He had no joy in receiving this letter but only a dread of something unwelcome inside it. He was often paranoid about his past and not knowing or not wanting to know irritated him. He was becoming more withdrawn and noticed that Emilie was concerned about him. Sitting by the night light in the living room, he read the letter. At first reading, he was not alerted, just curious as to why Joey would write so much about Joseph's family. Something drew him back to the letter and he read it again, slowly visualising the Polish family and their life there. He closed his eyes and could almost see the house as if he knew it.

"No, it can't be." He stood up and put the letter into his Bible.

"Tomorrow, I'll decide what should I do with it." He turned off the light and sat in deep darkness for a long time.

On the night that Jean read the letter from Joey, Ted opened his eyes to see only the blackness surrounding him.

Father, are you here? He tried to say it aloud but no voice came from his throat. It was his brain that was screaming. Since he was a child, Ted had experienced sleep paralysis; he was consciously aware of his surroundings but unable to move or speak. He knew that this state between sleep and waking would pass, but each time it happened, it frightened him with a feeling of something supernatural.

He searched the dark room with his wide-open eyes. Unable to see anything, he listened to any sound, any movement of the air and could not detect anything but the persistent feeling of his father's presence surrounding him.

His previous experiences had involved unknown people or demons, but this time the feeling was very clear; it was his father.

Are you here, Father? he repeated in his mind. *Are you here because you're still alive?*

At that moment, Ted heard a faint noise as if the wind had suddenly rattled the partially open window. He woke up and the nightmare was over. He couldn't sleep anymore; he was remembering every word Joey had said to him about his visit to Thionville. Lying in bed, not knowing the truth, Ted became angry at Joey, his father, and the entire world.

There's no point in thinking about it anymore. Too much uncertainty can drive me mad. Alive or dead he is dead to me. Ted decided that he would eradicate from his memory any thoughts of his father and would avoid looking at his picture on the shelf. He removed the small photograph of his father and was ready to tear it into pieces when he was stopped by the feeling of sin. It was sacrilege to destroy something that was part of his Father's life, even if he wanted to do it.

He rose from his narrow, foldable bed and lit a candle. Some time ago, he'd decided to sleep in his shop instead of the room he shared with Ania. Although the shop was in a large room, there was not much spare space between the cutting table, the ironing bench, and the shelves with some fabric. Every night he unfolded his bed in the corner, where during the day a mannequin stood partially covered by a jacket Ted was working on. Ted started laughing as he stared at the mannequin in the centre of the shop.

"Stupid me, it wasn't Father; it was the mannequin that I saw tonight." He went to it and covered it with a blanket. "No more nightmares."

He blew out the candle and went back to bed.

It was a late afternoon in October. Ted was on his way to pick up newspapers for distribution. He didn't do it on a regular basis, as others had stepped in to relieve him for other duties, but from time to time, he still did it. He always felt the adrenaline going through his veins as he carried the papers back from the printing shop. These newspapers were a source of the latest information about the war and the Allies' movements in Europe, as well as being a valuable propaganda tool for the Home Army.

Checking his surroundings, Ted spotted Erik nearby, walking along the river towards the bridge. Suddenly, the dark skies became even darker as Ted's mind became clouded with hate and the desire to kill and before he even realised it, he'd attacked Erik from behind and wrestled him to the ground. Ted was smaller than Erik but had more raw strength, built by years of hard work, discipline, and daily exercise. It would be easy to kill Erik. The river was rushing nearby, singing to Ted; *Kill, kill, kill, my waters will swallow him.*

He thought of Rose, hoping to win her heart when the war was over. To kill Erik now meant to make Rose unhappy. He couldn't do this to her.

"Damn you, German. Leave and never come back. I might kill you if I see you again."

Slowly he released Erik's neck and the skies brightened a little. Erik didn't move. He just lay there as if he was welcoming the punishment. That angered Ted even more. "Fight you cowardly swine!" He wanted to punch and kick Erik, but seeing him just lying there brought only revulsion, and he ran towards the river. The desire to kill was not over, and Ted jumped into the cold October water. The river took him in, swept his body into a bend, and he disappeared.

For many long seconds, he thought he was drowning, then a feeling of cleansing and a new beginning washed over him. He emerged from the water. The desire to kill was over. The hope for a better life had settled in his heart.

The fight with Ted was unnerving and Erik had to be careful meeting with Rose. Sometimes he wondered why she had not been punished for her relationship with him and that her beautiful hair had not been shaved off. Either they were both lucky or she was being protected by somebody. Perhaps it was Ted who protected her from the wrath of the underground. He suspected that Ted was in love with Rose and wasn't sure if he himself would act so honourably if it was the other way around. "Perhaps Ted is the better man?"

Erik didn't like his thoughts.

As the Russian Army kept closing on the Germans and pushing them west, many more injured and exhausted soldiers from the Eastern Front were brought to the town. The injured ones were quartered in the Town Hall that served as a makeshift hospital and others were placed in houses that were already overcrowded. Rose and other young women were enlisted by the Red Cross to help care for the injured soldiers.

As she walked between the cots, Rose heard a weak voice. "Rose."

She turned around and looked at the soldier covered in bandages. It took her a while to recognise him. "Hugo, is that you?"

"Yes, Rose, but just a shell of me."

"I didn't know that you were at the Eastern Front. How bad is it?"

"The Germans are losing the war but Berlin sends more young men to fight for their failed plans."

"Should I feel sorry for the German soldiers? We didn't ask you to come here."

"Forgive us Rose, but look around. Do you see the young boys just sixteen years of age? Do you think they had any choice? Germans went insane and even now, in the face of defeat, the older generation believes in their ideology of superiority. Did you know that my mother was Polish? I wish I had run away from Silesia before I enlisted. Instead, I joined them to escape the poverty of my family."

Rose looked around to avoid listening to Hugo but her consciousness was suddenly assaulted by the realisation that most of the soldiers lying around were just teenage boys, scared, praying to the God that abandoned them, and calling for their mothers in the delirium of the fevers that ravaged their bodies.

"Does Erik know that you're here?"

"I didn't see him, but he must have a list of all the soldiers sent from the front. The *Feldgendarmerie* is deciding who comes to the hospital and who is sent to people's homes."

"I'll tell him." Rose suddenly realised that she should not talk about Erik.

"Do you still see him?"

"Let's not talk about it. I must go attend to the others."

With many injured and exhausted soldiers transported from the Eastern Front, Erik and his men were busy with the logistics of accommodating them. Coming to the hospital and seeing the injured soldiers was eased by the opportunity to see Rose and talk to her, even if only for a moment. But even seeing Rose was no consolation for his distress when he had to send the recuperated soldiers back to the front.

"Officer, please don't send us back!" That was the most frequent cry, especially from the youngest soldiers.

There was no answer to such a plea, and Erik kept giving the orders as his heart was turning to stone.

It was near the end of the day when he heard a voice calling him by name. He turned and noticed Hugo sitting on his bed.

"Hello, Erik. I'm back." Hugo started laughing, making Erik uncomfortable. He wondered if Hugo realised that Erik was the Judas who'd betrayed him. He was almost panicking but Hugo just extended his hand and said, "It's so good to see you again."

Erik relaxed and shook Hugo's hand.

They talked about the Eastern Front and the senselessness of the war before Erik remembered that he needed to continue with his inspection.

"Did Rose tell you I was here?" asked Hugo. "She's looking after me and the others."

"No, she didn't. It's complicated. I'll see you tomorrow." Erik left full of remorse and hoping that he could come up with a plan to save Hugo from going back to the front.

Late at night, he hit on a plan that could help Hugo to escape. Next day Erik met Rose at the hospital and motioned to her to step outside of the building. "Rose, not long ago, you suggested that I leave the army and disappear as a civilian."

She looked at him, bewildered, but didn't question him.

"I need some clothes. Could you arrange it for tomorrow?"

"I'll do it for you, but come back when the war over."

"I'll always come back for you."

Erik avoided meeting Hugo at the hospital and kept busy all day inspecting soldiers stationed in private houses. Seeing the injured ones everywhere, all scared of the Russian Army but resigned to the fact that they would be sent back to the front, made Erik think about the escape.

꩜

Getting clothes for Erik wasn't easy. Franek would notice anything of his missing. He had just two pairs of pants and some old shirts, mostly hand-downs from his father, one light jacket, and one warm jacket. In past winters, he'd had to put on almost all his clothes to stay warm. Ted had repaired Franek's jackets and pants, adding some material to make extra cuffs on his pants and sleeves. Franek had grown during the war, but his clothes were mostly his old ones.

Every fall, Rose knitted sweaters from homespun wool bought from a sheep farm, and now she decided to take one of the older ones, hoping that nobody would notice. She always made them oversized to fit over many layers of clothes during winter and the large size would be good for Erik, she decided. Late at night, she went to the attic and rummaged through her father's pre-war pants and shirts, so old that even Franek wouldn't want them. As a bonus, she found a hat that she put in the box just in case the weather was really cold. She had brought the box from the hospital and fortunately, it had the Red Cross symbol on it.

It should be easy to smuggle it to the hospital, she thought as she packed everything neatly in it.

Not sure if she wanted Erik to leave, she couldn't stop the tears rolling down her cheeks. She cut a lock of her hair and put it in the pocket of an old jacket that her father had discarded a long time ago. She put the jacket into the box. As she looked around, pieces of leather string caught her eye. She took one from the hook, removed the engagement ring from her brassiere, and hung it on the string. She fastened it around her neck and hid it inside her dress.

I can look at it whenever I want without putting my hand in the brassiere. The idea cheered her up, and she took the box down the ladder and stored it under the bed that she shared with Hela. She looked at her sleeping sister, imagining that it was a different time and it was Erik gently snoring as she snuggled under the covers. The memory of their love in the river shook her body, waking up Hela.

"What is it?" Hela murmured through her sleep.

"Just sleep, my little sister. Better times will come." She said it more to herself than Hela.

She said her prayers and ended them as always with, "God help us to survive the war."

Early in the morning, Rose carried the box with the red cross to the hospital. She looked around, and satisfied that nobody was paying attention to her, put it under an empty bed. She was hoping that Erik would be at the hospital soon. It could be their last meeting. Her heart was aching and she almost regretted that she had suggested the escape.

Lost in her thoughts and confused between wanting him to escape or to stay here a little longer, she was halted by his voice.

"Is everything fine?"

"Check under the first bed near the entrance. I love you." Her mouth barely moved but her face showed the longing, desperation, and desire to be in his arms forever. She looked at him for a long time, then turned around and went to the supply area.

After dusk, Erik came back to the hospital and went straight to Hugo's bed.

"You'll be released from the hospital in two days."

"Straight into the arms of death." Hugo laughed sarcastically.

"They're sending everybody who's recovered back to the Eastern Front."

"The stories we tell you cannot reflect the true reality. It is hell on earth. It is better to die than go back there."

"There's a box under the empty bed with civilian clothes, food, and money. You may want to disappear tonight. Go south-west, far from the front."

"What about you?"

"I'm not being sent to the front like you. Good luck."

On November 10, 1944, the American Third Army, accompanied by some French troops, liberated Thionville. Jean prayed at home while Emilie and her children ventured into town to welcome the liberators. Like many people, she had secretly sewn a French flag, which her son was proudly waving alongside others with home-made flags. An hour later, Jean joined them, and they stood together in an embrace that released the stress of the last years.

Two days after the liberation, Emilie approached the shop just as the sun was rising behind the horizon. "Jean, somebody is asking for you." The autumn colours were already fading but still beautiful, proudly displayed on the hills behind their property. The crisp mornings were a prognostication of an early and severe winter. Jean and his crew were at work producing barrels for the late autumn harvest, which always yielded aromatic and sweet wines. The Germans liked the Alsatian wines and even now that they were losing the war, they kept a strong grip on the wineries, getting almost everything put into bottles. Rumours were going around that they were even confiscating barrels of wine and delivering them to the front lines to keep up the morale of the German soldiers still fighting in the northeast part of France. Jean was caught between a rock and a hard place, as Andreas often would say. They could not slow down production or produce inferior barrels because the Germans were still strong in Lorraine and Alsace and making sure that the wine industry was functioning as always. It would be devastating to survive the war only to be killed at the end of it. Although Thionville was free, there were people who still collaborated with the Nazis and were ready to do their dirty work.

Jean started walking towards the house alongside his wife. "Do you know who it is?"

"Never met him before, but he sounded as if he knew you well."

Fear sent a shiver through Jean's body. He didn't want to see anyone from his past; he didn't want to face another episode from his life that he could not explain. He lived in constant fear of a doomsday waiting for him, and he was tired of his feeling of uncertainty.

"Hello, Jean, glad to see you after four years." Michel Perrot extended his hand and to Emilie's surprise, Jean smiled and shook the stranger's hand.

"Please come in," said Jean. He introduced Emilie and asked her to bring two cups of tea.

Michel removed his overcoat and a hat and Jean hung them on the rack in the foyer. The coat was well worn but the quality of it was unmistakable, soft cashmere that smelled of good cologne. Jean himself liked to wear good clothes and the elegance of the blue shirt with a navy pullover over it didn't escape his eye. Michel was a different man than the one Jean remembered. The civilian clothes made him look younger than he had prior to the war.

Despite his hair being partially grey and a slight puffiness under his eyes, he looked no older than thirty and the civilian look gave him an aristocratic appearance. Jean was not surprised by this realisation. Prior to the war, he had sometimes wondered about Michel's rise to a high rank in the army despite his young age. Jean thought about his own life after the accident—his modest beginning and rise to successful businessman.

I owe everything to my and Emilie's hard work, not just a privileged upbringing, he thought. There was no bitterness in his mind, just a recognition of the reality. He'd always liked Michel and considered working with him a privilege, despite his reluctance to be involved in any spying activities.

"Jean, I'll be straight with you. France needs your service."

Jean took a sip of tea and slowly swallowed it. He lifted his head and asked, "What kind?"

"As you know, the Germans are fighting strong in the Vosges Mountains. French and American forces are pushing them towards Colmar in Alsace."

"I'm not a soldier; how can I be of any service?"

"You know the whole region very well. We need you to go to Colmar with a message to the underground fighters there."

Jean hesitated for a while before answering. He didn't want to go to any place that wasn't necessary for his business. He didn't look at Michel but with his head turned to the window, he said, "We were just liberated and you're asking me to go into a German-occupied area."

"The French underground isn't well organised. There are differences between the groups that make up the French resistance. Each has different origins, methods, and political aims. There are rivalries between the various intelligence organisations, including the Special Operations Executive." Michel sounded troubled and embarrassed by his words.

"What do you expect me to do about it?" Jean sounded a little irritated.

"You know Marc Kurtz."

"I haven't seen him for a long time." Jean sounded very cautious. He had been hoping that Marc had disappeared from his life forever.

"Marc works with us."

"Wasn't Marc your enemy that I had to spy on?"

"Times are different now. Enemies become allies and vice versa. He's working in the underground in Alsace. He doesn't know about our plans to push the Germans to the Colmar area and finish them there. We need you to travel, as you always did with your barrels for the late harvest wine, and contact Marc. I'll bring the plans for the final offensive and you need to deliver them to Marc."

"Can I think about it?" Jean answered in a frail voice.

"I'll be back in three days, be ready, Jean. That is an order. You're the best person to deliver the message to Marc. You're known to the proprietors of the wineries and to the Germans in this area as well. You've lived a sheltered life here because of your business. The Germans still want their wine and you can travel without suspicion on their part."

Emilie was upset when Jean told her about the mission to Colmar but put on a brave face to keep his spirits a little uplifted. Late at night, he prayed for a long time and asked God for forgiveness. He had the foreboding feeling that this was his last mission, that he wouldn't see his family again. He wasn't terribly sad; it was more a gloomy resignation that he wouldn't see his children grow up, and that he wouldn't hold Emilie in his arms, kiss her lips, cover her body with his, and make tender love to her. Emilie was a very passionate woman; she was not shy about her sexuality and used many ways to arouse Jean. Sometimes he was embarrassed by her openness, especially after his reading of the Bible, but her slim, soft body, her full breasts, and the smell of the garden in her hair always defeated his fear of God. He liked to allow himself to be led by her to the depths of passion that always left him breathless with his body trembling after reaching the climax of their union.

After their longer than usual lovemaking, his sleep was peaceful without any dreams. He woke up relaxed and ready to accept orders from Michel.

Delegating responsibilities to Andreas and giving him the authority to make any business decision in consultation with Emilie came naturally. Jean was surprised by how easy it was to delegate and not worry about the future.

As they packed barrels onto the truck, Andreas looked more anxious than Jean. "Isn't it dangerous to travel to Alsace when the Germans are fighting ferociously in the Vosges?"

"I'm not going that far south, and it might be even easier to move while the Germans are busy fighting."

Andreas' voice was subdued because he was concerned about Jean travelling alone. "Couldn't the Willmburg Estate find the barrels closer? Let me go with you."

"You take care of our business and Emilie while I'm away. I'm sure we and all of France will celebrate Christmas 1944 victorious. The Germans are done."

"Good riddance." Andreas looked at Jean and tried to smile, but it was more of a grimace that appeared on his face.

It was the middle of November 1944 when Joey got back to England. He submitted a full report from his mission to the Polish government in exile and was granted a week of leave to see Vera in Medmenham.

It was already late afternoon when he got to the housing compound where Vera and other women were quartered. He hesitated before entering the house. The absence of almost three months, the visit with his family in Poland, and time with Ted had made him unsure of his life here in England. He looked at the sky; it was cloudy with occasional sun rays trying desperately to break through the grey cloud mass hanging low on the horizon.

He missed the sky in Poland. He remembered it being brighter and sunnier, and despite the devastation of the country, friendlier than the one he was looking at.

Where is my home? he thought, looking at the horizon.

He was roused from his melancholy by the bright voice of a young woman in an army uniform entering the house. "Hello, soldier, are you coming in?"

Vera was in her room when he opened the door. She hesitated for a moment and ran into his arms. They held each other in a passionate embrace while Joey kissed her face as the tears flowed from her eyes.

He stayed for two days at Medmenham, spending most of the time with Vera. She was given one day of leave from her duties to spend with her fiancé, as he was known on the base. On the second day, after they came back from a long walk, they sat at the window and Joey continued to talk about Poland.

"The Borderlands are again under Russian occupation. They are now the liberators, but I think that there's no home for you to go back to."

"I've already accepted it and have no desire to go back. Too many bad memories."

He took her in his arms and stroked her hair, which was now very short but perfectly sculpted around her head.

She moved away from Joey and opened a drawer of the small dresser. "I received great news from the Red Cross."

"Red Cross?" Joey stood puzzled next to her.

"I don't remember if I told you that my family was dispersed throughout the world after we left Russia. I sent a query to the Red Cross missing-persons search and received a letter from them. My younger sister was located in an orphanage in India. Let me read you the letter."

Dear Vera Skarbek,

We're pleased to inform you that the Red Cross has located your sister Dana Skarbek in an orphanage in India. In 1942, Maharaja Jam Saheb Digvijaysinhij Ranjitsinhji, the ruler of Nawanagat, a state of British India, established an orphanage in the small seashore town of Balachadi, in north-west India. The maharaja has been a generous provider for many Polish orphans, not only with food and shelter in the dormitories built for them, but also with schooling in his palatial house. The children are safe there and will be united with their families when the war ends. If you would like to write to your sister, please send a letter to any location of the Red Cross near you and it will be delivered to India.

Sincerely,
Pat Hipkins
Red Cross.

"I know about this unusual orphanage in India," said Joey. "The Polish government in London organised deliveries of Polish books for the school they have there." He pulled Vera close to him. "I'm happy for you. Your sister will be part of our life one day soon."

Sitting at the table with the curtains drawn down, Vera's trembling hand touched Joey's.

"Here is the letter you left with me before your mission to Poland." She handed him the unopened envelope.

Joey took the envelope and looked at it for a long time. "There is no need to open it. I am back and alive, I will discuss my involvement in the child's future with Eloise."

She smiled "Please tell me again about your mission."

It was a long monologue never interrupted by Vera. She listened intently with her usual stoic face.

"I love you. I hope you will meet my family, Ted and Jean one day and forgive me for my confused life."

"Joey, you're my love and my best friend. Since I was a child, I kept losing my family one by one. You're the anchor that gives me the feeling of safety in this unsettled life. I'm not judging you; there is nothing to forgive. We're all children wounded by the war. You and I are the lucky ones for having found each other." She took him by his hand and led him to her narrow bed.

"Make love to me. I'm ready." She kicked the shoes off her feet and sat on the bed.

Emilie prepared a change of clothes to last for the long journey. She lifted each of Jean's garments to her face and deeply inhaled the fragrance of her husband. She worried about the travel but understood that trying to convince Jean to stay at home would be unsuccessful. She accepted that the barrel delivery was cover for the mission that he needed to complete.

Michel came in the evening to see Jean before his planned departure at dawn of the next day. "When you leave Thionville, stay on the main road to Metz. Somebody will meet you there to advise the best route to take to Colmar. Most likely, you may have to take back roads to Chateau

Seins, where you can stay for a while if the road is dangerous. From there, somebody familiar with the area will travel with you."

"The Germans are busy in the Ardennes and Vosges. Are your people sure that I can travel to Colmar?"

"Nobody is sure. You're our best man and if the situation on the road is dangerous, you can stop at some of the wineries along the road. You know the ones that are pro-France and they'll give you shelter. But you must get to Colmar to meet with Marc; otherwise, many people may die if they are not prepared for the final offensive."

"When do you expect me to arrive in Colmar?"

"In two weeks, by the end of November."

They went over the information that Jean needed to deliver to Marc. He wouldn't carry any documents of the planned offensive in Colmar. He would need to relay the plan almost word for word as Michel presented it.

"Give this Bible to Marc. We marked some dates and places; he knows the code to get them."

Fear entered Jean's heart as he realised that he couldn't take his old Bible, which had been part of him for years, bringing him peace and calm during difficult moments. The worn leather cover with almost invisible gold letters fitted perfectly in his hands. He knew every crease, every stain on so many pages that were so familiar. Taking two Bibles could be suspicious, especially if one was old and the other new.

The weather was unusual in the autumn of 1944. Sunny but colder than in other years. People were predicting a very cold winter, and Jean took his winter coat and boots with him. Among the many barrels, he stored containers with gasoline, enough to get to Colmar. Once there, he would refill them to bring him back home.

The first part of the road was quiet, and Jean thought about Emilie and the children standing in front of the house and waving goodbye. His mind drifted back to the beginning of his remembered life. He recalled Emilie bending over him to change the bandages while he pretended to be unconscious. He'd been so afraid of letting the people around him realise that he was awake because his mind was blank and his understanding of himself was only that he was a human. From the first moment he'd seen her, she'd become his lifeline, his guide, and his most treasured companion. The feeling of sadness slowly left him. He was determined to come back to his wife and the life he loved after completing his mission.

The countryside was beautiful despite the cold November weather. There were still remnants of harvest left on patches of land along the road. Before winter came, it would all be cleared by the migrant workers, who lived close to starvation.

His first stop was at the small town of Saint Augusto. He met his contact, a man in his early sixties, looking like a farmer with a weathered face and bright blue eyes. After a brief greeting and the customary small talk about the weather, Jean was led to a house with a wooden gate. His truck barely got through the gate into a nice courtyard hidden from the spying eyes of strangers. Although the war was ending, they had to take all precautions against collaborators or Germans passing by or through town.

Reluctantly, the owner of the house allowed Jean to use his phone. Jean had promised Emilie that he would call whenever it was possible. He wanted to tell her that he felt well and that the uncertainty about his mission had vanished and he had a good feeling about coming back home before Christmas.

He left the town before dawn, taking a route suggested by his contact. Although they never mentioned any names, he sensed that Michel was well known and respected in the underground network. The next few days, Jean travelled without any incident and the guides always directed him to travel the safest roads.

The landscape changed as he travelled south. Wineries were spread over the land, delighting the eyes with the beauty of late autumn, but the area was quieter than Jean remembered from previous years.

"The fall harvest should already be turning into wine, the sweet grapes of the late harvest waiting to be transformed into the famous Alsatian dessert wines." Jean dreamily looked into distant hills full of grapevines neatly growing in even rows like crouching soldiers. A shiver went through his body.

"Stop seeing gloom everywhere. This is your favourite countryside: the hills, the vines, and people harvesting ... " Jean stopped talking to himself. He'd realised that very few people were working in the fields and it had given him goosebumps all over his body from the feeling of uncertainty. Jean had the desire to turn around and go back home, he hesitated for a while and then sped up the truck. His ingrained responsibility wouldn't allow him to abandon the mission. People's safety relied on his arrival in Colmar ahead of the German Army and the advancing Allies.

His radio in the truck had poor reception and he often got broadcasts in German, French, and English. He considered the possibility to encounter German soldiers, but the first week passed and the back roads were clear. The war in Ardennes and the Vosges Mountains kept the German and Allied armies occupied. At each of his stops, people talked about the Allies' offensive and the war nearing the end. Some nights he reached the places that Michel had showed him on the map, but there were a few nights that he had to improvise and sleep in the truck hidden in the trees along the road.

They were the worst nights; he could hear the sounds of war in the distance and expected to be discovered by "something." He didn't believe in ghosts, but he was afraid of them. On nights like that, he clutched the Bible close to his chest and prayed to God for forgiveness, wondering what had happened in his early years to make him superstitious and afraid of the paranormal.

On the tenth day, he stopped for the night at a small estate that he knew from his past deliveries.

"Jean, we knew you might be coming this way, but in times like this, even the best of plans can go wrong." The proprietor, an older man with a big moustache adorning his smiling face, hugged Jean in a strong embrace.

"It is awfully quiet around here." Jean was finally able to release himself from the joyous embrace.

"You're travelling through a corridor of relative peace as the battles are raging in the mountais. But it won't last. You're slightly ahead of the Allies, who just liberated Strasbourg and the Germans who are gathering their troops marching east."

"Why don't they just surrender? They lost the war already."

"Hitler gave them orders to defend Alsace as they believe it is their right to this land. Some of them passed through our estate, marching south towards the Vosges. They acted as if they didn't want to cause much damage to the estates, believing that they'll own the region after the war and continue to get the great wines we produce."

Jean sounded tired. "If Hitler had been killed during that attempted assassination, the war would be over and many lives saved on both sides."

After a supper of wild rabbit in a tasty sauce with potatoes and roasted carrots, they enjoyed a glass of wine from the estate, talking until Jean's eyes were half closed. He slept well in a comfortable bed, free of any night-mares and filled again with hope for a better future.

He was in good spirits travelling southeast, thinking about last night and the generosity of the local people. Lorraine and Alsace were his favourite places on this earth, places that had allowed him to be prosperous even during the difficult war times. His empty gas containers had been refilled with gasoline that the estate kept hidden on-site, and he was planning on reaching Colmar in two days.

Lost in his thoughts, he suddenly noticed an army crossing the road in the distance. Consternation gripped him and chilled him to the bone. For a moment, he could not see if they were Germans or French, but soon it was clear to him. It was a large contingent of Germans and he knew that they'd noticed his truck. He stopped in the middle of the road. Should he turn his truck around or abandon it and run into the hills? His mind was racing and he almost allowed himself to panic. Then he noticed three motorcycles, one with a side car, driving towards him. He sobered up quickly and rehearsed his alibi.

They parked on both sides of the truck and at the back. He was trapped, not that he had any chance of escaping, he thought bitterly.

"Outside!" Two soldiers pointed their rifles at Jean.

He stepped out of the truck's cab and glanced towards the back. The two soldiers from the third motorcycle had already lifted the canvas cover and positioned their guns to shoot anyone hiding inside.

"*Hände hoch.*"

Jean put his hands up. The two soldiers from the back moved to the front and reported their findings.

"Why are you here?" a soldier demanded.

"I'm travelling to the Willmburg estate to deliver barrels for the late-harvest wine."

"Don't you know it is a war zone?"

"I do it every year. I'm a cooper and the estate needs my barrels."

"Hans, drive back and ask *Oberfeldwebel* Ross to come here. He was stationed in Alsace and is familiar with the wine business here.

"Bert, check the truck."

They waited for ten minutes—excruciating minutes that felt like an eternity to Jean.

Finally, Lieutenant Ross approached the truck on a motorcycle. Swiftly, he jumped off it and approached Jean. He looked at the documents handed to him by the soldier who was giving orders.

"Mr. Navarre, isn't it too late for the barrel delivery?"

Jean mustered his strength to sound confident. "The late harvest grapes are usually picked at the beginning of November. The farmers are predicting an early and severe winter and I hope to be back at home before the winter arrives."

"Bert, what did you find in the truck?"

"Barrels and containers with gasoline."

"Mr. Navarre, it is your lucky day. I know the wine industry, and I have heard of you as one of the best coopers in the whole region. We will confiscate some of your gasoline, leaving you enough to get to the estate. You can worry about getting more gasoline when you reach the estate." Lieutenant Ross handed Jean's documents back to him.

"Thank you." Jean was relieved but uncertain about what might happen next.

"Go, deliver the barrels. We like Alsatian wine. Soon we will be victorious drinking the wine that rightfully belongs to Germany."

Jean stood half-paralysed with fear watching them ride away. He went into the truck cab and started driving slowly towards the Germans.

Once he passed the soldiers, he felt safer when he realised that they were heading in a different direction from him.

He got to Colmar on November 26, sooner than expected. The city was still under German occupation but there was an air of quiet jubilation in the streets. Strasbourg had been liberated on November 23 and the people in Colmar and the area expected to gain freedom in the next few days.

To avoid any further risk, Jean sold his barrels to a local dealer and drove to an address that had been etched in his brain from the start of his journey.

"Jean, I didn't know that you were coming. I only knew that somebody was coming to deliver important plans." Marc sounded uncertain.

Jean was the first one to extend his hand. "I've had time to think about you, Marc. Times are strange and sometimes traitors become allies." The conversation was easier after that.

"Basically, you're telling me that the French and the American Armies are planning to push the Germans from all three directions towards Colmar and finish them here." Marc sounded very concerned.

"Michel Perrot said that you and others may choose to leave Colmar or stay behind and sabotage their position here in the area. He preferred that you choose the latter."

"What about you, Jean? Are you leaving?"

"Yes, I need to get some gasoline for my truck and some food supplies. I hope to get home before winter sets in."

"I'll help you to get what you need; in two days, you'll be able to leave. I and my people here will stay to fight."

Part Four

← DESTINIES →

1944 - 1946

S oon after Joey returned from his visit with Vera, he travelled to London to meet with Eloise's mother and his son. He was determined to be part of his son's life, but knew that the extent of his relationship with him depended on Eloise and Billy.

The site of London in ruins depressed Joey and his hope for seeing his son was slowly vanishing. Many houses were reduced to rubble that had to be carefully circumvented to get to another street. The distance from the train station to Eloise's mother's flat was not long, but it took Joey over two hours to get there. He decided to walk instead of taking a taxi as he wanted to absorb the devastation of the city that held so many happy memories for him. He passed a church that was destroyed by fire and looked like twisted arms stretching to the sky. A glimpse of a few people kneeling among the ruins of the church gave him momentary relief from his sadness. For the first time, he realised that life went on in the city. People were shopping in the few stores, some of them without windows; children were clambering over the piles of bricks and stones; and cars were slowly moving along some of the passable streets. London's heart was beating as the people with tired faces and shaggy clothes were showing defiance and hope for a victory. He reached the house and seeing it standing solid gave him the energy to run to the second floor and knock on the door.

"Good morning, Mrs. Kerr." He looked at her face aged with grief and his heart almost stopped. Although they'd never met, he was sure it was Eloise's mother. The resemblance between her and Eloise was striking; the same nose and the eyes, although sad, still sparkled.

"My name is Joey Wilk. Can I come in?"

"I know your name. Please come in."

He stepped into the small hallway and she motioned to the coat rack in the corner to hang his lined pilot jacket.

"What brings you here? Eloise is dead and Billy is with the army in Europe." She said the words slowly and the sorrow in her voice added to the grief that Joey felt immediately upon hearing about the death.

"I'm so very sorry about Eloise; she was close to me." Joey was shaken by the news about Eloise's death.

"I know, but I never thought that I would see you." She looked at Joey and something in the expression on her face hinted that she knew more than just his name.

"Is little Joey with you?" Joey's voice trembled as he spoke the name of his son.

"He's sleeping right now but will be up soon. Would you like a cup of tea?"

She went to the kitchen and Joey looked around the room. It was a combined living and dining space with a few pictures displayed on the antique mahogany credenza. The windows were adorned with heavy dark curtains lined with a black fabric that prevented any light from coming through. Everything in the room was dark and depressing.

He looked at the pictures of the Kerr family. Parents and two children: a boy and a girl. Eloise had never told him that she had a brother. Joey wondered what had happened to him.

"Tea is ready. I have some biscuits if you would like."

"Mrs. Kerr, I'll get straight to the reason for my visit. Joey is my son." He stopped and looked at her.

There was no surprise—there was even relief.

"I suspected that he might be yours when Billy told me that Joey wasn't his son. You see, I knew about Eloise's and your love affair. I didn't approve of it but I didn't say anything. The war made everything more intense and she was happy."

"I'm sorry," Joey said, looking away from her.

"I was surprised when she secretly married Billy and suspected that she was in a hurry to do so."

"I take the blame for the affair. I betrayed my close friend Billy and put Eloise in a difficult situation. I was hurt but accepted her decision to marry Billy, not knowing at that time that she was pregnant with my child."

"Everything changed with her death and Billy's clear refusal to accept the child."

"I'm here to talk about my son."

"What is there to talk about? You're a soldier and you'll be gone to war again; I'm the closest person to him."

"I would like to raise my son when the war is over. I have a fiancée, and she and I discussed raising Joey together."

Mrs. Kerr's face stiffened and she immediately said, "He is mine."

"We don't want to separate you and Joey; we would be happy for you to be part of his life."

After a long silence, Joey continued. "London is a very dangerous place to stay to the end of the war. My fiancée, Vera, works at Medmenham, one hour from here. There are estates nearby that house children and widows. We can arrange for you to move there with Joey. It's much safer to be away from London since it's still being bombed by the Germans."

There was still no answer from Mrs. Kerr.

"My fiancée will help you to raise the child while I'm at war. She has a full-time job in the army but would be happy to spend as much time as possible with you and Joey."

A child's cry filled the room.

"I'll bring him here." In a few seconds, Mrs. Kerr appeared in the living room with the boy in her arms.

Joey felt a sharp tingle in his heart. He didn't doubt that it was his son. The blue eyes, the fuzzy blond hair reminded him of himself in one of the old pictures.

"I'll accept your proposition. He is your son and we must think about his safety first. When do you think we can move?"

"I'll be here on Saturday with an army car to take you, Joey, and your belongings to the estate."

Two days later, on Saturday, Joey and Vera picked up Mrs. Kerr and Joey Jr. and left London. Nobody looked back, afraid it could make it difficult to leave the place where life had once flourished but turned into grief and misery.

Being a long-time experienced pilot, Joey was assigned to fly bombers over Germany. Each time, he found it difficult to drop the bombs over

German cities, he thought of devastated Warsaw, destroyed by the Nazis and its population mercilessly killed. This gave him strength as he whispered his gloomy prayer: "You deserve it. You started it. You did nothing to stop Hitler and the Nazis. One more flight, one more bomb." Sometimes it helped, but the long war, constant fighting and danger were wearing him down.

Jean left Colmar on November 29 in the middle of the night. Travelling in any direction was dangerous, and after discussing options with Marc and his people, Jean travelled southwest of Colmar towards the Vosges Mountains. The city of Mulhouse was already liberated—if Jean could get there, he would meet the French Army and even get help to move to safer areas west of Alsace.

The first two days on the way back home, Jean's journey was monotonous. The days were short and the wind beat against the windshield of his truck. In the early evening on the first of December, he drove into the small village of St. Theodore and directed his truck to the address given to him by Marc. An old farmer opened the door and after exchanging passwords, he ushered Jean in to pull his truck behind the barn. They covered it with dead tree branches and went home.

"You may have difficulties driving farther south," said the farmer after they ate a hot vegetable stew with a chunky slice of home-made bread.

"There is no other way for me to go."

"You could wait here for the French Army to arrive. They are pushing the Germans towards Colmar and you may run into either the German Army or go straight into the line of fire before you get to Mulhouse."

"I might be lucky and avoid the Germans," said Jean without really believing his own words.

The next morning Jean woke up to a heavy blanket of snow on the ground. There was no way he could get moving right away. The sky was clear and the shining sun blinded his eyes.

The clear air opened up the horizon and even the far away Vosges Mountains were visible, covered with white snow and looking like a group of brides in wedding dresses waiting for their grooms to come back from the war. Jean looked mesmerised at the snow-covered mountains. They were promising hope, a new and clear beginning. The white snow covered the atrocities of war and Jean took a deep breath and looked into the sky.

Suddenly, the earth trembled and black machines looking like deadly dragons appeared on the horizon. The farmer ran out of his house and looked in the direction of the darkness moving towards the village.

"German Army, come with me."

His wife, in her morning apron with a spoon dripping with porridge, stood in the kitchen looking at the two men entering the house.

"We must hide." The farmer dumped a bucket of water on the fire while his wife took the pot with porridge and handed it to Jean. They ran into the barn.

"Let's hope they'll pass our house and the whole village. They seem to be in a hurry." The farmer opened the side door to the barn.

Jean stopped, looking back. "We left tracks in the snow behind us."

"I'll brush them over with a broom and God help us that they don't notice."

Inside the barn was a trap door that led to a small cellar with a few blankets on the ground. They sat for a while, immobilised with fear until the smell of the porridge filling the cellar brought them back to reality.

"We may as well eat something," said the wife. She removed three spoons from the pocket of her apron and together they ate from the same pot.

Jean savoured the salty porridge, which tasted like the best food he'd ever eaten.

After a few hours, the loud noises of the moving army quieted and they left their hiding spot. The sun was high on the horizon and the blue of the sky was pristine with just a few white clouds lazily floating away from the mountains. They went to the house. It had been ransacked; chairs, bed, blankets, and food had been stolen.

"You stay in the house; I'm going to check with the neighbours about what is happening," said the farmer and he left the house.

Soon he was back with bad news. "The Germans are in the village, many of them. You should leave the house soon and go in the direction they just came from."

"I have to take my truck."

"They're busy resting and setting up fires to get warm. Let's hope they won't notice the truck driving away."

After putting on his winter coat, Jean went into the cab of the truck and started the engine. The farmer directed him to a narrow, unpaved road away from the main one. The ground was frozen and the truck rolled slowly towards the hills behind the village.

A new sound roared above them. A few French airplanes were surveying the area.

"Drive fast. The Germans may start shooting," he whispered, boosting his resolve to get away.

At that moment, several shells from German artillery dropped onto the truck, creating a small explosion and turning the truck on its side. Jean lost consciousness.

He woke up feeling warm. He struggled to leave the cab through the broken glass and exhausted leaned against the truck. The sun was low on the horizon but it was bright like a fire, blinding his vision. A sensation of floating in the air made him feel weightless. He turned away from the sun and a mirage-like vision appeared in front of him. Below was a house, smaller than his own but nicely designed, located near the main street of a town. At the back of the house was a young woman working in the garden, and next to her a little girl playing with the flowers. A boy was chopping wood but stopped and looked at the west horizon. His face was sad, as if he'd lost something precious to him. Jean looked around. It was a beautiful, late-summer day. The woman was picking some vegetables, but when he looked at her, she straightened and looked up into the sky.

As he was looking down at her, he felt as if a different person entered his body. He realised that he was Joseph Novak and below was his abandoned family. He raised his hand, attempting to wave but stopped as he looked at his wife Maria, making the sign of the cross.

Two days later, the French Army entered the village and found Jean's frozen body against the partially destroyed truck. His hand was raised and a faint smile was softening his rigid face.

December 1944 was unusually cold in northwest Europe and many were predicting that it would be a "Siberian" winter. Ted and George discussed the possible implications of winter with temperatures close to minus 20C. The Allies fighting in France had been slowed down by the low temperatures, strong winds, and snow over a metre deep. On the other hand, the Russians were pushing west and parts of eastern Poland were already in their hands.

"Will the Polish government in exile negotiate a deal with Churchill, Roosevelt, and Stalin preventing Poland from communist aggression?" That was the question that was utmost on their minds. The future outlook for a free Poland was getting worse with each day passing.

On December 2nd, after another depressing conversation with George, Ted took a shovel and mindlessly started removing snow, making a clear path to the shed. The late afternoon was beautiful despite the cold temperatures. The sky was deep blue, with a few white clouds slowly floating across. The sun was very strong, reflecting light in all the snowflakes, which were glittering like miniature diamonds scattered in the snow. He went to the shed to put away the shovel and an unusual chill went through his body. He pushed his hat down over his head and stepped outside. Walking toward the house with his head down, he almost bumped into his mother.

"What are you doing here without a coat? You'll freeze to death." His voice was alarmed.

Maria looked at Ted with a beautiful smile on her face. "Do you see the dark cloud?"

"All the clouds are white. Let's get home before you get sick."

She didn't move, just kept looking at the sky.

"Mother, what do you see there?"

She made a sign of cross, waved at the sky, and with a serene voice said, "Never mind."

In the next few days, Ted noticed a subtle transformation in Maria's conduct. She seemed happier, stopped complaining about pains, and the typical sadness on her face gave way to a frequent smile. Ted didn't want to ask what had led to the transformation, but every day he was amazed with the change. Ania noticed the transformation as well and asked her mother about it.

"I finally said goodbye to my husband. Joseph is in Heaven and is watching over us."

She hugged Ania as Ted stood there flabbergasted, wondering about the clouds from a few days ago.

Rose was going through the motions of everyday life, trying hard to suppress her feelings of emptiness and longing for Erik. She often caught herself whispering like a crazy woman, trying to rationalise the life choices she'd made. A week had passed since she'd seen Erik last, and slowly, she was coming to an acceptance of life without him.

Since October she had worked at the store with Wanda, a fifty-something woman who had escaped from Lublin and found shelter in Brusk. Wanda was like a mother to Rose, educated, elegant, and confident, not like her own mother, who was sliding deeper into depression.

"Rose, don't be miserable. Whatever life seems like now, it will be different a year from now."

"Did you escape in order to change your life?" Rose asked without interest in the answer, just to carry on some small talk.

"I never told you, but after my husband's death at the beginning of the war, I considered ending my life. We didn't have children, so life became senseless."

"But you're here now. What changed?"

"It isn't easy to end your own life, so I got involved with the underground, teaching university students."

"Were you a professor before the war?"

"Yes. Teaching again kept me alive, and I realised that no matter what we go through, we bounce back and find joy in life, a different one but still a joy. I left Lublin because after surviving the German occupation, I couldn't face the one coming, the Bolsheviks."

"But what will you do now? They are taking over Poland and the West doesn't care."

"I don't know, but what I wanted to tell you is that life brings new opportunities and new happiness, and you'll discover that."

Wanda left the store in the afternoon, and Rose had started sweeping the floor when the door opened and Erik's silhouette appeared in it. She stood with the broom in her hands, thinking that her madness had completely possessed her and she'd started seeing ghosts. He closed the door behind him and took her in his arms.

She accepted his explanation of Hugo's escape with joy. He was with her again and the future was not important at that moment.

The routine of Rose's life involved the hospital, the store, working at Ted's shop with Laura and Ania, and occasionally seeing Erik. The town was quiet on the surface, but underneath, it fumed with the fast-approaching end of the war. People gathered in houses, churches, and any out-of-sight places to discuss the inevitable collapse of the Nazi machine and the approaching Russian Army.

The orchard was one of the places where people gathered to discuss in whispering voices. Rose's father loved politics and he was one of the most outspoken men in the group. Women didn't participate in those discussions at the orchard, but Rose often hid behind one of the trees in the darkness and listened. In general, it was the same sentiment as during other groups' discussions. They hated the Germans and wanted them gone, but at the same time, they were afraid of the Bolsheviks. Often the discussion would slide into the history of Poland and the unjust treatment of the Polish people by other countries. Despite more than a hundred years of Poland's partition, they had never assimilated with the Germans, Russians, or Austrians. The Poles were different from their occupiers; they were independent thinkers almost to the point of anarchy, they were passionate, and they loved their folklore. They cultivated their language at home despite the German and Russian languages being used at schools. They wrote plays that had allegorical themes of history and culture, and they were disobedient to the rulers of their land.

At the end of each gathering, they repeated their pledge: "We will continue to be proud Poles, defiant of the rules of any oppressor until better times come."

Rose felt uneasy at such displays of patriotism and defiance. She thought about her patriotism, strong and deeply rooted, but the love of a German soldier had shaken that foundation. Her dream about a better life somewhere else was a sign that she didn't belong here. She felt regretful that all these intense emotions in her life had happened when she was very young and unable to make the right choices, including defying the love that had overcome her so unexpectedly.

She felt free from her guilty feelings when she was with Ania and Laura, making clothes and blankets for the refugees from Warsaw. Ted's house and his shop had an aura of conspiracy and contribution to winning the war. Rose felt good in their company, discussing current affairs with Ted. Sometimes he made fun of her, pointing out that she hadn't changed since she was a young girl reading her father's newspapers. It felt good to be teased in such an easy way. She sensed that Ted knew about her and Erik, but he never joked or said anything sarcastic about it. He was very mature, always making the right choices—not like her, she thought. *What choices will I make when the war comes to an end?* Lately, she often contemplated that question.

Everything had been a disappointment to Billy and he could not find any positive aspects to his life. Even his promotion to squadron leader seemed just a pittance and gave him no pride. He remembered that when he had joined the RAF, he'd expected a quick rise in the ranks, but it hadn't happened. He wasn't sure what events had affected his career, speculating that his marriage and fatherhood had played a role in its stagnation. He regretted his past and his unfortunate love.

On the first day of his new assignment as a squadron leader, his mood started to improve. His promotion had put him in the group of senior officers, even if his rank was the most junior among them. He had 120 people under his command, and he was flying again. His squadron was part of the 2nd Tactical Air Force, roaring through the skies, lacerating the retreating

Germans, and making the path to Berlin easier for the ground troops. The Allies, especially the Americans, showered the RAF with praise and admiration. The Spitfires and Typhoons were a match to any other plane, and together with the British and American bomber squadrons, prepared the ground below, destroying roads, railways, and bridges, preventing successful reinforcement by the German Army.

Often, Billy thought about Joey, who most likely was flying in the same campaign with even greater ferociousness, taking revenge for the destruction of his country. He thought about contacting him and even about rekindling their friendship, but there was never enough time or perhaps enough desire to contact Joey, so they fought in different squadrons, hoping to survive the war.

On Christmas Eve 1944, Billy, dressed in his warm winter jacket, stood outside of the house where he and other officers were stationed in France and looked at the sky towards England. He thought about the letter he'd received from his sister Lynn at the beginning of December.

> *Dearest Billy.*
>
> *First of all, I would like to tell you that we're all fine. It is surprising that amongst the frequent attacks by the German V-2 bombs, people in London found a way to survive and continue day after day with their lives. Father is serving our country by working in the Hawkers factory producing the Typhoons. We don't see him often as he is away from home most of the time. Mother decided to take employment in a local shelter, preparing boxes of clothes and non-perishable food for people that have lost their houses. I completed my studies and became a nurse. As you know, as a student, I already served in the Red Cross and gained a lot of experience in nursing wounded people. I'll be joining the Army and may even be sent to the front.*
>
> *Mother and Father send their regards and they miss you very much, as I do.*
>
> *Joey and his wife Vera arranged for Mrs. Kerr and little Joey to move out of London as it was very dangerous here, especially for*

an older woman and a toddler. They live now on one of the estates that shelters children and the women working there. Once a week, I travel by train to the estate and spend time with little Joey. Vera helps Mrs. Kerr as much as she can. She works for the RAF but it is a secret mission and I'm not privileged to know. Joey is seven months old now, and he is a healthy and happy boy. She loves him dearly and takes good care of him. I love him as well and hope to have a child of my own one day.

Stay safe and come back home soon.
Love Lynn.

"Stay safe and come back home," the last words of her letter were preying on his mind lately. He wasn't sure if he wanted to go back to England at the end of the war.

The British and American air campaign against Germany was still in full force in March 1945 when Billy received a letter from Joey. The first part of it was about Joey's work for the Polish government in exile and their desperate negotiations to reverse the inevitable takeover of Poland by the Russians and the establishment of a communist government.

The second part was about Joey's personal life. Billy realised that he was happy for his friend and it brought peace to his mind.

… Vera and I were engaged in November after I came back from my mission in Poland. You might be surprised, but you and Vera met several times while working in Medmenham. She was in training to be a member of the Interpretation unit. I told her about our friendship, which I still treasure very much and my fathering of baby Joey. Billy, if I could turn back time, I would change the course of events and never get involved with Eloise. It was wrong for me to romance her and push her on the path of betrayal. I loved her very much and I think of her fondly, but it was all wrong and I would like to apologise to you for what I did. I take full responsibility in that matter.

Vera and I convinced Mrs. Kerr to move away from London closer to Vera's station. She is involved in Joey's life and loves him very much, as do I. Mrs. Kerr is a great grandmother and has fully accepted my being the father. Lynn visits Joey as often as she can and she and Vera have a good relationship sharing their love for my son. I never met my biological father and want to make sure that my son is raised by me and the people who love him. We don't make long-term plans for our lives; we only hope that the war will end soon, allowing everybody a peaceful coexistence. I get updates about you from Lynn and I wish that one day we will meet again.

Your friend, Joey.

Although it was only half a year since Eloise's death, it seemed like an eternity to Billy. He didn't think much about her anymore and from the day of her confession, had rejected any attachment to the boy. Perhaps he would meet with Joey one day but for now, he was satisfied with his life and commanding his squadron of fighters was his purpose to get out of bed every day.

On December 28th, Erik came to Rose's house to say goodbye. The whole family was at home getting ready for dinner. He was invited to sit with them and share potato soup and an apple cake.

"We're ordered to move west in expectation of the fast-approaching Red Army," he told them.

They sat in silence during the meal and after they finished, Stan stood up and turned towards Rose. "You can go for a walk with him. Hela will clean the table."

Shivering in a thin winter coat, Rose led Erik to the frozen orchard, under the majestic apple tree.

"My love." He hugged her, stroking her back, trembling and kissing the tears flowing down her beautiful face.

She composed herself, removed the engagement ring from the leather string around her neck, and put it on her finger.

"It will always be with me waiting for your return."

"You're the only one for me, my love, my fiancée, my everything."

"Read this later. I wrote a poem for us." She handed him a folded piece of paper.

For a moment, he considered deserting and asking Rose to help him hide. The thought was short-lived as he knew he would despise himself for being a coward and Rose could lose respect for him.

The Red Army offensive restarted on January 12, 1945, against the German front in southern Poland. Soon after, the German Army was pushed out of Warsaw, on January 17, and the devastated capital of Poland was free. Fewer than 200,000 people were left in the city out of over one million pre-war. The celebrations were muted as people remembered the uprising and the Russian Army camping on the other side of the Vistula River, watching the burning city.

All winter, Erik and his battalion fought the losing battle. Their primary responsibilities were still with the *Feldgendarmerie*, but they were often involved in direct battles. Beginning in March, Erik arrived north of Poznań. Cold and hungry, he looked northwest toward the farm of his grandparents. His mother and father had planned to move there soon after his last visit to Gdańsk. He knew that the farm was not far away, around thirty kilometres from his location. Escaping the front crossed his mind again. *It wouldn't be difficult in the darkness of the night*, he thought. His mind drifted to Hugo, who had taken the chance and perhaps was safe with his family.

Thinking of Hugo and the possible safety of his grandparents' house put Erik into a deep sleep. He woke up at dawn and moved towards the fire, where some soldiers were warming up. The smell of ersatz coffee was waking up others and Erik looked at the men around him. He knew that he could not abandon them, that something unexplainable kept him committed to Germany, despite losing the war and the glory of the Aryan race. He recited Rose's poem, which he knew by heart now. It always helped him through the moments of despair and guilt of wrongdoing.

> *Born deeply rooted, soaked in the memory of generations*
> *Walked the streets painted with the patina of centuries*
> *Touched the imperishable walls of old buildings*

Dreamed in gardens under the majestic trees
Rested in the grass smelling of heroes' blood
Walked cemeteries with forefathers' souls in the tombs
Listened to whispers of strength, love, and death

Dreams of new land, new gardens, new life
Diverse, yet beautiful, young but strong
Buildings so high, reaching to the sky
Streets of windows and colours where all belong
New land inviting, waiting to explore
Home bright and thriving with lightness and love
Roots coiling deep from the saplings of old

December 28th was a day of sorrow, but at the same time, a day of resolve. From that day, Rose thought she would just wait for the end of the war and Erik's return. She didn't want to consider any other alternatives.

Just wait and the world will open the right path for me. That was the reoccurring thought in her mind.

Cold January weather brought some welcome relief to Rose's mother's health. The sunny days lessened her depression and she was more involved in the household chores, allowing Franek to get out of the kitchen.

She stopped to talk to him as he was fetching some wood for the stove. "Franek, you could check the attic. There are some things that you could use."

"What would be there for me?" He looked suspiciously at her.

"You always liked helping Father making horse saddles. There are a lot of materials. You could start doing them on your own."

"Yeah, our father will find out and forbid me from going there. Why is he treating me like I'm worth nothing?" Franek looked angrily at Rose.

"I think that he loves you and is afraid of losing you if you get involved in the underground."

"Little does he know that I'm already involved. I asked Ted to give me some responsibilities."

Rose was shocked. "What are you doing for them?"

"It is a secret, and please don't ask Ted. He's very important in the Home Army and I swore secrecy. He could dismiss me if he knew that I told you."

"I didn't know that Ted was so important. He never says anything about his role."

"Rose, since you met the German guy, you changed. You just work at the store and act like somebody important, and the rest of your time, you daydream or spend time with him."

"Don't talk to me like that." Rose pointed her finger at her brother.

"Don't you think that others might talk about you and him?"

"I don't care what people might say or not say about us." Her voice was loud and she stabbed at Franek with her finger.

"Why do you think your head wasn't shaved because of the German guy? It's Ted who has always protected you."

"Ted protected ..." She stopped in mid-sentence.

"Let's leave it at that. I'll check the stuff in the attic. Something useful might be found there." Franek hugged her and turned around, leaving Rose to her thoughts.

For the next few days, she avoided Ted's house, afraid of being judged by him. Looking back in time, she realised that he'd changed in the last few months and sometimes just looked at her without saying a word. He must have known many details of her relationship with Erik from Ania or even Laura. Rose became angry at herself for talking about her love to her friends. There was nothing she could do to change that; she would have to live with it.

On January 17, news about the liberation of Warsaw spread like wildfire throughout occupied parts of Poland. The atmosphere in Brusk was tense and full of speculations about the next events. It was already known that the Russians had outsmarted the Germans and one part of their army had gone around the trenches built on the banks of the river, taking by surprise the small contingent of German soldiers left to defend the fortified positions. The other half of the Russian Army was still days away from Brusk, approaching from the south-east.

Early morning of January 19th, Rose woke up to the roaring noise of German airplanes above the town. Everybody got up quickly and left their houses, scared and disoriented. The bombs were falling onto the houses, starting fires all around. Franek left without saying goodbye, leaving Rose and others staring at the sky.

"People are hiding in the church; the Russians are here," somebody shouted as they run by Rose.

Without much thought to her safety, she ran through the town towards her store. She needed to protect it from getting plundered by the escaping Germans and the arriving Russians. But she couldn't get that far as the bombs were exploding everywhere. She banged on the door where Wanda had rented a room and dived into it when the door opened. She knew the young couple and their parents living there. They were lying on the floor far from the window. An empty baby carriage and suitcases prepared for their escape were in the middle of the room.

Rose crouched behind the carriage and put her hands over her ears. "God forgive me for my sins and admit me to Heaven." She prayed, hoping to survive the inferno unfolding over the town.

They all screamed and the baby started to cry as the window shattered and bullets scattered around the room. Rose froze, watching the suitcase in front of her moving up and flipping over torn by the bullets. She closed her eyes and darkness enfolded her.

"Rose, wake up." Wanda was tagging on her sleeve.

"Are we alive?" Rose asked and fainted again.

She felt a cold towel over her head, and afraid to open her eyes, she grabbed the hand that was holding her head.

"We're alive. The suitcase saved you." Wanda smiled while stroking Rose's head.

It took a while before Rose recovered from the shock. She heard the bombs still whisking through the air, destroying the town, and her thoughts drifted to her family. Horrified, she realised that she'd left them in front of the house while preoccupied with her store. She felt a strong love for all of them, greater than any love she'd felt before. Powered by this love, she regained her strength and ran out of the house, not caring about the voices behind her, urging her to stay. Many houses in town were burning, with people running in all directions, looking for shelter.

She looked towards the church steeple and watched the bomb coming down toward it. She fixed her eyes on the bomb and everything around her was just like a silent movie where no words were spoken. There was just the loud, terrifying music of whistling, explosions, and shattered windows. The bomb appeared almost suspended in the air, then slowly touched the roof of the church at its lowest part and slid gently onto the grass in front of a cross. The seconds she waited for the loud explosion lasted for an eternity. She could not move. Paralysed, she stood on the side of the street until somebody pushed her out of the way with brutal force. All senses returned to her and she started running towards the church. She realised that her family had taken shelter there and her only thoughts were to save them. She entered the church calling her young sister's name. "Hela, Hela, are you here?"

The church was packed with people, many on their knees praying. Rose's loud voice turned many heads, and she felt strength entering her body. With a commanding voice, she spoke: "Leave the church and move away from it and the cross."

"What are you talking about, girl?"

"A bomb just hit the roof and slid onto the grass; it may explode."

A few young men took charge of the evacuation, preventing a stampede of people driven by fear. In a short time, everybody was out, running away from the church grounds. Rose spotted her family, and in a second, she grabbed Hela's hand and both ran out, followed by the rest. Without any thought to it, the whole family ran towards their house. Other than shattered windows, the house stood unscathed like a beacon of hope among the devastation. Rose's father went inside the house, Mother was crying, and Franek was looking at the shattered glass when Hela tugged on Rose's arm and pointed out to the end of the road. The sight ahead of them was like a nest of wasps swarming and moving towards the town.

"Franek, look." Rose pointed out the swarm.

"Russian Army." His statement bore no surprise.

"How would you know that for sure?"

"We've watched their progress in the last few days. They're here faster than we thought."

"Not fast enough to prevent the bombing by the Germans," Rose said quietly.

"They don't care about small towns or people; their mission is to get to Berlin as fast as they can."

Ten minutes later, the first trucks packed with soldiers reached the town. The procession lasted for many hours, bringing thousands of soldiers to town. They rode trucks, tanks, and horse-driven wagons, and many more of them simply marched on foot.

Rose and the family stood on the side of the road as more people appeared alongside, watching the Russians. The soldiers were friendly and shouted greetings at the silent people along the main street. Rose realised that the bombing had stopped a while ago and now the voices of the soldiers were filling the air. They looked battered and their uniforms were dirty, but they were smiling and waving.

Rose noticed that many of the soldiers were women, dressed in uniforms, driving the trucks or sitting on the tanks. That mesmerised her and she felt relieved of the fear of Bolsheviks.

"Franek, if there are so many women in the army, we should not fear them."

"Maybe."

Rose and Franek boarded up the broken windows to keep the cold weather out. It was dark in the house during the day now, except for some rays of light coming through the gaps between the planks of wood. When they were done, Rose left the house and walked towards the store.

The Russian soldiers had taken over the town. They put their wounded in the Town Hall that still housed the hospital, and many moved into private houses where the injured German soldiers had been quartered just a short time ago. Many more camped outside, warming up near the big bonfires they built and cooking their food.

The store was ransacked and all the food had already been confiscated by the army. Many soldiers were sitting around a stove erected in the middle of the store, some playing harmonicas, others snoozing or talking in their melodic language.

She stood for a while in the entrance door, and tears started running down her cheeks. So much work she had put into running this store; it was her domain, but not anymore. Some soldiers started talking to her, but she just looked at them, turned around and left.

"Why are you removing the windows?" Maria had learned to trust her son and knew that he had good reasons to take them down, but not asking would be strange.

"The Russian Army is coming and very possibly the German *Luftwaffe* will try to attack them and destroy everything in their path."

"Our town is in their path. When do you think they'll get here?"

"They're on the main road south of us, maybe day or two before they get here."

"Perhaps they'll go a different way."

"The Polish People's Army is with them and we talk to them. They are coming this way to avoid the trenches."

"God, what will happen to us?"

"Get some blankets and water to the cellar. You need to get ready to hide there with Ania if the bombs start falling."

"What about the windows?"

"I'm going to store them there, hoping that the glass won't shatter there."

"I'll help you; we need to board up the windows—there are many wood planks in the shed. I'll start bringing them."

Still amazed by her transformation, Ted looked at his mother as she rushed off to the shed. "You should ask Ania and Laura to help you."

By the afternoon, the glass windows were stored in the cellar along with any valuables, blankets, and water. Even Ted's supplies from his shop had been moved to the cellar, leaving little room for the family to hide there. The Germans were still in town, gathered in the main square, waiting for orders to leave.

"Ted, the Germans have started to move," one of the sentries posted near the square reported well past midnight.

"As planned, in the morning, we will inform as many people as possible to take shelter."

The last of the Germans were leaving the town in the morning when the first report of Russian arrival in the village outside of Brusk spread quickly through the town.

"Faster than expected," Ted told his mother. "You, Ania, and Laura go to the cellar. I'll check what is going on."

Before he'd had a chance to tell people to find shelter, the airplanes started roaring in the sky and the thunder of bombs near the town woke up people, who looked in disbelief at the rapidly changing situation. The first bombs reached the town on the west side, propelling some people to run back to their houses and others towards the church. Ted could not bring himself to hide in the cellar, thinking it would be a cowardly act for him. He stayed outside of the house, looking at the sky. He repeated the Home Army oath over and over again until he realised that some kind of madness was taking hold of him. Quickly, he ran to the house to grab a warm coat and raced towards the hills where two years ago, young people had hidden from the Germans. Other people were in the hills already and they watched in horror as the fires spread everywhere. By the end of the day, it was over and the Russians had taken over the town.

At first, the people of Brusk were suspicious of the Bolsheviks, but in a few days, they warmed up to their liberators. When the Russian soldiers defused the bomb in front of the church, the people organised a party on the church grounds, inviting the Russians to celebrate with them. There wasn't much food for the hundreds who attended, so the soldiers brought their own supplies and a lot of vodka. The celebration lasted late into the night until the fires died down and the many drunk people staggered back to their houses.

Rose kept to herself and didn't attend the celebration party. Her father had been very critical of the Russians ever since she remembered. Ted was fighting for the Home Army affiliated with the West, and it all made her mistrustful of the Russians. She stood a far distance from the church, thinking about the future and a possibly communist Poland when Hela materialised in front of her, happily shouting, "Look what I got." She had tins of food.

"Where did you get these?"

"People are trading with the Russians to get food, hats, and whatever."

"Slow down, Hela. Are people buying things from the Russians?"

"No, they are exchanging their stuff for whatever the Russians can give them."

"What did you trade?"

"Remember the toy watch I got from you last year? I gave it to a soldier for two cans of food."

"It doesn't make sense; did you steal the food?"

"I didn't steal anything." Hela started crying.

"I believe you; it's just strange." Rose hugged her sister and took one can from her.

"The soldier that gave me the cans had many watches on both of his arms; he didn't care if they were fake."

"You're so resourceful, my little sister. Maybe I'll hire you to work in my store."

"I'll have a better store, maybe with fashions from Paris," Hela replied, laughing.

"You're growing up fast."

Rose didn't follow Hela home. Instead, she went to the orchard and leaned against the "tree of hope," as she had called it since Erik left.

She looked up at the crown of the tree. *Was I blinded by love and lost touch with reality?*

Since meeting Erik, she'd lived in a dream, defying the existence around her, and daring to wish that the world would belong to them. She had often felt she was a better person than the people in her town. She dared to believe in finding her place in the big world and Erik was the man who could do it for her. She realised that she'd stopped being truly an independent thinker—that it was Erik who channelled her dreams and plans, that everything she could achieve was with him and nothing on her own. She'd repeated the mistake of her mother, who gave up her prospects of a good life for love, a love that brought only temporary happiness and a lifetime of disrespect and depression. Was Mother's love for a younger but dishonest man, like her love for a handsome but elusive man? She cried for a long time, her body shaking and losing feeling from the bitter cold around.

"Erik, you better come back and take me away from here. I'm lost."

She went home to search for more toy watches she had purchased from travelling vendors, since they once had been very popular gifts for kids. She and Hela found two of them and also an old accordion that nobody played, and a pair of sunglasses. The next day Franek and Hela exchanged them for two fur hats and a few cans of meat.

Even Father was smiling, looking at the treasures they'd brought home. "Maybe they're not bad people. After all, they are Slavic like us."

"Ania, what are you looking for?" Maria lifted a candle to look at her daughter.

"I had a toy watch and some rings; I want to trade them with the Russians."

"You won't bargain with the Russians." Ted stepped into the dark kitchen. "They are not our friends; others can do what they want."

In the next few days, Ted could not avoid contact with the Russian soldiers, despite the vague orders from London to stay away for now.

After they disarmed the bomb in front of the church, Ted decided to talk to the Polish soldiers fighting alongside the Russian Army.

"We need your help to detonate the mines in the trenches on the other side of the river. Can you take me to your superior?" Ted spoke with as much authority as he could."

"Do you have any information about the mines?"

Ted looked at the officer who'd asked the question as he entered the tent erected in the square and removed a few sheets of paper with crude sketches of the trenches.

The train to Warsaw was packed with people carrying suitcases, boxes tied with twine, or full canvas bags. Children were clutching parents' hands, their faces pale and tired of the world they could not understand. Ted and Laura stood near the window of the last wagon, enjoying being pressed to each other by the crowd of people.

Laura looked around the wagon. "People are coming back to their homes."

"Warsaw is in ruins; hope they have places to stay warm."

The late February day was cold, with snow crunching under their boots as they walked towards the Old Town. Ted carried Laura's suitcase and she had a backpack hanging over her shoulders. They held hands. They walked in silence, overwhelmed by the ruins all over the city. It was noon and many people were on the streets, busy with removing broken concrete from partially destroyed houses, cooking meals over barrels with fire, and greeting new arrivals.

"Welcome back home!" a young woman shouted to them. "Would you like some soup to keep you warm?"

Laura looked at Ted with a smile. "I'm home."

"You don't know yet if you have a roof over your head; everything is destroyed."

"The sky over the city is my roof. I'll find somewhere to stay warm."

As they walked along the main street, their hope of finding Laura's apartment intact was fading. Laura led Ted to a side street and they strolled for a few minutes along rows of destroyed houses, their tension rising.

"It's here." She stopped and pointed to an apartment building that was partially damaged. People were working inside, removing the rubble from a basement that appeared to be already occupied by families. Despite the cold weather, children were playing outside, building snowmen and throwing snowballs at passing adults.

"Let's hope that the children will have no scars of war as they grow up." Ted made a few snowballs and threw them toward the group of kids. He missed and laughter erupted.

"Hey, old man, try again."

Laura spoke to a few people she knew in passing. They lived on the same street but their building was destroyed and they'd found shelter in hers.

"You're welcome to stay with us. There is some space in the basement."

"Thank you, can I leave my suitcases with you?" she asked the young woman who offered her space.

"Ted, let's see my shop. Maybe it isn't destroyed. It's just around the corner. I walked to it every day for ten years."

Ted looked at Laura as they turned the corner. Sadness and hope were painted all over her face. She looked vulnerable and beautiful. He turned to her and put his arms around her shoulders.

"Not much left. Don't go any closer."

She lifted her arms toward the partially burned walls standing like guardians of Netherworld. "There was an entrance on the other side of the building. Maybe there is access to my studio. Not everything is destroyed."

She ran towards the building and he saw her disappearing inside the walls. He looked around, his eyes moving from ruin to ruin and settling on a big tree that had survived the inferno. Branches covered with snow were gently swaying in the light breeze and sunshine illuminated a few brown leaves still attached to the tree. Ted had never considered himself a sentimental person, but the tree brought tears to his eyes. "Like the tree, we survived the war and will come back to normal living again."

He followed Laura to the skeleton of the building and found her sitting inside a room with broken windows but intact walls. A sewing machine turned upside down, a mannequin without arms, and scattered fashion journals covered by dust were all over the room. Laura was sitting in the window with her head down and a letter in her hand.

Confused, Ted came close to her. "A letter in the ruins? Bad news?"

"Sit down, Ted. I have to tell you something." She looked straight into his eyes and folded the letter. A frown appeared on her face. "Don't say anything, just listen."

Ted nodded, not knowing what to expect.

"The letter is from my husband. He was an alcoholic and an abusive man. When the war started, he joined the army and left. I was not unhappy with his departure. He never wrote any letters, and I assumed that he perished in a battle somewhere. But he survived and he was here just a few days ago, leaving this letter."

"Where is he right now?"

"With his parents outside of Warsaw."

"Are you going back to him?" Ted looked almost accusingly at her.

"I don't know what I'm going to do. I thought he was gone forever."

"Go back with me to Brusk. We can talk about it later. You can't run into the hands of your abusive husband."

"I won't. I just have to resolve the problem on my own."

"Will you go to see him soon?"

"I have a sister who lives in Otwock not far from Warsaw. We're not close anymore because we argued a lot about me marrying a drunkard and staying with him. I'll take a train there and find her. I hope she still leaves at the same address. My mother is with her"

"Is there anything I can do for you?"

"I'm fine, Ted. Stay with me tonight." They stayed in the same room as three another people: the young woman who'd extended the invitation, her mother, and a young son.

They were given a narrow bed that belonged to the young boy while he slept with his grandmother. They were uncomfortable making love at first, but when the breathing of the others became regular, their bodies could no longer stay apart. The lovemaking was silent but passionate, inflamed by the notion that it might be their last time.

"I love you, Laura," Ted whispered after they both climaxed, keeping their hands on each other's mouths to quell the sounds of pleasure.

"I know, but you also love Rose, and she is the one for you. Win her. She is waiting."

The Russian Army left town and the days dragged on for Rose. She cleaned the store with Wanda's help and slowly restocked shelves with basics. Her father arranged that the bread baked in a small, partly damaged bakery was sold in the store. The morning hours were the highlights of the day, as many people gathered in the store to buy fresh bread. News of the Allies and the Russian Army closing in on the Germans dominated the daily conversation.

The hard work that engulfed her life was some form of liberation for Rose. She listened to people's conversation but preferred to force her mind to think about the next batch of soap coming to the store or about the potatoes that some farmers had stored away from the prying eyes of the Germans. She didn't want to think about her future but instead lived day by day, hoping for some kind of a solution to her existence.

"Rose, would you like to go with me to Lublin?" asked Wanda.

It was a sunny, warm, early-April day.

"Who will run the store?"

"I'm sure that your father and brother could step in for a few days."

"I don't know."

"Rose, come with me. I want to see what's left of my city. See if my house is still standing."

Suddenly, Rose felt a jolt of energy inside her and remembered the trips to Warsaw with Ted and Ania. She liked travelling. "I'll go with you."

Rose and Wanda sat on a train that was slowly moving towards Lublin. They had to change trains in Warsaw and the devastation of the city visible from the train was beyond comprehension. They sat silently until the city was behind them and the first signs of spring were visible on the trees and the farmers' fields around.

"Rose, you and many in your town lived rather a sheltered life until the last days of the war."

"What do you mean sheltered?"

"Brusk is located outside of the main roads, and didn't have any major industrial targets for the Germans to attack."

Rose sat with her head turned towards the window. There were no other passengers in the wagon as most of the travellers were going to the devastated Warsaw and not the other way.

"I would like to tell you about Lublin before we arrive there."

They sat listening to the monotonous sound of the wheels running on the tracks—*thump, thump, thump*—while Wanda gathered her thoughts. She spoke in a low voice that never changed through her story.

"Lublin was a relatively big city of over 120,000 people, and one-third of them were Jews. The city was under Russian rule after the Partition of Poland, but Lublin was unique because it was one of the major cultural and educational centres of the Jewish people. The world-famous Yeshiva Chachmel High School had been thriving since 1930. You could hear Polish, Yiddish, and Russian on the streets. Lublin was a major trading city before and after the Partition of Poland in the eighteenth century. Polish schools and colleges were well established and many scholars from Lviv University taught in Lublin. Lviv University, one of the oldest in Poland, was established in 1661 when the Polish king granted it its royal charter. It was a great privilege for Lublin University to host famous scholars. Above the city was a magnificent castle that was rebuilt by the Jagiellonian Dynasty and a place where the most important event in Polish history had taken place, the signing of the Union of Lublin, an act of the Polish-Lithuanian Commonwealth. Sadly, in the seventeenth century, the castle had been destroyed during the invasion of Poland by the Swedish king notably called "The Deluge." It was restored in 1828, ironically to serve as a prison for many years. The most horrible times were during the Nazi occupation when thousands of Polish resistance fighters and Jews were imprisoned and sent from there to the concentration camps. Hitler must have planned to subjugate and destroy the city of Lublin. After heavy bombardment on September 8, 1939, the German Army entered Lublin on September 18th and soon after the carnage began."

Wanda stopped talking and buried her head in her hands.

Rose remained silent for a while, concentrating on the staccato, rhythmic noise made by the train wheels. She felt scared and afraid that the Germans were still in Lublin waiting for the two women.

She moved to Wanda's side and put her arms around her. "I'm sorry."

"I'm fine. I'll continue my story." Wanda lifted her head, looked through the window to compose herself and continued. "Soon after they took over the city, many Jews were beaten and tortured and the Nazi soldiers robbed their shops and houses. Then they proceeded with the destruction of the Talmudic Academy and burning all the books from the library. The fire lasted for two days while the German band played happy music. In November, the German administration changed the names of the streets and parks from Polish and Yiddish to German. One of the main thoroughfares, Krakowskie Przedmieście, was renamed Adolf Hitler Park and the Stefan Batory College was renamed the Julius Schreck Kaserne. Polish and Jewish people were forcibly removed from their houses in the central part of Lublin to other districts."

Wanda stopped again but this time, she looked straight at Rose. "My family was forced out of our house and the renamed college became the headquarters of their propaganda centre."

"Was the college where you taught?"

"Yes, I was teaching European History and culture there."

"This is why you know so much about Jewish culture?"

"Not only that, but I also studied all of Europe's history from the times of the Roman Empire. Sadly, it has been filled with wars, hate, killings, and oppression."

"I studied history at the underground school during the war. I completed grade seven. Maybe I'll go to high school when the war is over."

"Let's hope that humanity has learned its final lesson and we will learn to live in peace."

They arrived at the Lublin train station after sunset. The weather was cool at this time of the day as they walked carrying their small luggage. The city was devastated, with buildings in ruins and only a few people on the streets.

"Despite the devastation, the city looks happier than when I left," said Wanda.

"What do you mean?"

"Look around, so many Polish flags on the buildings, no more German flags with swastikas."

They arrived at a tenement house that had been riddled by bullets but relatively intact. The entrance door to the hallway had been temporarily repaired and was not locked. They walked to the second floor and Wanda knocked at the apartment door, her face pale, not knowing if her family was still there. Soon a young woman Rose's age opened the door and a cry of happiness filled the hallway.

"Mother, look who's here!"

A woman in a dark dress rushed to greet them.

After much exclaiming and many embraces, Wanda searched the room for a sight of her brother. "Where is Antek?"

"He is dead, killed by the Germans in the castle's prison on the last day of their occupation."

Wanda's sister-in-law Kasia looked absentmindedly at the wall where a wedding picture hung.

"Couldn't he escape?"

"They kept the people working there without allowing them to leave and visit families. Three hundred people were killed before the Germans left."

"Oh my God." They were the only words spoken by Wanda before the women started to sob while Rose looked at them with sorrow in her eyes. She had never faced such tragedy. She'd heard of the mass murders but they were always somewhere at a distance.

"You must be hungry; I'll prepare some supper." Wanda's niece Ola broke the devastating silence.

Late at night, staying in a narrow bed while Ola slept on the second bed in the room, Rose thought about Erik, remembering that he'd been stationed in Lublin in the earlier years of the war. She had a vision of him involved in the atrocities against the people of Lublin, changing the street names and burning the Jewish library. She started to tremble under the thin blanket, terrified that she loved a monster, not the kind man that she thought she knew. She remembered Erik asking her forgiveness for the wrongs of his past. At that time, she thought that his wrongdoing was simply joining the German Army, but what if it was more than that?

"God forgive me and send me a sign that Erik has been a good person despite serving in the German Army." She whispered her prayers while holding to the little cross and the engagement ring on the leather string around her neck. She prayed, using her knuckles as imaginary rosary until she drifted into a deep sleep.

The next day Wanda and Rose went to the city. They rode bicycles, one that Kasia owned and one borrowed from a neighbour. The ruined city under the April sun looked less horrid than last evening. People were on the streets; stores were opening and the smell of baked bread struck their senses as they rode the bicycles. As they went towards the old town, the magnificent walls of the castle dominated the horizon on the hill in front of them. A large white and red flag was flying on top of the medieval tower, which stood taller than any building in Lublin.

They stopped their bikes in front of a large cross and knelt in front of it. The cross was erected as a monument to the massacre of Lublin's people. Wanda touched the cross and in a clear voice, she said, "Goodbye, my brother, you were the last of the male descendant of the Bukowski family. There is nobody left to carry the name of our long-lasting family." She stood in silence for a few minutes and when she finally turned towards Rose, unusual strength emanated from her face. "Time to go, Rose. We have places to visit."

The next stop was in the courtyard of the college, which was bustling with students coming in and out of the building, standing in small groups and talking intensely. From time to time, the laughter of young people broke, making Rose long to be a part of such a group, for learning and seizing any opportunity to be part of the big world.

"Rose, can you please stay here and guard our bicycles? I'll go inside for a short while."

She observed Wanda slowly approaching the building, looking around and smiling to herself. An older man extended his hand to Wanda. They embraced and both disappeared behind the massive door of the college. It was more than half an hour before Wanda left the building and they rode the bicycles to the centre of the city.

"Who was that man who greeted you?" Rose could not wait any longer, burning inside with curiosity.

"It was my professor when I was a student and later my colleague in the History Department."

"Are you coming back to Lublin to teach again?"

"I haven't made any decision; the war isn't over yet."

As they rode, Rose observed that all the German street names had been removed and new ones were erected. The main street, named "Krakowskie Przedmiescie," reminded Rose of a similar but much grander street in Warsaw before the war. She remembered Ted taking her and Ania for ice cream in one of the stores along that street. It was a time full of childish happiness and dreams about their future.

Why was she thinking about Ted, of all the people on the earth? He wasn't her childhood friend anymore; he was involved in all the right things and loved Laura. A little jealousy knocked at her heart, and she directed her attention to the buildings around. Wanda turned into one of the side streets and stopped in front of a three-storey building. Some windows were still intact and some were boarded up with planks of wood, but other than that, it had survived the war in relatively good shape.

"The Germans relocated my family from this building to the tenement house and took it over for their families."

"Was it your family house?"

"Yes, for many years. My great-grandfather moved here from Petersburg, where he served as a diplomat at the tsar's government."

"Was he Russian?"

"No, he was Polish, highly educated in France, and the tsar looked for people like him that would bring some reforms to his country."

"But the Russians were the enemy." Rose looked at Wanda in disbelief.

"He was a diplomat and chose to serve his country the way he knew best. He worked with emissaries of Tadeusz Kościuszko to start the November Uprising in 1830 and bring freedom to Poland."

"What happened after we lost that uprising?"

"He left Petersburg under the pretence of being sick with tuberculosis and settled with his family in Lublin before he was discovered and sentenced to death."

"You're from such an important family, yet you're so humble." Rose looked at Wanda with admiration.

"Enough talking about my family. Can you please stay here? I need to go inside."

The visit was short and soon after she left the building, both biked in silence. Rose sensed that it was better to avoid any questions.

Back at the flat, they washed their hands and sat to dinner. Both Wanda and Rose were famished after a long day of bicycling through the city.

"What do you think about the changes in Lublin?" Kasia was anxious to hear Wanda's opinion.

"Life is coming back to it; it seems almost normal, but it cannot be. The communists are in power."

"The Russians and the Polish Armies brought peace and the provisional government allows the opening of schools, stores, and trade, for now just with Russia. We even have American food and clothes that were sent to Russia during the war."

"I still think that the Bolsheviks are bad people and Stalin is as bad as Hitler. I'll just wait and see. Tomorrow, Rose and I have to go back to Brusk."

In the middle of April, Erik arrived in Berlin. The city was devastated by the bombing, the streets were deserted, and the hardship was written with invisible ink on the ruins of the buildings. He thought with bitterness about his plan to work for the *Wehrmacht* in Berlin, the magnificent centre of cultural and political life, the heart of Germany.

He had once visited Berlin prior to the war, and seeing it for the first time in ruins didn't break his heart. His bitterness that his advancement in the army hadn't panned out as he'd envisioned made him indifferent to anything that involved his past dream.

Upon arrival in Berlin, Erik was put in charge of controlling the city streets and enforcing the curfew. It wasn't long after his arrival that he learned about groups of men wearing swastikas on their sleeves who patrolled the streets of Berlin as well. Although they didn't have legal authority, they ruled by threat and violence. They were the blind followers of Hitler and his order that "The battle should be conducted without consideration for our own population." They entered houses to look for deserters; they intimidated people, forcing them to wear armbands with swastikas; and at any sign of disobedience, they killed men and women. Erik's work was made more difficult because of those groups of former SS soldiers and their young followers who were willing to die and kill others as ordered.

Whispers of Hitler's suicide spread through the city as the Russian troops were entering Berlin. The strategy of Hitler's successor, Donitz, was capitulation and saving as many civilians and German troops as possible. The fear of the Bolsheviks was propulsion for many to start moving westwards towards the American and British-controlled areas.

Erik and his small contingent of the *Feldgendarmerie* oversaw gathering and escorting people to leave Berlin. On May 5, 1945, Erik and his two soldiers were escorting the last group of people already walking safely outside of Berlin when he received the news that Germany had capitulated and the peace agreement was signed. Using his megaphone, he announced the news to the group of evacuees and in that moment, he noticed three men who had acted strangely from the beginning of the march raising their hands, clutching grenades, and shouting, "Heil Hitler." The grenades exploded simultaneously, and Erik fell to the ground.

On May 8th, Billy celebrated the surrender of Germany in Stuttgart. He took part in a campaign to ferry Allied POWs from German territories back to England.

A few German women with children stood along the streets as the Allied soldiers celebrated the victory. There was no joy on the faces of the hungry and tired women; they just stood there and watched the foreigners in resignation. Only the children were happy, running alongside the American soldiers, getting chocolates and chewing gum. Looking at the German women and children made Billy question whether the results of the saturation bombing of Germany had been worth the effort. There were only ruins as far as he could see on the way towards Berlin, even greater than the destruction of London through the years of war and the deadly V-1 and V-2 bombs.

Seeing the madness of war helped him to make up his mind about his future life. He handed in his resignation from the Royal Air Force and travelled to France. On a sunny day in May, he arrived in Thionville. He felt renewed, as if all the baggage of his past had left him and he was just an empty vessel open to new possibilities. He looked towards the direction of Jean's estate and smiling, he said out loud, "My friends, I'm here to build my new life."

Hitler's death and the subsequent signing of the capitulation on May 5th spread with lightning speed around the world. The whole of Brusk was celebrating. Rose joined Ania and Ted on the streets as they all sang the Polish anthem and danced on the wooden floor erected in the town's centre. Ted was serious as usual, but looked more stressed than even during the war.

"What is wrong, Ted?" Rose asked, pulling him to dance with her.

"It isn't the outcome we fought for. In the end, the Polish government in exile didn't deliver what the people fighting on their behalf expected. It's Churchill's fault for giving in to Stalin."

"The Polish government supported by the Russians might be fine," said Rose. "They promised reforms and land to the farmers. Is that so bad?"

"I don't want to talk about it." He left abruptly, leaving her on the dance floor. She was quickly saved by Ania, dancing with other women nearby.

Every day, Rose looked at her engagement ring, hoping to hear from Erik soon. By the end of May, she received a letter from Gdańsk, which was no longer called by its German name of Danzig.

With trepidation in her heart, she ran to the orchard and sat under her apple tree.

> *Dear Rose,*
>
> *Erik told me about you and his love for you. My husband and I loved him very much but we both saw different paths for him.*
>
> *Under the strong influence of his father and grandfather, he became a German soldier but deeply in his heart, he was Polish and loved Polish people and culture. Erik died outside of Berlin at the hands of the people that he served. Perhaps it was the only end to his life, as I'm sure he would live haunted forever by his choices. The only choice that he never regretted was loving you. We don't know where we will call our home after the dust of the war is settled; therefore, I'm not leaving you a returning address. Hope*

you'll have fond memories of my son and I wish you healing and good life ahead."

Rita Hermann.

The Victory Day celebration was a happy occasion for most people in Brusk and nearby villages. They could start rebuilding their livelihood under a sky free of bombers threatening their lives and the destruction of everything they possessed.

George and other Home Army members gathered at Ted's shop for their regular meeting. They continued to be guarded and use passwords before entering the shop.

George looked uncomfortable. "I received new orders from London."

"They still send orders?" Bolek said with slight ridicule.

"They ordered us to continue our fight, this time against the communists and their agents."

"Their agents." Ted started to talk but stopped as George had recovered from his hesitation and sounded authoritative. "Anyone who switched their allegiance and is now working for the militia or any form of local government."

"Can I say something?" Ted didn't wait for George's approval. "The Yalta Conference was the final blow to the dying hope that Poland could be saved from communism. The leaders of the Allied countries abandoned their support for the Polish government in London and handed Poland to Stalin's regime. They officially agreed that the provisional government created in July 1944 and backed by the Soviets would work on unifying the country, pending free elections."

"Ted, I'm providing the orders from the government in London." George was much quieter.

"The same government that failed to negotiate free and democratic Poland with the Allies? The same government that failed to negotiate with the Red Army to provide help to the Warsaw uprising? The same government that is still enjoying the good life in London and doesn't even know the true destruction of our lives, the hunger, the death? The government that left Poland as the war started and became lame as time passed? This government wants us to kill our friends because they took the only jobs available to them."

"Easy, Ted. Don't be so angry."

"I'm not going to listen to such orders. This Poland may not be what we fought for but the war is over and I won't spill the blood of more people to satisfy the government in exile. It is time to pick up the pieces, get married, start families, and create as normal a life as possible."

Ted looked around. The faces of the few friends who had served with him in the past four years were tense and unsure of the right way forward.

"You know my stance; I'm leaving the room now. Each of you can make the decision that is right for you without me knowing." Ted left the shop and stood outside, looking around. This time he was not checking for the Germans but for strangers who might be spying on the former Home Army members. He was suddenly tired of the war, of the new propaganda, of the uncertainty in his life. His friends of the past years slowly left the shop one by one without looking back.

The last one to emerge was George. "Goodbye, Ted. I'm leaving the area. Maybe we will meet again."

He extended his hand and Ted took it eagerly. "Goodbye."

At the beginning of May 1945, Joey read the letter from Emilie for the second time. His stone-like face didn't show the emotions that were ravaging his whole being. Sadness and guilt were his first reaction to the news in the letter, but once he finished reading for the second time, there was a feeling of the closure of something that was like an open wound in his heart, a wound that he'd tried to forget but always came back to hurt him. He looked at his son Joey, taking his first steps, and put the letter back in the envelope. *The past is closed now,* he thought. *Time to move on with unchained life.*

> *Dear Joey,*
>
> *Hope this letter finds you in good health. The war is over and life is slowly regaining normalcy. I would like to let you know that*

337

Jean isn't with us anymore. He died in December, fighting with the Allies in the Colmar Pocket. His body was buried there and perhaps one day it will be exhumed to be united with his family in Thionville. It isn't important to me where his body rests as I know that despite his troubled life, he is with God now, looking at his loved ones on this earth. His friend made a nice plaque with his name and it was affixed to the iron cross on Joseph's final resting place. Whoever is lying in this grave is acknowledged by the two names marking it.

While I was sorting Jean's belongings, I came across the letter you wrote to him last year. Jean never talked to me about it but I think it brought back some memories for him. Since your stay in Thionville last summer, I had some doubts about Jean's true identity but it could not be proven in any plausible way as his memory was lost to the darkness that had covered his life during the accident. I loved him very much and he was always Jean Navarre to me and our children. We will never know the truth and it is best to leave it this way.

I'm managing the cooperage business myself with the great help of Andreas. He was planning to go back to Poland after the war but with the communist government there, he feared for his safety and decided to stay in France. I'm planning to make him a business partner as the wine industry is picking up from its dormant state.

Our son Jean-Marc, who celebrated his fourteen birthday this month, is studying hard and one day, he plans to study linguistics. He is fluent in French, German, and English and already is learning Spanish and Italian. He would like to work for the government to advocate for peace for all future generations. Our daughter Marie-Ann is only twelve years old and happy to be at school with her friends.

If you and Ted would like to visit us here in Thionville, I'll be most happy to host you at our house.

Look after yourself.
Sincerely,
Emilie.

May 8, 1945, was a bittersweet Victory Day for Joey and the exiled Polish people in England. They had fought the Nazis to the end of the war, but losing their country to the communists and Russian domination was a bitter outcome. The peace agreement had swapped one dictatorship for another and Poles who had fought alongside the British in the hope of one day returning to their homes found themselves abandoned with no country to go to.

Since March 1945, Joey had worked for the Polish government in exile and was promoted to the rank of major in the Polish Army. With the imminent end of the war, the Polish government's efforts were increasingly desperate to secure a free and democratic Poland. Joey, referred to as Joseph Wilk among the government officials, was a valuable adviser on the Polish matter and his intelligence was respected not only by the Polish side but the Allies' side of the negotiating table.

For his service to his country, Joey was awarded the *Virtuti Militari*, the Polish Cross of Valour.

Joey and Vera got married in June 1945 and moved into a two-room apartment on the military base. Mrs. Kerr became a governess in a nearby estate and was able to spend weekends with Joey Jr.

In 1946, Europe was preparing to hold victory parades in many cities, including a big one in London. The British government initially invited the Soviet-backed government in Poland to send representatives to march among the Allied forces in the parade. The Polish forces who had fought under British High Command were not invited. Winston Churchill, some high-ranking RAF figures, and several MPs, protested the decision, which was a demoralising and cowardly concession to the communist dictatorship.

Finally, the British government invited twenty-five Polish pilots of the Royal Air Force who had taken part in the Battle of Britain to march together with other foreign detachments as part of the parade. Joey was among the invitees, but was almost certain that the Polish government in exile would refuse to participate. Last-minute invitations sent to the chief of staff of the Polish Army and the chiefs of the Polish Air Force and Polish Navy and various generals were considered an affront and refused. As a result of the political games, there was no Polish representation in the parade.

"Joey, are we going to wear the medals we received for our service in the RAF?" Vera was looking at the Defence Medal she'd received in May 1945, waiting for Joey's decision.

"The betrayal of the British hurt so much that I want to put the medals away and never look at them again."

"We earned them."

"Yes, we did. Perhaps we could put them under our jackets, close to our hearts but away from the eyes of the people who turned against us."

Joey took Vera's medal and attached it to the left side of her blouse, not the usual place on her uniform. She put her head on his shoulder and they stood for a while in silence.

Joey, Vera, Mrs. Kerr, and Joey Jr. stood in the crowd watching the parade.

"I'm sorry for the way the Polish heroes were treated, I'm ashamed of my country and its people," Mrs. Kerr said, holding Joey Jr. close to her chest. He was playing with the brooch that Billy had made in France, unaware of the trauma behind it.

With a quiet voice, Joey said, "We plan to emigrate to Canada; would you go with us?"

She looked at Joey, then at Vera, and smiled with happiness in her eyes.

"Will you marry me, Rose?" Ted sat next to her on the bench outside of her house.

His heart was pounding, rushing blood to his head. They had become very good friends after the war, talking about the shattered dreams of their youth and about new dreams in an uncertain world. They talked about rebuilding their lives, often realising that their lives had become entwined.

"Ted, I love you. I think I always did. Yes, I'll marry you." Looking into his eyes, she knew that his love would always be stronger and the driving force of their marriage.

Later that evening, Rose looked at the letter from Erik, sent soon after he left the town.

"My dearest Rose." She would remember every word of this letter for the rest of her life.

"Goodbye Erik, it is time to move on," she said to the flames engulfing his letter as it burned in the stove.

The next day she stood on the bank of the river where she and Erik had dreamed about the future together. Looking at the water calmly moving in front of her, she could almost see the images of her past life floating in front of her. When the last image of Erik waving his hand towards her disappeared behind the trees, she tossed the ring into the water.

She thought about Ted. He'd won her love with his gentle attention to her and his quiet understanding of her grief for Erik. Their love grew into a mature, responsible one—a love that promised a good life together.

With the devastation of Poland, a wedding dress was a dream not available to most. Ted's gift to Rose was the parachute he had hidden during the war. The silky white fabric was sewn by Laura into Rose's beautiful wedding dress. It was a reminder of the difficult years of war, but signified survival and hope for a good future.

Author's Note

This book is a work of fiction based on real-life stories spoken around the table by my parents and other family members throughout the years.

I relocated from Poland to Canada in 1983 and started my new life and professional career in Toronto. I love my new country and the life I've established here, yet the love for my homeland stays strong in my heart.

During many visits to Poland with my family, we continued our conversations about my ancestors and the turbulent history of the land of my birth.

After my father's passing, the conversations continued. During each of my visits, my siblings and I enjoyed sitting at the table drinking coffee and a little liqueur and listening to my mother's stories. With age, she remembered more of her childhood and youth times, and she loved to talk about it.

Many of her and my father's stories inspired me to write this book.

Ted's journey through the book is based on my father's real-life experiences. The Home Army resistance, the underground newspapers, the radio station in the church's crypt, the parachute drops from England, and many more of these events were the stories of my youth. I regret that I didn't ask questions about my father's life as a young, orphaned boy stepping up to be the "man of the house" after his father left for France. There must have been stories of bravery, anguish, and lost childhood. There is nobody anymore to answer these questions and this part of his life isn't well known to the family, so I have imagined what it must have been like for him.

Rose's character in the book was based on the real life of my mother. Her many stories were so intriguing and plentiful that it would require another book to write about all of them. The confusion and despair of the war at her young age, the closing of schools, the capture by the Germans and subsequent release, the general store she managed, and the parachute wedding dress, were all part of her young life. The story about her romantic involvement with the German soldier was mostly a creation of my imagination. There were some innuendos that while the half Polish and half German soldier was stationed in my mother's town, they were romantically connected.

Joseph's unusual story is partially based on my grandfather's life. Unfortunately, after emigrating to France, he died in an industrial accident, leaving his family in Poland grieving for the rest of their lives.

The mistaken identities of Joseph (Joe) Novak and Jean Navarre are fiction woven into the history of Alsace-Lorraine in France.

The story of Billy and Eloise was inspired by a brooch showed to me by my English friend. Her father had made the brooch for his wife from a burned fighter airplane during WWII.

Sometimes, as a writer, it is enough to have one piece of information to create a story around. That was the case with my fictional characters of Billy and Eloise. The truth in their story is the brooch and the fact that my friend's mother served in the WAAF and at one point during the war sewed parachutes used by the RAF. Who knows, maybe one of the parachutes she made became Rose's wedding dress?

Joey is a fictional character but his life, as depicted in the book, was lived by many Polish pilots who served in the Royal Air Force and played a significant role in the Battle of Britain in 1940 and many other battles with the German *Luftwaffe*.

The story of Vera, Joey's fiancée, and her family being deported to the Gulags with thousands of other Polish people by the Russians, is based on true events. Many died there from starvation and disease and many children, adopted by locals, lost their identities. I found it particularly interesting that Vera had been trained in Palestine as a flight mechanic and transferred to England to serve in the RAF.

The stories about the pilots flying the photographic planes and the people interpreting the photographs were inspired by the book *Spies in the*

Sky, written by Taylor Downing. The world knows a lot about the pilots fighting in battles, as depicted in many books, movies, and oral histories, but not much has been told about the pilots who flew the stripped-down planes equipped with cameras and just enough fuel to bring them back to England. Taking photographs of the German Army's positions all over Europe significantly helped the Allies to fight the enemy and win the war. One of the most important victories was the discovery of the German battleship *Bismarck,* hiding in the fiords of Norway, and its subsequent destruction by the British Navy in the waters of the Atlantic Ocean.

The facts about the Medmenham and its role in the interpretation of the photographs are fascinating, as is the fact that women played a significant role in deciphering the photographs; their keen eyes and ability to see minute details led to many victories.

The story of the aviation hero Sidney Cotton was also in the book *Spies in the Sky* and I became fascinated with his life and accomplishments. Each time I look at old photographs of pilots, my eyes are immediately drawn to their one-piece uniforms, designed by Sidney Cotton.

In my book I briefly mentioned the Lviv and Vilnius uprisings of the Home Army against the Nazis in the summer of 1944. The cities were part of the Polish-Lithuanian Commonwealth established in the 16th century. After the end of WWI and the Polish–Soviet War that ended in March 1921, they were part of Poland again. Both cities have a rich history of Polish, Lithuanian and Ukrainian peoples and cultures. Currently Lviv is part of the Ukraine and Vilnius is the capitol of Lithuania.

Among many unusual stories of the war was the one of the maharaja in India and his orphanage. He was a Hindu delegate to Great Britain's war cabinet and well aware of the troubles of the war. Thanks to his generous nature, hundreds of Polish orphans were saved during the war and many remembered him as an affectionate *bapu* (father).

The most earth-shattering atrocity of WWII was the torment of the Jewish people in Europe, inflicted on them by the Nazis and their collaborators. In my book, I wrote about their devastating treatment and planned extermination by the Third Reich. In order to reflect more deeply on the misery of the Jewish people in WWII, an entire book wouldn't be enough.

There are many books and historical accounts available to interested readers about the Jewish genocide at the hands of the Nazis.

One of the most beautiful parts of the book for me was the story about my mother's wedding dress. During one of my visits, my mother and I looked through some old photographs, including the pictures of my parents' wedding. As children, we often looked at them and listened to stories about the parachute and the dress, and then we put the photographs away and didn't think much about them.

As adults, we saw more and understood the narrative behind each story much better. I decided to write for my friends a short story about the origins of the dress and this story is woven into my book.

With the devastation of Poland, a wedding dress was a dream not available to most brides. The silky white fabric of the parachute was fashioned into my mother's wedding dress. Many young brides in town wore my mother's dress to their weddings and we always called it "The wedding dress from Heaven."

I hope that my book was of interest to you and perhaps has inspired you to learn more about the lesser-known facts of WWII.

I encourage you to talk to your parents, grandparents, and relatives about their life stories. There is mystery and beauty in many of the stories. We should cherish them and learn from them.

Printed in the USA
CPSIA information can be obtained
at www.ICGtesting.com
LVHW071739150923
758303LV00003B/417